OUTLAND EXILE

Thanks for reading
W. Clark Boutwell

BOOK 1 OF **OLD MEN AND INFIDELS**

OUTLAND EXILE

W. CLARK BOUTWELL

OUTLAND EXILE
BOOK 1 OF OLD MEN AND INFIDELS

iUniverse books may be ordered through booksellers or by contacting:

iUniverse
1663 Liberty Drive
Bloomington, IN 47403
www.iuniverse.com
1-800-Authors (1-800-288-4677)

ISBN: 978-1-4917-7565-3 (sc)
ISBN: 978-1-4917-7564-6 (e)

Library of Congress Control Number: 2015914856

Print information available on the last page.

iUniverse rev. date: 10/15/2015

To Lilianne, a young kinswoman who, in her short life, has had more pain, danger, trials, and triumph than I fear to know. Her parents have persevered, lost uncounted hours of sleep, reset their sails countless times, and given more than love may ask. I admire them.

ACKNOWLEDGMENTS

I would like to acknowledge the hard work and sage advice tendered me by my editors, particularly Patricia Kennedy. Any glimmer of professionalism in these words is due to their careful work and insightful critique, and any remaining gaffes are of my own crafting. I would like to thank all those who have critically read this work and offered their insights, especially James DiPisa, with whom I have shared food, stories, shelter, and danger. Finally, I must thank my wife, Cheryl, for her listening ear while hearing bits and pieces of this book. In addition, I swiped her name for the title. I hope that it doesn't mind.

PROLOGUE

The message impeded upon the gray man's notice unbidden. With the faintest suggestion of an interface, it rose up before him through his Outside-Above interface.[1] After years of use, the imperceptible biosensory device implanted in his brain, allowing him to use the Unity's CORE (Concepts of Reality Engineering Inc.) cyberspace, was just the habit of life.

In an earlier age, it might have appeared as follows:

To: ComOutOps

From: ComOutSig

Time/Date: 11.33.03.local_11_10_AU76[2]

RE: Unity Sensor Station 43.11.0/97_89.13.56/41 (SUNPRAIRIE)

---

[1] Further discussion of unfamiliar terms may be found in the glossary.

[2] Unity convention is hour.minute.second.time convention (e.g., local, Zulu, or time zone)_day_month_Anno Unitatem year.

Signal ceased SUNPRAIRIE 10.21.03. central_10_10_AU76

The gray man smiled, adjusted his uniform, signed the memorandum with his characteristic mental gesture, and began preparations for the destruction of Malila Evanova Chiu.

CHAPTER 1

HUNT

CORE, Democratic Unity of America
08.35.17.local_11_10_AU76

As her consciousness floated in the middle depths, she felt the freedom of her movements and enjoyed the surge of her predatory impulses. For a moment, Malila rippled the chromatophores along her four-meter length in pleasure before returning her borrowed skin to the pattern of the hunt. Her appearance now flowed second by second as sensors discerned the light falling upon them and mimicked the surface opposite to match.

Second Lieutenant Malila Evanova Chiu's mind tasted the salinity, the pressure, the faint rhythmic surge and flow of the waves around her, and ... her prey. In the instant of thought, she sent her winged diamond shape pulsing through the middepths, her skin adapting to the flow of water streaming over it, letting her slip along with barely a pressure wave. The designers of her avatar had subjugated all functions to the hunt, abandoning her need to feed, excrete, breathe, or pity. She saw in many dimensions of sight, sound, touch, and taste. Her sea avatar could harry, hunt, and kill even the largest animals on the diminished planet.

Reaching her selected rendezvous, she slowed and stopped. Although she had nothing as awkward as a mouth to disrupt her sleek envelope, she smiled. The prey were still oblivious to her, making a cacophony of clicking and splashing in the distance. It was time.

Malila Chiu mimicked a sound that had not been heard since the Meltdown. She stilled, waiting for the one animal aggressive enough to leave the group and give chase.

Once separated from the others, she could attack and kill her massive opponent unmolested. The beast would be expecting a flailing and disabled squid. Instead, he—it was always a male—would find a merciless killer. In the very moment the whale paused in consternation, she would thrust forward into his vital organs and sever the huge conduits of the heart.

She thrummed again and could now tell that all the animals had stopped—except one. She again smiled her bodiless smile and waited, listening to the rapid thrust of her prey's vast undulating tail as it forced the sea to part, pressing his attack upon her. By the noise, he seemed to be the largest Movasi she had ever taken. She moved away from her decoy sound and reset her chromatophores to render herself a mere ellipsis in the flow of water around her.

It was only then she remembered to reengage her sound filters. While she had passively listened for her prey, her sensors had been sensitive to the most-distant sounds, but now Malila needed protection from the din of combat. In that instant, the attack began. A rapid crescendo of focused clicks hit her like hammer blows. The concussions seemed to flatten her sleek shape, encasing her in a chaos of noise. Had she internal organs, the detonations would have disabled her. She drifted in the currents, trying to reorder her sensors. No longer able to hear, her courage in tatters against an invisible opponent, she fled.

Even as she sprinted away, she sensed the predatory green-gray shape, its forked jaws agape with its terrible scimitar teeth, sweep by to plunge into the volume of ocean from which she had just escaped. The sight of her huge opponent steadied her. She was turning to pursue when her returning sensors made her look below to see in the featureless depths the attack of the second whale.

It was no wonder the sonic signature was so large; the Movasi were hunting as a team. She had no strategy to confront them. She sprinted aside as the second whale, the greater of the two, rushed past, his wake tumbling her into confusion again.

She righted herself, with difficulty this time, but had no idea where the huge predators had gone … or from whence they would come again.

Malila considered abandoning the effort, but an unsuccessful hunt would condemn her fellow citizens to a cold, hungry winter. Other than the sharp beak at the leading edge of her body, she had no other weapons. Her defenses were stealth, speed, and cunning. To reduce her avatar's sonar signature, the designers had eliminated the squid's suckered and barbed arms in favor of her sleek shape.

Her dilemma was the same as every predator facing two adversaries. If she tried for a killing blow on one, she would be open to attack by the other. If disabled, she would be unable to flee; winning one battle, wounded, would be a death sentence.

Out of the buzzing of her returning hearing, she detected a murmur that might be the rushing charge of one of the whales. A thought gave her sudden confidence. Edie, her metaphract, a nonsentient translator between herself and the CORE, had found a saying: "If things go south, think sideways."

It would depend on timing.

Malila tried to calm herself. She was just able to see the glint of the recurved white teeth rising up from the depths before she acted. Launching one of her two drogue buoys, she backed away a few meters from the path of the attack. The drogue buoy jetted away before inflating with a subtle click. It hesitated, almost like a confused animal, before it began its increasingly rapid ascent.

The smaller and younger of the two Movasi whales, sleek, massive, voracious, and eellike, altered his course and followed the drogue as it appeared to flee.

As the leviathan careened past, Malila darted forward, cutting a massive slice along the muscular green tail, blood spewing out of the widening red mouth of the wound. The bull turned toward her attack even as she disengaged herself. Before the snakelike head could seize her, she thrust the remaining drogue buoy deep within his still-living flesh and fled up toward the warmth and light.

The great beast, no doubt, would find no difficulty in following her thin trail of cavitation bubbles in the water. At this depth, she knew, the wound she had inflicted would hardly slow the whale's next attack. Malila imagined jaws encircling her, the terrible teeth gripping her, even as she heard the Movasi surge toward her on his massive flukes.

She heard the buoy deploy.

Her hopes lay with the placement of the buoy deep within the whale's flesh. As it inflated, it would send a shock wave, like a small bomb, into the pressure-dense tissue. The whale's center of buoyancy would shift, the buoy's pressure and obstruction sapping his ability to propel the gigantic tail.

Moments later, the Movasi, seemingly disoriented, floated slowly past her, flailing toward the surface. The drogue balloon inflating even more as he rose, the wounded animal thrashed his huge pectoral flukes in agony, red and overwhelmed.

Her arsenal of drogues, meant to keep dead whales from sinking to rot in the abysmal depths, was now exhausted.

Where was the other whale? Malila cautiously lowered her sound filters again, forming a picture of the first whale's death throes from the cacophony of sounds. To her dismay, a sonar shadow lurked, obscured and silent near the surface noise. The other big male was waiting, pointing his snout in her direction. He was using his wounded partner to attract and distract … her.

Realization flashed through Malila, her skin prickling with the twin emotions of fear and rage. Again, she considered slipping away. Her top surface speed exceeded anything the whale might achieve. However, a strenuous and skillful fight did not fill any bellies; hunters were justified by success alone.

Sideways.

She regulated her buoyancy, adjusting it to become negative, and slipped into the cold, dark depths. Discovering a current of seawater running toward and under her remaining adversary, she let herself drift like flotsam, tumbling and turning. She took no action until she was almost beyond the blood plume. Righting herself, she rose wraithlike until she could taste the still-potent billowing blood.

Turning, flashing, bursting from the bloody cover, abandoning pretense, she darted forward toward the cloaking sound of the dying whale.

Surprise was almost complete. As she emerged from cover, she saw the splashes of gray and green of the Movasi's great flank and targeted him in the midthorax, halfway from snakelike head to trifid tail. Her quarry, finally sensing her presence, turned to meet the attack, his jaw serrated with back-curving teeth opening to seize her. Malila's hardened beak slid along the muscular side before she could disengage and turn to protect herself from his attack. A long wound opened up and added more hot blood to the cold sea. She reversed course, pushing away from the beast to circle around the smaller flailing animal. The old bull surfaced and, laboring, blew a plume of overheated breath, the cold air condensing it into a tall bloodless column. There was nothing to do but circle the two Movasi, awaiting the killing chance.

The end, when it came, surprised her. Taking her reticence for injury or timidity, the old bull rushed at her as she appeared around the bulk of his dying companion. She retreated and in her flight matched her speed to the old one's pursuit. As he accelerated, she led him away from the blood plume.

She taunted him, sometimes allowing him to approach closer if he appeared to tire, then lengthening the gap to make the whale expend the greatest amount of effort and blood to keep her in sight.

Finally, he faltered. Perhaps convinced that she was abandoning her hunt, the old bull turned to retrace his path. As he did, Malila darted forward and plunged her beak into the unprotected flank. An immediate rush of hot blood rewarded her attack. She thrust on and felt her beak cut through cartilage, bone, and muscle. Only when the gush of high-pressure blood sprayed across her beak did she pull out from the wound. The great bull spun once on his axis and was still. She swam to the still-struggling younger one to dispatch him and signaled the sea tugs to recover the carcasses.

In due course, the nation would learn of her victory. The recovery of both Movasi after combat in the open ocean was noteworthy by itself; her status as a mere E11—only seventeen years old—added savor to the story. Hundreds of her people would toast her hunting skills over whale dinners. She rendezvoused with the boats to take the whales in tow. *Malila was pleased.*

Malila moved the controls in her O-A, experiencing the odd but reassuring disorientation as she left the body of her sea avatar.

In a trivial way, or so it appeared to her masters, *Physeter movasii* and all the toothed whales, both natural and genetically engineered, had been extinct on this particular planet for the last fifty years. That was of minimal consequence, moreover, as Malila's sea avatar, the Movasi carcasses, the surface tugs, the crowds cheering from the shore, and, indeed, even the ocean evaporated from the simulation stage as soon as Second Lieutenant Malila E. Chiu reincorporated. Technicians of the CORE submitted reports, wiped the temporary data stacks, and started the next scheduled simulation.

CHAPTER 2

REINCORPORATION

Nyork, the Unity
11.01.35.local_11_10_AU76

Second Lieutenant Malila Evanova Chiu heard the bottom drop out of her vision and smelled burnt umber. She felt the clanging of cheap wine and retched from the taste of the creaky gate that had scared her as a child.

Could the Unity not do something to make reincorporation less disconcerting?

It was always the same when she reincorporated; her disembodied flesh sensed the trials her mind had endured … and suffered in her absence. It hardly seemed fair.

"Fathering muckers!"

Edie clucked at her as Malila groaned and sat up.

> *Don't be vulgar, squilch! You brought this on yourself, you know.*

Fecking frak!

The obscenity was meant to shock, and on cue, Edie grew silent. Growing up in the crèche and then the Democratic Unity Forces for Security (DUFS) barracks, Malila possessed a flamboyant repertoire of profanity, vulgarities, and obscenities. Her metaphract, of late, had taken a dim view of this proficiency.

Lieutenant Chiu donned the light robe she had laid aside hours before and, shivering, waited for her heart rate to glissade from the heights of conquest. A trickle of sweat worked its way through her short, military-style haircut and down her neck as she took a large breath to steady herself.

You're going to be late, squilch.

Give me a break, Edie. I just fought a battle ... two battles ... to the death.

That's nice. Your appointment is in seventy-seven minutes. You smell bad.

Malila rolled her eyes. No one was a hero to her frak.

<ED>[3] *Tell me when the comm'nets announce my whale hunt.*

---

[3] "The proper way to give a command to your new Turing Metaphract (ED v3.94) is always to begin on a new line. Announce to the ED that this is a command by the use of '<ED>,' and then give the desired command. Lines that do not begin this way will not be taken as commands, although, in time, your ED may act on them, once it gets used to you. You can guess the effect of your comments and commands by the 'verbals' you get from your ED, a new and exciting feature of Turing Metaphracts. Your ED will gradually learn how you speak mentally and will pick up your personal habits. This comes with time and practice. Don't be disappointed if your ED finds it too hard at first." Concepts of Reality Engineering Inc., *Beginner's Guide for the Turing Metaphract (Education Device [ED] v3.94)* (Passaic: COREprint, AU 64), 4.

Of course, Lieutenant Chiu. On an unrelated topic, we are getting full of ourselves—are we not, squilch?

Don't call me a squilch, frak.

Don't call me a frak, Second Lieutenant.

Malila thrust a gesture, equivalent to a small child with a wetly extended tongue, in the mental direction of her tormentor.

All right, metaphract, have it your own way.

<ED> Any messages?

You have received a number of offers on methods to improve pleasure-sex, another dozen offering to contact your spirit guide in the multiverse of your choice, one from a foundation requesting funds to combat the heartbreak of facial hair, and a message from Command Outland Signals.

I'm not going to deal with that now. Show me some music.

The Femtosense Grunge Philharmonic selection that Edie chose swelled within her. Malila experienced it in all her senses, feeling a breeze and receiving the sharp taste of spring rain. The music played upon her emotions, and she abandoned her will to its wanderings. Perceptions, which Malila interpreted as being "outside," slid over the input of her eyes, ears, and other senses. These were a level "above" what she detected with her corporal body.

Metaphracts like Edie originated as interpreters of the interface for those receiving the O-A brain implants as children. Most of the boys taught their metaphracts to play tricks on one another and discarded them with puberty. Most of the girls decorated them with childish fashions, retaining them after puberty but keeping them unused in their mental closets. Malila had been unusual in embellishing hers with wit, a face, and a personality … or at least as much as a Turing metaphract could imitate. Edie was, for Malila, a convenient construct of the CORE interface, coming when she called and doing the scut work of daily life.

In contrast to the metaphract, her O-A was a constant presence … with the constant potential danger of slipping across and becoming lost to reality. Those who ignored the warning suffered a living perdition. The first few victims had been immediately prohibited an interface with the CORE and had erupted in bloody rage. Thereafter the COREd-out had been left to dwindle away, lost both to the Unity and to their own shriveling personalities.

Perhaps it was just a tale, but some truth was embedded in it. The CORE interface was seductive. Once, when Malila had gotten too close, warning lights, a vile shade of green, had strobed across her inner eye. Now she only looked in that direction from the corner of her mind when she felt secure. Most feared to look at all.

A claxon sounded inside her head.

> *You are going to be late for your lunch appointment unless you—*
>
> *Fleckafather!*

Malila scampered across her room, shedding the robe as she went, knowing the chamber would retrieve it and sort it into the appropriate category: bureau drawer, closet hangers, or laundry chute. Malila stepped into her bathroom and quested, mentally accessing the CORE, with her O-A. The room warmed and misted to her specifications.

Within the hour, Lieutenant Chiu was dressed in the uniform of the DUFS: form-fitting black Produra cloth with the subdued holographic markings of her rank on her shoulders. This sleek envelope, surmounted by a black helmet covering most of her features, made her anonymous in the crowded streets of the Unity. Malila was ready to meet her friends for lunch.

Once on the street, Malila stepped onto the descending beltway and after a few minutes navigated to the express belt "For S24 and

Above Only!" Malila's specialist level, her rank within the Unity, was just high enough for her to use the belt.

Detecting Malila's presence, the beltway comm'nets blossomed with a weltering array of advertisements, PSAs, and lepto-mercials of numerous flavors. Malila ignored them as much as she could, seldom finding the enthusiasm for anything other than a few sporting spectacles, like her beloved kirshing, the daily melodrama of politics, and especially the news.

At that moment the news was showing two people, a man and a woman, both handcuffed, being led to a waiting DUFS skimmer.

> *This fascination with news borders upon the macabre, Malila.*
>
> *Nonsense, I'm being a good citizen. Does it occur to you that they brought it on themselves?*
>
> *You think they brought* that *on themselves?*

Bruises marked the prisoners' thin bodies. The woman's dress fell around her waist as she walked. The assembled crowd laughed at her attempt to cover herself.

> *They must have tried to resist arrest, frak. They were running an illegal phantom shop, after all.*
>
> *One you have used yourself!*
>
> *Edie, don't be difficult! Here come the policoms,[4] I need to see these.*

Major political analysts numbered about a dozen, and the long-time leader of the pack was James J. Gordon. He possessed an uncanny ability to ferret out scandal, hypocrisy, and political disloyalty in its

[4] Entertainment personalities masquerading as political commentators.

many forms, using the flensing knives of parody, innuendo, and sophistry for the loyal citizenry.

> *Best to keep your head down around here with people like Gordon about.*
>
> *That could be construed as a disloyal statement, frak.*
>
> *Then it is you that should worry, isn't it, squilch? I am but your humble servant, nothing more than your own program, am I not?*
>
> *So when does the humble thing kick in?*
>
> *I'm assertive only in your best interests, Lieutenant. Allow me to mention again that your messages await your attention.*
>
> *Not now, frak!*

Malila took an ascender and emerged immediately in front of the People's Museum of Natural History. A huge banner proclaiming "Triumph of the Will" emblazoned the entrance in the state colors of red, white, and black.

Entering, Malila looked up, as she did on most visits, to the three pale-blond stony depressions, surrounded by darker stone, far over her head.

> *I wonder why they chiseled them out in the first place, Malila. What could have been so obscene or seditious that they had to deface the whole building?*
>
> *There you go again, getting us into trouble, frak.*
>
> *No, I'm not! It was an honest question. For all I know it was done by the Sisis.*

The possibility that senile senior citizens, those who no longer contributed, had once more conspired to injure her homeland was distressing.

The wisdom of the Unity in retiring the elderly had been proven out time and again. Once removed from society, the role of the aged in past mistakes became evident. Even now, the practice of compassionate retirement ensured new ideas and new vigor came daily to the forefront of national life. Young and vital citizens had nothing to hinder them in their rise to greatness. In the past, it had taken decades of public service before younger leaders could ascend to their rightful level of responsibility. But now, citizens could assure their ascendancy if they were able to arouse the ardor of the citizens and to formulate most adroitly the aspirations of the state.

Malila brushed past the guards and into the lobby.

CHAPTER 3

LUNCH WITH THE GIRLS

Stealing a glance at the model of a blue whale suspended in the lobby, Malila avoided the packs of ululating children, E3 couples looking for secluded spots, and the state nannies.

One child, who had to be less than six years old, had unfastened himself from the harness and made a break for the worn marble steps. A nanny, brightly painted in a cheerful abstract, wheels smoking, cut him off before he gained the tactical advantage of the first step. The young malefactor was gripped, none too gently, and brought stumbling back to his place.

As they neared, Malila heard the nanny above the noise.

"Janes Brigham Cherbourg, you have violated field trip rule number three. You have brought shame on Créche Alinsky 188 … and you have made me very … disenchanted … with your behavior." The rest of the machine's remonstrations were lost in the bustle, but Janes Cherbourg did, indeed, appear penitent.

Malila entered the restaurant, and the gabbling of the children subsided.

Malila had first met her friends while they had all been crèchies. They each knew more embarrassing details about the others' lives than bore consideration. The table Hecate had reserved for them was delightful. Delicate gilt chairs surrounded expanses of white linen and shining silver. Nearby a string quartet played some Dutilleux. Exuberant vines wound around lattices along several of the walls, burdened with pale trumpet-shaped flowers that perfumed the whole room. Malila was the first to arrive, but she did not have to wait long.

Two of her friends appeared together: blonde Alexandra in her well-tailored academia-blue suit and Hecate in her government gray. Only after they had been seated did Lucy sweep in with a dramatic dark-red cloak, arriving with her glad exclamations and pointed accusations of neglect.

Lucy was still holding forth when their final component arrived; Tiffany, trotting with her head down, her long white coat fluttering behind her, always came last.

"Now we can all breathe. All present and accounted for! It has been so very long … six months? I was worried you all had forgotten me!" said Lucy, throwing back the red cloak and making as credible an imitation of neglected virtue as the small stage allowed.

"You don't fool us, Luscena! You have been the one that always has to sleep to noon and uses the 'I have a matinee' excuse, aren't you?" said Alexandra, smiling.

Before Lucy could respond, Tiffany cut in. "Alex, don't! That is just going to get you the 'I am merely a pawn of my craft … a victim of my artistic genius' soliloquy, you know."

Luscena opened her mouth briefly and closed it to peals of laughter.

Attentive waiters arrived and passed them elegant menus. Having already decided on the *filet de sole au citron vert* herself, Malila listened with plagiarized interest to her friends' choices and indecisions.

"Everything looks so good! I love the fettuccine here … but I'll just have the garden salad," said Tiffany Collins, to Malila's right.

Malila suppressed a smile, thinking her friend was on yet one more diet. Tiffany had auburn hair and was dressed in a pale shade of her league's green. She seemed even more professionally preoccupied than usual. As children, while Malila and Luscena had been egging each other on, Tiffany had been the one to mollify juvenile rage at imagined insults.

In contrast to Tiffany's soft and melodious voice, Lucy's projected to the corners of the room. Lucy used her talents well. Malila was pleased for her. As Luscena Kristòf, a rising star of the legitimate theater, she had just won accolades in the revival of *Memoir of a Protégé*.

Lucy, who was on Tiffany's right, ordered an herb omelet and a glass of wine without consulting the menu and immediately started her own interrogations.

"Alexandra, my love, I understand you are on the Art Task Force for this year? Are you going to fund the New-Artist Grants better? Phillipa—you know, Phillipa Dvorak—actually had to wait tables last year to make ends meet while she was staging her new thing. What's it called, Malila? I know you remember."

Before Malila could answer that she did *not* remember, the quicksilver of Luscena's interrogations had moved on to complaining about the woeful delays in the scheduling of aesthetic surgical procedures.

"It's not like this is vanity, Tiffany. I *need* my breast augmentation, you know. It is a necessity for my craft. After all, our bodies are our …" said Luscena, unwisely pausing for dramatic effect, allowing her companions to say in unison, and with choreographed dramatic poses. "*… instruments. They are the brushes we use to paint art on the canvas of the stage!*"

The women, absent Luscena, dissolved again into peals of laughter.

Tiffany, a health care provider, hurried on. "But, Lucy, the boob jobs are handled in turn. I have nothing to do with scheduling, honest." Tiffany, compassionate and hardworking, even if not the most astute, served her profession well, a young and vital population needing little medical care other than obligatory immunizations, euthanasia for the chronically ill, and plastic surgery. Tiffany was always authentically distressed at Lucy's dilemmas.

The waiter took the rest of the orders while Luscena pouted. By the time the food arrived, she apparently had forgiven everyone for their plebian attitudes and was delivering a convoluted tale that appeared to be merely an occasion for the flinging forth of Names.

Finally reaching a stopping point, Luscena paused to attack her omelet. "Fathercock! It's cold."

"Don't be crude, dear Lucy. It's only cold because you talk so much ... and we all want to hear every word you have to say, my love," responded Alexandra at Malila's left.

Malila laughed with the rest. Alexandra O'Brian had her own ways of grabbing attention. While very young, the other four children had adopted her when they'd fathomed the vicious wit she could deploy for the general welfare. Then cripplingly shy, Alexandra had been too timid to bend a breakable rule. She'd found her remedy in academia. After gaining a BA, MA, and two PhDs (theology and political science) at Yal-Vard, she had assumed the Sharpton Chair of Practical Democracy at Nyork City University in 73.

"You should talk, Alex. I see *you* on the 'nets more than I see Gordon," Malila inserted.

Alexandra smiled her trademark smile and patted Malila's hand. "Just trying to do my little part for the Unity when I'm asked." Malila always wondered who did the asking but admired the liberties it brought Alexandra. Malila self-consciously ran a hand through her short, straight black hair.

With her blonde shoulder-length hair, smooth brow, and large blue eyes, Alexandra always radiated a sincerity politicians lusted to emulate. More than once, she had turned down an offer to join the government, saying she could never make the hard choices that governing required. The solemn woman to her left understood.

Hecate Hester Jones was in government. She was medium: average height, medium-brown, and medium build. She and Malila had arrived at Unity Crèche Maddow #213 within days of each other, both "illegals," children raised by private citizens before being discovered.

Usually finding it difficult to break into the torrents of words issuing forth from Luscena and Alexandra, Hecate was satisfied to dabble in the back eddies of their conversations. Today she was even more withdrawn, Malila noted, but while arranging the luncheon yesterday, Hecate had been animated, even excited. The contrast disturbed her.

Malila's O-A, usually quiescent during meetings, came to life.

> *<Announcement> A hunt, concluding with the harvesting of two large male Movasi whales has been announced. The successful hunter has been identified as Second Lieutenant Malila E. Chiu, of the DUFS Battalion Thirty-Two, hunting in a sea avatar designed and built by the Unity forces with consultation with CORE Inc.*
>
> *Very good, Edie.*
>
> *<ED> Send the CORE address to everyone at the table.*

The combination of sights, sounds, and gustatory sensations rose up to overwhelm each of the others. Faces became fixed, eyes dilated, and hands carrying glasses of wine froze before returning to the table. No one spoke. After a moment, Malila played it for herself as well.

> *Once more breaking through the plume of blood to surprise the huge Movasi, her sea avatar attacked. She luxuriated again in the sharp metallic smell-taste of blood as she passed through it. She sensed the juddering thrill as her beak sliced along the smooth green flank.*

Mesmerized by what their inner senses were witnessing, all the young women paused. Luscena was the first to react.

"Father me, Mally! You are a fecking celebrity! How marvelous! Isn't that exciting?"

"And what a thrill to be able to use the best equipment the Unity has to offer," added Alexandra.

Tiffany turned a little pale but said, "Excellent hunting, Mally! That is going to fill a lot of dinner plates. You are so brave!"

"How could you be so courageous, Mally? Those monsters were

three times bigger than you, at the very least, and there were two of them!" said Luscena.

"So much blood, Mally. I had no idea they were so big," murmured Hecate at the last.

"That is going to get you a birth certificate for sure, my love!" continued Luscena.

"Do you think so?" Malila said.

"Absolutely. I got a birth certificate last month just for appearing at the Equinox rallies. You're a shoo-in, without a doubt," said Alexandra.

The comment took Malila by surprise. Birth certificates entitled the holder to the use of a state-owned breeder. She had never met one, nor did she wish to. They were gross, slow-moving puddles of flesh, Sapped—drugged to eliminate higher brain functions—and maintained for reproduction alone.

Another citizen with another birth certificate typically provided the other half of the genome. After that, all the messy business of selection, implantation, gestation, and birthing would be the duty of the Department of Reproductive Services. After its birth, caring for the child until it was at least E4 would be a crèche responsibility. Malila could put "certified parent of a child" on her résumé, and others would notice. The Unity was serious about its assertion that all production, even reproduction, belonged to the state.

"Who is going to be the father, Malila?" asked Tiffany.

"Don't be crude and sexist, Tiff. She hasn't even got the thing yet," Alexandra said.

"I'm not being sexist. She wants to have the chance of having a boy or a girl, doesn't she? You need sperm for that."

"They can always substitute a stock Y chrome. It's in the contract," Alexandra said.

"Believe me, you don't want any of the stock Ys out there. Get a Y from someone who is actually using his!" replied Tiffany.

"So who is it going to be, Mally?" asked Luscena.

"Oh, you know ..." said Malila, waving her hand in the air equivocally. In truth, she had hardly thought about it. None of her current patrons had ever expressed an interest in breeding. As a career move, the "parent" designation was desirable, but the idea of meeting a person in the future who had somehow been part of your own body was repulsive.

"Whatever you do, don't you go and use Oui-Donors. It's just too crass," added Luscena.

"I promise I'll have your approval before the dirty deed is done. Satisfied?"

The conversation drifted to Luscena's new project, her first as a director, for the revival of *The Cadre's Triumph*.

"That one has been out of production for maybe eight years, Luscena, dear. What makes you think you can resuscitate that old story?" asked Alexandra.

"Well, the censors might let you change some of the text—you know, make it more modern," said Hecate. Conversation stopped as all eyes went to Hecate. She usually did not have much to say about the theater.

"I didn't know you had this self-destructive streak. Bibberty James tried that in 66, and see where it got *him*," Alexandra replied and then smiled.

"Bibberty is so yesterday, my dear. He had no patrons deserving of his talent. This is going to be bold, new, untried. All I need are patrons and donors," said Luscena.

"I just read the original script of *Triumph*. What we think is the canon has already changed a lot compared to the original. I think you've a shot at getting it through, Lucy," Hecate said quietly. "I mean, they can't say that changes have never been done before," she added quickly, looking down at her mostly untouched fettuccine.

In the silence that descended, Tiffany asked quietly, "How did you know it was the original?"

"It was in a paper book, an old book."

"When did you start dealing in contraband, love?" Alexandra smiled.

Smiling back, Hecate said, "Nothing so exotic, Alex. You know Victor; he likes it when I tell him stories while we are in bed. He got me special permission to go to an old book warehouse. Lots of old data dumps but also books on actual paper. This one was published in 2060 CE; that's AU 8!"

"Father me, Heccy. It seems you have a real conquest there." Tiffany smiled quickly. It was an old joke among them. Victor and Hecate had been together for *ages*. This time Hecate took the comment at face value.

"You think? I just think Victor's a lonely man who will retire in eighteen months. Everyone he grew up with has already been denounced or retired," returned Hecate.

There was an uncomfortable silence until the waiters circulated some very good khat tea.

After everyone had finished, on cue Luscena rose, shrieking as she looked at her watch. Her personal skimmer was announced a second later. She swept out in a characteristic welter of air-kisses, insincere promises, and dubious threats.

The magic broken, Alexandra and Tiffany left, heads together, discussing some professional controversy. Hecate lingered.

Malila was pleased; Hecate deserved her undivided attention. The two women walked arm in arm into the lobby, stopping under the model of the blue whale. Malila took Hecate's hand to stop her, turning her around and looking into her solemn face.

"Heccy, you haven't said three words to me today. Tell me what's wrong?"

"Oh, Mally, it's work. Talk about a fathering screwup."

Malila's heart sank. "It's always work with you, Heccy."

Hecate gave a wan smile. "This is my first S22 posting, and I want to do everything perfectly!"

Malila took both her hands in her own. Hecate's hands were moist and cold. "Tell me what is wrong. You hardly ate anything. What has happened?"

Hecate looked down, away from the eyes of her friend, before looking back into her face.

"The numbers don't add up, and no one seems to care! A storm wiped out the maize harvest in Lankster in June, and we lost the krill farms off Negzed when the nets let loose. Fatherfecking workers! They let the nets rot in the water. It will be years before we build up the effusion again."

"Oh Heccy, you must be terribly disappointed!"

"On top of that, the algae plantation at Rawlee has been contaminated somehow, and the whole facility has to be shut down, flushed, and restarted. Even without that, our production has gone down the last three years, and no one knows why. We are going to have eight million tonnes less food this winter."

"Oh my. How do you think they will make it up?"

"They *can't* make up the difference this year. If they slaughtered all the animals, we'd still have a shortfall. Fathering feckers ..."

Malila let Hecate run on, though most of it was lost on her. Malila had no idea what an effusion was. What she did know was that her friend was in pain. Hecate had always felt things more than Malila. It had been one of Malila's unspoken delights as a child to hold a crying Hecate and feel the other child's sobs dissolve in her arms.

This time Hecate looked up, her eyes bright but tearless. "I asked my supervisor, Undersecretary Rice, what the Unity was going to do, but she just smiled and said not to worry, that they'd make up the difference in the wheat harvest ... But that's crazy. It's already in! The protein profile is all wrong ..."

"Heccy, Heccy, it's not your fault! No one can blame you. You are just doing your job. Someone will fix it once they know about it. Besides, I just added two whales to the larder, now didn't I?" Malila laughed.

Malila sensed Hecate's body stiffen.

"You don't understand, Mally! Whales are gone! People are going to die this winter, and the government knows it already. They aren't going to *do* anything!" Hecate stepped back, her stricken eyes seeming to hold Malila in their crosshairs.

"I'm sure the Solons know their business," Malila started in her most consoling voice, but she stopped at Hecate's scathing look at mention of the Solons, the ultimate rulers of the Unity.

Pity swept briefly across Hecate's face just before her professional mask clicked into place.

"Yes, of course, the Solons ... I'm sure all will be well." Hecate faded into the distance even as Malila held her hands.

Hecate disengaged herself and pantomimed looking at her watch, continuing without hesitation, "Oh ... look at the time! I should have been back at the department ages ago. Bye-bye, Malila. This was fun. We should do this more often. Bye for now."

Hecate turned, pushed through the doors, and almost ran down the stone steps under the scarred facade and out into the street.

Malila looked up into the serene gaze of the blue whale as the gray light of the city filtered down from the high windows above.

CHAPTER 4

THE MESSAGE

Troubled, Malila threaded her way back along the maze of beltways and returned to her quarters. The Unity was everything that she knew. She prided herself in how her daily labors furthered the goals and the welfare of her country. Hecate and the Unity were almost coequals in Malila's universe. It was inconceivable they would not coincide.

What did Hecate mean by saying the whales were gone?

How should I know, frak? I don't understand it. Do you?

Um, there are those messages, Lieutenant.

I'm not going to deal with that in the middle of a beltway, frak. Don't talk until I get home.

Malila exited the beltway at the Bedsty Plaza. She half-listened to the street argot she heard in passing. She was finding it an incessant trial to incorporate each day's new words that came and went from the deluge of inside jokes, comm'net comedian catchphrases, and hand gestures. It was like riding a tiger.

She had seen a tiger once—malevolent, solitary, and huge—at the People's Biodominium. The huge dome in Bronkz had once been a venue for sporting events but was now filled with all the improbable animals the Unity had been wise enough to exterminate since its rise. Those remaining specimens were maintained as a cautionary tale about the chaos of the outlands. As an additional mission, they demonstrated useful Unity animals: dogs, cats, horses, cattle, sheep, goats, and pigs. It was important, her teachers told her, to know the animals in the food chain, whatever that meant.

After her first visit to the Biodominium, while still an E2, the animals had terrorized her dreams for weeks thereafter. Huge bears with scythe-like talons and slavering jaws had awoken her night after night. Wolves' eyes had gleamed out of the darkness of her nightmares. Massive bison had trampled her in her sleep. She no longer went to the Biodominium.

Actually, she was professionally familiar with the dogs and horses. DUFS patrols used dogs. Nothing on foot escaped those beasts, all drool and teeth. Malila did not like them; the feeling was mutual.

DUFS used horses for crowd control. Last year Malila had done her six-month stint in a mounted troop. Her thighs ached at the memory.

Finally back to her apartment building, Malila took the ascender, stepped through the portal into her quarters, and then reconnected her O-A to the CORE.

Disconnection had not been an option with her first implant; it was always there to monitor her health and well-being. As an E1, when she had gotten it, she had been allowed to buy ThiZ, "the hallmark of a good society," or so Matron had said at the time. It was supposed to "produce dissociative and paradoxical endotactic emotions," whatever that might mean. It had been wonderful. For the first time in her life, she had not felt afraid.

Malila had only received the second implant, her O-A, when she'd started cadet training for the DUFS as an E4, ten years old. A slight flick of her eyes and a touching by her mind to a place in her thoughts was all it took to reconnect. It had taken her weeks to learn how to do that the first time.

Learn was an inadequate word. The implant had learned her as much as she'd learned it. They called it *questing*. It was like looking at the surface of a pond. She could see life reflected from the surface, but also she could see through it, move her mind through it, to another reality refracted on the other side. Her O-A was as much a part of her as her own skin. In a way, it was her skin, she thought. Questing now was second nature, and she barely noticed the differences between reality and the interface except in the subliminal way one sorts out reflections in a world of glass and mirrors.

> *Okay, Edie, I can deal with the messages now.*

> *<ED> Dump the advertisements. Keep all personal notes sorted into those from patrons, superior officers, and inferior officers. Show me the important message now.*

> *"... damage was presumed to have occurred due to nonfunctionality in electrical-signal distant-sensing devices (ESDSD/25.1-D through 37.7-A), which appears to some observers, due to the stereotypical repetition of the event, to be nonaccidental in nature ..."*

"Fathermuckers!"

Sunprairie was down—again.

She had been a young cadet when the Unity had voted to stop patrolling the outlands. The area was, properly speaking, a part of the territory inherited from the old republic, but it was unprofitable, undeveloped, and barren.

In place of armed patrols, the Unity had established a network of listening posts hundreds of kilometers within the outlands to detect any challenge to the rule of order. At her posting, earlier in the year,

Malila had accepted the common wisdom that the job of maintaining the station was a nuisance assignment.

It was supposed to require little of her attention. The actual work was supposed to be done by warrant officers as avatars (OAAs)—their personalities transmitted into real-world mechanisms—accompanied by a squad of Sapp-treated criminals, certified recycled neuroablated (CRNA) troopers. It was supposed to be a foolproof, unglamorous, but risk-free job for a newly minted second lieutenant. It was supposed to be fair.

Sunprairie had been anything but fair. Twice before, she had sent repair teams. Each time the OAA had found the pulse cannon depleted, the door blown, and random sabotage disabling the sensors. When retaken, the stations had been deserted. CRNAs had scoured the area within twenty klicks with no results.

If the 'net commentators singled her out for criticism, her short list of patrons would fade away. Demotion and denunciation would follow. Unless she wanted to commit professional suicide, she could not even suggest that the Unity's strategy was faulty, the station design flawed, or the technology defective.

"Fathering bizzles!"

Malila shook herself. It was too early for her ThiZ. The feeling of elation and self-actualization she got from ThiZ was enough to make her … not dependent … not that. ThiZ enlarged life.

She popped the little yellow pill unconsciously, without looking for a glass of water.

What's the matter with these knuckle-dragging savages? They hadn't challenged the listening posts for a decade. Sunprairie was the most distant station, farther west even than Lake Mishygun. What did they want?

> *<ED> Find strategic motives for attacking a fortified location.*
>
> *"Attacks on fortified sites are for the following motives: (1) the site is valuable or contains value that will be obtained*

or destroyed by occupation, (2) the site itself will become valuable after occupation or because of its occupation, or (3) occupation of the site will cause others to value it or bring value to it." Analects of Admiral Wescon.

Edie, do you know how silly that sounds? The savages just cut some wires and threw some paint around, like a bunch of crèchies!

Just following orders, squilch. Do you want more examples? Sergeant Hallux has some sayings about assaulting ladies' citadels of virtue ...

Not the same, frak. Let me think.

Edie, nonsentient, bordering on silly, was still a good mental grindstone for Malila.

The Unity wasn't getting very much from Sunprairie, but neither were the savages. In the prior two raids, they had not stolen as much as a length of cable. The stations had no value, contained no value, offered no value. Sunprairie hadn't detected any outlander occupation since it had been built.

Sunprairie had failed in its mission and was now consuming Unity resources.

And when she thought of it, there was her answer! Malila almost looked around to see if her thoughts had been overheard.

The solution was simplicity itself.

CHAPTER 5

THE FOUR RULES

With a tingle of excitement, Malila realized Sunprairie could be converted into a decisive stroke against the outlanders.

Like most decisive strokes, if she promoted this up the hierarchy, it would fail. One faction or another would get wind of it and find it easier to denounce her than join the effort. If she tried it solo, then again she would fail. She needed help from officers of her own level who would betray her in an instant if they thought it would gain them an advantage. If she were successful, all of them would appear to be part of a conspiracy. The comm'nets loved the idea of conspiracies.

> *"Small conspiracies fail, and large conspiracies are betrayed."*
> Analects of Juan Fugit.
>
> *Really, Edie? I am busy here. Shush!*

And her help needed to be just the right size.

Malila started a list and collected six, with herself making seven. She reread the list and struck off the second-to-last name.

Better to leave him out of it entirely.

Miramundo Morales had shown, of recent days, a little too much undeserved confidence. Not brilliant and with no notable accomplishments, he displayed too much arrogance for a young lieutenant. It smacked of a concealed liaison with a senior officer, and Malila was not going to share the fate of those who exposed delicate secrets of the top brass. Six was sufficient for her purposes.

Edie started sending the summons for the meeting.

Moving down the sinuous, shining mental corridors of her O-A display; passing the choke points; giving the right passwords and countersigns; bringing up data, statistics, images, maps, and video, Malila collected the elements of her *story. Rule 1: The story has to be absolutely true.*

Colonel Sophia Henchly, one of her first patrons, had taught her the four rules. Sophia had been a very crafty lady indeed.

In another portion of the CORE, an officer of the Democratic Unity Forces for Security sent a memorandum to his superior officer. This was all well, proper, and … invidious. He reviewed it with pleasure.

TO: Lt. Gen. V. Suarez

FROM: Lt. Col. E. Jourdaine

RE: Administrative actions in re. Unity Sensor Station 43.11.0/97_89.13.56/41 (SUNPRAIRIE)

14.17.32.local_11_10_AU76

As reported previously, failures at SUNPRAIRIE continue. Second Lt. Chiu is the officer responsible in re. SUNPRAIRIE operationality.

It has come to my attention that Lt. Chiu is contravening protocol in as:

She has inaugurated an ad hoc committee of inquiry for the failures at SUNPRAIRIE whose members include:

Herein the gray man included a list of a seven young officers of the DUFS.

Included for effect, if not for accuracy, was Second Lieutenant Miramundo Morales.

If Jourdaine's information and his conclusions were correct, Morales's name on the list of petty conspirators would trigger Suarez's outrage, plummeting young Lieutenant Chiu into the depths of the command structure. Like a great and unequal lever, Chiu's abrupt descent would elevate the slim gray man the short distance to the interior of Suarez's confidence.

CHAPTER 6

CONSPIRACY

An incessant pinging alerted Malila that all her committee members had arrived, each represented by a headshot looming in her O-A. The faces floated in and out of prominence as one or another factor played out in her thoughts. She started:

> *"Greetings to you all. I am pleased by your prompt response."*

Stock greetings, as expected, cascaded in, but even so, Malila detected the fleeting grimaces of several of them. They had come to get information, but they did not have to like it.

> *"Here is the situation as we now understand it. Station Sunprairie is down for the third time in three months."*

Malila listened to the rising babble, the faces surging in and out of prominence as one or another of her colleagues made or deflected accusations.

These people would fight each other until there was nothing left unless she gave them the setup. She rapped a mental gavel and killed all the audio outputs except her own.

Rule 2: The setup makes the story sing. A good setup arranged facts, simplified them, augmented them where needed, and gave the *right* facts structure and weight.

> *"Our best understanding about this outrage is that a dangerous new ideology has arisen among the barbarians. The natives have apparently decided that Sunprairie represents a gift from their spirit guides. They have gained ingress to Sunprairie, we have found, by sacrificing victim after victim to the pulse cannon, depleting the magazines, and using their stone weapons on the door. I cannot describe what obscene ceremonies are most likely being performed within this 'sacred precinct' even as we speak."*

Malila opened the audio, and the babbling among committee members accelerated right on cue. Malila smiled to herself.

> *"Hold your questions until the end, please.*

> *"We believe these events represent the rise of a new and radical band of shamans among the savages, a force that, we think, must be thwarted as soon as possible."*

Rule 3: Don't confuse people with too many choices. If she chose the right setup, told it correctly, then narrowed the options, subtly slanting her audience, they, like sheep, would come together into one box, all facing a blank wall … with but one gate. Once she opened that gate, the flock would crowd in, anxious not to be last to go through, lining up to be trimmed.

Now was the time to call in her "black capital," the mass of missteps and misdemeanors she'd collected on everyone. A little snapping at the heels to encourage them on would be proper.

"Unfortunately, and, Jorge, you may want to take note of this for the future, munition deliveries have been slow this month. That delayed our regular maintenance trip for three days. With this last attack, we did not have full magazines in the pulse cannon."

"Yes, but you see, Lieutenant Chiu—"

"Moving on," she said, "we have the matter of security upgrades that needed installing. Hari? You're taking over for Fillipa there, aren't you? I think I talked to her about that some time ago. She may have left notes. I'd check it out if I were you."

This time just a nod and no objections.

Malila went on from one to another, alluding to deficiencies of one or another department as she did. She would mention a name. A head would come up, looking startled, the look deepening as its owner apprehended the vulnerability, each face solidifying as the brain behind it evaluated its chances.

There were always deficiencies in the operation of these large departments. It mattered very little that the magazines were short a few rounds. The attack had emptied the entire magazine within two hours. No security upgrade would have protected the station once the savages had gotten close enough. Each of the half-dozen accusations, while true, was neither new nor outrageous.

Malila smiled to herself. At the end of her presentation, not one of her fellow officers was able to meet her eyes. She could lead them where she wanted to now.

"I think if we cooperate, we can come out of this unscathed, all of us. Moreover, we can get rid of a nuisance that is no longer serving the best objectives of the Unity."

"If this is such a good idea, why not send it up command and have them pass on it?" a voice said and chuckled.

> *"Oh, come on, Torq. You know the answer to that one. One faction or another will decide it is easier to attack any good idea than it is to cooperate,"* she replied.

Torq Hagken from Signals Procurement—tall, blond, and with a ready laugh—would under other circumstances be a good candidate for Malila's first liaison without patronage. Now he needed to be brought up a bit.

> *"Let's not be foolish. We represent here maybe three or four of the strongest factions, and all of us cooperate on a daily basis. Our bosses don't."*

There was generalized shaking of heads and wry smiles.

> *"Okay, saying that could be an accurate statement sometimes, maybe; what do you have in mind?"* replied Torq.
>
> Malila took a deep breath and said, *"Let me see if we can sum this up. Sunprairie is the farthest station. It sits in an uninhabited, untraveled wilderness. In the long run, the DUFS will probably abandon it.*
>
> *"However, the DUFS can't be seen to retreat before the savages. Agreed?"*

There was the expected bobbing of heads.

Rule 4: Don't be greedy. Let everyone win, and you can trim them again later.

> *"If the outlanders are so intent on Sunprairie, let's let them have it. Fix it up, get it running, pack in C24 until the walls bulge, then back away slowly. The savages break into it again, and while they are hooting and drooling, the C goes off, leaving a message even they can actually read.*

> *"We kill off these shamans. The survivors think it is their own evil spirits that have jibbed them. In a stroke we get the barbarians to back off, cut the head off their leadership, and rid ourselves of a liability. Questions?"*

> *"What about the loss of property. You are advising we blow up an entire installation to kill off a couple of hillbillies?"* asked Sharon DeWhit from Logistics.

> *"Look at the costs we have expended so far this year on fixing the place, Sharon. The operation would pay for itself in four rotations. The truth is we cannot hold Sunprairie. We either lose it for no gain, or we get some advantage from it and stop the hemorrhaging."*

> *"The loss of a facility is not going to go unnoticed. What happens when our bosses start looking into this?"* asked Hari.

> *"If"—Malila looked each of the others in the eye—"we stick together, it will be, at worst, only bad planning on Jorge's and my part: Jorge for overfilling a request for C24 and me for leaving it at Sunprairie. The best is that we ... all of us ... are given commendations. I will see to it that we all get rewarded."*

> *"Why are you so willing to sacrifice yourself—and me—for this? What's your angle?"* asked Jorge.

That was the question, wasn't it? *Sometimes to lead is to lose,* she thought.

> *"To tell the truth, I think your part in this is the least advantageous, Jorge. I can't see how we can blow up the station unless we get the C from you. That will always leave a trail. If things go south, you will take a hit before anyone*

else. At the same time, due to considerations not herein under discussion ..."

Jorge almost immediately looked as if he was going to vomit. Most of the others experienced enough of his dismay through their shared O-A connection to turn a little green themselves. Jorge's black-capital account with Malila was reaping dividends. Malila sent an encouraging message and documentation that his debt was now paid ... in part. He subsided.

"... I believe Jorge will stand nobly by my side in this hour of need.

"But," Malila continued, *"what's my angle? It is a legitimate question. Here goes: One, I think this will work. It will be seen as a victory, and I will get a lot of the credit. I will risk the fallout if it doesn't work. Two, it is the best for the DUFS. Sniffer stations are a bad idea, fixed fortification and all that. We would be better off patrolling the outlands in person ... and that means more combat missions for all of us. Our bosses have trouble making compromises.* We need to do this. *Three, if any of you rat me out, I promise you, I will rat out the rest. Do I make myself clear?"*

In the end, the committee made their peace with her. They would all be extraordinarily helpful in getting Sunprairie up and running one last time. They would all take a little heat from their superiors about their actions, if discovered, but it would not be career bending. Malila had just started the self-congratulatory preadjournment phase when Edie spoke up in her little-girl voice.

Oh-oh.

One and then another of her audience looked up, spoke a few unheard words, and disappeared, the image replaced by the Unity logo, an eagle grasping a *fasci*[5] in one claw and lightning in the other. Just then her own O-A went blank. She felt as if she had been struck blind. The subtle noise of circulation fans in her room stopped. Behind her, the portal latch locked with a snick.

Her heart surged, pounding in her ears, as her palms greased with sweat. Malila waited. It came almost as a relief when her vision filled with the looming face of her division commander, Lieutenant General Vivalagente Suarez. With steel-gray hair cut severely and pulled back into a flat braid, a hawk nose, severe eyes, and a hard mouth, it was a harsh face and currently not a happy one.

> *"Second Lieutenant Chiu, Malila E., E11, S24, 59026169, attention!"*

All her resources, of the CORE and her own person, came to taut singularity.

> *"Sir, yes, sir!"*

Then, to her horror, slowly, Malila sensed herself pressed down, crumpled from her posture of attention, bent, submitted, and reduced, kneeling before the image.

Her denunciation had started.

Observing through his O-A, Jourdaine thought it was the most profoundly humiliating seppuku he had ever witnessed. He quickly muted the emotional inputs. The discovery of Suarez's attachment to Miramundo Morales was reaping a richer bounty than he had hoped. Suarez viewed Malila Chiu as a dangerous but lightly armed adversary. Taking each of Chiu's sins, other than the real one, Suarez identified and cited the appropriate regulation. On her knees, Chiu was forced to recant, to plead, as every dignity and privilege she had rightfully earned was ripped away.

---

[5] Rods bundled around an ax; the emblem flanks the Speaker's chair in US Congress and is the source of the word *fascism*.

Suarez, even in her rage, never mentioned Morales's name, and Chiu would never know it had been added to her list of committee members. The real cause for her denunciation would be a lifelong mystery for Chiu.

Jourdaine had spent a great deal of time and influence uncovering Suarez's weak spot. Current Unity policies had not helped. Sexual liaisons of any imaginable number, composition, or equipage were tolerated. The only remaining sins, it appeared, were greed, failure, and favoritism. Suarez was inconveniently ascetic and awkwardly successful. However, to Jourdaine's surprise, Vivalagente Suarez was blessed with a younger brother.

Somehow, Suarez had been able to identify and connect with her sibling. She had arranged for his advancement well ahead of any demonstrated ability on the boy's part.

If seeming to include Morales in a plot, any plot, made Suarez react, it would confirm his suspicions. Her reaction to this counterfeit danger was so wildly out of proportion that it simultaneously confirmed Jourdaine's theory about Morales and ingratiated him with Suarez.

And Malila Chiu had paid for all the heavy lifting. No doubt, after rehabilitation, she would become a perpetual ensign in some outer district until retired. By then, Suarez would be a bad memory and Jourdaine himself a Solon … or better.

The immaculate poignancy of his success made Eustace Jourdaine laugh.

CHAPTER 7

SALVATION THROUGH WORK

Suarez pronounced sentence upon her. When the portal to Malila's quarters unlocked, a detail of CRNA guards entered, disarmed her, and took station ahead and behind as they double-quick marched her out of the building. None spoke.

Edie was gone; her O-A was now a buzzing blur of static.

All Malila could see ahead were the moving black backs of her guards. She caught glimpses of startled citizens watching her as she jogged past, their faces the odd mixture of horror and the quiet glee of the uninvolved spectator. The tramp of the soldiers' boots surrounded her. The weight of a full bladder made her fear shaming herself before men she might have commanded. Her lungs burned.

It was nightmare hours later before the heavy metal door closed behind her at Battry Island.

Malila found herself in darkness. Throughout that fetid, damp, and dark imprisonment, a thought animated her. She searched on hands and knees, finding no bed, water, food, or shard of glass. Only in failure did she weep. With no weapon, the satisfaction of leaving her tormentors with only a corpse was beyond her.

In the middle watches of the night, Malila's eyes adjusted, finding the cell not entirely dark. A single ray of light gleamed around the door, lighting a fingernail-sized patch of concrete floor. Malila emptied herself into watching the particle of light, small, like a faint star. Her nausea retreated. If she looked too directly, it vanished. By studious disregard, she was able to sit and watch its steady unmoving radiance. She was still crouched near it when they came to get her.

Again, there was the storm of barked orders, movement, nausea, and the clang of locking doors. She was thrust into a seat, hot light blinding her. Her O-A came alive. The face of a young ensign, an S16, loomed into her mental vision, capturing all her senses instantaneously.

> *"Chiu, Malila E., E11, number 59026169."*
>
> *"Sir, yes, sir!"*
>
> *"You are hereby assigned a rank of acting second lieutenant S08 without privileges, pay, or entitlements."*
>
> *"Sir, yes, sir!"*
>
> *"You are ordered to assume temporary command of Platoon Bravo, Second Company, Twentieth Battalion. They are to act as your security detail."*
>
> *"Sir, yes, sir!"*
>
> *"You are to repair station* 43.11.0/97_89.13.56/41, Sunprairie, *making it fully operational. You have rations for one week. Transport will rendezvous as convenient October 19, AU 76.*
>
> *"On completion, you will report to Correctional Facility 221c."*

"Sir!"

The O-A went dead before she could say, "Yes, sir!"

Nausea and the watery sensation of fear returned.

For long minutes, she heard only the whine of the engine and sensed herself rising, unable to withstand the sun's glare enough to open her eyes. Almost against reason, she grasped she was not going to be Sapped. She had been given a mission.

She opened her eyes and looked into the belly of the skimmer. It was filled with an unknown platoon of helmeted CRNA troopers. The CRNAs had paid their debt to the Unity, and anonymity was a way to preserve their usefulness after Sapping. CRNAs never removed their helmets in public, and one never entered their barracks unannounced.

Last night she'd had no opportunity to end her shame. Now she had an opportunity to redeem herself. She had a command, if only for the duration of the mission. She had a job, if only a dirty and trivial job. If she failed, she expected nothing but Sapp and a mindless life as a CRNA foot soldier. If she succeeded, perhaps a return to the active service. It was possible.

Acting Second Lieutenant Malila Chiu watched from the jump seat of the skimmer as it floated over the extended city of the Unity and headed west.

Malila tried to calm herself. She had always admired the design of the city. Stark-white residential buildings around neon-green community squares near black factory sections repeated as far as the eye could see. Skilled workers could walk to their jobs and return to snug apartment homes around parklike squares designed for trials, festivals, and celebrations. The pattern stretched away in every direction, accentuated by corridors left for water, sewage, power, and urban transit. The Unity was one city, from the southern stretches of sea sand to the rocky coasts of the North. Despite herself, Acting Second Lieutenant Chiu smiled at being under way and under orders.

"Ever see the farm belt, Lieutenant?" crackled the voice of the pilot, breaking into her reverie.

"No, no. Pretty much a city girl, sir!"

"Call me Jayden. Right seat here is Sofie. Wave to our supercargo, Sofie!" A hand fluttered overhead from the right-hand seat, which was turned forward, away from her.

A brown line edged up on the horizon. The farm belt stretched several hundred kilometers wide here, Malila supposed. It looked unpromising.

"Here it comes. They just got in the maize and soybeans, so it is pretty barren right now. You should see it in the spring," the pilot's voice buzzed into her headphones.

Even at this height, Malila smelled the reek of open brown earth, the tang of rot, and the pungent stench of manure. She had never been airsick before.

"Where are the animals?" Malila asked, trying to quell her stomach.

Jayden turned in his seat, his voice coming in through her headset.

"I've never seen them from the air. I suspect they are penned up below ground … saves land. What ya think, Sophie?"

"I think it smells like shit, Captain. Permission to increase speed."

Jayden shrugged at Malila and turned back to the controls.

Malila saw no people. She was watching a train with flatbeds carrying huge green machines moving north when she became aware of the band of abysmal blackness just slicing the horizon. No photograph, comm'net, or CORE sim did it justice. The power belt ran the length of the Unity. Underneath the kilometers-wide power panels lay the real heart of the Unity's energy: the storage farms that stretched under the landscape, far larger than the panels themselves.

"Behold the power that moves us all," intoned Jayden as the band filled the entire field of the windshield.

Sophie, a petite, freckled redhead, turned and rolled her eyes at Malila before turning back without saying a word. Malila smiled. It felt good.

With difficulty, Malila pulled her eyes away from the featureless blackness of the power farms back to the horizon. No-man's-land, interlocking sensors and integrated projectile-fire stations sweeping the free-fire zone, came next. As they neared, Malila saw small heaps of scorched feathers littering the plowed earth.

"Fall migration," said Sophie.

Then came the Rampart.[6] The Rampart itself was no longer made of anything so crude as concrete. It showed on the horizon as a single line from the skimmer's altitude. It loomed closer, unbroken and resolute. The pulse-cannon muzzles along a kilometer curve of the Rampart detected the approaching craft, moving in unison. Even at this distance, Malila saw the bottomless black stare of the weapons. She licked her lips.

"This is Charlie-Alpha-Tango-one-niner-niner. Requesting passage, two skimmers, Station one-one-Dog-Zulu-Bravo," Jayden said.

Malila heard a distant and imprecise buzzing in her earpiece.

"Whiskey-one, Quebec-November-three, Yankee-one-seven," Jayden said. There was another buzzing before Jayden finished with "One-niner-niner ... out."

Only when Malila saw the pulse-cannon muzzles drop away from the skimmer did she realize she had stopped breathing. She tried to cloak her too-rapid intake of air.

"Yep, it has that effect on most people the first time," Jayden's amused voice whistled through her headphones.

"You can't tell, but this section is the Western Gate. Try passing anywhere else except at gates, and it doesn't matter if you have all the codes in the world! Ka-phizzzzt!" he said before laughing.

Most pilots were ThiZed out most of the time, Malila knew; Sofie giggled.

The skimmers floated over the furrows of sundered earth and into

---

[6] "The Rampart was built just after the Scorching (October AU 3 to February AU 4). Thousands of savages from the final defeat of the outlands (AU 5) attempted to escape disaster by entering the Unity. Wave after wave died under our guns, but not without horrendous losses. It was then that the Solons proposed building the Rampart, and the people heroically responded. Over the years, the Rampart has grown, remaining the boundary marker between chaos and order, famine and plenty, dark and light. The Rampart itself has changed from a few strategic forts into a symbol of the Unity itself, its foundations washed at either end by the sea." B. Gore, ed., *A Young Citizen's Guide to the History of America*, 3rd ed. (Boston: Prometheus Press, AU 71), 210.

the outlands. Something grew out of the debris to rim the destruction with venomous green-and-purple tumors.

The skimmers' rate of climb was shallow, despite its ability to carry prodigious loads. Jayden took a circuitous route, following small waterless valleys, as they climbed and narrowed. Rank after rank of buildings, their black windows blown out, looking like gigantic stacks of dice in some unknown game of chance, passed underneath. Tall hollow towers, broken into thirds and lying amid the rubble of a mill, looked like ancient ruins. Despite all the simulations, the immediacy of the devastation troubled her. She fancied she could smell the stench of cold, wet embers and decay.

The skimmers reached the last curve of a valley and started a spiraling climb to pass over a series of ridges. Dark shadows of pines and hardwoods replaced the sere slopes and their relics. Before the Commendable Victory, when the People's Republic (now the Unity) had been forced to blanket much of the wilderness with herbicide, the outlands had supported a generous population, or so she had been told. It was impossible for Malila to imagine anything but primordial chaos, thrilling herself to a dose of domesticated horror.

Once free of the mountains, the landscape flattened. Crossing silver threads of rivers laced between dark forests, the skimmers pushed west. Malila made out faint rectangular traces among the trees. The land had memory, even if she did not.

By late afternoon, the skimmers approached their LZ. Despite the blaze of gold, scarlet, and orange leaves, the forest looked less exotic here. The bunker, at the center of a wide free-fire zone, was low and brooding, its four sides windowless and sloping to a flat roof spiked with antennae and weapons. It was an ugly edifice, an unvarnished statement of Unity power.

The skimmers landed. CRNA squads jogged out to secure the tree line. Three-quarters of an hour later, Malila left the skimmer to take possession of Sunprairie.

She was barely on the ground as she heard the ramp door closing behind her and the Skimmerhorn drives accelerating. Willing herself not to watch, Malila heard the skimmers lift free and speed away. It was a policy of the Unity that aircraft minimize their time at low altitude, ensuring that the barbarians never captured advanced technology. Apparently, acting second lieutenants were not a commodity the Unity felt compelled to conserve.

CHAPTER 8

SUNPRAIRIE

43.11.0/97_89.13.56/41 Sunprairie Station
15.52.07.central_12_10_AU76

The blackened door lay several meters from the portal, the rebar bent like grotesque writhing snakes.

"Sergeant Nelson, is the station secured? Any explosive devices?" Malila voiced into her headset.

"Sir. Yes. Station searched. No hostiles. Detected explosive devices: none."

"Meet me at the entrance, and keep a list of tasks."

"Sir!"

Nelson could at least act as a scribe. Most CRNAs could hardly talk.

Nelson and she strode through the base, which extended three floors below the hulking mass of the entrance. The first floor was all equipment and vandalized as expected. On the second floor, they passed through the landing into another room, crunching glass underfoot.

"Sir! Second floor, supplies and officers' quarters, sir. One bed, single; one command terminal, vid screen inoperative; toilet, unflushed; shower, nonfunctional; washbasin, occupied; cook surface, inoperative. Sir!" enunciated Nelson.

Malila examined briefly the damp feral sock that lurked in the washbasin.

"The colony is coming," in red dribbled paint, decorated the back wall. It surprised her. She had been unaware the outlanders had the written word.

"Sergeant, have this room cleaned; repaint these quarters."

"Sir, yes, sir."

Malila was beginning to feel that her world was becoming understandable ... until she started down to the men's barracks on the lowest floor. A dark and foreboding pool of fetid water opened at her feet.

"Sergeant, the men will bivouac outside until we get their quarters pumped dry. Do we have cover for them? What is the weather forecast?"

"Sir! Shelters, food, water, and latrine facilities sufficient, sir. Weather report: fair weather, five days, minimum temperature four degrees standard, sir."

"Good enough, Sergeant. Let's keep going."

By the time she finished the inspection, Nelson had a long list of menial jobs for the men. Malila sent him to organize the perimeter.

It would take days to pump the station dry, bring the computers online, reestablish the network, and finally synchronize the signals with headquarters. The actual work was hers; CRNAs were only her bodyguard, nothing more.

Malila began work on the pumps, emerging an hour later dirty and wet after crawling around service conduits and rewiring the connection through the panel. She would be listening to the pump's low rumble for most of the next two days.

The weather was good for autumn, and the men would be comfortable outside. She was just as glad. CRNAs always made their quarters smell foul after a few hours. As a cadet, she had called them "the rank and vile." Malila smiled.

Other than the intermittent sound of pulse fire, the rest of the travel-shortened first day was uneventful. Malila guessed there would be an abrupt decline in the local rodent population. The judgment of the CRNAs was poor. The rifles were locked to the platoon by fingerprint readers on the triggers and ID chips embedded in the base of the thumb. It kept them from losing them. They even had the antifratricide subroutine to keep the men from firing at each other by mistake.

CRNAs were the bone and muscle of the DUFS. They were hardy, loyal, and dumb as a sack of hammers, but they fired quickly and accurately and took staggering losses before losing combat integrity. The use of their bodies, absent the higher functions, was the price the Unity had prescribed for their crimes. Lieutenant Chiu climbed up to the destroyed portal.

"Sergeant Nelson!"

"Sir, yes, sir!" rasped into her headset.

"Feed the men, and set a perimeter. Reveille at 0600."

"Sir, yes, sir."

She felt better when she was issuing commands.

Her quarters were now clean, and the plumbing worked. She ate some rations, showered, threw herself onto the cot, took her ThiZ, and was asleep almost immediately.

The first night was quiet, but fatigued as she was, Malila did not sleep well. She had her dream, waking her in the darkness with its usual panic. Once awake she could not sleep.

All her hopes balanced at some point in the future. In time, she would watch the balance lever slowly drop her down into the depths of oblivion or lift her back to where she had been only hours before. Strangely, she missed Edie. Malila had created Edie—well, had designed the accent, the speech, the subroutines, and the commands—and yet she missed her. The useless O-A hummed in her head.

She finally got up at 0200 and walked along the picket line. She found the CRNAs' brisk challenges reassuring. She returned to her bed an hour later and was able to drop off again with the monotonous hum of the pumps sounding like a huddle of distant voices.

She awoke still grumpy and a bit dazed. Even the CRNAs were

having trouble getting started in the cold morning air. It took repeated orders to get them to respond. With luck, she thought, the men would be under cover tomorrow.

Despite her weariness, Malila set to her task with eagerness. Her path to rejoin the DUFS, reenter the Unity, and retrieve her career led through the dank and dimly lit corridors of Sunprairie. In a way, she found it a pleasure to fall back onto her skills as a warrant officer, doing her own work and depending on her own computations. She spent the day fixing one problem only to find another that had been undiscoverable until she had fixed the first.

Every few hours she went to the surface to give a new task to Sergeant Nelson and the CRNAs.

She worked through the afternoon and into the evening before she caught herself nodding. Then she ordered Nelson to wake her at 0530, took her usual hit of ThiZ, stripped down to her skivvies, ate some rations, and threw herself onto the bunk in a haze of exhaustion.

She slept well until, hours later, she awoke in the dark with a hand over her mouth and a knife to her throat.

"Don't move, lass," hissed a voice. The hand moved enough for her to breathe, if just barely. She heard the muffled sounds of what might be commands, several loud reports, and then single shots at longer intervals. After the first few, Malila counted thirty-seven shots fired. She felt a jab in her thigh and then nothing.

CHAPTER 9

HECATE

Nyork, Unity
12.47.11.local_11_10_AU76

Hecate ran down the stone steps of the museum and into the street without looking back, glad that a real excuse compelled her to leave Malila and go where she might think. She hurried along the sidewalk under the awnings put up to catch the buildings in their inevitable decay. After taking the descender for the belt trip uptown, she looked at her watch. She'd get back only a few minutes early, and it made her nervous. She would feel much better if she arrived at her usual fifteen minutes before the end of lunchtime.

Maneuvering to the fastest belt, she started walking whenever she could, dodging small groups of people as she went, and emerged into the towering lobby of the People's Building at 148th.

Malila was so frustratingly dense at times! It came from her finding things so easy. She had never needed to study at school, had never needed to practice. It gave her a blind spot, almost a cruelty. It also made Malila blind to the failings of the Unity. Hecate supposed that was only reasonable for a DUFS. The whole society heaved and groaned, toiled and struggled, merely to give the soldiers their next shiny toy. Certainly, no one was going to dispute their position of supremacy. Data readouts and ponderous reports were no match for a couple of pulse mortar shells lobbed into a ministry.

Hecate absentmindedly walked to her elevator and announced her floor before settling back into thought.

She had gotten much up too upset about the krill farm and could not blame Malila, or her boss, for not sharing her concern. She supposed Undersecretary Rice herself was engaged in an unseen battle with her own superiors, just as Hecate was engaged with Rice. While Hecate had to contend with awkward facts coming in from the field, Rice had to contend with a couple dozen S22s, like Hecate herself. Rice had to keep the S22s moving forward and had to make her own bosses happy with an analysis of the analyses. Hecate wondered if she would ever have the ruthlessness needed for Rice's job.

Exiting the elevator, Hecate entered the bustle of her office, dodging the kid from CORE as he sped by on skates.

"Kazzen! Can I talk with you?" she said to the disappearing back of the computer tech.

"Get back to you in a minute, Jones," echoed back to her in the nearly empty office.

She finally was able to wend her way to the small desk in a windowless corner, and her stomach lurched.

"Jervani-ah, can I help you?" she said, and the young man looked up, startled.

"Oh, uh, hi, Hecate! I was just looking. Nice holos, really," he said, rapidly putting the holo he was holding down. Then he moved it and put down a paper he was carrying. "I should check up on something ... Bye," he said as he walked off.

Dumb and clumsy, Jervani-ah was somebody's new henchman. It might just be a mind game, but it might be someone trying to gather the innocent coincidences that fueled office politics. It had taken Hecate only a short time to realize that politics was the true product of her whole division.

Rearranging her pictures back to where they should be, she picked up a holo of her friends and herself in a frame she'd made in school as a child, all improbable flowers and pink hearts. A younger Malila smiled back at her from midair as the projection sensed her regard and activated itself.

The image, giving her a faint buzzing feedback as it appeared to rest on her palm, enlarged as she moved it nearer. Malila smiled broadly at her from an age ago. Malila was the true believer of the group and never saw the problems others did. If she led, people followed.

Luscena, next to her in the holo, possessed the sheer vitality to lead, but her talent had seduced her. She preened herself as long as others applauded. Alexandra, next to her, had the smarts but not the personality to make a stand on her own. Alex spun stories to spec, fooling the less wary … and herself along with everyone else.

Hecate moved a finger along the contours of the holo to the last of her friends, Tiffany's auburn hair off-color in the image. Tiffany was such a good person, bumbling along with her head down, doing good things for less worthy people, and not looking where she was going. It was always so good to have them together again, just like today. It spoke to old times and confidences.

She loved them all, with a childish ardent love that she could never really examine. And she loved Victor.

Hecate's coworkers started arriving, coming back from lunch the usual thirteen minutes late. She put the holo image down; it faded slowly as she moved to the next holo of Victor himself, looking a bit absentminded as he received the Osmian Prize in 74.

Doctor Victor di Lorenzo was her first patron … her only one for the four years since they'd met. He was one of the people her teachers had helped her choose among the more senior staff when she was an E7, just finishing government guild school.

The whole thing had terrified her younger self. Hecate could see the utility of the system easily enough, of course. Take the new kids straight out of school and have them mentored by the experienced bureaucrats. In exchange for guidance and protection, the thirteen-year-olds provided loyalty and pleasure-sex.

But Hecate had not enjoyed offering herself. It must have shown. In the morning, after each submission ceremony, the other patrons-elect had wished her well and wished her elsewhere. None had accepted her as a protégé.

Victor had been an S31 and an E28 when they'd met. She'd followed the protocol precisely: disrobing, then enunciating the submission speech while looking into his eyes. Victor had held her by the hand before leading her to his bedroom.

He'd held her all night in a warm embrace, listening to her fears and hopes, sharing stories of his life, and letting her sleep. She had risen the next morning to leave, thinking he had rejected her as a protégé, only to be surprised as he gently pulled her back to his bed and told her of his acceptance.

They had been inseparable ever since. He was not a particularly good patron for someone in her division. His area of expertise was in bacteriology, but his work was important and well regarded. Their prolonged relationship had amused and then concerned her teachers. It was a joke among his friends. Neither she nor Victor cared. They were both happy to remain each other's sole pleasure-sex partner and nearly constant companion.

Victor reminded her of Tiffany, in a way. He was a good man who dealt with the problems at hand and expended little regard for the commotion of life around him. He lived, in his way, a life of quiet seclusion: doing his experiments, collating the data, writing his insightful papers, publishing them, and defending them with humor and dignity. Fame surprised him.

With Victor now an S33, their lives should be easier, but Victor was probably not as good an administrator as he was an investigator. He depended too much on others' good will and integrity.

Her world revolved between these three centers of gravity: Victor, her friends, and work.

Work ... She had found her work fulfilling until Undersecretary Rice had arrived. Her last boss, Wiscoll Root, had always maintained that their job was to get the best information into the most understandable package for the ward leaders and district supervisors to argue over and let the chips fall where they may. As long as the information was sound, he did not care what happened to it.

Undersecretary Rice cared what happened to it ... sometimes. She would devote endless efforts to craft a report one day. On another, she would shovel critical findings into an obscure footnote in a huge routine report. Victor had sniffed when Hecate had told him Rice was her new boss.

Hecate replaced Victor's holo in line and straightened them all again before sitting down to start the report for the now-defunct krill farm. It would be a short report.

A group of touring schoolchildren had arrived to discover the entire effusion was dead or lost back into the ocean. The nets had rotted in the water. The workers had been long gone, their names fictional, the manager a well-protected career bureaucrat in Nyork who most likely had no idea where Negzed was located in the first place. Victor had somehow known something was wrong.

Victor always knew a great deal more than he admitted, which was odd, as he was so nonpolitical. Even granting he was a brilliant man, his influence seeped into odd places, like the book warehouses. Hecate always wondered why they had not just burned the books for fuel during the chaotic days of the Meltdown. Instead, the books had been bundled up and tossed into old warehouses near the wharves. Victor had obtained the pass on a whim when they had been lazing away a Sunday morning in bed.

The volume of old books, the really old ones on paper, was huge. Many had been destroyed by mildew and rats, but some of the books in the interior of the bundles had been saved from destruction. Those she read. She brought the stories back to Victor, and he loved them ... but then again, Victor loved her. Hecate mined the warehouses for tales and stories to make Victor laugh and, on occasion, to make him appear as young as when they'd first met. Victor would be forty years old in April AU 78, eighteen months from now. Then he would be gone.

CHAPTER 10

SUAREZ AND THE GRAY MAN

DUFS Divisional HQ, Nyork, Unity
07.11.43.local_18_10_AU76

The skimmer accepted its passenger and traced a seemingly random pattern on empty streets before entering the S30-and-above armored carriageway under the city. It delivered its passenger to an anonymous beige office building three minutes later.

A senior officer of the DUFS strode through the lobby and to the elevator. The elevator moved. Lieutenant General Vivalagente Suarez remained brooding.

The Chiu woman had delivered another black eye. The failure of a sensor station was a triviality, and if Chiu had admitted her failure instead of trying to ape her superiors, nothing more would have occurred … other than her demotion. Foolishly, Chiu had jeopardized Miro, knowingly or unknowingly, and there was nothing for it. It had taken years to find him, and Suarez was not going to let this girl mess it up. Looking after Miramundo was the least she could do for her dead parents.

But she had let her anger affect her judgment. In a moment of pique, she'd sent Chiu to fix the station herself. A squad of CRNAs and an OAA would have been sufficient, and Chiu should have been able to put the station to rights in a few days. Instead, the jumped-up little fool had gone missing. Most of the platoon identifiers had winked out within minutes of each other. The scout craft had discovered Sunprairie still smoldering. The few operating implants had come from the bottom of a mass of charred bodies in a half-submerged stairwell.

It had taken a day to ensure that Chiu was not within the death pit. After recalibration, they had picked up her O-A signal. That had led to a wasted day tacking back and forth across a patch of muddy water on some nameless river in the outlands.

As she stepped from the elevator, she said, "Get Jourdaine in to me as soon as you can, Adrianna," without breaking stride as she entered the security portal of her office. It was time to see what her new adjutant was good for.

Lieutenant Colonel Jourdaine noted the summons and, turning, emptied the contents of his desktop into a secure drawer. He fastened his own ElectoMag lock onto it and pressed his thumb to the surface to secure it. He left his austere office and began to trot the several floors to his audience with Suarez.

Eustace Tilley Jourdaine, lieutenant colonel, DUFS, E21, S29, had made himself a very useful man, he thought. He had made his career by being useful to his superiors, to the DUFS, and to the nation. One commanding officer after another had given him the jobs that had no glamor if a success and immense disgrace if a failure.

Yet nothing about him had ever seemed to snag the recognition of his superiors. He had gone a full year in General Suarez's staff before she'd remembered his name reliably. Nonetheless, after his recent elevation to adjutant, he would be the officer to whom Suarez gave the jobs that required subtlety, judgment, and ingenuity. Her demands would serve him well … for a while, at least.

He never stayed within any one command very long. They

would name him to a post, he would be quietly proficient for a year or so, and then he would quietly start the rumors. Sometimes his superiors had taken excessive liberties in the distribution of spoils. On other occasions, unit money had been misapplied. Sometimes exposés of darker political ambitions among his fellow officers had surfaced. There was always something. With some clever manipulation, Jourdaine could enlarge any potential wrongdoing and expose the perpetrators. Then those higher up promoted him and quietly transfered him to another unit. His old commander retired "for the good of the service." Thus did Eustace Jourdaine prosper.

Jourdaine smiled more broadly at the irony of it as he exited onto Suarez's floor.

Even as Jourdaine was shown in, Suarez said, "Tell me about Sunprairie."

Jourdaine came to parade rest.

"It was a trap, sir. An entire platoon is dead, and Lieutenant Chiu is missing and presumed captured. I assume that was the object of the outages all summer long ... to capture an officer for questioning."

"How many pulse rifles were lost?" she asked.

"Uhh ... forty-two."

"They weren't recovered when the sensor station was retaken?"

"No, sir. Just the lieutenant's sidearm, sir. We had to excavate the stairwell to recover the bodies ..."

A faint grimace of distaste crossed Suarez's features. "Spare me the details. Any disfigurements of the bodies, Colonel?"

He stopped for the beat of a heart. She already knew! "Yes, sir, the right forefingers were removed at the DIP joint, as well as skin and tissue of the thenar eminence."

Suarez looked at Jourdaine and raised an eyebrow.

"Ah, DIP ... They cut through the first knuckle ... here. And the thenar eminence is where we insert the ID-chip on version S72." He indicated the base of his thumb.

"So how many signature chips have these savages obtained?"

"Forty-two, sir."

"How many weapons with their signature chips have we lost in the outlands prior to this?"

This was not going as he had expected. "I don't immediately know the answer to that question, General Suarez."

"Five since the start of the Unity. Five total. So now the savages have forty-two Springfield model 72s, our best field weapon. Chiu has delivered this disaster into our laps. I hope for her sake she's dead."

"May I ask, General, what you propose to do?" Jourdaine kept his face bland for the woman to inspect.

"I plan to give you the problem," she said finally.

"Yes, sir. How would you like me to proceed? Shall I call a committee meeting of ... 'interested' parties?"

"Good start, Jourdaine." She gave him an odd look, hawk-like. He was beginning to feel increasingly mousy.

"Keep me posted," she said. "The advantage to this is that the disaster is big enough that most other commands within the service will want to help us minimize the damage."

"Yes, sir."

"Now, Colonel, tell me your views of the Aroostook Campaign."

The hawk was showing him her talons, but he'd come prepared for this one.

"Sir, the Aroostook Campaign is winding down. The Quebecers have pretty much gotten what they wanted. My opinion is that the war has been a nightmare and was probably never winnable. Getting a rail line to an ice-free port is a realpolitik goal for Canadians. Northern Main is just blueberries and pulpwood for us. My understanding is that General of the Army Emanuel is awaiting a vote of confidence."

Suarez smiled. "So suddenly, the Unity has a stable northern border, and we will have to recycle these troopers within eighteen months," Suarez said.

"Recycle?"

"If you are going to be an effective adjutant, there are a few things you should know. You have just passed into the senior staff, Eustace. Here is point number one: CRNAs don't last more than about four to six years after Sapping. They do improve with training ... slowly, of course. So currently, half of our experienced troopers will be compost in eighteen months." She looked down to brush at her sleeve, as if giving him time to consider.

"Then it is imperative that we use the army now rather than waiting."

"You understand. Excellent. Where would you use them?" she asked quietly.

Jourdaine hesitated. Anywhere from the ruins of Detroyt to Bangor, Main, would be part of a treaty settlement with the Canadians. An attack anywhere west of the Rampart, roughly the crest of the Applach, from Pensy to NorKarolyna, would require logistical support through the Unity's own farmlands and power grid. A counterattack, although improbable, would be damaging to the Unity's breadbasket. Moreover, the entire area west of the Applach had been Scorched and was still useless for agriculture. Attacking west, they would be fighting uphill, at risk, for nothing more than ashes.

"Aytlana, Jorja Province," he concluded aloud.

The Scorching had not been as devastating farther south. Jorja remained a prize now that the Unity was to make peace with the truculent Canadians.

Suarez smiled. "Excellent, Colonel. Tell me how you would proceed."

Jourdaine hesitated before continuing. Suarez's question might be a trap. A little too much candor in a subordinate was not seemly. He looked at her and caught for the least slice of time her rapt expression. Her eyes gleamed, and she licked her lips as she waited. He suddenly understood that Suarez wanted a partner in this, someone with whom she could share the hard decisions. The way ahead appeared clear.

"Make an air strike to take power and communication centers in Aytlana, infantry with munitions and pulse cannons following up on the ground before the dust settles. Then fortify Aytlana and wait to receive a counterattack."

"Why would they attack us? Why not just seal us off and starve us out?" the hawk asked the mouse.

"It's classic Unity analysis, sir: Center of Gravity. They would have no choice but to attack. Aytlana is the center of all ground transport in the region, a manufacturing center, the capital of Jorja, and a bastion against an attack on Florida. They either attack or surrender."

"Then what?" she asked.

"They would attack and lose. As they retreat, we pursue and destroy them in detail. We would have a hundred and fifty thousand hectares of new land."

"Problems?" asked Suarez.

"You have to convince the council and avoid the Solons' veto."

Suarez smiled.

Go for broke, he thought.

"You have three obstacles," he said. "One is that the Unity has become complacent, and the other generals will not like being reminded of it. Since the shooting war up north cooled off in 72, the DUFS has become more a police force than an army.

"The second is that the outlands have become an enigma, and no one likes walking into a dark room. Once we stopped patrolling the outlands, we lost touch with the tactical situation. Forty-two sensor stations work well but never show any activity whatever. Sunprairie works only when the barbarians let it, and then it sees nothing until the next attack.

"And finally, with all due respect, the third reason is you, sir. You will gain power if the council approves the plan. Concentrated power in one individual makes the council nervous. You have had too much success in the past to make them want to give you more."

Suarez looked pleased, and in turn, Jourdaine was pleased—for different reasons.

Suarez stood from behind her desk for the first time. "The council will have to agree, Colonel. The Unity is at its most fragile state since the start of the new republic. Food reserves are falling, despite whatever the gray suits tell us. We need more food and more power production. Both those things need land."

"Why don't we just get rid of the Sisi? Fewer nonproducers could only help us sooner, General."

"That's the one thing we dare not do, Colonel!"

She explained.

"I see, sir. We are in a trap, aren't we?" replied Jourdaine. Obviously, a new balance needed to be reached.

"Pretty much, Colonel. But it is worse," Suarez continued. "Recruiting all the men and infertile women we can only nets about one in three as a CRNA. The other two enter a sort of catatonia and have to be recycled as fertilizer. Last year, we changed the process, sacrificed a little of the operational specs for better recruitment and longer life span, but that only helps a little. We need more land and water in the short run and better recruitment methods in the long run." She paused. "Sit down, Colonel, and let me show you the plans for Jorja."

Jourdaine accepted the seat gratefully. "What of the Solons, General?" he asked.

Indeed what of the Solons? The council discussed, planned, and proposed. The Solons disposed. The original Solons had offered stability in return for loyalty. Now they were anonymous, selecting their members from those about to retire.

"What of them, Colonel? I expect they can do the math as well as we can."

"Don't you think they will be unwilling to drop one war just to pick up another somewhere else?" Jourdaine was authentically curious as to what his commander might say.

"They don't think like us … or maybe they do," Suarez said. "What happens in an offensive war, Colonel? You spend men and matériel on the chance you get more resources to feed the survivors. If you win, the country has more food to share among fewer mouths, less likelihood of a rebellion but more of a coup d'état from your successful generals."

"I see, sir, and if you lose, you can eliminate your most likely competitors, the generals, but will be more likely to suffer a rebellion with less resources to put it down. But you still have fewer mouths to feed."

"So as a Solon, if the Unity wins?" asked the hawk.

"Placate the generals with bribes and honors and then make them the face of retribution with the people."

"And if we lose?"

"Execute the generals and placate the people with the resources of those killed already," Jourdaine said promptly, exhilarated, looking behind the curtain of power.

"So, Colonel, given the information, do you think the Solons will agree?" Suarez asked. Jourdaine could detect no right answer from her face or attitude.

"They will agree. Regardless, win or lose, they will have fewer mouths. In the long run, they win, as CRNAs are always improving."

The hawk smiled at the mouse and called out for tea.

Two hours later, after leaving his commander's office, Jourdaine took the stairs three at a time. Suarez's desire to bury the news of the Sunprairie debacle was predictable. As a loyal subordinate, Jourdaine would work tirelessly to accomplish that end. He would also have one more piece of black capital when it came for her denunciation. Suarez, if he pitched it to the right people, would show herself to be the architect of an embarrassing Unity defeat and cover-up. Moreover, he now had an idea of Suarez's real goal, and that fact was invaluable.

Returning to his office, he entered and locked his door, checked the telltales for any unauthorized entry in his absence, and unlocked his desk. The Chiu woman had played her unenviable part in his own elevation. She was a messy detail. If alive, she could show, if anyone asked, that she had never intended to implicate Miramundo Morales in her own plot. That would lead Suarez to discover how he, Jourdaine, had faked the original committee list. That would, in turn, be ... unfortunate.

Inside the Unity, he could have contained her. She was no longer contained, if she was alive at all. The odd behavior of Chiu's implant indicated a certain amount of craft. It suggested that she was a great deal more resourceful than expected or that someone else thought her worth the effort. This required his immediate Presence.

Jourdaine composed himself at his desk and contacted Major Rajesh Khama via their mutual O-A contact.

Khama was a lucky early discovery of Jourdaine's, useful beyond expectations. No faction claimed him. To Jourdaine, it was like having a direct line to an unknowing coconspirator, the adjutant for General Ingamar Magness, a man noted for his political longevity and careful avoidance of both risk and excellence. Any action from Major Khama would be imputed to Magness and discounted as trivial.

On the surface, Khama and Jourdaine's relations were cordial if somewhat distant. After some banter, Jourdaine's Presence skipped across the connection and ransacked the recent memory of the other officer. He numbed the growing panic and increased the appropriate neurotransmitters a bit before placing the necessary command and erasing Khama's labile memory of himself. Instead, Khama would have warm, fuzzy thoughts about Jourdaine for days.

CHAPTER 11

THE PRESENCE

Divisional Shop, Nyork, Unity
07.42.19.local_19_10_AU76

"Guess what jag Major Khama is on today?" Technical Sergeant Iain Dalgliesh reported as Gunnery Sergeant Jasun Ciszek entered the ops center for Battalion Thirty-Nine.

"Haven't a clue, fecker. Stopped eavesdropping on that ensign, has he?"

Iain laughed. "Nope, this is on top of that. Ya know that maintenance platoon that went missing last week? Well, it appears the looie's implant is still skidding around the bottom of some outlander river. Khama's intrigued."

"One less hero of the Unity. Imagine my sorrow, would ya?" said Ciszek.

"Funny thing, Gunny, is that the lieutenant was an S08, bottom of the barrel."

"Well, how Major Khama amuses hisself is none of my nevermind. What's he got ya doing anyway, Doggy?"

"I set up an auto ping on the looie's plugjob every few hours. If she comes within two hundred klicks of the Rampart, we get a signal."

"I need to do anything?"

"As if I could trust you, Gunny." He smiled. "Nope, the signal goes to Khama himself."

"Sounds good to me, Doggy. Let's sit down and go over the new enunciation protocols before ThiZ time, okay?"

"Aye, aye, Gunny!"

Feigning work, Iain watched as Jasun walked over to his workstation and reversed a blue folder from its habitual place. Someone from Ciszek's faction would notice, no doubt, and would report the odd occurrence to his handler. Iain was sure to meet his own handler, a woman he knew as Shirley, within the day.

The factions were quiet for now. That was good. He had come to like Jasun, even if he belonged to the wrong faction. He really wanted things to be peaceful for a while, at any rate. He was distracted.

Monee'k was quite a distraction.

Jourdaine's Presence was his own discovery from years ago while he had been a mere ensign. He had told no one about it since. Jourdaine did not have a foolishly generous character. Really, he thought of it as the unintended reward for attempting to rescue the COREd-out protégé of his commander, Major General Divny. For reasons that escaped Jourdaine, the old man, almost a Sisi himself, had decided to rescue his E7 boyfriend from a CORE coma.

"You know him, don't you, Eustace? He was a classmate of yours at the academy, wasn't he? Olevar Thimosen? You could talk him out of it. It was a mistake, I'm sure. I shouldn't have been so harsh with him. A bit too much ThiZ, and he looked into the CORE. I found him at my apartment, dead to the world. He's at Bellvu now. We have to do something!"

"It would mean trying to go into the CORE myself, sir. I-I'm not sure, sir." Jourdaine had sensed his heart pounding in his ears.

"I'm not a fool, ensign! I have a CORE tech on the strength. He has an idea. The implants have their own ID number, of course. He can reprogram your implant. Get you to poor Olevar's locus in the CORE in one shot. Olevar trusts you. He'll listen to you, and we can put a tracer on you … give you a way back. It'd mean a promotion for you, just for trying. I know I'm asking a lot, but if this works, think what good it would do for all the other COREd-out citizens?"

Jourdaine indeed knew young Olevar. They had been more than classmates but less than lovers. Olevar had abandoned him the month before Jourdaine had gone off to Officer Training School.

After an admittedly long period of self-loathing, Jourdaine had bounced back to what he'd hoped was a competent sober officer. When Olevar had joined Divny's professional family as a protégé, neither of them had acknowledged their previous attachment.

"Yes, sir. Of course, sir. For the good of the service. I am sure he will know me. I consider it a great honor, sir."

His stomach lurched at what he was saying.

"That's my boy! I'll contact Pippitte right away. He's the CORE tech. One more thing: When was your last ThiZ? Pippitte wants the attempt to be done cold, off ThiZ at least for forty-eight hours."

"I haven't had mine today, sir."

"Good, it will give us some time to set up. Go see to transferring your assignments, and we will contact you. Dismissed."

Taking ThiZ was the only way he knew to navigate the rest of the day, and now that was taken away as well.

"Sir, yes, sir!"

After the wrenching diarrhea and nausea of the next two days, the little of Jourdaine's confidence had drained away with the toilet flushings. Nevertheless, he came when summoned.

Pippitte turned out to be a dark little man who talked to himself. Jourdaine was required to wear some sort of orthodontic apparatus that allowed him to hear Pippitte even when he was in the CORE.

The first few attempts were futile. The CORE illusion using the standard O-A was of gleaming mental corridors, branches, turnings, doors, passwords—a net of connections, passages, and information. Jourdaine easily slid along the illusion at Pippitte's direction, his nausea subsiding as he went on, even as the man's mutterings grew less helpful. In the end he ignored them.

He reached a blockage. Pippitte's plan was foolish, really. No two consciousnesses could occupy the same locus at the same time. Jourdaine was preparing himself for failure when he glimpsed the dark line along the wall. It should not have been there. Questing along the line, it moved to his command.

He pushed again; it opened to blackness. He looked around to see if anyone noticed.

He moved through the gap more from frustration than curiosity to find himself in another reality. Nothing was "up" unless he told himself so. He looked back at the defect he had discovered. The bright corridors of the 'net stretched around him but were different from this vantage point, "the outside." It looked like patchwork, as if made of plates. He expected it was code segments.

He had escaped the interior of the 'net; he was outside. His disembodied bowels began to rebel. He was floating free. He would be lost … like so many others. In panic, his mind yearned … quested … to touch the merest edge of the crack from which he had just emerged, to find a handhold, something solid … and it was so. Gracefully, his Presence swept back to the fissure, and Jourdaine reached out a "hand" to run along the edge. It sizzled coldly at his touch.

Finding Olevar was just as easy. Jourdaine thought of his name and was drawn the short distance to the locus. He could tell it was Olevar somehow; he had the right smell. However, the tornado of swirling thoughts surrounding Olevar battered Jourdaine away. Olevar recognized him.

> *"What are you doing? Why are you here? Useless. I'm so cold. Where are all the pencils? The general … wanting … Don't! Why? Go away! Og ywaa?"*

Olevar was continually terrified of falling, but his frenzy was like a buzz saw to Jourdaine's touch.

Pippitte's urgent mutterings broke through to Jourdaine, even here, and ordered him to return. Once back, Jourdaine just told them he had been successful in contacting Olevar. The general was pink with hope. Pippitte wiped his mouth on his sleeve and asked for his apparatus back.

Jourdaine went again. He had to. Divny demanded, cajoled, and eventually ordered him, then fell to wringing his hands during Jourdaine's attempts. Later, Jourdaine's questing mind went unsupervised. He stopped using ThiZ. He was learning.

The CORE, outside the limitations of the Unity conventions, was a great temptation.

The lights, sounds, concepts, and jangle of identifiers flashed by, oblivious to Jourdaine's freed Presence. In the CORE but outside Unity restrictions, Jourdaine claimed a new world as his own.

Sitting near Olevar's turmoil, Jourdaine watched huge magenta engines of commerce chunter by, flaking off RFPs in the same color that scattered in six directions. Svelte ellipses of the arts in myriad colors teemed in a large scintillating ball in the distance, waiting for sponsors, occasionally fountaining off into smaller groups, then recombining. Individuals appeared to him, at a distance, to be wraithlike squiggles, nodes that, while appearing to fill the space, were invisible when he looked past them, varying in appearance only once focused upon. Whole dimensions of meaning were somehow compressed into the scene, obvious to him but near impossible to describe once he had exited.

Only with difficulty did he go back to Olevar.

> *"Olevar, it is me. It is Eustace. You know me. You liked me once. Remember? You don't have to do this. You can come back with me. Everything will be all right. Divny wants you to be happy. I want you to be happy. Just take my hand … Olevar, it's me,"* he said again and again.

At first that had slowed the maelstrom of mirrored thoughts, but only at first. Olevar had stopped talking after the first few times. At intervals, he lashed out with bursts of sensation: heat, cold, a stench of death, quinine bitterness, and pain. But far worse were the memories: memories of Eustace being taunted by his crèche mates, Olevar's own abandonment, Olevar's ascendancy as Divny's protégé, his smug disdain for the plodding Jourdaine.

> *"Olevar, it is me. It is Eustace. You know me. You liked me once. You don't have to do this. You can come back with me. Everything will be all right. Divny wants you to be happy. I want you to be happy. Just take my hand ... Olevar, it's me. It is Eustace."*

It was all he could offer, unarmed as he was before the mounting violence of his friend's circular thoughts. Battered, he would leave for a few hours, only to be forced back by Divny's mounting anxiety and threats.

Jourdaine recounted to Olevar his own memories, random but always containing something that he should recognize: a teacher, a matron, a lost friend. Eventually, mercifully, it worked. Jourdaine never knew what it was that stopped Olevar's whirling intensity of self-loathing. The chaos slowly petered out like a dying top.

For the first time, Eustace saw what had become of Olevar in the mirrored corridors of his thoughts. Wizened, sapped of vitality, feral, his face in the illusion of the CORE was nevertheless unmistakable. Jourdaine still shivered anytime he thought about it. The face was there, the same smooth brow and gentle mouth, but now creased with rage, guile, and savagery. In repose, the face relaxed almost to beauty—until Olevar recognized Jourdaine.

> *"Little Useless, come to fumble, have you? Clueless Useless, fathering baby. Feck off someplace and fumble yourself!"*

> *"Olevar, I came to help you come back."*

> *"You help me? Help* me*? You have nothing! Nothing to help* me*!"*

Jourdaine had tried again and again, but that one thought was the only one he got from the creature that Olevar had become. Pippitte told him to return. By then, Jourdaine was weary and repulsed by the creature.

In his disgust, Jourdaine did what was necessary just before he left.

Sacrifices had to be made.

The boy's body died a few days later. Jourdaine's report to the general described how the damage was too severe. It gave no mention of the illusion of Jourdaine's hand sliding along the slender silver tether of Olevar's life and severing it with a paroxysm of disgust.

The exercise had gained him rewards. Divny had given him an excellent efficiency report and, after being denounced, had not suspected Jourdaine's betrayal. In his grief, the man had no longer cared.

Thus, Jourdaine learned to be a thinking Presence, a resident phantom in a land peopled by tourists. He alone had plumbed the possibilities of the CORE. He could project his Presence into the CORE itself and thence to another O-A recipient.

Cadets for generations had been warned that they might contract CORE fever. He wondered if the CORE had been warned that it might catch a case of Jourdaine.

CHAPTER 12

THE SISI

Environs of Sun Prairie, Wisconsin Territory, Restructured States of America (RSA)

Late afternoon, October 14, 2128

Malila awoke, her ears ringing and too dazed to move. The air was redolent of wood smoke. She lay in a small campsite on her side in a lean-to crafted from still-green boughs woven onto saplings rooted into the ground. An ax and sheathed knife threaded onto a broad leather belt hung from a small branch near her head. Only when she moved to retrieve them did she comprehend she had been bound, her wrists tied behind her back and her legs tied at the ankles. A shiver coursed through her when she found she was naked as well. On hearing a faint scuffling behind her, Malila closed her eyes, calmed her breathing, and relaxed her body, sagging into the bonds. She felt the slight breeze of someone's entrance and then heard nothing but the forest.

"You are awake, lass." It wasn't a question. "Open your eyes, or I start to take off toes."

She detected an alien soft-burred accent. After a few seconds, a hand gripped her left foot by the instep. Her eyes shot open, startled, all pretense lost at the immediate threat.

A Sisi was crouching back on his heels, holding her foot, an odd short, curved knife in his other hand, his face concealed in a grizzled beard, his skin burned muddy brown. Over his left cheek he wore a series of blue streaks, faded and indistinct. His hair grew out from under a knitted cap of uncertain design: abundant, lank, white, and to his shoulders. He filled the small space.

After a second to regard her, the old man dropped her foot and turned back to working a small piece of leather. "There you go, lass. Much better. Let's have your name. I can't be calling you 'lass' all the time, can I?"

Malila calmed herself, waiting until she was confident of her voice. Before she could answer, the old man looked up at her from under his thick eyebrows with such menace that she squeaked, "Chiu, Malila E., E11, S08, lieutenant … acting second lieutenant … serial number 59026169."

The old man tilted his head back, his face split to show brilliant and sound teeth. He started a low vigorous laugh, stopping after he dabbed at his eyes with a square of rough fabric taken from his leather tunic.

"You should see yourself, lass, trying to look official and all, lying bare-ass naked and trussed up like a prize sow."

He wiped his eyes again, and his face sobered. "Let me tell you what you've told me, so far, Acting Second Lieutenant Chiu, Chiu, Malila E. You are seventeen years old. You've been sent on this shit of an assignment because you messed up, and they broke you down a rank or three. You have been given the chance to redeem yourself … if you don't screw up, as you just did. You have been in the service for seven years, and you think you are hot stuff, which you ain't, as we wouldna be having this here conversation otherwise.

"You have a small scar under your chin, another over your left shin, and one under your right tit, which I should remark is pretty enough, although personally I prefer a little more. The scars under your chin and on your leg are no doubt from training accidents. Your hair is too short for my taste. Your facial features are regular and rather pretty in an exotic way, lass, nice shade of blue in your eyes. Once upon a time, you broke your left forearm as a child from a fall on an outstretched hand, due to some fool game, I should think. You have never birthed a baby. You are sound in heart and limb, but I don't know about your head yet. Your nutrition could be better, and you would do well to add a few pounds for aesthetic reasons. Have I missed anything, Lieutenant?" he said, again transfixing her with his pale eyes.

Malila's features creased in revulsion despite herself. A sense of violation inundated her as fear, adding a watery sensation, arrived unannounced. Her empty stomach sent bile surging into the back of her throat. She swallowed but then started coughing.

The man was at her side almost at once, cutting her hands apart and lifting her to a sitting position.

"There you go, Lieutenant. Can't have you dying on me," said the old man, almost gently.

Her nausea subsided. She tensed her elbow to swing back into his throat now that her hands were free.

"I wouldna, Malila. I really wouldna do that," hissed the old man. It was then that she again sensed the cold of the knife pressed against her back. The watery sensation returned.

"Put your arms behind you, lass."

She complied, and the man bound her wrists again. She took several deep breaths. It seemed to help. The day was almost spent, the scene becoming more hostile and surreal as the dimming light filled it with ominous shadows.

Elderly of the Unity were shepherded into their own enclaves on their fortieth birthday. While Malila supposed they enjoyed their retirement, she and the larger society had little use and scant respect for any of the old, used-up, and worn-out Sisis. That one of these ersatz humans would rise up to touch … to violate a citizen … a DUFS officer … was impossible to imagine.

"I need some water. You, get me water!" she demanded.

She used her command voice, thinking that and the simplicity of the request would gain her the old man's compliance. If she could get him to abandon his script for even a moment, she increased her chances of escape. If given an opening, her years of training in the killing arts would make short work of this ancient savage. The elderly were supposed to be differential and obedient. This old obscenity needed a dose of reality. The look of dismay on the old face would go far to heal her humiliation.

"I need some water, you fathering Sisi piece of shit."

"No, Malila, you don't. And watch your language; there's a lady present!"

Malila looked around but could see no other person.

"Where are my men? You can't keep me from my men," she said, trying to keep her voice low and flat with menace.

"Your troopers? You were given a platoon of dead men, lass. We just did them the kindness of burying them."

She heard a sharp, gritty sound as a spray of incandescent sparks spurted in a short arc in the darkness. The sound repeated a few times. For a heartbeat, the sparks showed the old man crouching studiously in the dark. After a few attempts, he took up something from the ground and blew on it. It erupted into a red blossom of fire in his hand and the old man placed it back onto the ground before adding small twigs, creating ghastly shadows in the small space. The old man's eyes became mere pools in a death mask. A moment later a small lamp flared, and the old man hooked the light onto the lattice of the lean-to, illuminating the dirt floor.

"Are you going to rape me now, you fathering twisted Sisi?" she shouted.

The old man shook his head, more in disgust than negation.

"Why is it that all young women think they are going to be ravished at the drop of a blouse? But no, lass, not yet … even if you ask nice. And watch your language."

"Flecking moron! Fathering Sisi!"

The blow caught her by surprise, her teeth cutting into her lip, the metallic taste of blood filling her mouth.

The old man smiled. "Now, lass, have I got your attention? Talk nice!"

He went behind her and lashed a hide rope around her bound wrists, leaving a long bight as a lead. He then worked loose her ankle bonds and pulled her to her feet.

"Walk. I'll tell you when to stop." When she hesitated, the old man slapped her buttocks with his free hand and pointed the way.

Malila stepped into the dark, one bare foot in front of the other in the heavy, expectant gait of the seldom shoeless. After long minutes, her night vision returned somewhat, and she was able to see that they were in another large meadow, surrounded by a dark line of trees.

"Okay, empty your bladder, and if you can move your bowels, you'll be more comfortable tomorrow."

She found to her embarrassment that the mere mention made the sensation of her full bladder overwhelming. Grateful for the darkness, she crouched and relieved herself. As soon as she was finished, the man started to pull her backward off her heels.

"No mischief, girl. I didn't have an attack of stupid," he said, stopping her attempts to squeeze her wrists from their bonds.

"Is this how you get your pleasure, old man? Watching women pee?" she hissed.

Rather than responding, the old man told her to walk back to the light.

When they returned, he left her so he could rummage in a pile of skins, coming back with a greasy and malodorous cowhide parcel. After tying one of her ankles to a sapling, the old man released her hands. Malila stood facing him, her breasts quivering with her ragged breathing and the chill air.

He tossed her the parcel.

"Rub this on your chest, girl. Use lots of it."

When she did not immediately respond, the old man pulled his sheath knife into the lamplight. The blade had to be over twenty-five centimeters long. Its edge blazed in the firelight and moved in small arcs in the old man's hand. Malila, finding she could not hold his gaze, opened the greasy container and scooped out a small handful of oozing matter. Retching at its rancid odor, she self-consciously spread the soap over her breasts and under her arms, scraping off the excess into the container.

The old man approached her, and Malila's reserve withered, cringing at his close approach. Malila yelped as he sprayed cold water onto her from a water bag. He threw her a faded square of fabric.

"Scrub it in well, lass."

CHAPTER 13

RECOVERY

Malila woke feeling as if a wall had run over her. The rest of the night had been a nightmare. Her last firm memory was the old man stabbing her thigh again. She was sure she had been asleep for days, but she also had a blur of disconnected images: a knife, the old man, naked to the waist, his muscled chest covered in blue. There was pain, fascination, and the red of her own blood.

She discovered her hands and feet were free and the old man was gone. Lying there, she felt comfortable until she tried to move, and then a searing pain in her right side made her groan. Exploring the smooth contours of a soft bandage there, she winced as she fingered a small area under her right breast. Any attempt to rise left her gasping. If she did not move, she had a pleasant fuzzy sensation that left her limbs feeling leaden.

Rousing when the old man returned, she realized she had slept again. He approached her, knelt, looked into her eyes, and felt her forehead. "I'm glad to see you back, lass. Let me know if you hurt too much, and let me help you up. I can give you something to drink now if you feel up to it."

She focused with difficulty on his face.

"You cut me, fathering moronic Sisi!" she said, her tongue viscous and clumsy in her mouth.

"Yes, I did, lass. And watch your language." He smiled.

The old man stopped further conversation by lifting her up to a sitting position. After the wave of pain subsided, he brought the water skin to her lips and let her drink a few gulps. Spasms of pain and confusion obscured the remainder of the day, her ears humming like a taut wire in a high wind. Her mouth tasted woolly and fetid. She had odd fantasies of the old man sitting by her head giving her mouthfuls of a bitter liquid or crooning a simple melody. It reminded her of the image of a small soft-bodied woman, a faded memory of her childhood.

Malila awoke in the thin light of early morning. Gray specters of ground fog danced across the meadow in the hectic breeze. The old man was already moving, collapsing the gear into a big green nylon pack with a welded-metal frame, out of place with his leather and homespun clothing. He saw her moving and threw a bundle of cloth at her.

"Best get dressed, lass. Moving day."

A thin strip of braided leather rope led from a large tangle of branches and encircled her waist, knotting at the small of her back, impossible to decipher by touch. This new arrangement allowed her to dress, even as it ensured her confinement.

She unrolled the bundle to find a rough and oversize homespun shirt that fastened with antler buttons, a pair of soft leather pants, and moccasins. She had to roll up the cuffs of the pants several times to expose her feet before she could even try to insert them into the rough moccasins. These, after several attempts, she got to stay on her feet. Nevertheless, it felt good finally to be clothed around the old man.

Her chest wound was tender, but she could move carefully with little pain. By the time she was finished dressing, the old man was ready to leave, a stolen pulse rifle over his arm. *If the demented Sisi only knew how useless it is to him,* she thought. She had no obligation to volunteer the information. She smiled at the old man, and after a second he smiled back. He dropped the rifle onto his pack and walked over to her.

Without prologue, the man unbuttoned her shirt and let it drop around her waist, unwound the bandage, and exposed her to the cool morning air. Malila shivered as he washed his hands and then started examining her wound, pressing her flesh and muttering a noncommittal *hmmm* at intervals in self-absorbed concentration. Her growing rage was cut short when the man retied the bandage, making her wince. He rebuttoned her shirt for her before she could complain.

By this time, the lean-to was a mere suggestion of a tangle in the underbrush. All the woven branches were gone, and the rooted saplings were slowly recoiling to their normal posture. The man took a fallen branch and smoothed the dirt floor before scattering dried leaves over the area.

Malila had imagined, initially, that the Unity's hand of retribution was reaching out to crush this arrogant savage, but no skimmers had appeared in over two days. Uneasily, Malila remembered how the Unity was quite capable of ignoring inconvenient facts. She was now an inconvenient fact.

The old man hefted his huge green pack onto a raised knee with a grunt before swooping it into place. He retied her hands in back, leaving a long leash of the braided rope, and, grabbing up a final bundle in his other hand, set her walking ahead of him.

"I'll make it easy for the first couple of days, but we have to meet Percy. I'm sure he's anxious to be off."

Stepping out into the meadow once more, the old man indicated a chink in the forest edge as they approached, and Malila found that it concealed a faint trail through the alder and willow. The old man followed far enough behind her that any branch she released failed to whip back into his face, but close enough to urge her on with the free end of the lead flicked onto her behind. Deviation from the path, however slight, earned her backside a stroke with the leash.

The air rapidly warmed, and Malila began to sweat with the pace required of her. Doubting now whether the old man was some subhuman outlander, she thought he must have escaped from the Unity, surviving by his tattered wits and lunatic delusions. His imaginary companion, Percy, had not materialized by midmorning, and Malila was beginning to worry how he would respond when his delusions abandoned him.

In the Unity, the Sisis were no longer citizens; their opinions and preferences were no longer anyone's concern. Most old people just faded into the background, and when you looked up later, they were gone. Those were the good Sisis. The demented Sisis were the ones you had to look out for.

This old man was definitely of the demented variety.

CHAPTER 14

PERCY

I'm going crazy, she thought. With its choking, closed horizons; identical green-gloomed panoramas; moist, dark tree trunks disappearing overhead; and the unending brambles waiting to grab her clothes, the forest depressed her. Malila refused any of the old man's bitter draughts now. The pain was tolerable, and she wanted as little of the maniac's home remedies as she could manage.

The old man had no idea who he was up against. She started studying how best to escape. She would have had a good chance ... if her body had not chosen that time to betray her.

Her heart rate pounding in her throat, the spasms of colic, the grinding sensation, and the ever-tightening pain in her head accelerated into panic. She realized the problem only afterward. She had never gone as long as two days without ThiZ; it had been over fifty hours since her last hit. Her nausea came in waves that warped further and further up the beach of her well-being. Sensations of heat and cold wrapped her in drenching sweats or shivering tremors within minutes of each other. Spasms of colic bent her over in pain, relieved by noisy and liquid evacuations under the eyes of the old man. Her breathing became ragged. An unseen insect flew into her mouth, and Malila dissolved into a paroxysm of coughing. For the first time in years, she wept.

The old man let her cry on the ground for a minute before shaking the rawhide lead.

"Get it out of your system, girl, but do it while we walk. We are almost there. Percy will be waiting."

He retied her hands in front to lead her on. Malila closed her eyes to her tears and stumbled on behind him. It was not until they stopped that Malila fathomed a river was near, splayed out in front of them, brilliant in the noonday sun.

Entering a well-used campsite, the old man tied her to a tree. Even so, she could see a pool, crude and man-made, connected to the river by a narrow stream barred by stakes driven into the bottom. The old man dropped his burdens and rummaged under some bushes before emerging with a wooden shovel and a bundle of green sticks. Malila crumpled down to rest, watching the old man.

Without explanation, he started digging along the lower side of the pool until water flowed down into the river, cutting a new channel. He toppled the bundle of sticks into this new sluice. It proved to be a net, a partition of poles, held together by twistings of vine and surrounded by ropes that he staked down with forked branches.

He had only just finished when a fish, perhaps forty to fifty kilograms and armored like some prehistoric leviathan, surged from the murky water of the pool. Malila cried out in sudden panic. The fish surged into the small channel, and the old man rolled the screen neatly over it before hoisting it out of the water with the help of the ropes. Nevertheless, he was gasping with exertion by the time the fish was secure, flapping wildly several feet above the level of the water.

"Malila, meet Percy. Percy … Malila. Percy here has been kind enough to volunteer in our escape. I thought we'd give your friends something to chase."

"You have no idea what you have done, old man."

He laughed. "Here's a way to find out, lass."

With that, the old man withdrew from his shirt a plastic capsule about one centimeter long, with several small studs along its length. He attached a short length of fishing line with a hefty hook to it, and, turning, he threw himself onto the gyrating fish, his short knife held in his teeth. When he removed himself several minutes later, the capsule decorated Percy's dorsal fin.

It took the old man another half an hour to sledge the giant fish into the shallows and release him. Turning back, the old man stripped off his leather tunic.

He did not look like the Sisis she had seen on training sims. He was a good twenty centimeters taller than most men she knew and wider. She guessed he massed ten kilograms more than the average Unity officer, and the mass was devoted to meat. Intricate blue tattoos, with curlicues inside rectangular cartouches, covered the old man's chest and back. He climbed back up the bank to her smiling.

"Mose and I caught Percy here a couple of weeks ago. I got the idea to pen him here. If you hadn't come when I'd called, he might have wound up trail rations. Now he gets to migrate south for the winter, if he doesn't sulk too long."

"What was that you attached to that poor fish?" Malila asked as the old man put on the shirt.

"That was your implant. You might not even remember getting that one."

"You're telling me that was inside me? That is why you drugged me and mutilated me and then mutilated a fish? Pathetic!" she hissed.

"It wasn't me who mutilated you, girl. That was already taken care of before, wasn't it? You could say thank you anytime now, lass, if you was properly brung up." He smiled a toothy, contented smile.

She responded with a vulgar and unlikely imperative.

"Watch you language, Acting Lieutenant Chiu. But do you think I'd risk my skin hanging around for my own amusement? I need your damned so-called Unity to take off in the wrong direction." He spat as if the word itself were distasteful.

His answer added to her disquiet. He could not have carried her far from the station. Her confinement, anesthesia, and surgery so near the scene of his ambush made no sense if it were just a staged event.

"What was that implant supposed to be?" she asked.

"It *is*," he said, pausing, "several things, lass. It changes the drugs you take into any number of interesting agents. Your keepers can change what the drugs do to you. You poor Unis take that trash for amusement, while your masters tailor what it does to you. You haven't had an authentic emotion or a conviction to call your own since you were six years old. Welcome to thinking for yourself, lass."

Malila was not amused, in part because of the old man's jolly demeanor. When she didn't respond, he turned to pick up the bundle he had been carrying and added over his shoulder, "Have you ever seen one of your troopers without his visor?"

Before she could think, she barked, *"No!"* It was almost an obscenity.

"Would you like to?" He turned and underhanded the bundle to her.

She caught it without thinking. Pushing aside the coarse fabric, she found the familiar shape of a DUFS helmet and, feeling its weight, turned it over. Instead of the dark, obscuring helmet shield, the startled gaze of an old man stared at her from the helmet of NELSON, James P., platoon sergeant. A neat and bloodless slice divided the larynx, spinal cord, and spine. A faint odor of decay arose from the thing in her hands.

She dropped the helmet and heaved, retching up the taste of bile and green acid. The old man sighed but was again by her side, wiping her mouth with his red kerchief after each convulsion. He gathered the repellant burden into its bag and helped Malila to her feet.

"At your age I wouldna believed me neither. I figured your sergeant might be more convincing."

Uncertainty rose and washed around her. She had grown up with the CRNA troops and had applauded early and often the severity of their punishment. The troopers never complained, and that had given her permission, somehow, to accept their enslavement. She expected

CRNAs to be young, coarse, brutal, but James P. Nelson's face was so ... old.

The man returned to the river and threw the helmet far into the opaque water before washing his tunic and putting it on wet.

Malila led the way, away from the river, until sundown.

CHAPTER 15

JESSE JOHNSTONE

That night, the old man settled them into a small clearing, guided by the lingering light in the sky. He tethered her around a root of a massive oak, throwing down a soft doeskin for her before starting the strange ritual of fire making. They had a hurried meal of some sort of stale bread and a bitter hot tea. Malila ate little, but the old man allowed her to drink as much as she wanted.

Afterward, the old man sat back against the oak and began talking. "It'll take us a few weeks to walk to the summer camp. Moses took off right away with the horses and the pulse rifles you brought for us. He may still be there when we arrive. Then we ride back in style … if Mose is still there. Ask me any questions you want. I can answer them now."

"Who are you, and why are you doing this to me?" Malila's voice surprised her, hoarse, insistent, and with the tinge of panic.

"My, my, the narcissism of youth! I'd have done this for anyone who answered my call. You were just the lucky winner."

"You called me?" She heard her voice sound incredulous.

"And it took me knocking a third time to get you to answer the door! Courting you has taken most of my summer, lass. But third time pays for all. The first two times we knocked out that station, you people just sent a robot to fix it!" He sounded affronted at the neglect. "Then you volunteered so nicely. Just in time too. If you hadn't come, we'd have had to leave to beat the snows."

"What do you want with me?" she asked, trying to gain time to digest the information. *He may be mad, but he's intelligent.*

"Remains to be seen, doesn't it. My superiors need a platoon officer to interrogate, whether they know it or not. That, it seems, is you, lass."

He paused for a moment. "My turn to ask questions," he said at last. "Where do you think you are?" He turned to face her in the gloaming, his voice sounding mischievous.

"The outlands. Anything outside the Rampart is outlands, isn't it?" she said, noting with odd satisfaction her own patronizing tone.

"Wrong, lass. You are in the great state of Wisconsin. We are traveling to Kentucky, another great state, I might add, but Kentucky is favored above all states and nations as being the home of that great American, Jesse Aaron Johnstone."

"Who's he?"

"He's me." And then he laughed.

"What are you talking about, you fecking old father! You're crazy. Do you know how much trouble you are in? When the Unity catches you, you're gonna get Sapped. You damn pathetic senile bagman, you're gonna be drooling within a day!" she screamed. It felt good to get it out, to reset the order of the universe. She waited for his face to register the new disaster.

The old man backhanded her and waited for her to look him in the face before slapping her with his open palm on the return. Malila recoiled from the blows and braced herself. The man's face showed no anger but something else; she did not know what.

"You are a slow learner, lass. I thought you might be smarter. *Talk nice*. But to answer your question, Lieutenant, yes." He seated himself again.

The old man's voice changed, as if reading from some manual. "I do know that I have obtained by subterfuge, violence, and the threat of violence a junior officer of a power hostile to my own country. I'm returning you to my lines for interrogation and eventual repatriation at the end of hostilities."

Malila's face stung. Sisis were a tractable lot, as a rule. A man as elderly as this should have backed down and pleaded senility for his actions.

She'd expected immediate rescue, with Unity forces falling from the sky and welling up out of the ground to retrieve her. Almost three days had elapsed since the attack, with no signs of pursuit. No skimmers crisscrossing overhead, no loudspeakers warning the old goat to give up. A week ago, she had been a promising young officer, slated for early company command. Now, because of this tattooed horror, she was a hostage to the madman's idea of some extinct republic.

"You can't just grab me, take me away from my life, kill my command, keep me tied up, strip me naked, drug me, cut my boob, and do whatever else you did while I was asleep! You ..."

The old man's smile increased during her rant until mirth burst out of him as laughter. "You object to your treatment because it is immoral? What would your zombies say about that, I wonder?"

Her answer had just reached her lips when she stopped. Malila understood what immoral was, of course. The net'casts were always going off about "Unity subdirector succumbs to the immorality of simony" and the like. *Morals* was a media word. Sapping convicted felons was fair; numerous plebiscites had confirmed its justice. Malila was proud to be a defender of history's—democracy's—finest flower. Those who worked to defeat the Unity, whatever their motive, deserved justice.

"The CRNAs deserve to be Sapped. They're all criminals!"

"Numbers don't add up well, you know. 'Less everyone is a crook or a traitor or lives forever, how can you Unis have that big an army ... or police for that matter? What is it, about ten cops for every thousand people?"

"Don't be absurd, old man. Only nine. Where do you get your absurd data? Ignorant savage!"

For a maniac, the man was well informed.

He laughed. "Okay, Lieutenant, educate me. Do you really think all those old people go to live happy little lives in Implausible Acres Retirement Home?"

"You answer me one, Sisi. How did you get by my platoon?" Malila asked, hoping to change the subject.

The old man smiled. "Yes, that was a bit difficult. Have you ever heard of the Trojan horse? No? I didn't think so. I shall not sully your ignorance. Mose and I figured that you people would respond in about three days from when the station went down. I spent most of a day giving you a cascade of things to repair so that you'd be stuck there for a while. Separating you from your bodyguard was easy enough. We reckoned that you'd not refuse a nice soft bed and would let your zombies sleep rough."

"Don't call them zombies. They are neuroablated, not some superstition of yours!" Malila inserted, trying to derail his answer now that the old man was taking pleasure in the telling.

"Don't be rude, lass. My story. You use whatever euphemism you want when it's your turn. As I was saying, Mose and I made a wall in the back of the storage room and built us a hidey-hole. It's been there since the first outage, if'n any of you woulda bothered to look. The storage room was the one place we didn't damage, and I doubted you noticed that it was a couple of feet too short. But let me tell you, living with Moses and a honeypot in a hole in the wall is above and beyond," he laughed grimly.

"We just waited for you to pass out and then I neutralized you. Mose took your helmet and throat mike. Your zombies aren't good about refusing orders, are they? Mose just ordered them to come in one at a time and put them down as they got close. We dumped them down into the bunker, reversed the fans to give it a draft, and topped it off with a fire. Mose took the rifles and lit off south to our rendezvous. He's a good man; I doubt he'll have any trouble. As for me, I had to make you safe before I brought you south, now, didn't I?"

It startled her. Up to the very moment of her capture, she could have turned the tables on this barbarian. Her private consolation was the trouble they were wasting on the pulse rifles. The Unity was very careful with its technology. No equipment left the Unity without being tied to its user by embedded ID chips. No weapon lost to the outlands was useful to them. They were welcome to expend as much effort as they wanted.

She smiled at the small victory, despite her own disaster.

CHAPTER 16

SLEEPING WITH THE ENEMY

The light finally deserted the sky, and the stars came out. Malila seldom noticed them at home. The old man threw new fuel onto the fire, the heat washing over her.

"Let me tell you a story, my young friend. Once upon a time, this was one country from the Union in the east to the republics out west. What you call the outlands is still the same country. We call it the Reorganized States of America."

"You are wrong there, old man. This land belongs to the Unity," Malila said, glad to stop the lecture.

She could easily see his smile, even in the darkness.

"Well, lass, y'all welcome to come an' git it anytime you want. Seems to me if it was yours, we wouldn't be talkin' now, would we?" He yanked on her tether, making her start.

"Any road, a few generations ago, there was an awful war. Young men made up most armies then. By young, I mean older than you. They were headed by generals who were old, meaning younger than me. Our country, yours and mine, went to war in some godforsaken piece of desert—and we lost."

"If they depended on senile generals, that was bound to happen!" she said. The watery sensation in Malila's body grew. It could not be true.

The old man ignored her.

"Those pagans set off enough nuclear bombs to wipe our forces off the map. No one came home from that war … not a one. The whole world turned in on itself then. The pagans pulled the house down on themselves, 'course. They got their glow-in-the-dark caliphate, but commerce disappeared. For the first time in fifteen hundred years, they had nothing to trade: no spices, no slaves, no silk, no salt, no oil, no water, and no guilt remittances from the rest of the world. I suppose the stories of cannibalism could be bogus, but I'm not sure I can blame them, can you?"

"What are you talking about? The Unity rebelled against the old republic when it showed how decadent and corrupt it had become," she said, now angry with the old man for inventing the absurd story wholesale.

"Not quite right. Decadence and corruption were there, I grant you, but this country doesn't do well with defeats. We ignore the ones we can and just call them victories. If we can't ignore them, we blame somebody. This time we blamed the old for the death of the young … not entirely unfair, I grant you. It worked, as usual, but it started a new war. This one, everyone lost."

"You mean the Great Patriotic War. The Unity beat the reactionary forces into submission. I'd have liked to have been there!" she said.

The old man's voice took on an edge.

"*Everybody* lost. The Unity as well as America. I understand it was worse back east. There was a takeover by the Coasties, only ones with any military organization. They were the first Solons. They declared a new state you call the Unity. Something like that happened out west as well. Different name, the Demarchy, but same disease."

"The first Solons were selected by acclamation of the people, Sisi," Malila said when the old man drifted off for a moment.

"I 'spect you was there taking notes, then, lass?"

"Don't be absurd; of course I wasn't. That is ancient history."

"Perhaps not so ancient as some would like you to believe, but long ago as the Union counts time, I'll grant you."

"Unity, Democratic Unity of America, old man."

The old man laughed easily.

"'A word ... means just what I choose it to mean—neither more nor less,' said Humpty. Cut something longer, grow shorter, maximum increased negativization, secede from the country but call the result a Unity. Black be white and white, black. Evil is good and good, evil. All to the tune of the masters' pipes. Amen and amen." His arms moved against the stars.

"You are talking crazy, Sisi. Let me go!"

He ignored her now. "I guess there was a difference this time. The coup just killed the scapegoats, people my age, I suppose."

"It seems we were good enough, back then, to defeat you savages. You are all still running and hiding, aren't you? Living useless little lives in the ruins," Malila spat back at him, giving the self-satisfied old horror a bit of his own.

The old man threw some branches onto the fire. As they flamed up, his form emerged from the darkness, preceded by his toothy smile.

"Excellent. Well done! 'A touch, a touch. I do confess 't.' A point in your favor, lass. But not the story I'm telling.

"The Solons declared that no drugs were illegal anymore. Lotsa idiots went right out and bought enough shit to blow their minds up several times over. Your masters no longer had to worry about controlling the unproductive; they were doing a good enough job left alone. Your Union pukes dropped the cost of the drugs and even started supplying them free if people got an implant, the forerunner of the one I tickled out of you. Time came that you could not buy fuel, rent a room, get services, or show your face to the sun without an implant.

"What do they call that stuff now, by the way, lass?"

"ThiZ is a great boon to humankind. It elevates our existence, enlarges our imaginations …"

"Makes you crap your pants. Yes, I noticed the wonders of ThiZ on the trail. Did you notice the other great triumph of the Union pharmacology today?"

The old man stopped and cupped a hand around his ear.

"Sorry, Lieutenant, we old people get hard of hearing. What was that you said?"

"I'm not playing your games any longer, Sisi," Malila said, trying to rise and getting one leg under her before the old man pulled her back. She sat down painfully.

"Sit and be sociable. It's not a request. Your sergeant was about an average zombie for your platoon. I have to ask you, what could anyone do to deserve what *he* got?"

The question sounded familiar to her. "Only criminals get Sapped. It's the law. They pay back to the Unity for their crimes."

"Well, that at least was true at the Meltdown. They emptied the prisons and made theirselves a brand-new army. They put down the food riots. Then they invaded the rest of the country, the rest of America. They went through here like we was made of paper. They burned from Cleveland, Detroit, and Chicago down to Peoria. By then the American army had been mustered, such as it was; we held them off at Springfield.

"Even so, they never found my family's homestead. Your average zombie army lacks personal initiative, doncha think?"

Malila refused to answer. Sisis could have quite extensive hallucinations, she knew. She was not going to feed into them anymore if she could.

The old man shrugged and threw another branch onto the fire and flicked a few stray coals back into position before starting again.

"Like I say, the East Coast and the West Coast probably lost the most—their souls. Parts of what you call the outlands were Scorched. It was some sort of chemical weapon. It killed plants but not animals. It'd have been kinder had it killed everything. Most everyone died that winter or the next spring when crops withered as they came up. The plants that did come up, come up *changed*."

"You savages got what you deserved," Malila said. Somehow it felt unfair, though.

"People survived in the outlands, but I was just a kid, so don't ask me how. Don't wanta speculate. I had my family, and they had weapons and a cabin in a hollow. Most of the hunger mobs never knew we were there, and the few that did ... never shared the information."

"Why should I believe any of this shit, old man?"

"No reason at all, Acting Second Lieutenant. None whatsoever. Far be it from me to educate the unwary, the uncaring, or the stupid." The old man laughed a little before standing. He left the circle of light, returning with armfuls of dying ferns, dry and yellow, to make a pile. From the depths of his pack, he pulled out a coil of hard-used, thick climbing rope, unlooped the fifty meters, and coiled it down flat onto the ferns, before piling furs and skins onto it.

The old man pulled Malila to her feet by her lead and wound the braided leather around her waist again.

"Undress ... You need to wash."

When Malila started to object, the old man pulled out his short knife and prepared to cut the clothes from her. Malila raised her hands and began to disrobe. Once she started, he turned away and busied himself with the fire. She was shivering in the night breeze by the time he threw her a water skin and the soap.

"Wash. Be thorough, lass. If you get the furs dirty, you'll freeze when the weather gets cold."

"Gets cold? I'm freezing now!"

The old man grinned.

"I suggest the shortest route to a warm bed is a cold bath, lass."

After she had washed to the old man's satisfaction, he indicated where she should lie and covered her with furs. Gradual warmth washed back into her. By then she could hear the old man washing himself as well.

She steeled herself for the inevitable.

Pleasure-sex with her patron, man or woman, was, of course, only natural and predictable. Her education had been enlightened. As an E7, her teachers had helped her choose among the more senior cadre and select the best patrons based on influence, preferences, and likelihood for further advancement. A grimace flitted across her features before she noticed.

It pleased her, at times, that men and women thought her attractive and, at least, an adornment to the life of power. Malila's skin crawled to think how her counterparts in some bygone era would have had to endure coupling with the ancient patrons of old. The Unity had saved the nation from the tyranny of the elderly and saved her from sharing her body with some hideous Sisi ... until now.

The old man, naked, stepped onto the sleeping skins next to Malila, sat, and brushed off his feet before pulling back the hides. Malila felt the cold night air quest along her spine. Jesse tested her lead with a brisk pull before wrapping the cord around his wrist and lying down next to her. Malila stiffened.

Within minutes, she heard the heavy breathing of sleep and, later yet, slept herself.

That night she dreamed of holding Sergeant Nelson's severed head inside his helmet, the eyes opening and the mouth trying to speak to her, making only hideous moist appeals. She awoke gasping, a cry half-heard in her sleep. The sky was ablaze with an intense blue-white star and a waning moon low in the west. Their light gave an icy cast to the scene, and the wind moved the tufts of grass just enough to suggest furtive motion. She looked around at the old man. Starlight reflected from his open eyes. She mumbled something and settled herself again. Her O-A hummed in her head. Edie's absence made her uneasy. Despite her fatigue, she watched the crescent moon founder into the horizon.

CHAPTER 17

TRAILS TAKEN

Malila was slumbering when Jesse flicked the hides off her.

"Rise and shine, Lieutenant; daylight's burning!"

Her detailed and profane response made him laugh.

Jesse kept the southeastern direction for three days before turning full south, although, in those first few days, they walked every heading of the compass. She realized that each step taken was a step down, a step into darkness and obscurity and away from the light of the Unity.

A routine soon developed. At first light, the old man roused her. He dismantled whatever shelter he had made, hid the evidence of it, packed his huge green pack, and swooped his shoulders into it before buckling it down. They walked for about an hour before breakfast. Malila led the way, bound. There were few ways to retaliate.

Before eating his own food, she noticed, Jesse closed his eyes and mumbled a few words. Malila decided it was some superstitious ritual, and at the next meal, she thought to parody his silly practice. Thereafter, she ate alone.

They ate what she first took to be leather. She had initially refused.

Jesse had smiled and dropped her portion into his grinning mouth with all apparent satisfaction. At the next stop, she had taken the scrap and, after gnawing, been able to swallow it. It had a smoky, salty taste.

"Jerky ... venison. For the record, Malila, if I wanted to kill you, poison's not my style. You are tied up; knives are durable, have easy instructions for use."

"You don't scare me, Sisi."

"Wasn't trying to, lass."

Daily for a week, after washing his hands in the malodorous soap and making her strip off her shirt, the old man examined her wound, lifting and probing her flesh. After some days, he removed the binding and covered the wound with some boiled cloth, sticking it to the wound with aromatic syrup that dried to a tacky brown surface. In a few days more, he removed her sutures.

"That is going to be a pretty little scar."

"Are you done?"

"Just admiring my handiwork, lass. All done."

"Then stop pawing me."

He released his grip on her right breast and looked briefly at the offending hand.

"Sorry, lass, no insult to your maidenly virtue was intended. Just trying to get some light on the site of interest."

"Sorry if my tits overshadowed your 'site of interest.'"

"Nothin' ye'll need worry about, Lieutenant. Nae yer fault," said the old man, moving to help her dress.

Malila smacked his hands away when he tried.

The following morning, the old man shoved a rucksack into her arms, containing her sleeping skins, a water flask, and some of the food.

"This is yours, lass. Time you started lifting your weight around here, doncha think?"

With a defiant look, Malila let the pack fall to the ground, folding her arms. Her duty was clear; to cooperate with the enemy was to betray the Unity.

"No matter. It's your stuff. Carry it or leave it ... all the same to me."

Malila glared at him. His face was unreadable behind its alien bush of white beard and blue tattoos. When she did not pick up the pack, he shouldered his own, bound Malila's wrists in front of her, and walked off. They had passed out of view of the campsite by the time she fathomed her mistake. They were a few hundred meters beyond that before her defiance crumbled.

"I get it. I get it, old man. You can turn around now," she demanded.

Jesse's pack advanced ahead of her, his legs churning underneath, as if she did not exist. After a few more moments, Malila dug in her heels and pulled on the lead, throwing her full weight into it. She toppled over and was dragged for a meter or so before Jesse stopped.

"Sorry, lass. Did you say something?"

"I understand. Let me get the pack."

"Well, now, lass, that's a problem. If I walk back for your pack, I carry my bag three times over the same ground, don't you see? It only seems fair that we share the load. You walk it back, and I'll take it once we get to yours. Sound fair?"

"Not really. Will you let me go back if I don't carry your pack?"

"No." And Jesse smiled his toothy smile.

"Okay, if you are going to be like that."

"I'm going to be just like that."

Malila grunted under the impossible weight of the old man's pack, the distance expanding in front of her with each step. Her sides burned, her legs ached, and her breath came in dry rasps. She got about halfway back before she stumbled and fell to her knees. Jesse leaned over and offered her a hand.

"Nice try, lass. You can leave it there. Stand up, and we can go back without it."

Malila followed him in silence and let the old man help her into the smaller pack before they started again.

"Lesson learned, lass?" he asked over his shoulder.

"Don't piss off the Sisi."

Jesse laughed before yanking on Malila's leash and making her stumble.

"Watch your language, Lieutenant, but you were close. 'Accept instruction, that you may gain wisdom.' Perhaps with contemplation, you might come up with a more philosophical answer."

"You aren't making any sense, old man."

Jesse laughed and walked on. For a Sisi, the man seemed to have too many layers.

They passed derelict buildings and rusted devastations that she took for bridges. Many of these last stretched over mere streams, suggesting destroyed dams or a more hostile climate.

During the late afternoon, the old man slowed his pace to investigate bivouac sites. Once camped, their main meal was various combinations of hard bread, jerky, dried berries, and the luck of the snares. If there was still sufficient light, the old man did small tasks. His movements were delicate and dexterous while repairing clothes or working on the small patches of leather that he kept in a buckskin roll in his pack. At other times, he soaked the pieces in a malodorous solution that he kept in a thick plastic satchel. Unidentifiable gray objects swam in the turbid yellow liquid.

Before turning in each night, Jesse performed three rituals. Malila understood the elderly liked their little rituals. He first brewed up an effusion from the contents of a leather pouch, bitter and tasting of some unidentifiable dried berry. It made her teeth feel furry. He drank it as well. She surreptitiously discarded it until Jesse caught her doing so. His blow stung. She had to drink it down in front of him thereafter.

Jesse's second ritual was odd. He sang, recited passages from memory, and told improbable stories. It mystified her as he did not seem to care whether she listened or not. All his speeches were odd, but the long passages of cadenced words he called "poems" bewildered her completely. She heard about Horatio defending his father, who was also a river; a man loitering among some yellow flowers; another talking to a skin parasite; another watching for a flag; another about someone named MacPherson holding up a floor with pipes; and an academic railing against the arrival of a pool in a table. It was all very silly.

The last ritual before retiring was bathing. Jesse had some excuse, but Malila could see it was just to humiliate her on a daily basis. She would have to strip, soap up, and sluice off before Jesse would allow her to dive shivering under the sleeping skins. He followed suit, damp and shivering under the furs as well. When Malila understood that the old man did not expect her to service him, she welcomed the warmth of the sleeping arrangements and slept well ... except for the dream.

During the interim of fatigue, while she warmed the bed to allow her body to sag into slumber, Malila was able to think. The old savage acted as if her abduction was a clever prank. She knew better. She was disgraced. The Unity boasted it had never lost a war or suffered an officer captured in the seventy-four years of its glorious history. If she were part of history at all, Malila would star in a great cautionary tale told to new recruits.

Malila ran through the great narratives she had known as a recruit. The Unity immortalized sagas in which the individual sacrificed for the glory of the country. Dying soldiers praised the Unity with their cooling lips. Martyrs succumbed only after striking a courageous blow to confound the enemies of freedom and democracy. Not one heroine had been caught in her underwear by a demented Sisi.

The Sisis were vile, worn-out, incompetent, incontinent, selfish, and dim-witted. They were beneath notice or contempt. She must be an unknowing fraud to have let herself be captured. She was a failure with each kilometer she walked, each kilogram she carried, and each meal she accepted.

Malila imagined how she might become a martyr for the Unity before this lunatic Sisi could show her off as a trophy. After her glorious death, her friends would mourn her and count themselves blessed to have known her. Her patrons would gain heroic cachet that their fellow officers would covet. Her crèche would have a tasteful brass plaque placed on her old bunk. However, as each of her imagined exploits to martyrdom played out in her mind, Malila returned to the same dilemma: as far as the Unity would ever know, she was alive, swimming around some muddy river of the outlands. She would waste her last words on the dementia of an old man. It was just too grotesque.

One night, after she stopped shivering, Malila asked, "Why are you doing this to me, old man?"

"I am a man under authority, and I have men under authority to me. To one I say 'Come' and he comes, and to another I say 'Go' and he goes."

"That isn't an answer."

"No, it isn't. When I start answering those questions, lass, it means that I no longer think you are going back to your damned Union alive. Do you want me to answer your questions?"

"No!"

"Good ... Sleep."

She slept, somehow comforted.

CHAPTER 18

TRIP WIRE, SPRING, TRIGGER, JAWS

Nyork, Unity
19.51.31.local_19_10_AU76

Monee'k is different from the other girls, Iain thought. That would be obvious to anyone who bothered to really look. Her body floated, while all the other girls merely danced. He knew his attraction, his addiction, for her was getting out of hand. All his spare pay, not that there was a lot, went to buy time with Monee'k at the Night Lite Ballroom. If he got there early enough, he could dance with her the entire night … or until his money ran out. She smiled at him as they shared a few words dancing, his hands caressing her warm skin as they moved. He shivered.

He had seen her arrive at the club once before. Even with her clothes on, she had been easy to spot. She had a bounce in her stride that he would know anywhere. Iain had been waiting across the alley from the stage door in the rain, his service coat buttoned and his collar turned up. He hunkered down into the coat, trying to warm himself against the wind coming in from the river.

A group of women started down the alley to enter the stage door, the lights from the street making them unrecognizable silhouettes. It was only when the others turned to go in that Iain saw Monee'k at the back of the group. She stopped. When she smiled, Iain felt himself breathe again. He waved, stopped, his hand still up. She walked across the alley, smiled again, and took his hand. She held it as they talked. She was special.

"Nice to see you, Sergeant."

"Call me Iain. Can I call you Monee'k? That is a pretty name."

"My name's really Heather. Monee'k is like a stage name … Iain. You've been coming here a lot lately."

"I've been here before, but I started coming back when I noticed you."

Heather had laughed, and it had made his heart skip. Once inside they had danced until closing. Heather had paid for their last three dances.

To Hecate, Malila's disappearance had been wrenching. At the museum, Hecate had been too brusque with her, the memory of their abrupt parting haunting her even before she'd learned of Malila's disappearance. Then, Malila's apartment vacant and O-A terminated, Hecate had imagined a purge inside the DUFS. Malila would never have seen it coming. Even as she was bending the rules in unimagined ways, Malila could be blindsided after a not-quite-agile-enough maneuver. Someone would find it so easy to denounce her.

Hecate had made judicious inquiries through the governmental back channels, but to no avail. Malila had just evaporated.

Then Victor had been denounced. To watch his slow, public evisceration at the hands of lesser creatures had been agony. It had been a mercy when he killed himself.

Since then, the one remaining bright spot for her was the book warehouse. To her surprise, Victor's suicide had not canceled her access. She was spending more and more time within its high dusty walls, staying all night before returning to the ministry.

She found and inhabited worlds of hope, despair, joy, sorrow, and delight. Eventually, it scared her, thinking she might lose herself to the books. There was so little to keep her here otherwise.

"Doggy, I can beat Khama's last jag!" said a grinning Jasun Ciszek as Iain arrived.

"Given up on loser lieutenants, has the old man?"

"Seems he has changed from looies to loos," said Jasun.

"Makes sense when you think about it, Gunny. Whata we gotta do now?"

Jasun slipped into official bureaucratese. "Our section is to direct all resources to evaluating and revising policies and procedures for the care and maintenance of all sanitary facilities in the command."

"You're kidding me, yeah? We are supposed to feck off everything to make sure the toilets flush?"

"By the authority bestowed by rank and custom … yes."

"So what do I do with the Chiu data?"

Ciszek was ready for him and passed over a small scrap of actual paper.

"Just post it to this address, Doggy, just the raw data. Let's get a move on. I need to get this new shit started before my ThiZ break. We gotta have something to show by retreat today."

Iain gave a smart salute before slouching into the seat at his console. "Ours is not to wonder, Sarge, why these bizzles are in charge."

Jourdaine smiled his bodiless smile as the Presence. He supervised Khama, unbeknownst to the man or his sergeants. In the CORE of the Unity, secrets of state, encrypted industrial correspondence, and even a low-level data stream were free for the taking … to Jourdaine. The best security procedures were no match for a Presence that could move outside the mirrored corridors of the 'net. With little danger to himself, he had been able to have Khama not only initiate but now disassociate himself from the first step of his trap for Chiu. He had his trip wire—the auto ping.

It was a start. Unlike any usual trap, however, this one possessed parts that never would appear to connect with any other part. It would never look like a trap. Anyone climbing up the data stream would find people ignorant of any connection they might have with each other. It was not complete yet. He still needed a spring to energize it, a trigger to set off the capture, and the jaws to seize his prey.

With that thought, the next item on his scavenger hunt would be a spring, to magnify the tentative vibrations of the trip wire. In the vast landscape of the CORE, if you could view it from Jourdaine's perspective, there existed all sorts of oddities and back alleys with bits of program or personality that had gotten lost or corrupted. Becoming cumbersome over time, the CORE techs had found it easier to assign a distant and silent block of memory to them, letting the bits fight it out among themselves.

The n-dimensioned space assigned to them frothed with danger, of course, but it was always worth a look. Sometimes, the bits of program acted like rats, burrowing into otherwise protected file dumps to retrieve a datum or two. However, there were some things you could not get rats to do.

For those jobs, you needed graduate students.

Dr. Waylan Swartzbender, the Rodman professor of the Heidegger School of Practical Theology of Columbia University of the People connected with Jourdaine via a video interview. Jourdaine needed no O-A for this. Everyday coercion, fear, and duplicity were quite sufficient for academics.

"Colonel Jourdaine, I must say I am a bit surprised. My meeting was with a … Undersecretary Chilton … about the funding?" said the E30 S30 man in the rolled-sleeves, red-shirted uniform of a tenured professor.

"Yes, Professor Swartzbender, it is about that we need to speak."

Jourdaine was pleased with the several beats of eye blinking that his words provoked. *Good start.*

"Is there any problem, Colonel Jourdaine?"

"I do hope not, Doctor. That is why this interview is what we must consider … informal. It would be unwise to make known this conversation outside ourselves. It would look like … favoritism."

The academic smiled on cue. *Sometimes it's too easy.*

"Well, then, Colonel. The funding proposal was in order, surely? It is almost the same as last year, plus COLA, capital fund, pedagogical allowances, the usual … isn't it?"

"Yes …"

Jourdaine waited for the professor to blink. He blinked.

"Who is BethanE Winters, Professor Swartzbender?"

The professor's eyebrows flicked up in surprise, and he looked down, rather than up, recalling her. The man was working from notes.

"Why, I was unaware there was this level of inspection into the academic process, Colonel."

"Who is she, Doctor?"

"Just a graduate student."

"Indeed, a graduate student … just. What is her area of study then?"

A hurried number of keystrokes later, the professor said, "The superiority of ethical immanence to the concept of transcendent ethicality with the deconstruction of the modern city-state as text."

"Now, Professor, I am hardly a man of your learning or insight, but I had thought that concept a bit played out?"

"Indeed, indeed. Rather hackneyed, expected more, distracted, don't you know … government contracts. But … why is this important?"

The professor looked up into Jourdaine's eyes. His chin came up; his lips thinned.

Excellent, Jourdaine thought. *We finally come to what he thinks important. Time to set him up.*

"Are you familiar with *The Vital Realism,* by John Baudrillard, Professor?"

The older man's eyes dilated, and there was a slight intake of breath. *Jackpot,* thought Jourdaine.

"I was a very young scholar at the time, Colonel. The book was on the Correct Readings for Consumers list then …"

The professor subsided as Jourdaine raised his hand and shook his head. *Take your foot off the accelerator briefly; makes the turning easier.*

"It is not your ... reading habits ... we are questioning, Professor. Citizen Winters seems to have acquired a copy from her current liaison with a Malik Mafee. What is your opinion of the work, since you admit to having read it?" *Now let him hear the trap snap shut. It will focus his efforts wonderfully.*

"Oh, derivative, totally derivative. Old-fashioned. Knew it at the time, of course," the professor said, rather too fast.

Just a little frenzy, as expected, of course.

"So glad to hear you say that—and, of course, your loyalty and ... orthodoxy ... have never been in serious question. But this Citizen Winters ... another issue entirely. I think I would feel very much better about her advancement if we could judge how loyal and cooperative she is," Jourdaine added, waiting for the response. *Open a gate and see how fast he rushes to it,* he thought.

"Yes, assuredly, Colonel. I could have her do some of my classes," the professor said and actually looked away to write something.

"Hardly, Professor." Jourdaine laughed but did not smile.

The man looked up, startled. The man needed his priorities rectified.

"I think I will provide the test," Jourdaine said. "A little discrimination test for her." Jourdaine sent the file to the professor as he spoke. "She is to review this data stream, and when it matches these parameters, here, she is then to set this flag in the CORE. Her thesis would be unwise to accept if she fails, don't you agree? She will find the task tedious but untaxing. Is that acceptable?"

The look of immediate gratitude on the man's face was unfeigned. It had taken so little. The professor disdained money and thus lowered his own value to the cost of an impoverished scribbler. He disdained politicians and thus became a bad one.

The remainder of the interview was painless. By the time Jourdaine broke the contact, Swartzbender was practically rolling onto his back to have his belly scratched.

The same day, a good deal less unusually, at Columbia's University of the People, a graduate student's thesis advisor assigned her to do a task that was completely useless.

Now Jourdaine needed a trigger. Questing around the frothing edge of the CORE, he had seen how an anomaly dimpled the surface, darkened it, and distorted the landmarks. He swooped closer and could tell it was Charlie. Inside a swirling vortex of the CORE sat what had been a promising sports personality.

Even Jourdaine, not a fan of the usual blood sports, had heard the reports that a defensive lineman, one who had just been given his O-A, probably a little too late, had almost immediately COREd himself out. His owners were furious.

Jourdaine's Presence sat near the lineman, close enough to hear but far enough away so as not to be hit by the backwash of the man's emotions.

oHw ddi I gte ehre? Ewehr si eerh?

No! I said that wrong.

How.did.I.get.here? Where.is.here?

The trainer had given him some of the yellow pills and told him not to take them all at one time.

I sohudl avhe lenisted!

No! Not right.

Thoughts and images swirling around him, he could get no fingerholds for his own ideas. He kept falling, falling forever. His flesh melted and reformed as he watched. He saw his guts clench and move, pink and writhing like a newly killed hog.

The O-A had been such a great new toy when they'd put it in. They'd said that it was going to improve his game. It had taken a lot of hard work to get the thing to work, but it had been fecking amazing. He had been able to see the game like a bird and feel the ball move before he could see it, feel how the quarterback was going to move by how he pressed against the earth.

They had told him not to look into the CORE. He had understood that.

What he had not understood were all the willing, enthusiastic, exceptional women who had undressed for him every time he'd turned around. He could just eat them up … the girls. They had come with their pills and the pills with their visions, and he'd eaten those too.

Mi' llafign!

Charlie watched his fingers morph into staring alien eyes before they dissolved into a fetid, sticky mass. It hurt so bad.

He was aware of the Presence for a while as he watched his fingers regrow.

> *"Charlie, Charlie. You aren't falling. Look at me, Charlie. You are here with me, and I am not falling. I can make it all go away. You don't have to do this Charlie …"*

Charlie looked over and could see only the barest swirl of darkness in the shadowless noon of the CORE. He didn't have to say anything. The Presence calmed him. He was grateful for the brief respite from his torrent of sensation. He clung to the Presence and wept, for the first time since that night when they had found him raving.

He had tried to hide from them in the CORE. Now he wept. Just having the Presence there gave him an anchor. Once he stopped falling and stopped crying, the Presence told him what he had to do.

> *"Charlie, you can listen to me, Charlie. I can get you home. You will stop falling. It will all be easy, but you have to do your part. You know how to execute, don't you, Charlie? People depend on you. You have always done your best for a teammate, haven't you? I'm your teammate, Charlie. Just one more assignment, and we can go home.*

"Just watch the flag. See the line marker. When it comes up, just throw the switch. It will send you home. But you have to wait. It isn't time yet. It is too dangerous to test the switch until the flag is set. Do you understand, Charlie?

"Yes … und'stand: assignment flag home."

"Excellent, Charlie. At the right time, the switch will send you home."

Trip wire, spring, trigger … only jaws were needed. The trap was coming along.

He would be ready for her: Khama to order the auto ping to be tripped if Chiu's O-A came within range, an agent of his own in the shop to create the auto ping, an expendable E20 graduate student to read the raw data, her thesis advisor ready to denounce her if needs be, Charlie to trigger the switch, and, easiest of all, a snatch team. Anyone working on any one link was unable to identify Jourdaine himself: no program code to be unearthed, no data dump to be gone through by some enterprising eprovost. Jourdaine's programming had been in people, and when people died, their memories died with them. Chiu, if she surfaced alive, could dispute her last disastrous meeting with Suarez. If anyone took her seriously, it might expose Miramundo Morales. Jourdaine wished to reserve the pleasure of that revelation for himself.

Of course, it was probably unnecessary. Chiu had already been missing for three weeks. He'd give it six months and then dismantle the whole affair. His coconspirators would go back to whatever they had been doing, never knowing they had been a part of a conspiracy.

But this had been a good deal of trouble for one jumped-up second lieutenant unless … she might be recycled.

Palace coups required audacity, brutality, and the ability to draw people to his cause. Power blocks in academia, the government, or the arts were fools to contest a change in government against a unified military. Barring kitchen knives and makeshift cudgels, only the DUFS had weapons.

However, the DUFS was hardly unified. It seethed with intrigue. Like a magnet, any leader powerful enough to succeed induced polar opposites to dispute that success. Disinterest combated enthusiasm, disaffection contended with popularity, and combinations of lesser powers blocked a greater one. Jourdaine would have to be seen and unseen, exceptional and unremarkable, decisive and compliant.

For this coup d'état, then, he needed not supporters but metasupporters, those who were unaware how their actions might forward his plans. Many were in place already, Jourdaine's spiderweb of subordinates. None of his people knew another. None of his human tools would ever be able to report more than an odd enthusiasm or quirky behavior, and Jourdaine would remain a bland smudge on their recollections.

But at some time the virtual must become real, and for that he needed a face.

CHAPTER 19

DEATH WALKER

Illinois Territory, RSA
Late October 2128

The leaves, at first just tinged with yellow and scarlet, were now gaudy, floating down to swirl around them as they walked. The air was scented with the musk of loam, sunshine, and the promise of winter. Autumn in the Unity was merely a different shade of gray. Malila was ever more grateful for the warmth of the old man as she slept.

During the second week, as they reached the crest of a long slope covered in scrub, two tilted and paved plateaus appeared, fading to the horizon, left and right. Woods separated them in many places, and stray vegetation punctuated the pavements themselves.

Jesse grunted and, stepping onto the hard surface, started walking south without comment. Malila adjusted her gait, letting her legs swing free, and hitched her pack higher. The consistency of the tread allowed her to look around without tripping. She could then enjoy the unfolding of the landscape: the changing shape of a copse of trees, clouds and their shadows, and the slow flow of the land under her feet—ridges, shallow lakes, and bomb craters. At their first stop, she asked him about the trail.

"It's the old Eye-39, lass. Due north-south for a while before we have to head east to pick up Eye-74. Don't much like using these roads. It's a little too easy to see us coming."

"What are you worried about, old man. We haven't seen anybody since we started."

"Doesn't mean that they haven't seen us, lass. When Mose and I came up here, we took side roads, as we had horses … didn't want to offer too tempting a prize to your Unity scabs. Now we are fighting south before the snows; fewer sharks to feed on us this time of year. We can hazard the highways for a while."

Despite his anxiety, the old man took time to show Malila new skills. She learned to make fire, set snares, skin the game, and much else. Out of the corner of her eye Malila would catch the man watching as she demonstrated some new talent, a vigilant brittle gleam in his eye and a smile on his face until she turned to look at him. Then he would harrumph at her efforts before turning away. She found herself laughing at the absurd old man. He laughed as well, then.

One skill she had not successfully acquired was setting up a bear bag, hauling food out of the reach of "critters." Malila had tried to learn how to select the right tree branch and toss the line so that it did not get tangled. On the occasion of her first attempt, the counterweight, a large machine nut, had swung around, giving her a black eye. Since then that job had been left to Jesse.

She was still a prisoner. She wore a tether while they walked and slept. At night, Jesse still recited his long cadenced elocutions to the fire, he still made her drink the tea, and he still made her bathe, despite the cold.

"This must be the highlight of your day, old man," she said as she started to disrobe at a small cove along a stream, the water black in the light of the first quarter moon, shining low in the west.

"You get to humiliate a Unity officer in the name of good hygiene. How pathetic is that?"

"For the record, I'm obligated to supervise prisoners, Acting

Lieutenant Chiu. I'd like nothing better than to preserve your maidenly modesty, but the company strength is deficient one provost marshal's matron, if'n you ain't noticed."

"Seriously, Jesse, you have me tied up naked. Where am I going to go? I just want some time without you looking at me."

"The eye cannot trespass, my friend, but ... do you promise not to try to escape? If I accept your parole, I come back and you are still tied up here waiting for me, right?"

Malila almost smiled. In the Unity, they were so past this. The government made many promises, only to break them, all for superb and cogent reasons. The people could vote to change any regulation, deny any privilege, and revoke any liberty. Promises were "a bookmark for progress." Personal promises fared rather worse. Anyway, Jesse was not a citizen. Grateful for the dim light, she hoped her voice did not betray her.

"I promise I will not attempt any escape, Jesse. I'd just like a little privacy."

"Okay, lass. I'll take you at your word."

Jesse threw the long line of her tether around the root of a big tree overshadowing the pool and tied it off before leaving. Once he was gone, Malila finished disrobing and threw her clothes onto a bush and herself into the cold water. It should have been frigid but wasn't. Working upstream, she found a patch of warmth and followed it to its source, a ten-centimeter-wide opening at the floor of the pool.

Malila luxuriated. That was when she saw the lights.

They were the first lights she had seen at night since her capture, two yellow lights weaving back and forth above the leafless scrub. What supported the lights she could not see, but the light of the moon seemed to gleam off a surface that reminded Malila of dark, brushed steel. She heard no rotors or the hum of a Skimmerhorn drive.

She stepped forward and gasped in pain; a singeing feeling sliced along her instep. Malila pulled her foot back, allowing herself to float. The pain remained steady, and her immediate fear subsided. She slid her fingers down her leg gently, finding a small, sharp shard of something still protruding from her instep. Malila swam back to the bank, reluctantly leaving the warm current, and clumsily hauled out onto the tree root. A green glass shard was still sticking out of the wound. Without a thought, she pulled it out and could see the stream of darkness—her blood—wash into the dark waters. The wound was neither deep nor long, and Malila had no difficulty walking back to where she had left her clothes.

Dressed and still damp, she moved through the brush to find a place where she could see the lights but was brought up short by her tether, within a few meters. With little thought, Malila spun the rope around her waist and began slicing through the braid with her newfound glass knife. Within a few cuts the tether parted.

Malila worked her way through the scrub along the banks of the stream toward where she thought the lights had gone. Using it as cover, Malila crept near the bole of a large, dead tree.

She should have known that the Unity patrols would patrol at night. Low-light technology let them scan large sections of the outlands, while the savages were slowed by the darkness. The overwhelming might of the Unity would descend out of shadows, and in the morning only stories of mysterious lights in the night sky would remain.

She moved out from behind the tree trunk.

The lights were just meters away from her. The moon silhouetted two serpentine stalks, twisting and writhing above her in a complicated dance. A light surmounting each stalk like an eye turned down and seemed to inspect the ground. She could no longer breathe. The stench of ammonia hit her. Her eyes watered, and her vision started to fade. She retched as the yellow lights halted, turned together, and started to advance toward her, emitting a scritting noise as it came.

The blow took her just below the ribcage. An arm snaked around her waist and began to drag her off. Dazed, she was surprised that the yellow eyes began to fade away in the night before the trunk of the dead tree blocked her view. A dark shape stood her up against the bole of the tree, pressing her against the rough bark. The shape stooped and put an arm between her legs before painfully grabbing her wrist and hoisting her. Malila's world spun as she was turned upside down and bounced on the old man's shoulder back to their fire.

Jesse dropped her with a thump onto the skins before turning on her.

"Li'l Miss I-Just-Want-a-Little-Privacy got mair than she was bargainin' for, seems like, ye damned Uni gowk! Now I've gotta burn out a Death Walker. Th' thing is gonna stink fur days. What 'xactly wur ye thinkin', lass?" he shouted.

When she didn't respond, the old man threw up his arms before frisking her, rapidly and thoroughly, and tying her up, facedown, onto her skins. He built up the fire and transferred red coals onto a makeshift shovel made from tree bark before starting back down the path from which they had just come.

Sundering screams from what Malila took to be a running battle with the creature punctuated the darkness. Strange cries rent the night and subsided into groaning agues of noise. Jesse returned to stoke the fire with fresh fuel, shoveled more coals out, and again disappeared into the dark. For a time, the old man was getting the worst of it. Screams and smoke assaulted her where she lay, always coming closer. After that, however, the cries of the creature, sounding like a thrown belt on a major beltway, started to move off. The stench of smoke and ammonia sullied the air.

Jesse returned just before dawn. Even by the dim light, Malila could see blisters on his hands and burns marking his face. Jesse slumped next to her and let his head droop, his beard smudging the soot on his tunic as he rested his elbows on his knees. He coughed, an extended, emphatic liquid cough, which left him breathless.

"What was that?"

"It was a gift … from our … friends … 'cross the Rampart … I didn't think … they got … this far west … Call them … Death Walkers … Showed up after th' Scorching … kind o' fungus … Got to burn … 'em out … They need meat … attack at night."

"Is it dead?"

"Pretty much. Don't live … long … blinded. Tried to eat … one, once. Tough … taste like they smell … 'Spect they'd … say … same of me."

The old man started laughing and was again seized with a fit of coughing that drove him to his hands and knees. Blood streaked across the back of his hand after he wiped his mouth.

The old man coughed for a week thereafter. That day, they walked hard, away from the site of the fight, and Malila, again bound, found herself running to keep up.

CHAPTER 20

PAROLE

The day following the forced march away from the battle with the Death Walker started with crystalline sunlight. High fleecy clouds arched up and over them as they walked. By late morning, however, the sky turned threatening. Almost on cue, the highway disappeared into a confusion of rubble with rusting steel erupting into frozen fountains of splintered metal. They spent the afternoon retracing false starts and bushwhacking new trails.

Long before his normal time, Jesse scouted out a bivouac on a slight rise in the lee of a stand of old trees and built a hut rather more generous and sturdy than usual. A cold wind set the woods to groaning and rattling in protest against the wind.

"We are in for some dirty weather, lass. With this high a wind, it should not last too long. Best we hunker down and ride it out for a day. I could use the rest."

He coughed. After the rain started, Jesse built a small fire and lit the lamp as he sat, cooking stew. The rain added a frenzy of noise as wave after wave of the storm beat against the jury-rigged roof.

Malila started shivering. Jesse arose, unasked, to fetch a couple of deerskins to drape around her and himself before regaining his place by the fire, working another small patch of hide with the short knife as he stirred the pot.

A stray gust of wind whipped under the eaves and swirled the air with smoke and sparks. Blinded, her eyes stinging with tears, Malila coughed until she was exhausted.

In an instant, the whole grotesque burden of the day descended on Malila, the cold, the wet, the fatigue, the frustration, and now the smoke.

"You made a mess of this, old man! We are both going to die because a demented Sisi thinks he can beat the Unity! Why didn't you kill me the first day?"

Jesse, recovering from another fit of his visceral coughing, wiped his mouth.

"Why indeed, lass? Be careful what you wish for. Dead is for life, I'm told."

"You should know, Sisi; you must be half dead already!"

"I love you too, lass! But I wouldna be so anxious to end it all. You are tired. You will feel better after a night's sleep, my friend."

"I'm not your friend, Sisi! How would you have any idea how I feel?" she shrieked at the old man.

Jesse looked up, spearing her with his pallid eyes even in the dim light. He pulled the small pot off the flames, set it aside, and waved a finger under her nose before Malila could consider she might have gone too far.

"How would ah know? How am ah suppose ta be sae damned auld 'n' ne'er hae bin young, once upon a time? Dae ye think ah wis born auld, ye arrogant boot pup? How much dae ye put inta th' pot ye eat from, Acting Lieutenant Chiu?"

Malila inched away from his anger, antagonizing him further.

"Who dae ye think is keeping yer sorry bahookie dry richt noo? If it weren't fur me, ye'd be cold and drookit in some hollow o' a tree someplace!"

The old man dismissed her with a flourish of his hand when she gave him a bewildered look, turning his back on her as he replaced the pot on the fire.

"If I'm such a burden to you, why don't you let me go?"

"Humph … You don't mind being abandoned to die o' starvation and exposure to the elements? Good to know, provender being at low ebb for the moment."

"Is that why you tie me up every night? So you can find me when you want to butcher me?" She knew that was unfair, and it pleased her to say it.

"I tie you up because of you being an enemy soldier. I haven't decide about roasting you … yet."

"Look, Jesse, I'm a city girl. Even if I could get away, I don't know how to get home. I'll make you a deal. Don't tie me up, and I promise not to try to get away. Let me loose, or let me go! Do one or the other, old man, if you are telling me the truth!"

There was silence for a second, and then the old man turned to look at her.

"Well said, lass. But how do I know you won't try to kill me?"

"Would you believe me if I promised?"

"Your promises don't mean much to *you*. You showed me as much back there. Why should they mean anything to *me*?"

Malila stopped. Her actions, when she had cut herself free at the hot spring, had not been to escape … at least she had not been sure she could escape. She had dismissed her promise to Jesse before she had made it. Jesse had not, apparently. For the old man, the promise had had actual substance. To him, she had betrayed him. It had never occurred to her. The new realization made her feel empty. She was left with no response for the old man except one. In grim determination, she stood. The Unity procedure was straightforward, even if Jesse did not know the long history of it. Over the weeks, Jesse's restraint, despite his interest in her, had grown perplexing and, in its way, demeaning.

Malila faced him and waited for him to look up at her. She undressed herself. Jesse did not look away, and it gave Malila hope. When she finished, she remained standing, the cold wind plucking her flesh into tight peaks.

She announced the formulaic declaration in a voice made uncertain by the cold. "Jesse Johnstone, I offer you the freedom of my body and my faithful service in return for your protection and advice."

In the Unity, the patron-elect would acknowledge her act and words with a session of animated pleasure-sex before announcing his or her decision. Malila waited. She had to admit to herself that the idea of a Sisi as patron was grotesque, but oddly, it no longer filled her with disgust.

"This is how we ask someone to become a patron. I offer myself to you in return for your looking out for my interests … Talk, old man. I'm getting cold!"

Jesse again moved the food off the fire and stood facing her. Malila gratefully took his hand and pressed it between her breasts, moving his dry, warm hand against her softness. Malila stepped closer, feeling warmed by his nearness, and smiled to herself.

The old man had finally shown himself to be no different than her other patrons. It had been difficult for a naive thirteen-year-old Malila to present herself the first time. Defenseless and friendless, the desirability of her body had bought her protection and power, of a sort. After weeks of uncertainty, life was becoming understandable again.

Jesse spoke without moving, low and unhurried. "We aren't about ta dae this, lass. If ah dinna tak yer words, ah wouldna shame ye by taking yer body. Ah think ye should git dressed."

Jesse's words at first made no sense to her. She pressed herself against the old man and was reassured by his growing reaction. Malila touched him, feeling she had at last gotten a purchase on the rocky slope of the old man's personality.

"Malila Chiu, git dressed!"

He spoke it as a command. It startled her. Cold air circled around her as she stepped back.

"But …"

"No, lass. Git dressed. Please."

This time is was a plea. In turmoil and confusion, Malila stooped to gather her clothes. Jesse stood watching her, his face impassive and unmoving until she was dressed.

"The question was why I should believe a promise from you, Lieutenant Chiu."

Malila looked up at the stolid face of the old man. "You should believe me because if I kill you, then I die alone. Everyone I've ever known will think I drowned in some river out here. I don't want to die alone."

After a few moments of silence, the old man gave her a wooden spoon and a cup of the stew he had been cooking.

"No one should die alone, lass. Mak' me a promise nay ta escape or ta harm me or yourself, an' I will take your parole."

"I promise, Jesse."

"Enough said, lass. Eat your stew."

CHAPTER 21

BISON

Malila sensed the ground tremble in a bowel-loosening crescendo. Small stones bounced in the dust at her feet. She looked up into the oncoming terror, bizarrely shaped animals with huge forequarters tapering to slender hips and massive misshapen heads covered in horn and dark fur. They bore down on her with wild eyes and lolling tongues, arcs of spittle flicking across their flanks. Into the chaos, the old man sprang up, flapping a hide and ululating across the prairie in a clear, high voice.

The herd veered off, circled back to a small clearing, and slowed. Malila knelt and aimed at one of the smaller animals. The crack of the pulse rifle echoed back from the trees. The animal dropped to its knees before falling to its side. The herd set off again, charging along the edge of the woods and returning to the wider reaches of the grassland. After she could no longer feel the shuddering throb through her feet, she ran to the kill site, arriving just as an exultant Jesse did.

The old man scooped her up and spun her around. For an instant Malila, transported by her success, enjoyed Jesse's delight, feeling his strength elevate her face into the warm autumn light. They stopped laughing, and the old man let her slip down and out of his grasp. Malila had enough time to realize how her body stroked along Jesse's before her feet once more found the ground.

"Wonnersome shooting, lass. I dinna think ah seen better."

It was only then Malila appreciated just how enormous the beast was, the chest coming almost to her shoulder. Jesse took the pulse rifle from her, put it back into his pack, slipped his long knife out of its sheath, and set to work. He stripped to his waist, rectangular tattoos absurdly contrasting his pale skin. Jesse cut a long gash in the animal's belly and began pulling armfuls of steaming entrails out of the bloody cavern. Malila was predictably queasy.

They left the carcass, minus tongue, hide, haunch, liver, and shoulder, to the wolves and ravens. Improvising a sledge from the hide and springy saplings cut from along the tree line, they made good time, pulling in tandem until the sun was almost down. Jesse had them bathe when they found a stream and then abandon the sledge. He cut a few long green branches from a tree, and they hiked into the forest along the stream. They camped that night at a bend with a wide sandy beach.

Jesse, using the short knife, cut a generous circle of the raw bison hide, wiped the blade, and flipped it to her so that the handle hit the ground at her knee.

"Strip the bark off those branches, lass. We are going to have a delicacy."

Malila finished her task in time to watch Jesse finish pegging the bloody hide to the ground and start to scrape it free of flesh and hair with a tool from his kit. She was fascinated, not for the first time, by the delicate handling and deft touch he used on what was, to her, a foul and bloody souvenir.

"Now make a loop out of each branch, the ends together," he called to her.

Once scraped clean, the old man folded the raw hide into a more or less flat-bottomed cone and fastened the loops of green wood around the edge, folding the edges of the hide under one and then over the other. Pouring some water into the bottom of the cone, he placed it into the fire.

"Why bother with all that if you were just going to burn it, old man?"

"Watch and learn, lass."

Some of the residual fat rendered and flamed, sending up a spiral of oily smoke. Malila expected the whole thing to incinerate at any moment. Jesse, building the fire up around the cone and adding water, remained unperturbed. When the cone was about half full and the water boiling, he threw in some salt and a handful of weeds that he had harvested along the stream. Then he lowered a portion of the skinned bison tongue into the cone, the water rising perilously close to the rim.

When she did not respond, he added, "Admit it, lass: it's a neat trick, doncha think? Water boils and keeps the skin too cool to burn. The handles catch the hide between them and keep the shape to hold the water. The hide cooks into shape to keep the handles together. So I got a boiling pot."

"For an old man, you are such a little kid."

"One of my many endearing qualities, lass."

Within minutes, Malila inhaled a savory smell. Jesse hoisted the piece of tongue out and carved the coarse meat crosswise into slices. For the first time in weeks, Malila's mouth watered. He offered her the first slice, and she grabbed it, the flesh tender, hot, and sweet. The tang of the seasonings gave a relish where hunger had provided appetite. She chewed it briskly before swallowing, waiting for Jesse to offer her another slice.

They spent the evening eating tongue while the old man sliced the haunch and jerked it over the fire. For the first time since her capture, Malila experienced an odd sensation of satisfaction. Together they had brought down a great animal and were sharing in the success of their efforts.

"I want to commend you, lass. You took down a moving buffalo. You are a better shot with that weapon than I could hope to be."

"Thank you, Jesse. I am, aren't I?"

He gave her a smile, a genuine smile, and Malila saw the young man Jesse must have been once. Without much thought she asked, "Why do you have all those tattoos?"

"They mean things to people as know how to read them."

Malila placed three fingers next to her nose and drew them down and away from her. "What do those mean, then?"

Jesse raised a hand to his face, touching the blue stripes absently. "They tell people that I've killed three men, righteously."

"In war, I suppose."

"No, not in war."

"Then it was murder."

"No, lass. Jury saw it as righteous. The way you tell, Lieutenant, for future reference is if I were a murderer, you'd not see me at all. We can't afford to have murderers around isolated farms with kids for the taking. If we catch one, he dies."

"What if he gets away?"

"Then we don't see him at all. If we do, it's shoot on sight, no jury, thank you. If we find a body, then a jury sits to decide if it was a righteous killing or not. Righteous, it earns you a mark, so that people know you on sight. Killing changes a person, righteous or not."

"But three?"

"I amn't going into the tales for your titillation, my young friend, but one was a man who I shot in the back as he was running away."

"You shot him in the back? You could have let him live!"

"I could have. He left behind the body of my wife and was dragging away my daughter, perhaps I might have mentioned."

His whisper came to her from a distance she could not see. Malila's chest tightened spasmodically. She knew no children other than her distantly remembered younger self and her friends. She had no vocabulary for sorrow, no words for regret, pain, or loss. The Unity's response to loss was rage and scorn. Malila reached out to touch the old man's hand as it cupped his knee. She had failed to express her feelings, unnamed as they were. Jesse started as she touched him, coming back from years and miles away, pulling his hand away from her. Her sudden flow of tears surprised her.

Jesse pressed one of his red handkerchiefs into her hand as Malila struggled to calm her breathing and distance herself from this unseen quicksand of emotions.

"You must have done something terrible to earn the big tattoos on your back then!" She smiled, handing back the handkerchief, making it a statement.

Jesse explained to her another odd practice of the outlands. He pulled up his tunic near the warmth of the fire to display one and then another of his decorations. The oldest, smallest, and most faded tattoo was his graduation certificate from a secondary school. Even so, it was meticulous, elaborate, signed, and numbered. By outlander standards, Jesse was an accomplished scholar. Degrees in engineering and medicine were duly exposed, admired, and discussed.

"What is a doctor of medicine?" Malila blurted as the last one was explained. This tattoo occupied the upper portion of his right chest, ornate with curlicues and shadings.

"You don't have any doctors in the Union?" exclaimed Jesse. "Who takes care of the sick?"

"An HP—health care provider. You get a doctorate of government or philosophy but not health care. No one gets a doctorate in that."

Jesse tapped the blue patch reflectively. "Getting that was painful … and the tattoo wasn't much fun neither! Family tradition and all."

"I thought you were raised in a hollow by your parents."

"I was. Both of my parents were docs, but they were hiding out when the Union attacked us. It wasn't for years they felt safe enough to come down. If the Union didn't shoot you, the hunger mobs would find where you holed up. The militias didn't make it really safe until I was half-grown. My folks both had the teaching gene as well, it seems. By the time I was twelve years old—that's when we came out of hiding—I started my sophomore year in high school. My sister and her family still live in St. Lou."

"Why not just put the certificate on paper?" asked Malila, truly fascinated despite herself.

Jesse shrugged. "People skin is cheaper than sheepskin, I 'spect. My parents had all theirs on parchment. After the Meltdown and the Scorching, people had to be a lot more mobile. Big cities like Chicago burned. Detroit was leveled, first by the rebels and then by the Canadians. Anyway, people started inking themselves to prove they had done what they claimed they had. No worries about getting your papers burned or lost and no worries if the city where you went to school was a smoking hole in the ground."

"So you are marked for life. You can't go anywhere without everyone knowing who you are and what you've done?"

"Why would I want to, lass?"

The idea was chilling. In the Unity's crowded streets, Malila felt like a stone in a stream, unremarked amid the citizens sliding around her. The people were supreme in their will but anonymous in their persons.

Jesse offered her another piece of bison tongue on the tip of his long knife. She moved closer to the old man, feeling his warmth as they shared the bounty.

CHAPTER 22

LAKE OF BLOOD

They went to bed with bellies rounded by the meal. Malila slept well … for a few hours.

The dream, when it came, was like all the others: Malila was thigh-deep in warm blood, redolent and thick. The sky, lighting the sea and its empty horizon, was a yellow hue from pole to pole. Malila was walking, had been walking. She sensed the viscous blood clinging to her legs, exhausting her. Each time she stopped, the vista was the same. The oddest thing about the dream was her apathy, watching herself trek through the hideous, shallow sea of blood without a qualm.

A shiver ran through her, and she turned sharply. Immediately behind her now was a stone temple of some ancient and derelict design. Approaching the vast stone steps, she started to climb. Her feet slid at first, but she got her weight over them and mounted. The steps were steep; she could not see what lay at the top. She never could. She climbed until exhaustion overcame her.

She turned again to discover the lake of blood was gone and the stone steps extended down to lose themselves in haze. She turned back to find she was at the pinnacle with no sight of a temple.

Overhead, the yellow sky stretched to the horizon. She reached up a hand, scraping it along a surface like plaster. Once touched, the sky at once began to descend upon her. Only now did terror assault her. Turning, Malila tried to retreat to the invisible sea of blood. She could hear the sky chewing up the stones behind her ... and gaining. The nausea of adrenaline surged within her. The final panic awakened her, as it always did.

Malila sat, her heart racing and her skin sheened with terror. A sensation of wetness spread along her thighs, and she rose with a start, wondering if the fear had made her incontinent. She threw off her sleeping skins to find blood fouling her legs and bedding. She screamed.

Jesse leaped up in alarm. The sky was yet dark, but dawn was beginning to overpower the fainter stars in the east. Malila looked to the old man's face for explanation and reassurance. His expression flitted from alarm at her scream, to reassurance, to anger at her waking him, and then the mask of professional concern clicked into place.

"It is all right, lass. Nothing bad is happening. I know it looks bad, but nothing bad is happening."

"There's all this blood. How can this be all right? What is happening to me?"

"Did your mother never talk to you about this when it first happened?"

"Don't be absurd. When would I have met my fecking mother? It hasn't happened before! Look at all the blood!"

The old man paused and lapsed into quiet efficiency, leading her away from the sleeping skins and toward the dark ribbon of the stream, his calm lessening the watery sensation of her fear.

Jesse said in a quiet monotone as he helped her bathe, "The bleeding is going to go on for probably a week the first time, lass. You aren't sick. This is what most women go through. You are going to be fine. You've just started monthly bleeding cycles, is all. Most girls begin when they reach puberty. I'm guessing your implant stopped you until now. Women's bodies are ready to get pregnant for much of their lives, lass."

"You're telling me I'm a breeder?" said Malila. "That's fecking crazy. I haven't been Sapped. I didn't do anything wrong. What have you done to me?"

"Believe me, lass: you have done nothing wrong. Since you were ten or eleven, you've been a breeder. I don't know what your keepers have done to you or why, but this is what most women are. It's really pretty amazing," he finished with a smile that encouraged Malila to return one.

Malila lapsed into shivering silence and let the old man dry her before draping his own dry skins around her and leading her back to the cold fire ring.

He roused a blaze from the ashes. Malila's shivers subsided as Jesse went on to outline the peculiarities of human reproduction, explaining her biology in alarming detail.

"Every month! How can that be efficient? I waste that much blood every month for nothing?" she asked.

"I dunno, lass. God has no' asked my opinion of late," he replied as if Malila might think it amusing.

She did not. It was not credible that half of humankind was required to watch the calendar with more than idle interest.

Jesse washed and dried her sleeping furs, arraying them around the flames on a framework he contrived from branches and vines. Despite the fire, Malila shivered. Her body had betrayed her. She would now be shadowing the phases of the moon with the rhythms of her body, a captive to the mechanism of her own flesh. If she believed what the old man said, this bloody cycle would stop eventually. By then she would be a Sisi and no longer worthy of her own consideration. She shivered again.

Returning from gathering wood, Jesse also brought along an armful of tawny yellow lichen. By the time she was warm and dry, he had fashioned a lichen-and-doeskin pad to protect her clothes. Jesse promised that the next bleeding would start in about four weeks and not last as long. It annoyed Malila that this old primitive should be giving appointments to her body to keep.

They did not travel that day, Jesse using the time to jerk the rest of the bison meat. By the following day, both packs bulging, they retraced the route to the site of the kill. There was little more to harvest as far as Malila could see. Animals had already stripped the carcass, the ribs shining as white as a gruesome picket fence. Jesse, however, grabbed up the massive head by the horns with a grunt of satisfaction. Again stripping off his shirt, he began to bash the skull with his ax. Finally breaching the skull, the old man scooped out the brain and added it to the noxious concoction in the plastic satchel.

Malila stood upwind.

As the weather grew colder, their appetites grew ravenous. They stopped less frequently now. The food was monotonous, bison jerky at every meal and every stop. Jesse still made her drink his bitter tea, although he no longer could stomach it himself. Adding a new ritual, most nights, Jesse worked on the buffalo hide, scraping the dried flesh off the underside, stretching it to shave the thickness of the skin and then working the reeking brain-mixture into the hide. After a couple of weeks' work, Jesse built a small and uncharacteristically smoky fire before wrapping the now-supple hide around it. After a few hours, he pronounced the hide cured and ready for use. He never told her from what condition it had recovered.

Jesse's evening orations increased with the lengthening nights. After a vehement recitation about some ancient battle's "volley and thunder," in the quiet before sleep, she finally asked, "Why are you saying all those things, Jesse? Are you getting senile?"

Malila expected no answer whatever and was startled when she sensed the furs quiver in what she took to be outrage. It was some time before she grasped that the old man was shaking with laughter.

"You are most likely right, lass. But it pleases me. I like the sound of the words. Don't any of them move you?"

"Move me?"

"Do they affect your emotions at all? The words have a rhythm but a meaning as well."

The old man's voice lilted softly into her ear:

> And still of a winter's night, they say, when the wind is in the trees,
>
> When the moon is a ghostly galleon tossed upon cloudy seas,
>
> When the road is a ribbon of moonlight over the purple moor,
>
> A highwayman comes riding—
>
> Riding—riding—
>
> A highwayman comes riding, up to the old inn-door.[7]

Malila suppressed the involuntary shiver traveling her spine. "I don't understand it. It's old-fashioned. Why should I try to understand it?"

He sighed. "Why indeed, lass? Go to sleep."

A few minutes later, she heard his steady breathing. Two stars in the east caught her attention as they climbed the sky. One was a brilliant blue-white that flickered as if it were a mere spark while the other, fainter one, keeping pace, burned with a constant ruddy gleam.

Why had she lied? Why had she dismissed it all because of its age? The old man had shown her something, and only her body had understood.

---

[7] Alfred Noyes, "The Highwayman," *Collected Poems* (1947).

CHAPTER 23

THE UNDERPASS

Crossing of US 41 and Interstate 74, western Indiana Territory
November 11, 2128

Off the road and near a small huddle of hemlocks, under the thin gray sky, Malila sat. The temperature had plummeted since sunup, and the wind had backed into the northwest. Before noon, low clouds had obscured the sky. She could barely swallow enough of the frigid slurried water to satisfy Jesse's watchful supervision. Within the last hour, the old man had spotted a road to the south, calling it Old 41, telling her it ran under the highway they were following, Eye 74, one more of the roads that stretched across the prairie from horizon to horizon. The savage names were always so picturesque.

Jesse, after giving her their cache of food, left her in the lee of the evergreens.

"If I am tardy now, lass, let's say past sundown, walk back west and take the last road we passed going north, on your right."

"I know which way is north, old man. But I guess, since I have the food, you will find me."

"My thinking precisely, my friend."

"I'm not your friend!"

He took the pulse rifle with him.

Malila ducked her face into her jacket, breathing her warmth back into herself, glad for the weight and warmth of her backpack shielding her from the wind. Her O-A hummed painlessly in the background, the annoying mental irritation she had noted during the first week now gone.

They had met no travelers. She'd seen no smoke, no tracks other than animals, and smelled nothing but the coming winter. All the rivers they had crossed flowed west or south. Unity maps showed the outlands as a narrow belt of Scorched and waterless land between the Rampart and the western republics, in most places no more than 150 klicks wide. However, Malila reasoned there must be a great river between the highlands near the Rampart and the highlands out west. Jesse called it the Mississippi River, a name too grotesque to take seriously.

Malila jumped as Jesse joggled her out of her doze.

"Nice to see my absence has not made you overanxious, lass."

Malila grimaced at him, staggering to her feet as the old man repacked his pack and hoisted it with his usual grunt. She followed him down the long, oblique slope to the underpass, then through it to the opposite side, the dim light slipping into the space like a beggar. When they had reached the north side of the underpass, Jesse motioned for her to stop as he continued farther north, up the side, and out of sight.

In a few minutes, he was back, beaming. "No one home. It looks like we have a place out of the storm."

"How long do you think it will rain?" she asked, hoping for a day of rest, snug out of the wind.

"I don't think it will rain at all! Have you never seen it snow?"

"Of course, I go to VerMon all the time to train."

"Big difference between a noun and a verb, lass!"

"Even so," he continued, "it is early in the season. It shouldn't last for long. If we had skis, we could make some real time, but as 'tis, we are stuck here for at least a day. I'll get wood enough to last us a while."

The old man emptied their jerky into the small cook pot before taking the remainder of it with him, hoisting the meagre remains of their food cache into a tree while Malila went to start the fire.

By the time Jesse returned, the first flakes were drifting down. The fire, stoked with the new fuel and illuminating graffiti of obscure provenance on the crumbling walls, did little to warm Malila as she shivered in the cave-like corner of the underpass. She wrapped her clothes around her, even grabbing some of the sleeping furs as she watched the fire.

Jesse set about cooking her share of a meager meal, a stew of sorts in the single small pot he carried. Malila's stomach grumbled as the last of the jerky, scraps of trail bread, and some roots that Jesse had dug up that day bubbled in the pot.

"What do you call this, old man?"

"Specialité de la maison, ragout avec de bison et detritus, mademoiselle."

"Sounds appetizing," she said as she made a face at him.

"If we can't move and run out of food, what are we going to eat?" she asked between bites.

Jesse grimaced but answered, "While it snows, not much. I can scrape some tree bark, and there is a stream to the north with cattails. Dig the roots and bake 'em. Maybe dip the stream for fish."

Malila ignored the look and the comment and returned to eating. It was horrid. She forced herself to swallow, knowing that she needed the energy just to be warm enough to sleep. When she finished, Jesse set about cooking another batch in the small pot for himself.

Malila watched the fire, warm, with a full belly, wrapped in the obscurity of the swirling snow. Every day's trek had exhausted her, but today was worse. The cold wind eroded her well-being, and the noise in her head, even dulled to a barely perceptible hum, still bore upon her. Whether it was the cold or their dwindling supplies, Malila felt used up. Orange tongues of flame licked along a small branch, building and adding their glow to the whole fire. The heat, splashing across her face and hands, settled her. Jesse stirred his own meal without comment.

Malila awoke with a start. A dribble of drool chilled her chin. The fire was still burning, but the branch she had been watching was now just a few disconnected gray coals. Newly added branches sent sparks drifting up into the dark beams raftering their camp. Wavering shadows showed a drag in the shin-deep snow along the lowest point of the underpass to the north—no sign of a footprint. The small pot, already clean, was upended near the fire. No doubt the old man had gone to get firewood.

She looked down. Jesse's odd short knife was out of its sheath and on the ground in front of her: it was a round-backed, drop-point blade with a small back bar for fine work and finger rings in the handle. The old man never left his blades unsheathed, except when he was using them. The blade, looking molten in the firelight, pointed at her. He had not woken her as he'd left. Malila tried to control a shiver as she scooped up the knife, sheathed it, and wedged it into the waistband in the small of her back.

There must have been a noise; Malila looked into the swirling snow to the south side of the underpass. Outside the cone of the fire's light, the white flakes were a chaos of motion. She stared into the maelstrom, still muzzy from her nap and annoyed at the old man for leaving her.

It was then she saw the hunched darkness against the black. It shuffled, turning from side to side as if smelling the trail. There was no head, just a huddle of shapes, ill-defined and ominous. As it drew nearer, Malila could make out the shaggy coat. A pair of lifeless eyes rested on the top of the heap of fur. The form lumbered into the light.

CHAPTER 24

BEAR

The man was of average height, but there was an adamant solidity to him, Malila thought. He wore the skin of a large bear, the muzzle fur skinned out and tanned, making a gruesome hood, with the eyeless eyes perched on the man's head. His hair was as black as the bearskin and hung cowl-like around his face. Dark eyes lurked under bushy eyebrows almost hidden in the grotesque hood.

As the figure moved nearer her fire, the man's large hands shucked off the leather shooter's mittens and spread open to grasp the heat of the blaze.

"Good evening, Miss. I was hoping to share your fire. The name is Edward Phillips, but most people around here call me Bear."

He looked sideways at her. It was several seconds before he smiled.

Malila had no idea how to respond. All people of the outlands had reverted to savagery, she knew. The old man showed that much to be true. She understood her choices here: take this unknown man into her confidence or remain in captivity with Jesse. The might and wealth of the Unity should buy her a welcome almost anywhere. Fear and greed were durable motives. Her choice was obvious. *The enemy of my enemy is my friend,* she thought.

Just before she spoke, however, another saying resonated inside her head: *Better the enemy you know than the one you do not know.* In the moments she had to choose, the man's fetid smell decided for her.

"I'm Jane. My friends are coming back in a minute," she said perhaps a little too late.

This greasy man looked around the campsite, hesitant and uneasy at first. Without invitation, he sat on his heels near the fire, the flames glinting from his eyes. He rocked on his heels and again spread his raw-boned hands over the warmth. He licked his lips as he looked into the flames and started questioning her.

"Where did you say you were coming from, Miss?"

"I didn't. We are coming from Wiscomsin and going to Kentucky."

It did not sound quite right. She looked at the man without blinking. It was always good to keep as much truth in a lie as convenient, she knew.

"And your man, where is he? Seems he took his pack with him when he left."

"He is coming back soon. I'm not sure you ought to be here when he comes back. He mightn't like it."

Malila had missed the fact that Jesse had taken his pack, a clear indication he was abandoning her. Her face froze as she tried to act nonchalant. She had been foolish to brandish the possibility of returning companions.

"That isn't very hospitable, Miss. The night is cold, and the weather's ugly. No one should be denied shelter on a night like this," Bear said with a reasonable smile.

Malila had no idea what constituted outland hospitality. By no means should she let this man get too close to her. She ought to make an escape herself. Jesse had said the snow would not last.

Stringing together phrases that she hoped sounded like Jesse, she said, "Okay, I guess you can bed down over there. We are out of food. I cannot offer you anything. But you can have some coals and dry wood to start your fire over there." She gestured again across the underpass to the far side.

The man did not answer, but his head swiveled to look at her. His appearance had altered in the few seconds since he'd last spoken. He looked up at her through black, bushy eyebrows and wrenched his face into a grimace of amusement. He fished a small orange whistle out from under layers of dingy shirts and blew three short blasts.

"I like the fire and the company well enough here." He stood.

Almost at once, dark shapes, hunched against the wind, climbed down the slopes at both ends of the underpass, half-walking, half-sliding in the shin-deep snow, carrying skis and long guns.

Within seconds, Malila was surrounded by men stamping snow off their legs. Most wore beards. Even in the cold, Malila smelled poorly tanned hides and unwashed bodies. Her O-A's low-level hum had risen to a keen inside her head.

Bear rose and smiled as his men approached.

"Let me do some introductions, Miss. These gentlemen are what you might call my fellow travelers. We sort of patrol this stretch of the I-74 to keep it free of … hazards to navigation. As it happens, the weather has reduced our prospects. That is, until George noticed your fire. So we're just being friendly-like and welcoming you to the neighborhood, you traveling alone and all. Boys, this here is Jane. I'll let you introduce yourselves … in private."

While he was speaking, several of the men had started emptying Malila's pack, throwing the contents onto the frozen ground and pawing through them. Malila tried to move to one side of the men. A hand reached from behind her and gripped her across her breasts. A yelp of surprise and pain escaped her lips and fixed the men's attention.

"Easy, boys, the rules are the same. Equal shares and double for the captain, just like we agreed."

Bear was aiming a sidearm toward the ground negligently, but the threat was immediate and well understood.

"Just checking the inventory, Bear, no harm done," said a large man with a ginger beard and an uncertain smile.

The man's huge belt buckle ground into her back, moving Jesse's short knife on occasion.

"'Course not, Jimmy. No harm at all. George is the lucky one to get her first. He sighted the fire. Harry, you go find him so we can get started. The sooner he gets done, the sooner we all get a piece," Bear said in a reasonable, businesslike voice.

Bear turned to another man. "Pete, let's get some food up. You others go get some more wood. This pile won't last us through the night. I think our lady friend here will want the fire nice and warm. Isn't that right, Miss?"

"I'm an officer of the Democratic Unity Forces for Security! If you take me to your authorities, no harm will come to you." Her voice sounded shrill, even panicked.

Jimmy paused in midmolestation as all heads turned to watch how Bear would react.

"Well, Miss Great and Powerful General, ma'am, you appear to be out of uniform and in enemy territory." At a nod from the man, Jimmy pulled her shirt open, spilling her breasts into the dim light of the fire. The men grinned and hooted their appreciation.

"Worse and worse, ma'am." Bear shook his head. "I think you must be a spy!"

It was obvious to her that fear or favor of the Unity did not extend to this patch of nowhere. Pretending to lapse into apathy and keeping her head down, Malila counted nine men, plus the absent George. She surprised herself at her revulsion at these leering men.

Since she was an E7, she had found pleasure-sex enjoyable enough with her patrons. This would be very different; this would be a grunting obscenity. She could not have put a name to it before. There was an incorrectness … a wrongness to it. These men wanted to hurt her and to make her fear, using her own body to do so, like overgrown children tormenting smaller ones by making them hit themselves with their own fists.

She had never understood the meaning of *evil* in her life. *Evil* was a media word for the losers: "Unity District Conquers the Evil of Hoarding." The malefactors paraded before the 'nets were always small, frightened, and grubby; this evil was rank and brutal. Her heart started racing, almost pounding out of her chest. Jimmy still held her, moving his hands over her breasts and between her legs despite her best efforts to cover herself.

The man sent out to fetch George and start her serial rape returned. He kicked off his skis and went over to the fire, spreading his hands to the enlarged blaze. It was a few seconds before Bear asked him, "Harry, is George coming?"

Amid some hesitant chuckles, the man, blinking, looked up, snow melting from his wool cap and beard.

"I didn't find him. I saw some tracks and figured he had come in to get his first piece. Isn't he here?"

The men stopped laughing and looked up. The only sound was the low moan of the wind and the hiss of falling snow.

A muffled crack of a projectile rifle echoed through the darkness, along with a sound that could have been a man's wail.

CHAPTER 25

WHISTLES

Jesse had just tipped up the pot to dry by the fire when, above the wind, he heard the whistle. The old man grabbed his pack and picked up the pulse rifle. Before he left the campfire, he pulled out his short knife, unsheathed it, and placed it squarely before the dozing girl. It would have to serve.

A whistle told him at least two men lurked in the swirling darkness, a darkness for which the firelight left him blind. A signal also said they came from more than one direction. The intruders' advantage lay in their numbers and firepower. Jesse's advantage must lie in his ability to take back the night—to force the others to hunt him. For the time being, Malila would be hostage … and perhaps plunder. If he had brought Malila with him, the men would have hunted them both down, unwilling to linger by a ready-made fire with the prospect of a weak victim or a strong enemy in the neighborhood.

If hostile, they would try to block his escape. What he needed now were more weapons and many more diversions. One lone man not did inspire fear.

Pushing on into the teeth of the wind, Jesse pumped his legs through the deepening snow, north to where he might find some combat-ready weapons. It was blinding, painful, and cold, as it would be for his pursuers.

They caught you out good this time, didn't they, old man?

The interstates were a wager. The odds should have been good this time of year.

Think maybe the size of the bet is bit too big, old fool?

Jesse had scouted the stream before the storm had closed in but approached the verge with care now. Being careless climbing over the snow cornice at the edge might send it and him to the stream below. Once negotiated, Jesse pounded down a firing step in the snow below the rim before clambering up to the roadbed again. After flailing around in the smooth snow cover, he again crawled back over the edge to his prepared step. Anyone coming after him would stop to read the narrative in the snow. The old man moved along the cornice until he could look back on his own trail unseen. He stamped down the snow to make another firing step and waited.

Think you are going to fool anyone with that old trick, old man?

Don't have to fool him, just slow him down a mite.

A weak hand, bluff; a strong hand, sandbag. That is your strategy?

We play the cards we're dealt.

The attackers would never miss his trail in the snow. Jesse hurried to harvest some winter-coppiced hickory shafts below the rim and some withies from a willow near the stream. One never knew when finding one's way in the snow was going to be dicey.

He was sharpening the second shaft when he heard the man's skis hissing along. His pursuer's vision would be narrowed from the wind and snow and, most likely, from a close-drawn hood. Rather than hiding, Jesse froze in place, one more snow-covered shape.

His hunter approached and slowed, took off his skis, and kneeled to decipher the chaos in the snow.

Jesse waited.

When the hunter started to negotiate the snow cornice, the old man moved. Hammering the butt end of the spear into the man's face as he looked up, Jesse toppled him into the ravine, the rifle shot and the man's wail echoing around him.

CHAPTER 26

WAILS

To Malila, Bear's demeanor was more irritated than concerned.

"Did that fool go and cross his skis someplace?" asked Bear.

Bear ordered three of his men to go together to find the missing George. Jimmy, her molester, earned himself a berth in the search party, leaving Malila alone with Bear and five other men. Jimmy, despite his enthusiastic mauling of her, had missed the short knife wedged into her belt in the small of her back. Malila sat by the fire and draped the bison hide around herself, trying to rebutton her shirt. Bear came and sat beside her.

"This can go bad or worse for you, girl. You can't expect to travel alone with no protection. I'll keep you with us until we get back to High Ground, and if you've been nice, we will probably sell you to a house in town, uncut. The boys will be tired of you by then. You will just be tired."

Bear chuckled and stretched his hands toward the fire.

The other men shuffled around, the size of the fire growing as first one and then another threw more wood onto the flames.

It was then Malila heard the cry. The hairs on the back of her neck stood on end. A piercing, bizarre shriek continued for long seconds and worked its way into her marrow, rising and falling as if in agony.

"What was that, Bear?"

"Hush up, Billy; can't be. Ain't no wolves here."

Trying to make her voice flat, Malila said, "When we started out, there were four of us. The wolves got the rest of my party, dragged them away as I slept."

Just then, two of the search party returned on foot, dragging a body, presumably the "lucky" George. The third man of their party was bringing up the rear, burdened by the others' gear. Malila watched the vague silhouette of the last man stumble and fall in the swirling darkness to the north. What was happening?

It was a while before the winded men gave Bear their account. They had followed a trail of ski tracks. It stopped or, rather, disappeared into a ravine. They had descended to find George dead at the bottom. His rifle must have fired as he'd fallen, and it was now, no doubt, at the bottom of a half-frozen creek, along with his skis and gear. George's neck was broken, and his face was bloody and disfigured.

"He never was that smart. He was just supposed to cover us as we came in," muttered Bear as he examined the body.

"Looks like he won't be able to get first crack at our lady here," observed a small ferret-like man, making an emphatic gesture.

The other men laughed.

"Where is Junk?" someone asked.

"He was right behind me as we was coming in," said Jimmy.

Again, the weird cry echoed around them, reverberating inside the confined space. Despite herself, Malila huddled inside the bison hide, imagining death in the jaws of a savage outland animal.

"Maybe Junk met up with a wolf on the way back," murmured someone from the back of the group.

Thunder echoed in the distance.

"Which one of you fools said that?" Bear asked.

Bear walked to Malila and slipped his hand through her hair, now long enough to offer him a purchase, and turned her face up to him.

Malila gasped from the pain.

"Where was the camp where you lost the men to wolves, girl?"

Malila had her answer ready. "It was right here, last night, before the snow started. I was too afraid to move. I just planned to build the fire up and stay here. I don't have a rifle; you can see that."

Malila did her imitation of a cringing civilian. The man stared into her eyes before flinging her head down.

"Gentlemen, we aren't going to be enjoying Jane here if we have to worry about those wolves. If we go out now and kill a couple, it should make the pack scatter. The first wolves to attack are the leaders. Kill them, and the pack will have to sort out who's top dog. That could take days."

As Bear stared at each man, heads dropped in unenthusiastic submission. Malila used their distraction to ease the short knife from her belt and push it under the log she was sitting on.

"Harry, Jimmy, Pete, and you three ... yeah, you, Jose, Manuelito, and Billy. I want you all to go out with the Knapps. Sam and I will keep the shotguns and make sure Jane don't go anywhere. Go out the other way, south. Stay within a few feet of each other, like a pheasant hunt. Don't let anyone get out of your sight. Got it?"

After a muttering of agreement there was a general bundling up, the men ensuring they could work the triggers of the rifles with split-finger mittens or gloves.

Jesse, no doubt, had run away when faced with overwhelming odds, saving his old blue skin, she thought. The first man had died from a fall, and the second one had disappeared. Junk might have a grudge against the others and be using the blizzard to settle scores. These men were beyond any law. Life was cheap in the outlands.

Bear looked down at her and licked his lips.

"Strip. Do it now!"

"What? It's freezing. I'll be dead of exposure in minutes."

"Just my point. I need to watch my men, and I don't need to be worrying that you're going missing on me."

"Okay. Take my moccasins."

"And the rest of your clothes ... this is not a parley."

"At least let me keep the bison hide."

"Okay, but do it now, or I'll use a knife. Got it?"

The unequal bargaining left Malila feeling helpless. Finding a log still warm from the fire, she kicked off her moccasins as she stepped onto it. Bear followed her, and she looked him in the eyes as she unbuttoned and removed her coat and then her shirt and pants.

The man smirked as she disrobed.

"You really are cold, aren't you? Here's your buffalo robe."

Bear took her clothes with him, standing guard at the other end of the underpass, staring into the dark, swirling snow.

The other men, after critiquing her body, collected their rifles and moved off in a group. Within half a minute, they were invisible. Malila, despite the thick robe and the fire, began to shiver, her jaw shaking, making her teeth click. Jesse was gone; she was alone.

Malila heard a cry … very human this time.

Jesse went through the dead man's pack, scavenging food and ammo before pushing the pack into the stream. Sprinting away on the waiting skis, he saw a shadow of men approach out of the swirling snow, following the first man's tracks. Heads down, the three men did not notice him.

Now, after circling back closer to the bridge, the old man waited for the next hand to be dealt. The odds on this one were against him. Risks were a part of the game. Jesse howled.

Frightened men returning to a bright, warm fire do not look too close at a random pile of snow, he thought. The last man in the queue was gasping for air even before Jesse stood up from his hiding place. It took strength to make the garrote a silent weapon. They might have caught him if they had been smarter. Jesse was well away from the light by the time he dropped the second body and went to make a shelter.

You just better hope you can get that rifle to fire, old man.

Jesse nodded, pulled off a mitten, and fished the firing glove out of his jacket. The scrap of deer skin was oddly shaped, just enough to cover his trigger finger, the back of his hand and the base of his thumb closely.

Jesse tied the glove on, pulling the knot tight with his teeth. He could feel the little window of human skin he had carefully tanned and sewn into the finger of the glove, tight against his own finger. A slight bulge for the ID chip nestled into the base of his thumb. Placing his hand onto the firing position of the rifle, it immediately showed the small telltale blink—red, red, red.

And then—finally—green.

He fired.

The pulse bolt disappeared into the snowdrift. Jesse's heart sank at the thunderous report. He was about to sprint away when he noticed water gushing out at the entry point.

The tunneling laser had generated little cavitation in the snow, but the pulse itself had been massive and energetic. This Union technology was what the brass wanted from Sun Prairie in the first place.

The old man carved an entrance with his long knife, making it just wide enough to admit him. At the end of the tunnel where the bolt had buried itself into the frozen earth, Jesse carved away snow from the roof to raise a sleeping bench. The cold air would now drain away from anyone lying inside. He threw in the excess baggage and backed out, throwing a deerskin, fur side out, over the hole. The snow would cover the hide in minutes.

He was still in the card game. He had won two hands, but the odds were still eight to one against him. The next deal would be for the biggest pot, Malila herself … and it would be his deal.

Wrapping his climbing rope around the stiffening corpse and dragging it well east, he turned and climbed back along the smooth ascending slope of the east-west interstate until he was directly over the flickering shadows of the bushwhackers. It left him gasping for air. With two men down, the hostiles would break or send out a reconnaissance-in-force. He hoped they had a little more sand.

Avoiding knocking any snow down and thus alerting those below, Jesse stuffed one of the spears through the corpse's belt and positioned the stiffening body, after a little preparation, on the edge of the overpass south of their camp. Jesse wedged the butt of the spear into the corroded railings and looped his own climbing rope to the butt. He moved to the north side, Malila's side, and restarted the wolf calls. Swirling winds and fearful minds, he hoped, would confuse his location. With the rope in place and a self-belay set, he could set off this bit of drama at his leisure, whenever the number of men guarding Malila was at a minimum.

Until he had Malila away from them, he had to keep the men agitated—convinced that their enemy was not just one old man. If they settled in, Malila would suffer. If they thought she was an accomplice, she would suffer ... and then die.

She will hate me for leaving her.

If she lives long enough to hate you, old man.

Malila had such odd holes in her knowledge. Lucky for them both, actually. Tanning fingerprints, grisly as it was, was fine work and had to be done as soon as you got the fingers. With a city girl, Jesse had been able to tan her platoon's fingerprints under her nose without suspicion. The last thing he wanted to worry about was her mucking it up to strike a blow for the "glorious," damned-to-hell Union.

Smart and pretty enough, Malila was like bad corn liquor: all fire and no finesse.

He waited.

A line of dark shapes passed beneath him.

CHAPTER 27

JUNK JUMPS

The despairing cry came to an abrupt end amid the crunch of breaking bones as a man plummeted to the ground. Rushing to the body, Bear and Sam turned him over.

"It's Junk! Where are his eyes, Bear? The wolves took his eyes!"

This is insane. There is something about the cry, she thought.

Malila stooped and grabbed a smoking log from the fire before she ran into the swirling dark, the robe tied across her back. For long seconds, she ran before she fell for the first time. It was not until then that she sensed the cold … and the fear.

There's something about the cry. She heard the three gunshot blasts behind her, hunched her shoulders without thinking, and ran on. She knew she was not choosing her death well. What were the chances she could hide someplace with just the bison robe for warmth? The unknown dark chaos was somehow better than an ever-narrowing certainty in the light and warmth of the fire.

She staggered on, her heat bleeding off into the darkness, snow foaming up to her breasts as her numbing legs churned beneath her. She fell again, the cold clogging her mind, deadening her reason.

She rose again and knew she was dying. *So soon!* She staggered, her knees a memory, her feet an illusion.

A sullen black shape emerged on her right, lean, predatory, rising up out of the snow itself. She stopped and took the log in both hands, the robe slipping off a shoulder. She steadied herself, like walking on stilts instead of her frozen feet.

The apparition advanced, and she slashed at it, putting all her will and force into the gamble, leaving nothing for a counterblow to fend off savage teeth and claws.

The dark form grunted with the blow, deflecting most of it, letting her fall headlong into the snow.

"No way to treat a friend, lass," Jesse said as he stooped and peeled up a section of snow.

Almost at her feet, a large black hole in a snowbank opened up. She allowed the old man to get her up and bundle her in without a word.

It was a measure of her confusion that Malila crawled on unfeeling knees into the blackness. She found a light stick glowing when she entered a small chamber at the end. A narrow raised bench covered in hides, furs, and discarded clothes almost filled the space.

Jesse followed her in with the buffalo robe. Shivering uncontrollably, she allowed him to cover her up and slam an oversize and malodorous hat onto her head. The old man loosened his belt, pulled up his tunic, and grabbed her feet, holding them next to the naked skin of his belly. She felt his warmth as if from another lifetime.

"Damnedest thing, taking off lik' that, lass! Ah was nae sure how we would dae it. But you solved that right well! Yer a wonder on earth, my friend."

"You … you … left me for them to f-find! They … they were gonna f-fuck me, muckingfather! I coulda been killed, and you le-let them get me!"

The old man's face bowed into the shadows in the eerie light of the cave.

"Forgive me for that, lass. I did what I thought best. You are the bravest lass I ever met and no mistake," he said, his voice flat. *Timid?*

"You le-left me fo-for those me-men," she stammered on.

Despite herself, Malila stopped her rant when the meaning of Jesse's words defrosted a part of her mind.

"It is God's ain truth, my friend, but you took an awful chance. Tell me, how many men are there? What kind o' weapons?" Jesse asked in a rush.

"T-ten, no, no, eight now. Ri-rifle ... fire s-slugs. Not p-pulse," she forced through tortured breaths.

Jesse nodded and examined her feet, feeling the pulses and noting the pink flow of blood again. Malila, moaning as her feet warmed, now more fatigued than cold, allowed the old man to maneuver her under the pile of coats, tucking her in. He thought she was asleep when he kissed her and left the cave.

"N-not y-your friend," Malila said to the muffled sounds of the wind before the shivering again shook her to exhaustion.

She lost track of time before her breathing steadied, allowing her to take several deep breaths. It stopped her shivering, getting around the oppressive edges of the cold. She readjusted the furs, sighed again, and slept.

Her dreams, fractured images of grunting men and the terrifying cold, woke her hours later. It was better to be awake. Light filtered in along the tunnel entrance. It wasn't cozy here, but she had been colder in the wind near the fire than she was now, surrounded by snow. To her relief, when she wiggled her fingers and toes, all digits reported in as operational. Throwing off one heavy jacket, she frisked the pockets, finding trail bread and a water bottle. She tried to think.

The old man was at war with Bear, some outlander rivalry, she guessed, and she had become a pawn in their game. Bear had tried to keep her a prisoner of the cold, but Jesse had given her the keys to her prison: clothes, food, water, and ... weapons? Bear had miscalculated her daring. Jesse had miscalculated by abandoning her—twice.

In the dim light she sorted through everything left in the chamber, cataloguing food, water bottles that hadn't frozen solid, clothes, furs, and a sheath knife to replace the one she had left under the bridge. In the dim light, her hand closed on the cold barrel of a rifle.

Malila smiled. It was a projectile weapon. She had trained with them as an ensign. Malila checked the magazine and went through the other coats, retrieving almost two dozen cartridges. The rifle would make her autonomous, free of these primitives' feud, and impervious to the old man's abandonment. For the first time in weeks, things were falling her way.

Malila ate, ravenous after her near miss in the cold. Only then was she warm enough to dress. She got into a pair of nondescript wool trousers and a plaid shirt, wincing as her still-tender breasts chafed against the coarse fabric. Stuffing the bulky shirt inside the pants, she found a wide belt to hold everything together. She cut strips of coat lining to keep oversize mittens from wandering around her hands and wider strips to wind around her feet in lieu of boots. They would have to do for now. Once ready, she spent long minutes listening for the sounds of movement outside her shelter.

It was time to move. The snow cave gave her no vantage point and no lines of retreat. Slipping the handy knife into her coat pocket, Malila racked a round into the chamber and put the safety on. Lieutenant Chiu was ready to reassume her proper role as she crawled out into the sun.

CHAPTER 28

BAD NIGHT AND DAY

It has been a bad night for a good conscience, Jesse thought as he skied back toward the underpass.

Immediately after leaving Malila tucked up, asleep and warming, he had started following her panicked tracks in the dark, back to the underpass. If the bushwhackers came his way, he might take a couple down before they got him ... long enough for Malila's cave to go unnoticed in the continuing snow. Bushwhackers' woodcraft was brassic at best.

Instead, under the bridge, he found a chaos of men making hurried preparations for departure. Their sand had run out.

He dropped the first man into the fire and the second too. That served to keep the bandits nicely grouped and anxious to seek opportunities for shelter elsewhere. Bushwhackers, townies with guns, always had some place to hole up, warm and dry. The guy in the bearskins gave orders.

Once Jesse knew which way they were going, he set his traps. A mound of snow with a stick, on a dark night, became a waiting sniper.

Firing just by the sound of the shot kept the hostiles from gaining too much ground and spread them out, while shots from the sides set them off killing each other in terror … a one-man Jerubbaal. He liked that. There were two more dead men from that business, making six.

The damned-to-eternity Union tried to rule here by threats and bribes, dividing people's loyalties. The three survivors he found were a good example. They were small, frightened, wounded men by the time he called to them out of the dark. "Halloo, the camp. Don't fire!"

"Who the hell are you?"

"The man who can drop you right there if you raise that rifle one more inch."

The man ducked below the rim of a snow pit, near the fire that had made him night blind.

"You are surrounded. We can pick you off, one by one, like we did under the bridge, or you can throw out your weapons … now. Oh, and your captain comes with us."

"Bear, damn his soul, took off hours ago, and he ain't come back yet."

"That so? Well, throw out your weapons, and then we will see what to do with you. Where you boys come from?"

"High Ground, sir. Leastwise I do. Jose and Manuelito are Demarcians, but we all started from there."

Six rifles and two shotguns arced into the darkness, and there was silence for a space of time. Stars appeared through rents in the clouds overhead.

"Okay, speaker … You come out of the pit with your hands up. Walk backward until I tell you to stop."

A small Demarcian came next, and after turning out their pockets, Jesse had both men kneel in the snow, their hands bound to their ankles. He entered the snow pit. Without a word, he examined and redressed the gunshot wound of an older Demarcian. He would live.

It was only after he regained the anonymity of the darkness that Jesse bellowed back to the frightened men, "The old man tells me that you're a pretty sorry sight. Why shouldn't we just scalp you and collect the bounty?"

There was a hurried chorus of counterproposals before Jesse stopped them, saying, "We will let you all go if … one of you shows us your cabin. We will burn it, and you'll go back to Terra Haute and tell them that this here stretch of 74 is off-limits to your kind. Anybody gets caught from now on gets a face mark … or worse. Understand?"

The bushwhackers chorused back agreement.

"One more thing: if we find Bear, he dies. Okay, speaker, you go with the old man to the cabin. The other two stay put and keep your heads down. I see the hair on the end of your nose above the rim of that pit, and you get shot. Everybody understand the rules?"

After another chorus of agreement, the old man emerged from the darkness to unbind the two men and escort the younger Demarcian back to the snow pit. The rest of the night was simple. Jesse remained silent; the bushwhacker remained compliant. When they got to the cabin, Jesse let his guide have a sled, medicine, and some food. After taking some supplies for himself, Jesse burned the cabin and its arsenal. On their return, Jesse directed the bushwhacker to retrace his own tracks, slowly letting him get ahead in the dark before the old man angled away. Following the stars, Jesse started back to the underpass. The new day would be cold and clear.

He would feel a lot better once he got back to her.

"Stop or die!"

Malila tried to pull back into the snow cave, just before the hammer came down on her head. The absurd hat absorbed some of the blow, but she groaned from the pain. Bright light blinded her as the hat was pulled off and a booted foot kicked her over. Bear stood over her, licking his lips.

"Hello again, Jane! You ran off last night without saying goodbye … hurt my feelings. Now, crawl out, and no tricks this time."

While she was still trying to get to her feet, Bear hurled her to the snow outside the entrance and waved a knife blade under her nose.

"Where are the shooters?"

"I don't know what you are talking about."

He backhanded her. He looked pleased to see her blood come away on his hand. He licked his lips.

"Not very convincing, Jane. After you run off, someone killed four more of my men ... and here you are. You know anything about that?"

"You outlanders kill each other all the time. You were going to rape me and sell me!"

Bear slapped her again. She moved with the blow. It hurt less.

"You're in luck, Jane. We can still get that done. It is gonna be a few days before we get back to High Ground. I 'spect we will be really good friends before then. After that, I've a business proposition for you. Now get up, take off the coat, and turn around, real slow."

He chuckled when he found the knife in the coat pocket, shook his head, and knocked her down. She felt unsteady, her neck aching from the blows. This time, when she rose, Bear motioned her to walk back toward the underpass.

Trying to ignore the veneer of hunger that masqueraded as nausea among those who labor between dusk and dawn, Jesse pushed on into the morning. Pulling all-nighters was getting old.

If the girl could be coaxed to ski, he thought, they could go fast and far as long as the snow lasted, maybe three days this time of year. At least it gave them a chance. He had to admit, the girl had done well last night. Malila's desperate breakaway from the fire, bootless and naked in knee-deep snow, was unbelievable. In an instant, she had turned the two of them from jackals to panthers.

The snow cave would be safe if she stayed put and didn't act stupid. Stupid? No. Never stupid. Immature, partisan, and dismissive, yes. She had never acted stupid, despite what he told her. She just needed some manners.

He had not acted entirely civilized himself. That was the problem with age, Jesse thought. As a kid, you guessed you could do better with time. As a man, you thought you could do better with experience. As an old man, you knew that you were never going to want to be as good as you thought you should be.

Jesse skied into the woods west and south of the I-74/Old 41 junction, following the withies he had placed the night before. Removing his skies, he crept through the tangled underbrush until he could inspect the interstate.

It was a long, exposed expanse of whiteness he had to cross if he wanted to get north of the junction and into the snow cave. His silhouette was a perfect target, and once across, he would be so easy to follow.

No use waiting, old man.

Almost noon. We are going to lose a whole day fetching her, he told himself.

'Course, if you'd left her in Wisconsin, we'd be toasting our feet in front of a fire at home by now! Old fool!

Jesse replaced his skis and then cut a few branches from several hemlocks along the verge, tying them together. He dragged them along behind as he zigged and zagged across the wide-open area of the abandoned highway, through a break in the rusted guardrails, and over the remaining distance. He made it to the woods on the north side, confident that anyone coming across his tracks in the next few days could mistake them for a deer, a hog, or a large wolf in the deep snow.

Once in the woods, however, what with blowdowns and snow-covered bramble, his progress slowed. Jesse finally gained position north and west of the junction, looking across at the underpass itself.

He settled himself to watch for a while before he would venture to the snow cave and Malila.

It was then he saw the sniper. Right at the junction, the highest point, blossoming up and hanging for a mere moment, was a plume of steam.

CHAPTER 29

SLAVER'S BLADE

Malila's mind raced. Bear skied along behind her, easily keeping pace as she postholed laboriously toward the underpass with its burden of dead men. Bear was good at this: he was not so close that she could lunge at him nor so far away that she could make a run for it. Dripping wet despite the cold, Malila was about to duck into the snow-free cover of the bridge, when Bear motioned her to climb to the highway above.

"Up you go, Jane. We can go through the leavings after I am done with you. Right now, I need good light ... and a good lookout."

The snow here was deeper. Malila flailed on all fours, crawling to reach the highway while Bear paralleled her climb on the skis, stepping up lightly as she lumbered. At the top, while Malila was gasping for air, Bear again threw her down onto her back. He waved a small blade, no more than a fingernail of bright steel, under her nose, his voice becoming low, reasonable ... almost friendly.

"Whores are a valuable commodity in the outlands, Jane. However, you being part rabbit is an occupational disadvantage, wouldn't you say?

"We outlanders have a solution. My brand goes on your belly so that a man knows what you are and who you belong to. I 'spect the wound will heal in a few weeks if you are careful. The scar will look real nice if you don't move too much right now. I'd hate to kill you—by mistake."

His knife wavering before Malila's eyes, Bear ripped at her clothes. She moved to stop him. Bear punched her, clicking her teeth together as a sour metallic taste invaded her mouth, and her vision dimmed . A dusting of snow washed across her breasts and belly, chilling her flesh, reviving her. Dazed, Malila watched Bear's face against the dazzling sunlight. Sunlight flashed from the small blade ... *mesmerizing.* Bear licked his lips.

The first cut was the worst, an electric singeing sensation as Bear made a short cut before stepping back to admire the effect. It was then that Bear's face changed, his gaze jerking up to look at the horizon, his jaw hardening.

"What the ... Must be one of them bastards! Look at him go!" he said under his breath. He dropped the knife, grabbed up a rifle, and raised it to aim into the distance. Malila watched the look of concentration on Bear's face and saw his trigger finger, coated in her blood, tensing and beginning to squeeze.

An echo-less voice, odd, distant, and childlike, sounded in her head.

Knife!

Malila closed her hand around the handle of the knife where Bear had dropped it ... *cold ... slick with blood*. She drove the small blade into the back of Bear's knee, her arm arcing into him with all her weight behind it. Bear went down with a muffled cry, almost tearing the knife out of her hand. She felt more tendons sever as he wrenched himself away, falling backward. Bear would never walk on that knee again, without remembering her.

"Fuckin' bitch!" The rifle came up, aiming at her as if in slow motion.

Detached, emotionless, empty, Malila swept the barrel to the side and rolled onto the man's supine body, kneeling on his wounded knee. Bear roared a wordless obscenity and jammed the stock of the rifle into her belly. He forced her back before rolling on top of her, crushing the breath from her. His hands encircled her throat, warm and slippery. Bear cut her breathing off in an instant. Almost at once, a mad hunger for air burned her lungs, and blood pounded in her ears. Her vision dimmed as she looked up into Bear's grimacing face. He was yelling, but she heard nothing but the pounding. Even her limbs felt foreign to her now. In the smallest part of a thought, she knew she still clenched the tiny blade in her numbed right hand. She watched mesmerized as the short blade flashed up to the pulsing white flesh of Bear's neck, writhed with blue veins. In slow-motioned indifference, the brightness furrowed into his flesh, fountaining red blood. She slashed on, like her sea avatar, coating herself in gouts of blood as she sought the killing blow.

She was again in the cold ocean, tasting the hot blood of her prey, feeling the scalding surge of life gush around her. When it stopped, she floated, lethargic, too depleted even to signal for help.

Malila's vision blurred and went black.

The woods ended in the ravine, which, Jesse thought, should give him cover from the sniper. Winds had carved the little valley into long ridges of deep snow. The old man saw no trace of the death struggle from the night before, as a lowering sun left the ravine in deep blue shadow … slowing him further.

He slogged a hard-fought hour along the wall, above the icy stream. He stopped. He was sailing blind. He needed to check his position, make sure he was past the sniper. Jesse sidestepped up the slope, his head just below the level of the road … invisible to any sniper.

The snow cornice, even more precarious now than when he had taken the first bushwhacker, bulged out to meet him. He leaned in, piked a ski pole into the snow, and sensed it punch through to the other side. Clearing it of snow, Jesse placed his eye to the hole.

"Damn."

A good fifty feet separated him from where the curve of the road would hide him from the sniper. Another hour's worth of work lay ahead before he could retrieve Malila. Leaning over to clear ice from his ski binding, Jesse felt the bullet hit.

CHAPTER 30

SNIPER

By the time icy water trickled down the back of Malila's neck to awaken her, she was stiff with cold. Once she had freed her arms, she pushed up into the squalid dead mass of Bear. His clotting blood had coated her face and shredded clothes. With more satisfaction than disgust, she heaved his dead bulk over onto his back. Malila crawled to an expanse of clean snow and tried to get as much Bear off herself as possible. She was still getting back handfuls of red snow by the time uncontrolled shivering stopped her.

This victory was not like her others. She felt achy, sick, cold yet feverish, somehow. The wound Bear had given was just a centimeter long, just above her pubic hair. It had already stopped bleeding, but it burned. *These savages like to label things.*

Bear had given her the first taste of leering evil in her life, she thought. Before, the word had been only an advertisement of her country's displeasure. Now, evil would carry Bear's face. She saw again the knife stabbing into the back of Bear's knee and his answering bellow ... *Very satisfying.* The strange disembodied voice she had heard, the voice reminding her of the knife, had sounded like Edie, but that, after consideration, worried her all the more. *Hearing voices means you are going mad.*

Malila shook herself. It was after noon. Jesse hadn't returned. She left Bear lying on his back, his eyes open to the skies ... and the crows.

Malila plunge-stepped down to the underpass, letting each stride slow her while allowing her to watch the bleak whiteness for enemies. Nothing moved under the bridge. She slid beneath the rusting edge of the underpass and, sitting on her heels, surveyed the area before creeping down and rummaging among the debris. The fire had long since died out. Corpses in various positions, destroyed weapons, discarded cooking utensils, abandoned packs, and stray clothes were all that remained from the previous evening. Malila shifted her grip on Bear's rifle. There were four bodies. Two, she could account for: "lucky" George and "diving" Junk. Two others lay collapsed over the fire. Grabbing a ski pole, she pushed the top body off the smaller one. The top one was the oaf who had pawed her the night before. A large exit wound of a pulse rifle bolt gaped at the top of his head. She smiled. The man beneath was unrecognizable. Most of his face fell off into the fire ring as she turned him over. The disturbing smell of grilled meat wafted into the cold air. Malila backed away until her belly subsided.

Turning away from the sight, wrestling with the smaller man's frozen feet, Malila eventually recovered his boots, sturdy and hobnailed. Ripping a flannel lining out of another coat, she folded covers for her feet before putting on the boots and stamping to check the fit. Malila went through the rest of the debris, collecting her pack and clothes that were not soaked in anyone's blood. She retrieved Jesse's odd short knife. Somehow, she would hate to tell the old man she had lost it.

In time, she found most of the items she had been carrying and added two water bottles, some better gloves, a hooded parka, and some very thick and invitingly woolly socks. That and the additional food she scavenged made the bandits' raid an economic bonanza. She found nothing of the old man's possessions in the debris. For the first time in almost a month, she felt safe.

Malila sat and gnawed on some trail bread. Jesse was gone—good riddance. The old Sisi had finally shown his true colors: abandoning her, leaving her as bait, capturing her again, and leaving her for Bear, no doubt as some peace offering. *Trading her or discarding her like so much trash!*

She had escaped naked into the snow last night and was eating the bread of her one-time captors today. These outlanders died just like other men. If Jesse ever wandered back, the old man would expect her to follow him to some savage prison pit or, worse, to a barbarian trophy stand. *Not going to happen!*

Malila watched her anger boil up in front of her. It felt good. Jesse didn't even want what she was willing to give him. He had humiliated her for the last time, rejected her for the very last time. After today, even death was preferable to being the disgraced chattel of the old, creepy, strange, impotent—well, unwilling—hallucinating, humiliating Jesse. Malila liked how that sounded.

She was armed, well clothed, well watered, and well provisioned. If the ignorant old man could survive in the outlands, so could she!

However, she had to admit she was not a good skier. She couldn't leave here laying an obvious trail to be caught up and picked up by Bear's men or whatever it was Bear had seen before she'd killed him.

In the end she decided to stay, just until sundown. But to stay, she would need a killing field and camouflage, just like her sea avatar. Looking around, she noticed the wind had created a massive snow cornice between the two ribbons of concrete on the west side of the underpass. *The top of the column of snow would make an ideal sniper nest, protected from the sides and a little above the level of the highways,* she thought. Shoveling her way to the top of the cornice, stamping down the snow in order to move up and forward, Malila was finally able to throw herself down into the small bowl of her blind. She jury-rigged a deer hide as a cape with the hair outside to cover herself. Throwing handfuls of the light snow over herself and the rifle, she again eased herself down into the shallow cup. She peered over the edge. Nothing moved.

She wanted to ripple her chromatophores in pleasure but settled for a satisfied sigh ... and instantly regretted it. A large plume of steam rose above her and blinked out almost immediately.

Malila fussed at herself for such an amateur mistake as she wrapped a scarf around her face. A plume of steam like that could have alerted the enemy. She settled in for the inevitable wait. A good hunter learned how to wait. Malila was a good hunter.

She let her eyes unfocus, a trick she had learned in sniper training. She looked at nothing but became more sensitive to movement everywhere. Motion was enemy.

She supposed it was hours later; the sun was behind her and near the tree line, casting most of the land into long blue shadows—*movement!*

A shadow, on the edge of the roadway, the very limit of her field of fire.

Past her own tracks, the north-south road was a uniform blanket of snow up to where it disappeared in a curve, which must be the ravine George had fallen into. She guessed the range at a thousand meters. She had used projectile weapons but rarely. Nevertheless, the grooves of this weapon looked sharp; the air was still.

She chambered a round and swept along the crest of the snow with the rifle's reticle. The shot was almost due north; the Coriolis effect would make the slug veer right about ten centimeters and up perhaps half that. As she adjusted the crosshairs, she saw more activity, movement behind a neat round hole. Malila aimed for a center-of-mass shot, fifty centimeters below the hole. She took a breath, released it, sensed her heart beat once, and fired.

The sound of the shot echoed back from the woods on either side. There was an eruption of snow at the site. The edge slid away, and she saw flailing distant dark limbs. Malila always smiled at the death of her enemies.

Once she was sure there was no more activity to her front, Malila retreated to the center of the shallow bowl of her stand. She found some of the trail bread and gnawed it until it blunted her appetite. Despite making her head throb, she forced herself to gulp the slurry of ice from a water bottle. The worst was almost over. With the coming of night, she could set out. Her mind wandered as she watched the sapphire shadows lengthen against the black woods. The humming in her head subsided.

It was good to be free at last. She would go east, stay away from anything that looked like trouble, and get up to Pensy. She would take a bison before she left the grasslands. She would survive ... *fecking, fathering old Sisi.*

CHAPTER 31

NOBODY ANSWERED

Jesse toppled, flailing as he fell down the steep slope, the cold, dark water churning at the bottom, waiting for him. Facedown, he skidded to the very edge of the water. The ice creaked under his weight. The slug had destroyed the shaft of his ski pole, scattering splinters of carbon fiber along the line of his descent.

You deserve to be knocked on your ass, scorbutic old cretin!

True enough, but it's always good to be alive-er than your enemy thinks you are.

Jesse released his pack, kicked off his skis, flipped onto all fours, and pushed the heavy pack over the ice and close to the edge of the roiling stream. He lifted it away. If someone came looking, it would seem the icy creek had claimed another body.

All he needed was time.

An hour later, finally out of sight of the sniper, after crossing Old 41, Jesse was able to get into the cave unseen.

That's disappointing, he thought.

Picking up spectral points of light from the dying sun, the woods took on a look of spun glass.

In front of her, a scraping sound intruded into her thoughts. Malila had been hearing it for seconds now. She saw no movement. The sound was definitely coming from the direction of the snow cave. She could see Bear's tracks and her own start at a snowdrift. She heard the scraping sound again and then nothing. Malila centered the rifle's reticle onto the ridge of the drift and waited for a target.

"Halloo, the bridge. You missed us back there. Give us back the girl, and we won't bother you."

Jesse? And the old man thought she was a prisoner! Malila grinned to herself. Yesterday's killings would not gain him any new friends. No doubt, Jesse was anxious to leave the area before accounts could be settled.

Malila had accounts of her own. Jesse had humiliated her for the last time—had rejected … abandoned her for the very last time. Old, strange, unwilling, humiliating … old Jesse. The humming in her head increased.

"Jesse, it's me. I … I'm all right. They … they haven't hurt me. They say for you to go away."

"Good to hear you're alive and well, lass. Who is it you're talking for now?"

Just a bit too slow she said, "Andre. He says his name is Andre, and his squad will be coming up to relieve him at sundown."

In a stand-up fight at twenty to one, Jesse would die. The smart move for him was to retreat and travel fast enough to hide his trail.

"Are they coming from Kankakee or Sheboygan?"

Malila tried to localize the voice, but the snowbank was too large a target.

"He says he won't tell you."

This was not going right. Jesse had not shown himself, nor had he just backed off from the prospect of an overwhelming opponent. Malila thought she had handled the question about those places with the grotesque names adroitly. No one gave out information to anyone for free, especially to an enemy. The humming in her head felt like the tingling of an old scar.

"Funny that, lass. Kankakee was blown away generations ago. Sheboygan too, now I think 'bout it."

"Fecking Sisi, go away!" she yelled. Jesse's condescending arrogance had brought this on himself now.

"Watch your tongue, lass," he replied.

The tide of the old man's laughter rolled across the snowfield, deep, rich, uninhibited ... insulting.

"Fathering old Sisi!"

Malila looked through the reticle for a target. The sun had already cast the snowdrift into a long shadow. She inhaled, exhaled, waited for the quiet between heartbeats, and ... saw movement to the right. More by instinct than thought, she aimed and fired.

A thin voice ... or an echo of a voice ... rang back to Malila in the silence after the shot.

No!

The first crack of the pulse rifle made her jump in astonishment. The old man was not dead; he had foiled the signature lock on the pulse rifle, and he was willing to kill. In the last several weeks, she had convinced herself that Jesse would never harm her. It had earned her disdain. Her head keened with sound.

Malila sighted through the reticle and placed another slug into the snow cave as she noticed another small movement. *Not going to be that old man's pet prisoner ... ever.* The duel continued, and that surprised her again. She answered every pulse bolt with another slug, and each slug was answered with another thundering crack of the pulse rifle, ineffective as the others. There were no near misses, no scorching overhead rounds. The man seemed to be firing into the ground for all the good it was doing him.

Malila was down to her last few rounds before it stopped. *He's wounded, without a doubt. Fathering Sisi.* She would wait until he bled out before she wasted any more ammunition. Malila moved to the middle of the shallow cup of her nest to retrieve a water bottle. Her next surprise occurred as the snow opened up and swallowed her whole.

It was warm work, Jesse had to admit. The girl kept a steady fusillade going, definitely pissing off the Sisi. The snow cave was deceptive, however; the ground sloped away from the side facing her fire. He was able to shelter somewhat as he moved from side to side along the length of the cave, aiming through holes made by the slugs meant to kill him. He had to place his own shots well, even as Malila shot back.

When she screamed, Jesse stood, broke through the snow cave, and sprinted the hundred yards to the base of the cornice. Small holes left by his pulse bolts were spouting water. Like the snow cave, the bolts had expended their energy deep inside the cornice, melting the snow as he'd planned. He heard the girl splashing around inside the snowbank, newly turned into an icy death trap.

"Malila, can you hear me?" he bellowed.

All movement stopped.

"Yes."

Malila's voice had already begun to quaver from the cold.

"You are going to die in there unless I help you." It was not a question.

"Y … yes."

"I'll drain out the water and get you out. Understand?"

"Y … y … es." Almost unintelligible.

Jesse hammered at the soft ice with his ax as if it were rotten concrete. A small stream and then a spout of water appeared, then slowed and stopped.

"Clear the rifle and hand it out, butt first."

He listened to the sound of the clip being removed and again as the action was worked. A rifle butt appeared in the hole. He grabbed it and tossed it away. Jesse's small knife came next. Shortly thereafter, Malila was delivered from her ice womb by a double footling breech extraction.

CHAPTER 32

PRISONER CHIU

Jesse arose, dressed, and left the warm, sleeping form of the girl as sunlight just tinged the walls of the new snow cave.

It had been dark by the time he'd led Malila away last night, surrendering final possession of the underpass to dead men. He had found enough dry clothes from among the dead to replace Malila's sodden gear, but she had been too cold to dress herself, her teeth had been chattering, and her limbs refusing to obey commands. He had carried her down the slope to the new snow cave in the ravine. Even with all the furs, the buffalo robe, and his own heat, she had felt like a shivering corpse as he'd held her throughout that long night. He'd woken her at intervals to make her drink water, melted from his own heat.

By the time he left, she was warm, soft, and drowsy, like a new love.

Twice in a single day she had gotten dangerously cold. Malila would awake exhausted and tied to the snow cave by her nakedness. Jesse still had work to do at the underpass.

Camping there, not one of our better decisions, old man.

If I could predict the future, why would I bother to work?

Losing time too! Mid-November and we're still north of the Ohio.

"You give me much good counsel. I am tired of it."

Once he regained the road and started along the broad swath of snow, Jesse was careful to make new tracks and not to cross those he and Malila had made the night before. Snow would never hide your presence, but it might be convinced to lie about you to others, overestimating your numbers.

As he approached, Jesse noticed the trail of broken snow leading up to the interstate on the right of the underpass; he hadn't made those marks. Curiosity was one bad habit he had meant to kick. He sidestepped up the slope, following the tracks already there, crusty with ice.

He could now report the final fate of the enforcer leader. The dead, pale blue lips were already pulled back from chipped teeth in the rictus of death. The man still wore his bearskins, but the hood was a frozen mass of blood. With difficulty, Jesse lifted the dead man's chin to examine the wounds. There had been only two cuts, but one had fileted the carotid artery on the left for over four inches. The man's blood pressure must have dropped like a stone. Most of the bleeding was next to the corpse rather than underneath it; the body had been moved, flipped onto its back after death. Jesse looked at where the man had died, mentally canceling out the blood pool, looking just at the shape of the cavity. It revealed the form of a body … a small, familiar body.

The old man widened his search away from the corpse and found the wicked little blade. He grunted.

"Slaver's blade," he hummed. Except for some of the peace-loving Muslim states, the institution had officially been interred before the twentieth century. When the Meltdown had occurred, American slavery had stretched, yawned, and resurfaced, invigorated by the brief rest.

They were now in the no-man's-land of Indiana, and the practice was alive and well. The old man had wondered about the odd wound Malila had collected just above her pubic hairline. It looked deliberate. Despite how much she put on about her sexuality, the girl was still naive about the sexual cesspits available for falling into.

"Everything is about sex, except sex. Sex is about power," Jesse thought.

So Malila had killed the man in a hand-to-hand fight. She had also made two credible attempts to kill Jesse himself with an unfamiliar weapon, one at a range of over 1,100 yards. If his kith and kin were not to be deprived of his sparkling personality, Jesse needed to keep Malila under very close guard. Damn.

It was late morning when Malila awoke. It took her a few minutes to orient herself inside the horizonless whiteness of the cave. She wondered how many of the experiences of the day before had been dreams. Had the old man really abandoned her to rape and enslavement? Had she run off naked into the snow and been attacked by a wolf that had turned into Jesse? Had she killed Bear? How had she come to be swimming encased in a column of ice?

She found herself again naked under warm furs inside a snow cave. The old man had not seen fit to leave her any clothes this time. Malila checked her fingers and toes, finding them flushed, warm, and tingling.

Sometime later, she heard Jesse glissade down the face of the ravine. He pulled aside the deer hide covering the entrance and, without a word, threw in some clothes, the woolly socks, and her still-damp new boots. Malila dressed, despite the occasional dark, stiff stains she found on the clothes, and emerged. The old man grunted at the fit and pulled the coat's hood up, closing it around her face.

"We hav' ta shift, Lieutenant. Gimme any more truck, and I'll leave ye fur th' wolves."

"What?"

"*Wolves*, lass. Do ye want to meet them for real?"

"No!"

"Clever lass."

Malila waded up the snow slope with difficulty, followed by Jesse.

Then Jesse had her load her pack and put on skis, the old man adjusting the bindings until he was satisfied.

"J'ever use skis lik' this afore, Lieutenant?"

"No."

"Show me what ye kin do, lass. Gang down twenty meter or so, and come back."

Before she started, Jesse put a hand on her arm and waited until she was looking at him.

"Just for th' record, I'm fagged out, and right now I don't like ye over much. I have this new Knapp. Not tried out yet. *Don't piss off the Sisi.*"

Malila nodded.

"Learn to ski wi' the pack, and we get on the trail sooner. Let the skis carry ye. This ain't snow walkin' by a long sight."

It was still snow walking for Malila for many attempts thereafter. She got the hang of it before the sun was down, the old man's burr improving in step with her skiing.

They headed north on the smaller road until well after sundown, when they rested. By the time they were moving again, the rising moon shed an eerie light across the landscape. During that lurid night, each time Malila looked over her shoulder, she saw Jesse's dark form silhouetted against the blue-lit snow, like a specter bearing down, as if to run her over.

At dawn, they had made several false trails to either side of the road. Jesse then directed her to backtrack a kilometer before heading to a bivouac. In the cold camp, Jesse once more bound her before they slept. It was midafternoon before she awoke and dusk before they set out again.

The hard-driving dash lasted for three long nights. She rose exhausted, the days too short to repair her fatigue. When the snow melted too much, Jesse started again to hike during the day. He never talked to her now. Days passed with nothing more than a nudge from a boot. His silence drained her life away. Even the hallucination of Edie's voice had abandoned her after that last protest. She had acted like a child lashing out in anger … in frustration. The old man had then turned to save her. She felt shamed by her actions but could not put a name to the feeling.

For the first time, Malila saw the two of them in comparison to the vast unpeopled prairie, a life raft on a sterile sea.

CHAPTER 33

DEVIL'S BRIDGE

The cold rains of November swept across the plains as Malila and Jesse huddled under a small lean-to near the river Jesse had refused to name.

They had reached the banks that evening. Pruned of its leaves and limbs by death and the wind, an immense cottonwood tree had fallen across the small river that blocked their line of travel.

Malila, without asking, hopped onto the trunk and started walking forward.

"Get back, you fool."

She turned to look at the old man. Since Bear, Jesse had seemed to shrivel within himself, older now than she could imagine. His eyes became dull, his hands bore livid bruises when he took his gloves off, and he winced with each mouthful of food. He had become vague and indecisive. The only unchanged condition was her bondage. Jesse was still scrupulous in tying her up and watching her movements.

Looking back at Jesse, Malila bounced on the log, taunting him, her long lead sending sine waves back and forth to Jesse. "Losing your nerve, old man? We have a ready-made bridge."

"A devil's bridge, more like. Kill you quick enough if you try to cross."

"It's a dead tree!" Malila jumped up and down again lightly. "See? Nothing to worry about."

"Okay, nothing to worry about. I'm not going to cross on it. Any road, we are stoppin'—now. Understand, Prisoner Chiu?"

Malila shrugged and retreated from the trunk to follow Jesse up to the lee side of the river's bluff. Jesse was getting old before her eyes.

After constructing a shelter, the sound of the roaring water still audible, the old man acted exhausted, stumbling as he collected firewood to store dry, nodding if he sat for even a few seconds, and refusing to answer her questions. After he threw her some jerky, he went to bed, without fire, food, water, or bathing. Falling asleep almost at once, every few minutes Jesse would fret, groan, wake, and reposition himself. Malila was left to consider her hunger and isolation. Clouds scudded over them, extinguishing the stars before the sky even grew dark.

It started to rain within the hour.

Despite her hunger and the dismal weather, Malila slept. The next day Jesse was even sicker. Trapped, Malila was forced to roust the old man whenever she wanted to pee or get water. At last, Jesse, drawing his long knife and brandishing it clumsily, worked the blade between the knot and the small of her back and released her. Jesse collapsed back onto the furs, and Malila skittered away into the dull, sodden landscape.

That day and the next, Jesse lay abed, fretting and moaning. Malila scrounged enough food to keep herself nourished as the rains continued and the river rose. The old man moved only enough to drink and piss. All he ate were the berries from which he made his loathsome tea.

It looked as if he was settling himself for a slide toward a fetid death, like an old picture of a sinking ship. At home, they would have euthanized him by now. It would have been kinder. He stank.

That third night, with nothing to do all day but watch the rain and listen to Jesse die, she could not sleep. She tried pulling Jesse's arm over her waist to console herself, to warm him. He groaned and rolled away from her, leaving her colder than before.

It had been five weeks since her capture. Jesse had abducted her only to die in his own Sisi way, leaving her in a half-drowned wilderness. The thoughts of what might have been played nightly in her imagination. Every time she drifted off, Jesse groaned and moved.

At dawn, exhausted, Malila arose and dressed, leaving Jesse to his fretful but now less-noisy sleep. It must be getting close to the end. Throwing an oilskin around her shoulders, she left the shelter barefoot, her light footprints filling with water. Once free of the shelter, the roar of the water almost overwhelmed her, and she followed it to the river.

The cottonwood that Jesse had feared to use was still there. The rising river now crested over the massive trunk, generating a monstrous standing wave of dirty water. Malila stood mesmerized. Debris sped along in the peat-colored water before being sucked up and over the aged trunk to disappear into the maelstrom below. Caught in the flood, uprooted trees and swept-up wreckage fountained into the endless cascade.

Upstream a dark object caught Malila's eye. It moved within the torrent, and she could not tell if it was alive or dead. As it swept into the cataract and over the trunk, she could make out the carcass of a bloated and decaying young bison. It rose high on the wave but caught, for a moment, at the very crest. Malila could see the sodden head of the beast. Short horns protruded above the lolling putrescent tongue, the belly ballooning obscenely, the legs bulging away, as if fearful of its rupture. The bison pivoted in the torrent and was released, plunging over the spume and spinning away downstream.

The cold no longer bothered her. She thought how inexorable would be the plunge. The decision simplified things to a single point. She need no longer be a failure or an embarrassment. A single decision solved it all.

The huge spinning mass of her life swung back and forth over a malevolent darkness. Malila crawled and climbed up the roots to the trunk of the cottonwood and turned toward the river before standing.

Through her feet, she felt the thrill of the surging water as she inched forward. A few small steps and she would snip the single corroded fiber that bound her to life. She moved forward. The trunk swayed as the river surged. The brown opaque crest of water overtopping the trunk hypnotized her, her life ... squandered ... too damaged to cherish.

Glimpsing a dark shadow on the shore, she hurried forward another two steps as if afraid that death might take her uninvited.

Malila, come back!

"Malila, *come back!*"

The two voices echoed each other inside her head and confused her. The voices were mingled: old and young, without and within. She hesitated.

Jesse swung up to the trunk, and she felt it shudder under their combined weight. She moved forward once more, no longer waiting, afraid to look back at what Jesse might have become. The Unity was already counting her among the dead. The oblivion of the cold rushing water beckoned to her. She stretched forward her bare foot ... and felt the cold water close over her head.

She gasped and inhaled some water. Darkness enclosed her as she struggled to the surface to cough, the water burning her lungs.

"Stand up, lass!"

She opened her eyes. The naked scrub trees were turning lazily around her. She put down her feet, and cold, soft mud squished between her toes. Rage flared momentarily within her. Jesse, clothed in just his oilskin, jumped off the trunk, waded in, and disengaged the length of hide rope she found tangled around her neck, arm, and legs. As she dully tried to pick the line away, she recognized it, the thin line weighted with a machine nut to suspend food away from nighttime scavengers. While she had been consoling herself with the idea of her death, the old man had thrown the line to ensnare her. Jesse had pulled her into the backwater of the cottonwood, a quiet spinning pool despite the cataract beside it.

Without a word, the old man was beside her, pulling her up. Standing in thigh-deep water, he hugged her, almost crushing her, and sobbed. Numb and in the throes of her thoughts, Malila, for long seconds, stood with her arms at her sides before starting to beat at Jesse to release her. When he turned her to face him, his face frightened her, rain or tears furrowing down the man's features before dripping onto his oilskin.

"I'm sae sorry, love. Ah haven't been keeping ye right. Ah promise ta keek after ye, hereafter, na matter what."

Malila stared at him.

Jesse retrieved and shouldered the rope before grabbing her by the wrist. Malila allowed herself to be half-pulled and half-led up the bank and along to the shelter. She let the old man strip her, wash her, and maneuver her under the furs, before he kindled a fire with the stored dry wood.

She awoke in what she knew to be a dream. She had returned to the blood lake, the steps, and the sunless, brittle sky. She had not had the dream since her first bleeding. The dream was different this time, even from the beginning. There was a sharp texture to the air. She was grateful for the warmth of the blood as she moved through it. She still dreamed she was climbing the steps to gain the temple porch. When she reached the top, the breeze smelled of the sea. She was wearing a long white gown of some soft, clinging material. Looking out, a forest spread into the distance. She raised her hand to the sky and watched her hand disappear as through a wall of fog. She felt the cold, wet breeze on her hand, dew condensing on her fingers to run down onto her arms. The dewdrops were the color of blood. She awoke with a start.

Jesse hushed her as she rose. "It's all right, lass. Just your dream."

He pulled her down to the warmth of their bed and arranged the skins over her again before settling himself. He rested his arm, thick and solid on her waist, and Malila hugged it to herself, letting the old man feel how her heart pounded.

"It will be all right, my friend."

She sagged into his warmth and was again asleep.

Over the next several days, they scouted south until they found an ancient weir, fouled with debris but sturdy enough to offer them a footpath. They never camped near a large river again.

CHAPTER 34

THE RIVER

Crossing of the Ohio, Indiana Territory
Early evening, December 6, 2128

Malila sat tied with her back against the furrowed trunk of a tree, the ground littered with dried pod-like fruit, telegraphing her every motion. Since her attempt at the devil's bridge, Jesse's concern for her welfare had been almost endearing, making her ashamed to have ever thought he wanted her merely as a trophy. He kept her under "close arrest," as he called it. She did not blame him.

In so many other ways, however, the old man was not playing fair.

He was an enemy. He was strange, old, and uncouth. Even so, Jesse had, without her permission, refilled her empty cache of self-esteem. Over the last week, ever since he had pulled her back from the devil's bridge, it had become clear to her: somehow, the old man reminded her of forgotten childhood images, best forgotten … perhaps.

Regardless, the idea of causing grief to the old man was now somehow distasteful to her. Her own life had a worth because of the old man's concern, their bondage now mutual. For a while, he had talked to her at every opportunity, expending his grand eloquence around every campfire, holding her close at night in the increasing cold.

But it had not lasted. Over the last few days, Jesse had started the same vague, slow descent into senility. He could no longer eat except by cutting the meat into small bits and swallowing without chewing. Malila had taken over cooking. Jesse forgot things … or no longer cared. The voice that had echoed with Jesse's, calling her back, had not surfaced again.

She had no illusions. If Jesse died, her own death in this wilderness could not be long delayed, just more gruesome; she would go back to the devil's bridge.

It had been two days since Jesse had talked to her.

Tonight he'd abandoned her at dusk, bound. She was not sure he could remember where he had left her. Darkness rendered her blind. Her ears picked up every sound: the fall of a leaf, the faint cracking of a branch in the distance, a distant bird crying unanswerable questions. She could see nothing. No doubt her body, producing a plume of scent down the wind stream, attracted any animal or plant with a taste for flesh. In the dark, her imagination invented slavering horrors circling her. Malila felt a breeze on the back of her neck.

Behind her, without a rattle of a pod, a voice whispered, "Get up."

Jesse retied her hands in front of her. He showed no hesitancy in the gloom of the forest, his gait smoother and more assured, even as Malila found every exposed root to trip over. Eventually, she looked up to see an opening in the blackness. The forest parted to reveal a broad expanse of river. Jesse led her along a bluff and down to the water's edge. A small skin boat waited for them. Jesse tethered her to a seat in the bow with their packs lashed amidships. The old man settled himself aft and, after groaning effort, pushed them off with a short paddle.

Jesse negotiated rather than paddled the boat across and down the wide river. Washed out by the full moon, the sky showed just the brightest stars as they slipped along between shadowy lines of forest. Within a few minutes, a little break in the tree line on the opposite shore proved to be a juncture with a smaller stream. Water foaming white even in the uncertain light, the old man pointed the bow toward the point and shoved the boat forward. He paddled them close to the port-side shore and continued upstream. Within minutes, a small light appeared, flashing in triplets. Jesse leaned back and turned toward the light before running onto the shingle of a small beach.

"Halloo, the shore!"

A dark form separated itself from the mass of the trees and caught the rope the old man threw into the dark.

"Halloo yourself, you old fool. What took you? I've been exposing myself with that damned light for almost an hour."

"Well, all's well, Mose. I got our supercargo here. Malila, please meet my friend, Moses P. Stewert. Moses, meet Chiu, Malila E., acting second lieutenant." Jesse's apathy was gone, replaced by a brittle brightness, like a shard of mirror in the dark.

"You will pardon me if I don't curtsy, and stop wasting time, you old coot!" said the voice in the dark.

The two men unloaded the boat onto a beach and lifted it bodily out of the water to walk it up the bank.

Malila heard the occasional soft scrape of a tree branch as they moved. An errant breeze carried a pungent smell that she vaguely remembered. After a great deal of opening and closing of gates and doors, Malila found herself inside a building, the air close and warm. Jesse removed her makeshift hood after tying her to a post. A small fire glowed a sullen red in a river-rock-and-mud hearth but revealed nothing of the space until the man called Moses lit a crude candle.

The dim yellow light revealed a large dirt-floored room. Moses appeared a few years older than she and was tall, with competent hands and a prominent Adam's apple. His almost somnolent eyes looked at Malila without pleasure. He was clean shaven except for a few days' growth. In the way of tall men, he walked in a crouch.

As Moses added new fuel to the hearth fire, Malila could see the rest of the room. Alcoves with raised sleeping platforms lined three sides of the long, narrow space. The ceiling was tall enough for Malila to stand and displayed a collection of drying herbs, tools, and food left hanging from the rafters.

"Glad to see you, old man. You were beginning to worry me," said Moses.

Jesse grinned his grin. "Glad to see you can outrun the bears."

"I don't have to outrun the bears, old man ... I just got to outrun *you*!"

The men embraced, hugging each other for long seconds. Amazed, Malila saw a gleam of moisture on the old man's cheek as they parted.

After a scant pause, the old man said, "Are you gonna let me die of thirst, young man? I know your momma, and she would be ashamed of your manners."

Moses laughed and, without a word, retreated from the lighted circle, only to return with an earthenware jug of considerable size and an odd shape. Its flank displayed numerous looped handles, and a gray glaze showing the mark of the potter's hand as its only decoration. He placed it on a makeshift table. Moses poured two portions of clear liquid into metal tins before the two men rattled them together, without a word, and drank. There followed a profound silence before a smacking of lips, inrush of breath, and low hoots of amazement.

"Where did you find this?" Jesse asked in hushed awe.

"Booker Tolliver came by last week. He had orders to take all the animals that I couldn't use to Lex'ton before winter. His missus sent it along with him as a special present. You know, Jess, I think the lady is sweet on you, you old dried-out stump of a man."

"Just a delayed payment on services rendered, Mose. And see ... no good deed goes unpunished!" Jesse gave a small salute with the tin cup.

Moses laughed for a moment before his face sobered. "The railroad has been cut again. Up near Lou'ville, place called Muddy Fork. Lost a loco and most of the hospital cars. It was on a siding, so some of the docs and nurses got away ... and some were with their patients."

"Anybody I know? Dorothy Partridge used to go on that run as part of her job, but I think she has a practice in Covington now ..." Jesse's voice petered out, and he sipped, his face now in shadow away from Malila's sight.

Moses had no response but took a knife and carved a slice from what looked like a lump of wood hanging from a low rafter and offered it to Jesse on the tip of the blade.

"Black-bear ham, smoked with some applewood I found."

Malila's stomach growled.

Jesse accepted the morsel and ate it in silence. He took another slice, and the two compared notes on wild gastronomy.

"What are you going to do with Miss Anthrope over there?" Moses asked as he cut another piece.

"That is a puzzle, is it not, my friend? I don't suppose you have more applewood by chance?"

"Tell me again, Jess: Why do we want to compromise the whole mission just to capture a real-live, bone-and-sinew Union butter bar? It don't make much sense to me if what we get is still kicking and spitting."

Jesse shrugged.

"We can get a message to the regimental head shed, but without the rail line, I surely don't care to have to transport her to corps HQ in winter on horseback. But let me see something," said the old man, turning to Malila, her face barely illuminated in the dim light. "Lieutenant Chiu, answer me a question."

"Chiu, Malila E., acting second lieutenant, serial number 590261697."

Jesse sighed and asked anyway, his pale eyes now bright. "Have I told you any lies?" he asked.

His question made Malila uneasy. It almost sounded like a plea.

"You said you were going to eat me."

The old man sighed and looked down for a second before looking up. "Yes, ma'am. I said I might … and we still ain't home yet."

Moses hooted in the background.

"As far as I know, you've been truthful," Malila said in a childish singsong.

Jesse rolled his eyes and went on. "How many times could I ha' killed you?"

"That's against the rules of war," she spat back.

"Well, we savages don't read no rules. Do we, Mose? I ain't read no rules of war. What about you?"

"Shucks, Jesse, you know I cain't hardly read," Moses replied, grinning mischievously and shaking his head.

"How many times could I have killed you, Lieutenant Chiu?" Jesse repeated.

"Anytime you wanted. Is that the answer you want?"

The old man nodded and continued more slowly, "Tell me the truth, Lieutenant: Do you know how to get back home?"

"No," she said after a pause.

Jesse turned to Moses and said brightly, "Moses, I have a real hankering for fresh vegetables. Have you got any?"

"Sorry, Jesse, I was eating up the reserve, trying to close up the station. I got some pickles. Would that do?"

"Sure, if you are sure it won't be any trouble."

"No trouble at all!" The younger man rose and went outside. Malila could hear him moving around in an adjacent room.

Jesse asked softly, once the outside door had closed, "Are you going to try to kill me again, Lieutenant Chiu?"

When she did not respond immediately, he sighed.

She paused and searched her own character. There was a time when she would have killed Jesse without remorse. She had wanted to hurt him for capturing her, for abandoning her, for making her trust him while he was playing her for a fool, for making it seem that he was concerned for her.

She had gotten used to his peculiarities. No, that was unfair. She missed his confidences. She saw him floating away into senility. He had wanted her but, even then, had rejected her. He should have stayed with her, at the underpass, at the river. Even just the last few days, he had been distancing himself. Every time she'd needed him, he'd vanished. When she tried to analyze the events, the images slid and spiraled away from her.

Jesse was still staring at her.

"No, Jesse. I'm not going to try to kill you."

"Do you mean it this time?" he asked in a quiet voice. Moses's rummaging stopped, and Malila could hear him returning.

"Yes, Jesse, I mean it this time. I'll not try to harm you or Moses."

"Or yourself?"

"Or myself."

Moses entered with a glass jar of ancient pickles, held on high, in triumph.

"Then have a drink wi' us," said Jesse.

CHAPTER 35

MOONSHINE

Malila rubbed her wrists, long since chafed and callused from the bindings, as Jesse kicked a box near the ring of light, gesturing to her to sit. Moses shrugged and retrieved a small jar into which he poured a finger of the clear liquid before giving it to Malila. Jesse tried to open the jar of pickles before letting Moses complete the process. Jesse took a bite of a pickle and made a face that nearly made Malila laugh.

A second later however, his face sobered and he raised his cup in salute. "Here's to Percy! May he swim farthest, swim fastest, see more ladies, and sire more babies than the rest."

Moses laughed and clicked cups with the old man and with Malila before swallowing with gusto. Malila sniffed at the contents of her jar. A noseful of fumes made her sneeze.

"To Percy."

She upended the glass, downing the contents to get the absurd toast over with as quickly as possible.

Moses's smiling face froze, and he nudged Jesse.

Silence reigned.

The fire in her mouth, throat, and lungs, like a body blow, wrung the breath from her. She could breathe neither in nor out. Her vision started to narrow before a paroxysm of coughing threw her off the box and onto her knees. Jesse was at her side, pounding her back as she gasped for a breath through her still-alcohol-saturated mouth. Another frenzy of coughs seized her, tears streaming down her cheeks. She slowly recovered, breathing carefully through her nose.

"Smooth," she lied.

The men dissolved into relieved laughter. Malila found herself smiling as well. Alcohol in its many forms was available in the Unity. The infinity of names, brands, colors, and adulterants confused her. The DUFS frowned upon its use. Some of her age group had been found drunk and disorderly when she was an E6. They'd received no reprimand, but then again, all had washed out within eighteen months. She'd never seen them again.

She took another sip. This time, negotiating the liquid past her reflexes, she grinned back at the expectant glances of the men. Between sips and slices of pickle and ham, the three of them talked about the eternally safe topic of the weather. Moses told jokes, and Jesse obediently chuckled, before explaining them to her.

She perceived no effect of the drink other than a warming action in her near-empty belly and an improvement in the quality of the humor. Her drinking companions were becoming excellent hosts.

Jesse started to tell his friend of the events of the last six weeks. He gave an account of Malila's surgery, Percy's release, and Bear's attack. The old man improved upon her performance during the bison hunt but mentioned nothing about her attempt on his life, the devil's bridge, or her bleeding. As the jug passed around each time, Malila's opinion of the old man as a traveling companion, scholar, and benefactor improved.

The conversation passed on to local news from back home.

"... and Wesley Sanchez just bought the Zimmerman place in Cabot's Town after Philip was near killed by some bushwhackers ... broke his leg," Moses continued.

"That's a shame. The association[8] doing anything?"

Malila interrupted before Moses could reply. "Tha'd never happen in the Unity. Mus' be horrible to live in diz country. What I don' understan' is why you don' just join the Unity," spat Malila, becoming annoyed that her viscous tongue had taken to wandering as she was trying to speak.

"Other than I'd be turned into one of your zombie troopers, you mean?" sniffed Jesse.

Malila dismissed the comment with a wave of her hand.

"Nothing is so law-abiding as a conquered country ... peace of the graveyard, is all," returned Jesse.

"How can you say we're con ... con ... beaten? You're the ones that have to run and hide, old man." She poked Jesse's chest for emphasis.

"Oh, I think both of our countries have been beaten, lass. Ours after the Scorching, but yours had already been conquered by that time. The buzzards were the only ones to win that war."

"*We* won the las' war ... Glor'ous War of Liberation!"

"I had no idea you were such an authority, my friend. From whom were you liberated then?"

"From the old people who were hoarding all the wealth and, ya know ... stuff!"

"And did these wealthy old people have rights?"

"You don' understand rights." Again the fluttering hands. "Individuals don' have rights. It's the *people* who have rights. No one has the right to hoard the wealth of the people for their own benefit!"

"So it was not so much that they were old as that they had something valuable? Was that their crime?"

---

[8] "Due in part to the unequal campaign waged against them ... many Christian groups atrophied, leaving their buildings to litter the landscape with archaic or outrageous architecture both great and small. After ... the remaining believers consolidated, organizing around local congregations and the congregations around regional associations ... Few will ignore a directive from the association. Any dispute, sacred or profane, can be referred to the local congregation or association." Kim Eun Sung, *History of the Church Resurgent* (St Louis: St. Louis University Press, 2066), 7.

"You can't understan'! It's com'licated. That was then, ol' man. The Unity is based on rights, after all!"

The old man's grizzled eyebrows went up in mock surprise. "Oh, well now, it's based on rights. I didn't know that. Educate me, lass, if you would be so kind."

"We have the right t' vote, t' believe what we want, t' be free of being offended, t' say anything we want long as it doesn't offend anyone else, the right to food, work, housing, transportation, and medical care. After we retire, the Unity takes care of ever'thin'! It's guaranteed."

"Do you have the right to be foolish?" He cocked his head to the side, like a fox.

"Of course not. Who wants to be foolish?"

"Who indeed, lass? Everyone should be protected from being foolish. So a question, my wise friend: Is gambling wise or foolish?"

"Only the foolish gamble ... so you mus' like it, Sisi!" She laughed, throwing her head back and nearly falling.

"Mose, when did you start your homestead?"

"Five years ago, Jesse. Is your brain giving out? You were there helping me pull stumps, weren't you?"

"Yes, now that you mention it, that was you, was it? I musta mistook you for the south end of the northbound mule I was working. Tell me how many times people have tried to homestead that same parcel before you."

"Two others. Some guy named Fletcher—he was murdered in a Unity raid—and a family of Swedes as come down from Minnesota. They started too late to get a crop in that first winter, and then they lost most of their pigs to some disease. They threw in to go stay in town somewheres. Jesse, you know all this. Why am I telling you?"

"Bear with me, Mose. Why did you think you could succeed where those good folks failed?"

Moses shrugged his shoulders and tipped the box back so that he was leaning against the wall.

"I had done it before ... with you. You were staking me, and you said you'd help me if needed. I chose to prove out my section here. Where can you get cheap bottomland anymore?"

"Wasn't your choice a foolish bet? You put up your money, sweat, and time on the chance you could bring in a harvest to pay your note. You had no guarantee, right?"

Moses laughed. "Some people might think it foolish—Sally's mother for one. Of course there was no guarantee! I wouldn't o' been able afford it, if'n it was to be guaranteed. It was a bet, like most everything! I guess. That's how someone like *me* deals with the future. I *bet* that I could prove out the section, and I have.

He turned slightly, including Malila in his comments now.

"My folks didn't have nothing to give me by the time I set out, miss. I left with nothing but my clothes, an old rifle from my uncle, my books, and my tools.

"Jesse here hired me to help prove out his farm in Bath County, and I saved some. With that and with what Jesse staked me, I had enough to buy what I needed to homestead. If I hadn't tried to homestead there, I'd have gone out west. The soil and water are better here, but it is closer to the damned Union, begging your pardon. I suppose it was a gamble, but it was *my* gamble. I bet the farm … everything I had, but I knew the odds, and I knew the stakes."

Jesse smiled. "Always make your own bet …"

"… and never take someone else's bet. Cut the deck when you can, and …" Moses replied.

"… smile when you lose!" they said together before grinning at each other.

"Last question, Mose: Have you paid me back?"

"Well, the note for this year doesn't come due till New Year, Jess, but we can pay you now if you need it."

Jesse held up his hand to the younger man and turned back to Malila. "Should we have prevented Mose from being foolish, lass?"

"Tha's different. Back home the gov'ment makes sure everyone works 'n' is paid good wages." She smiled.

Moses gave a short, barky chuckle.

"And if you don't like your wages, you go to the *other* government in town ... right?" asked Jesse.

Malila gave him an uncomprehending stare before Jesse said, "I think I need some sleep, Mose. Must admit I am tired. It's been long hours on short rations since you left Sun Prairie, and the liquor has wagged my tongue for me."

Moses took his cue, adding, "We should start as soon as we can in the morning. Never know how the trail is this time of year."

Moses collected the cups, and Jesse pointed Malila toward the latrine. She relieved herself without undue disgust, and on her return, an old piece of towel, a cup of soap, and a bucket were laid out next to the rushlight. She leaned over the top of the bucket and was surprised by the warmth wafting up. Several large river rocks bubbled in the bottom when she passed the light above it.

Moses's voice emerged from a dark alcove. "That hot water is for you, miss. The rocks will keep it warm for a while. You can take the lamp to bed if you want. You've got your privacy, Miss Malila. Jesse and I are gent'men."

She could just make out the younger man in his sleeping furs rolling away from her. She glanced over at another pile of furs that was already breathing heavily.

Since she had left the Unity weeks ago, she had not had the luxury of hot water. Shucking her moccasins, pants, and shirt, Malila indulged. She had forgotten how opulent it felt to bathe in hot water, even standing up on a stone hearth. She shampooed her hair, no longer DUFS short. The wound from Bear had healed well, but it was still a centimeter-long pink streak of tenderness. On an impulse, when she was done, she soaked the old shirt in the lukewarm water and wrung it out before draping it before the banked fireplace. Naked, she located her sleeping place. Blowing out the rushlight on its stand, Malila snuggled into the cold weight of her furs, shivering before she got them warm. It was odd to go to bed without the reassuring warmth of the old man.

CHAPTER 36

ARRIVAL

Malila sat up and moaned. Her head, feeling twice its normal size, throbbed in retaliation. She sensed something had died, died a slow, pestilential death, in her mouth. Remembering a dinner of pickles, bear ham, and alcohol, she barely had time to dress before staggering out and vomiting into the tall grass.

Jesse found her as the last heaves subsided, leaning over her to block the too-bright sun with his shadow, and tsked. He pressed a red bandana into her limp hand. The back of the old man's hand showed a new livid bruise. She almost asked him about it.

"We have to move today, lass. Rest while we pack. When you feel up to it, we will get you something to make you feel better … when it will stay put for a while."

"You poisoned me! I'm going to die here!"

"I'm sorry, so sorry, lass. I don't know what I was thinkin' … bear ham, pickles, and 'shine. I am truly sorry."

Malila had an appropriately scathing response on her lips, but the thought of the food, again, wrung her out, making her retch bile-green slime into the grass.

In time, Malila recovered enough to stand and wash out her mouth from a bucket left near the door of the dugout.

Moses, grinning, approached her with a large tin of clear liquid.

"Jesse said for you to drink this. Make you feel better if'n you can keep it down." It tasted vaguely salty but bitter.

Moses showed her to the corral. Jesse had finished saddling three horses and had leads on two others loaded with their gear. The old man, looking gray, finished wrestling a pack into place. Malila smiled at his discomfort, matching her own.

"Okay, miss. This here is Arab. He's about as gentle an animal as I have," said Moses. "Do you want a leg up?"

Malila nearly fell over backward looking up to the saddle. Unity horses were never this massive. She took the leg.

Once mounted, acrophobia replaced nausea for a season. Jesse mounted with Moses's help as well.

They left the rendezvous station deserted, the doors barricaded against animals and the coming snow, for what Moses said would be a three-day ride to the colony.

By early afternoon, Malila was better and worse. Her nausea gone, she could devote her misery to a more fundamental pain. Moses shortened her stirrups, a name she suspected he had just invented to annoy her. As the sun sank, they moved south, a little higher out of the river valley. The high country already wore the brown gray of a winter landscape, although, here and there, near the river Malila still saw the greens, crimsons, and yellows of autumn. Occasional spires of blue smoke rose up until kited away by the wind.

The riding trip, like the foot trek before, rapidly assumed a sameness. Moses nudged her before dawn as he went to collect the horses. Jesse stirred up the fire from the night before. The three broke their fast with a bitter black effusion of what appeared to be charcoal. Malila was given some glutinous gray material in a shallow bowl that she refused to eat until she saw Moses and Jesse lather into their portions dark sugar and handfuls of dried fruit. Jesse cut his fruit into small pieces. Malila found it remarkably filling.

The trail reached ever eastward along the river valley, sometimes cutting off a large loop as the river twisted and turned. They stopped, much as they had afoot, to share out small portions of jerky and water about once an hour. Now both men mumbled their superstitious formula before eating. Malila chose to make no comment.

On the morning of the third day, the two men neglected breakfast and set out while it was still dark. As she rode, frost-rimed branches littered ice back into her face. After weeks in the wilderness, Malila began to see small signs of civilization growing around her. Wagon tracks multiplied, to left and right, joining their tracks to deepen the ruts. Horse tracks wove back and forth across the trail until it intersected a hardened road nearer the river. The few travelers they now met on foot and horseback greeted them, weapons prominent but the greetings friendly enough. Malila was told not to speak. Later in the morning, the greetings included laconic inquiries and replies. Most of these travelers wore clothes that were woven rather than skins. Here and there on the wagons were shiny cook pots, well-used machinery, and the occasional whip antenna of a broadcast radio in a jet-and-silver case. Malila saw children: dirty, fat, and dressed well against the cold. They giggled at her. Jesse talked to them, making them laugh.

By late morning, the three of them arrived at collections of buildings, clustering closer together as they moved on. There were more people. Long, penetrating stares greeted Malila. Jesse generated the most hootings and hailings along the way. Riding down a lane between fenced enclosures, they entered an unpaved plaza, one side dominated by a building with a louvered tower and pleasing symmetrical proportions. It displayed no sign except "Parsonage in Back." The other buildings appeared to be shops. One fresh-painted green clapboard building boasted a sign that read, "James Uhuru Robertson, RSA Congressional District #19." She thought it all impossibly squalid.

Once they had stopped, people converged. For the most part, the townsfolk ignored Malila, greeting the men with hugs, friendly insults, backslappings, and kisses.

Malila watched from the periphery as the crowd parted for a young blonde woman holding a bundle. The woman approached, staring fixedly at the new arrivals. Moses, turning when the crowd grew silent, whooped and burst through the remaining ring of people to scoop the woman into his arms. He hesitated when he saw the bundle, stopping with an uncertain look on his long face. The woman broke into a glorious smile that spoke to Malila of pride, tenderness, and longing.

Moses folded back the corner of a blanket. A small face grimaced from the light. Moses bent close, as if smelling before looking up to the woman. She spoke softly, then gently smiled, which in its quiet wisdom reminded Malila of Moses himself. He gathered up the bundle and started to turn, his cheeks streaked with moisture, when the woman stopped him. Wordlessly, she wiped his face.

Turning again, Moses proclaimed, "Hallo, old man! Come meet Ethan Graham Stewert!"

The crowd erupted; Ethan responded. The woman smiled broadly before gathering the baby into her arms once more. She clucked at Moses before trying to soothe her infant's objections.

Malila was stunned. She had never met a breeder. Most of the Unity's surrogates survived only a few pregnancies. The burden of childbearing was so great that no sentient Unity woman would endanger herself. But this woman's health and pride in her new son shone for all to see. Something plucked a chord in Malila she had never played.

As the baby's wail escalated, his mother scooped a breast from her gown and presented it to her son. The baby yawned open his mouth and homed in on the engorged nipple with seeming expertise, shaking his small head before clamping down in earnest. Malila felt ill at the grotesque display until she heard the sounds of lusty infantile satisfaction. Men and women of all ages looked on smiling as the newest and least productive member of their community was cosseted and cuddled.

Within minutes, the plaza was almost deserted. Jesse had gone to talk with a man in a peaked hat and an odd military uniform. Malila could see Jesse surrendering his precious buckskin roll to the man, prompting a good deal of discussion. Moses and the baby's mother had moved off and were already in deep conversation.

Malila was alone and looking at the best path to escape when the dogs found her. She almost panicked. She had always hated the vicious animals. With floppy ears still dusty from their late-morning naps, the outland dogs sauntered over and started to snuffle Malila myopically. In terror, outnumbered, fearful that she would be rapidly brought down by the jaws of these outland monsters, Malila stood and endured.

Jesse and the military man continued to talk; the old man was more animated than he had been since the devil's bridge. Within a few minutes, Moses and the baby's mother were called back for a hurried conference.

Malila's doggy examiners, having finished their examination, sneezed and went to sleep on her feet. Malila closed her eyes to the ordeal.

Some minutes later, she was rescued by the old man.

"Get on, you two; find someplace else to nap!" he said and wiggled a foot under each as he encouraged them to leave.

Without a preamble, Jesse pressed something into her hand. "This is for ye, lass. Ah wouldna want ye a beggar. See it wages for yer time."

"You are leaving me, old man?"

"It seems I am. You'll be staying wi' Moses and Sally. I hope that is a better fit for you."

"When will I see you again, Jesse?"

"See me again?" Jesse said, his eyebrows lifting in what she thought was surprise.

"Never mind, old man. Go!"

Malila looked down at the object, finding that he had given her one of his red bandanas, washed and smelling of wood smoke and Jesse. Tied inside was a hard fluted black disk with impressions on both sides. By the time she looked up, Jesse had turned, gathered up his green backpack, and was walking out of the square. He seemed to shrink as he walked, his head bowing and his gait growing wider. When he reached a lane leading from the square, he staggered and put a hand out to the clapboard wall to steady himself. Malila looked away as if she were violating a privacy. When she looked up, Jesse was gone.

CHAPTER 37

BILLET

Malila asked, "Is that your son?" as Moses and the blonde woman approached her. Malila had never in her life expected to ask so rude a question.

Moses smiled. "Yes, or so my Sally tells me." The woman was within hearing distance … and striking distance, fetching Moses a sharp jab in the ribs, to which he gave an exaggerated reaction.

The breeder extended her hand to Malila while juggling the nursing infant.

"I am Sally Stewert. I'd be an old woman before Moses'd think to introduce us. This is Ethan Graham. He's our first."

"Acting Second Lieutenant Chiu, Malila E."

Sally looked a little blank.

The conversation stopped until Moses said, "The captain tells me that he has to question you for the next few weeks. I am to give you room and board. I 'spect you should help around the homestead if I feed and house you. Is that all right, Miss Malila?"

Malila nodded. Moses, noticing her looking at the baby, said,

"Here, let me introduce you to Ethan." Before Sally could object, he whisked the baby away from her, leaving Sally to replace her breast into her gown.

Having satisfied most of his appetite, the baby writhed slightly in his father's hands, pursing his lips before smacking them experimentally. Malila leaned close enough to shade his eyes from the late-morning sun and was rewarded with a dark-gray quizzical gaze. She inhaled his soft foreign-familiar scent and offered a finger to the small clenching fist. Ethan's idle, fleeting smile seduced another victim with the charm of the newly born.

Sally sat cuddling Ethan as the wind whipped about them, pointedly not listening to Moses. The girl was relegated to the back of the small wagon, mercifully out of the way, at least for the time being. Jesse had left Sally with a little souvenir of his summer adventure. The man was impossible. And just like every other time, Moses carried on as if his trip with Jesse had been some lark. It was too much to abide.

The girl was now, she supposed, their prisoner … her prisoner. Moses would be in the fields, and the enemy soldier would be added to Sally's burden. Ethan was a week old. It was all too much to bear.

Moses's forced jolliness sputtered to a slow death, and they finished the trip, winding through the winter-gray scrublands of their parcel in silence. It was getting on to late afternoon before they approached their homestead, nestled in its pleasant copse of trees.

The strange girl would probably notice the house needed painting, Sally thought. She probably would not notice that it had a second floor and chimneys at both ends of the gabled roof, one of only six in the county. The Swerdigans had built it, but Sally had made it a home.

Moses halted in front of the house, and Sally, after handing Ethan down to him, alighted before he could move to help her. Plucking the baby from him, she stalked into the house. The baby needed changing. She had work to do.

Sally had sorted out Ethan and started to set the fire to rights when the strange Uni girl finally entered the house, looking as if she were afraid to touch anything. *It was time to set some rules!*

"Mose tells me that we have to billet you while you are being questioned by Captain Delarosa. It isn't fair, and we are on winter rations already. They tell me we'll get some provisions from the army for you, but they can't say when. While you are here, you work. We don't run no boarding house. You sleep in the loft, and the washout and privy are out back. Do you understand?"

There was no use in sugarcoating it.

"Yes, sir, I understand, Sally, sir!"

Sally grimaced at the reaction, inspecting the unkempt girl for signs of criticism. The seconds stretched on. The Uni girl was actually at attention, staring not at her but apparently at a patch of blank plastered wall.

After a spell, Sally relented. "Don't call me that. Call me Mrs. Stewert when people are around; otherwise, call me Sally. Tell me your name again."

"Acting Lieutenant Chiu, Malila E. … Sally! Request permission to speak freely, Sally!" the girl barked out.

"Of course you can talk, Malila. Free country, after all, isn't it?"

The girl was beginning to get on her nerves. It was as if someone had thrown a switch and turned her into some sort of a robot. Sally was feeling put upon. For the sake of her country, she could accommodate an attractive and unattached woman in her home, but it annoyed her to have one around while she herself was preoccupied with a new baby. It was barely tolerable, but apparently unavoidable, to have one around her long-absent and handsome husband during the forced inactivity of winter.

What she would not abide was the girl-bot barking at her.

"Sally, sir, what is a missus?" Malila asked.

"Oh my, girl, it means I'm Moses's wife. Don't you Union people use *Mrs.*? Relax and sit down! I'll make us some coffee before the baby starts crying again," she said as she turned away from the robot-girl.

"Sally, sir, what is a wife, sir?" The girl remained standing, and if possible, she seemed to straighten herself one notch more, reminding Sally of the faceless horrors of the Union.

Once again, she studied the girl's face for the faintest taint of sarcasm. She had married Moses just two years before. They had both come up as hardscrabble kids with almost no family and no inheritance other than their hands, heads, and backs. When the old man had staked Moses to prove out this parcel, despite her dislike of him, she had urged Moses to take the chance.

After paying off his first note, Moses had walked the fifteen miles to Georgeville and proposed to her. The same day, they had walked back as husband and wife. She had only just imagined she was pregnant when Moses had left to follow that Jesse "Let's Go Get Us Some Rifles" Johnstone to the wilderness of Wisconsin.

She was all for fighting the Union. The godless black horrors had killed her father and a younger sister only seven years ago. She and her brothers had buried their scorched remains by the road without even a marker, for fear of a return raid. But now, the horrible old man had brought a little piece of the Union back to haunt her.

"Humph … I might have known!" she said and turned again to make the coffee.

The girl, still standing and staring at the wall as if her mainspring had stuck from overwinding, looked paler. *Money can't buy people respectability,* Sally thought. *Folks' husbands aren't safe with people like this around.* Sally turned back.

"Just a word, girl: come on to Moses, harm me or my son, and you are out of here that very day! Captain Delarosa or no. Understand?"

Hearing the words, Malila felt her face flush hot, her heart pounding.

"Sally, I … yes, Missus Sally. No coming on to Moses, no harm. Yes, sir!" she blurted out.

The hope of an end to her hardship was slipping away from Malila. She just wanted to stop moving. She wanted to wear clothes that were not stiff with dirt and blood. She'd hoped this was an end to her trek, but instead, the missus threatened to turn her out into the wind and wet. Malila did not know what "coming on to Moses" even meant. Ever since that terrible day when Suarez's face had welled up into her vision, nothing had gone right. Even Jesse had finally abandoned her completely. Every fixed point in her universe had come loose in her hand. She sensed herself falling. Trying again to come more perfectly to attention in order to placate this angry woman, Malila's hot tears streaked across her wind-chapped cheeks and prismed her vision.

It might have been the heat of the room after the weeks in the open. It might have been that she had not eaten since the night before. It might have been the catharsis of having at last arrived, or it might have been the company of another woman, no matter how hostile.

Malila found herself flittering back to consciousness. The pain of her split lip and the fleeting memory of blissed-out daydreams mingled briefly. Sally was at her side where she had fallen forward into the wall, a bright smear of blood marring its whiteness.

"Malila, Malila, honey, come back, come on now ..."

Malila felt patting strokes on her hands as she resurfaced to the worried face of Sally hovering over her.

"I'm so sorry, girl! I didn't mean to snap at you. It doesn't matter. You can't help how you're raised. It will be okay ..." Sally cycled through her platitudes. Groaning, Malila sat up and saw Sally for the first time: only a few years older than herself, and drawn with the concern for her baby, her husband, and, now, a sharp anxiety for Malila herself.

Malila, to her own surprise, sat up, embraced Sally, and started to sob. Malila had learned not to cry in the crèche; it had drawn the unwanted and cruel attention of the older children. It had offered no remedy. Malila sobbed now, clutching Sally's warm form. She sobbed for the cold, for her ignorance, for not knowing what a wife meant, for the pain of her split lip, for the horror of the fight with Bear, for the despair of her near suicide, for Jesse's abandonment. She sobbed for all the sobbing she had not done as a child. She sobbed for her lost homeland and the kindness of this stranger. She sobbed.

Sally, after a moment's hesitation, hugged her in return. The two women embraced on the floor of a primative homestead in the outlands of the Unity and the Stewert farm of the New Carrolton Colony of the Reorganized States of America until both women were crying and laughing in turn. Minutes later, a shrill declaration of neglect by Ethan made both women rise to his summons.

CHAPTER 38

CAPTIVITY

Over the next two weeks, Sally listened to most of the girl's tales. Malila needed the chance to say all the words left unsaid from her trip, her capture, and, maybe, her entire life, Sally thought. Malila retold her solitary memories of early childhood: a soft-bodied woman; a tall, thin man with spectacles; and the windblown clapboard house on a hill against an empty gray sky as it disappeared in the rear window of a government skimmer. She talked about her hopes, her patrons, and her return to the Unity.

Sally asked questions about the things she could not know and kept from her face the reaction to what the answers revealed. Some things she would never fathom. The patrons, whom Malila discussed so openly, filled her with outrage, showing her Malila as a naive victim of a repellant system.

But that first day, Sally interrupted her as Malila's clothes, warmed by the bright fire, began to liberate the odors they had captured over the weeks of hard use.

"Let's see if I can find anything of mine I can alter for you, honey.

We can't have you walking around in that old man's cast-offs, can we, now? Looks like the only thing worth keeping are those boots."

"Yes, Missus Sally."

"Call me Sally, honey. Let's get you out of those things before they crawl away on their own. We'll need to get you some undies too, I see."

Sally had seen violence visited upon flesh before. However, she was not prepared for the bruises and healing wounds she found on the slim body of the girl. Malila had a black eye just fading from green, bruises from leg to shoulder, and abrasions on her face and hands. The girl was muscular, but she was painfully thin, her ribs and hip bones protruding. Besides the small healing wounds that went along with life on the trail, the girl had deeper scars under a breast and above her privates. Her eyes spoke of long days and insufficient rest.

"You've had a hard trip, honey. How long did it take you to get here? Just put your arms up, and I'll drop this old gown over you." A swoosh of gingham interrupted Malila's reply.

She repeated it as her face cleared the neckline. "About six weeks until we crossed this last big river; then we met Moses and rode here."

"You mean the Ohio? Big, I suppose, but you should see it in springtime! Those scars look new. What did you get caught in, leaving you so marked?"

"Jesse did the one under my right breast, and the other one was when he abandoned me for another man to take. That was Bear. I don't know what the mark was really supposed to look like. He said cutting me was to show people what I was and who I belonged to. You know what a brothel is, Sally?"

"Yes, I do, but we don't generally talk about it among civilized folk, honey."

"Oh, really? We don't have brothels in the Unity."

"No, I see where you might not. Hmm ... looks like I'll have to take it in a bit up top and round the hips. I'm not going to make it fit too tight. I'm thinking you might gain a little back now that you are off the trail."

"Jesse said my boobs were too small too."

"That old goat, he said that? They look just fine, honey. You have a sweet shape. Men always think they want more than they can get their hands on."

"He didn't seem to want them when he had them, missus." Malila sighed.

"It's Sally, honey. Did he? I mean did Jesse touch you?"

"Of course he did. We were sleeping together ... oh, not for pleasure-sex! Father me, no! He watched me, especially when I had to wash. He got, you know, interested. Did I tell you he made me wash before bed every night, even as cold as it was? And he watched me. But I guess he didn't like what he saw."

"Must be tough to fight off a big man like Jesse. Brutish is all I have to say."

"I guess he doesn't have much interest anymore. I'm told Sisis, old people, are like that," said Malila with a smirk.

"Jesse? I wouldn't take that bet, honey," Sally chuckled. "That old man ... I'd not trust with the virtue of a spinster. He's already run through three wives that he admits to."

"I guess it is just me he doesn't like, then. That must be why he abandoned me, again," said Malila. This time her smile was wan. She looked away.

Sally looked at her without answering, and Malila, turning back, explained. "Jesse abandoned me over and over as we were walking. First, a Death Walker nearly got me. Next, he took off during a snowstorm. A band of bandits saw my fire. Before they could rape me, I ran off into the snow. Jesse found me, but then he just stuffed me into a snowdrift. He left me there and didn't come back until after dark the next day. Even when he was there, he wasn't there. Do you know what I mean?"

"I know something of that. Moses went off with Jesse at the beginning of summer this year. I was just beginning to figure I was expecting Ethan. Jesse said it'd be a few weeks, and it turned into months. The Sentinels kept me up to date, so's I didn't worry, but I couldn't get a message to Moses. We, Mose and me, need to talk about that. I'm not happy about how he abandoned me to go keep house at Morganfield."

"What was Moses supposed to be doing during the birth?"

Sally laughed. "Far as I know, he's supposed to look worried and keep out of the way. Men are pretty useless when it comes to birthing their own babies. They need to be there so's they don't get the idea this is just a woman thing and to know what women go through so that they, the men, can have a child."

Malila looked confused, and Sally waved a hand at her before continuing. "Men want children as much as women do, whether it shows or not. It's a whole lot more complicated for a man to get a baby than for a woman. Boys don't understand that, of course. They're just rutting. It's only when they grow up that men realize they want to bring up a child in this world of sorrows—see they turn out to be good people. The gladdest people I know are the men who are proud how their kids turned out. The most sorrowful ones are the ones who failed for not trying."

"But Moses abandoned you when you needed him."

"I can thank your friend Jesse for that. They were supposed to be back by middle August."

"He's not my friend. He abandoned me too. He abandoned me in a lot of ways."

"Well, if it hadn't been for Jesse, Moses would've been here. I expected Mrs. Parker to help with the birthing, and she brought along her girl, Simone. What an annoying child. Moses could've saved me from her, if he'd have been here."

The conversation subsided as Sally, with a mouthful of pins, concentrated on the alterations.

How much to believe of the girl's wild stories was anyone's guess. Jesse was not above a little fabrication at the expense of the gullible. What was certain was that the old man had been too rough with a young, weak, and vulnerable girl. Considering how casual she was with sex, it would not surprise her if Jesse had taken advantage of her on the long trip south, whatever Malila said. Sex was an issue between them; that much was obvious. Sally was not so naive as to think rape was rare in a wild and lawless country, but she would be damned if she allowed the vile man into her house again.

Sally saw how much good it did the girl to talk, wrenching as it was to hear how the old man had treated her. No matter that Jesse Johnstone was a legend of the frontier and the first of the "old ones." Since his childhood, he was supposed to have aged slower than anyone in recorded history. It was all part of some science experiment[9] around the time of the Meltdown. The good news, at least for Sally and those she cared about, was that aging was now a disease like the red measles or lockjaw. You got a few shots, and it did not happen. The old man had helped make it possible. It did not mean she had to like him.

Malila's evident pride in her country and its institutions were even harder for Sally to understand. Sally knew herself to be uneducated. Schooling for her had ceased with the murder of her father when she was thirteen. She could read and cipher. She could run the agro-support differential equations, run the diagnostics for the power panels, manage her household programs, and program the farm machines. She knew enough machine language to create her own market-prediction programs. Beyond that, she read for her own pleasure and that, for the most part, in English. There had been little room in her life for earning "merit" or admiring "the rule of the people" either.

She worked for possessions, things to ensure the safety and welfare of herself and those she loved. She would much rather have money than "merit." As for other folks messing with her business, she was

---

[9] "Ageplay is a project that may have the greatest effect on health since the discovery of vaccines. A couple who have been marooned in a summer cabin since the Scorching have finally returned to civilization, bringing with them their four children.

At the time of the invasion, Saint Louis native Dr. Alyssa Elizabeth Browne, MD, PhD, and her husband, Dr. Alexander Rodney Johnstone, MD, a native of Dumfries, Scotland, escaped to what they hoped would be a safe refuge in eastern Kentucky. When the Unity invaded, they became isolated. To protect the only functional specimen of the Ageplay agent, they administered it to their youngest son.

The Ageplay treatment may increase vigorous lifespan to 170 years ... For the time being their son provides the only source of the agent." Bella Trelagen, "Promising New Treatment," *St. Louis Post-Dispatch*, July 22, 2063, Sunday supplement, 3.

quite willing to tell them what she thought about such busybodies if they tried.

The most mystifying aspect of the girl was her baffling fascination with Ethan. The strange, alien girl, if left unsupervised, stood and watched him for hours. Malila scrutinized each of Ethan's fleeting grimaces as they cycled across his face, watched the slow dance of the small hands as they writhed even in sleep. She talked incessantly about how sweet he smelled, newly laundered and freshly attired. Sally had quickly instructed her about replacing his diaper when he was not so sweet-smelling. She seemed to enjoy the privilege. Strange girl.

CHAPTER 39

INTERROGATION

The day after she arrived at the Stewert farm, Malila's interrogation began. Her inquisitor was the man she had seen with Jesse in the village square. He was sparse with intense dark eyes behind rimless spectacles perched on a hawk-like nose, generous lips rescuing his face from severity. Instead of a close-fitting suit of black Produra, as she expected of a soldier, he wore a drab forest-green camouflage pattern with shoulder patches and "Captain Delarosa, Xavier C." over the right breast pocket. He seemed harmless enough as he accepted a cup of Sally's coffee and a fresh-baked biscuit. After a short while, Sally made some excuse to busy herself and left the front room to them. She made it clear to the officer that she was never farther away than a loud voice might summon.

Delarosa looked down at his coffee cup and rotated the handle clockwise by a few degrees, picked up a morsel of biscuit with a remaining smear of blackberry jam on it, and popped it into his mouth.

"Sally makes the best biscuits I know … Has she shown you her secret recipe?"

"Chiu, Malila Evanova, acting second lieutenant, serial number 59026169."

Delarosa smiled.

"I see that Sally's secrets are safe. A shame. The world would be a better place if we ate more biscuits together, don't you think?"

"You are speaking nonsense. It is absurd talking about biscuits; you waste my time trying to make me betray the Unity."

"That is saying a good deal, you know, wasting the time of a failed junior officer sent to the middle of nowhere. Sent because you were more expendable than a machine?"

"I am a loyal member of the Democratic Unity Forces for Security."

"You are the first prisoner of war I have interviewed. And that explains nothing. But I must say you have made quite an impression on Captain Johnstone. It is not very frequent that Jesse voices such strong opinions."

"And where is Captain Johnstone now?"

"Captain Johnstone asked … well, was given … a detached assignment in Lexington. I don't know when he will be back. It is me you have to deal with, Lieutenant Chiu." He did not smile.

After talking with Sally, Malila had recognized just how worthless the old man's assurances would be. He had promised to look after her when they arrived, but instead he had managed to get assigned somewhere else. She should have known. Sally had said as much.

"If I'm such an incompetent, why don't you just send me back to the Unity?"

"I would if I could, Lieutenant. We have not had any contact with the … Unity in generations. If we get close to your wall, they send hunter-killer teams after us. It is not the best way to negotiate."

"Then let me go near the gate, and I will find my way."

"We have tried that in the past. Those not shot out of hand were captured, restrained, and injected with something that gave them seizures. What might that be, do you think, Lieutenant?"

"That is just an outlander lie! Sapp hasn't produced seizures in years."

"Sapp? That's the agent that you give your foot soldiers, isn't it? Makes them zombies. It still doesn't sound very good, does it?"

"I don't know what you mean. CRNAs are loyal troops. They no longer have the cognitive abilities that got them into trouble in the first place."

"I see. Very poetic. I didn't think you Union types had a sense of humor. I was wrong."

"Do you have anything to ask me, Captain Delarosa?"

"That's more like it! Brittle, formal, and hostile to lower life-forms. Maybe I can answer a question of yours, instead?"

"What was in the buckskin roll that Captain Johnstone gave to you when we arrived?"

Delarosa's eyes shot open. "Right to the point! You really don't know? Okay, Acting Lieutenant Chiu, since you asked so nice. How do you think Jesse used the pulse-rifle without a registered fingerprint and ID chip?"

"I don't know … He never said."

"He harvested the ID chips and the fingertips of all your troopers after he captured you. That should be obvious. He tanned them in some awful stuff he carries, like salt, acid, and oil. The ID inserts have to be shared among your troopers, right? Anyway, he made a glove to use with the rifle. Man's clever; you gotta hand it to him."

Malila heart sank. Jesse had been carrying the key to the signature locks under her eyes … and nose … since she'd first awoken in the lean-to, bound and naked. The old man was no doubt telling all who would listen about the gullible Uni he had captured. Malila swallowed her shame.

"Thank you for pointing out my failures, Captain. I had not noticed," she said as icily as possible. Delarosa's candor struck her as ominous.

"Are the outlands so chaotic that they don't try to hide their defenses?" she asked.

"Is the Unity so blind as to what constitutes a defense?" Delarosa replied, smiling.

"You talk in riddles. I am done for today. You may starve me or beat me. I will not say anything more."

"Admirable, Acting Second Lieutenant Chiu, admirable! Let's get another cup of coffee while I schedule you for flogging. If we are lucky, we might find cookies."

To Malila's surprise, Delarosa neither coerced nor threatened. He asked direct as well as subtle questions about her, her unit, and the Unity. He shared far more information than she did: he was a city kid from Saint Louis, a town situated on the same Mississippi River Jesse had mentioned, as absurd as that seemed. He had grown up in a place called the Hill with his breeder-mother, donor-father, and siblings of the same parentage. The arrangement made Malila queasy.

"What are you doing in the outlands, Captain?" Malila asked.

"A good question, isn't it? I'm not much of a country boy, but my wife, she was a farm girl from Illinois … so that is where we went to live. I worked as a federal marshal, and she and her brother ran the farm. It was a nice arrangement … as long as it lasted."

Delarosa turned to look her in the face, his acute eyes capturing her own. "She was killed in the Meridosia Raid ten years ago. I'm guessing you've never heard of it. War breeds a lot of casual death."

Malila had no answer to this and hurried on to her real point.

"Jesse acted as if the outlanders were all like him … old, primitive. Why are you telling me about the city?"

"I think he might have figured he was protecting you. He was operating kind of off the lead. He didn't want to let the genie out of the bottle. Good policy that, in general."

"Oh sure, protecting me from the truth … that does sound like him."

Malila glimpsed an odd look on the captain's face.

"You don't like him much, do you?"

"Why should I like him, Captain? He captured me, cut me, beat me, and nearly killed me. Why should I like any of you?" she flared at him.

"Depends on how onerous you choose to make your captivity,

Acting Lieutenant Chiu. Jesse suggested that you might enjoy the company of a woman close to your own age. Sally Stewert is a nice lady. I think you may have fallen onto your feet here, Lieutenant."

"I like Missus Stewert very much, but if it hadn't been for Jesse, I'd be back home! He made me miserable for weeks. He almost got me raped and sold to a brothel."

"You *do* know our two countries are at war, don't you, Acting Second Lieutenant? He doesn't *owe* you anything."

Before she could answer, Delarosa shrugged and changed the topic to Unity sidearms. Malila was delighted, as she was able to refuse to answer.

It was her anticipation of Delarosa's visits that surprised her. Unity men were either her superiors, sizing her up as a protégé, or her competitors, watching for some chink in her defenses to exploit. Worst of all were her subordinates. They were ingratiating, saccharine, and looking for eventual patronage from a rising star of the Unity. Malila sighed. The hope of her having any patronage to distribute had vanished months ago.

However, Delarosa amused her. At first, he challenged her to tell stories of her homeland. Malila related the few narratives she knew, the Storming of the Hoover Building and the Battle for Wilmington, confident Delarosa was already familiar with them. Then she went on to tell him of her friends and Maddow Crèche #213, all useless information to him.

Delarosa reciprocated, not by telling stories but by relating wonders. He would set the scene with words and the pitch of his voice. He impersonated each character with distinctive accents and phrases.

"Who goes there afoot on my land, you bold foeman? Approach, if you dare, and be tried by the Strangler," boomed an alien, brutal voice.

Malila felt her heart race.

"Oedipus of Corinth, out to seek my fortune, to foil a worse fortune at home than abroad. And what of this trial to each stranger you give, O Sphinx?" said another voice, smaller yet manly, forthright, and noble.

"Mere words, fainting man, but the forfeit is death. Take you the wager?"

Dread seized her as the foundling Oedipus endangered himself to save his family. Malila applauded Oedipus's cleverness, his success, his noble struggle with Apollo's plague … and wept at his downfall. It left her exhausted.

In turn, Delarosa became a dying emperor, a Saracen maiden, the village drunk, and an oriental sage. Soon Malila gave up all pretensions at exchanging stories and just listened as she was moved to laughter, tears, and longing.

Malila had thought she was sophisticated. With Luscena's help, she had experienced the best of Unity performing arts: magnificent productions of light and sound. With each elaborate program, a boutique ThiZ, tailored for the performance, was distributed. The shows had been marvelous, but Malila couldn't remember them now. Her heart pounded as Delarosa painted with mere words.

She was always sorry when Delarosa left for the day, usually with several of Sally's cookies wrapped in a handkerchief in his jacket.

CHAPTER 40

INTRUDER

After two weeks at the Stewerts', Malila saw that some special event was approaching. Moses cleared out a barn before throwing sawdust on the floor. More confusing, he cut conifer boughs to decorate the house and the barn. Wagons arrived with townspeople, who assembled long trestle tables. Sally made more succotash than they could consume in a week.

The Coming, as Sally called it, was a great day of celebration, leaving Malila's ignorance undisturbed. She meant to bring it up with Xavier the following day, but it slipped her mind when Moses insisted on showing off the new milking program to Xavier and her.

On their return, nearing the front of the house, they heard muffled shouts. The front door banged open. A hunched figure of a man in a black-and-red-checkered wool coat hastened out, scolded and savaged by the diminutive Sally wielding a broom. The man halted only when he found himself outflanked by the woodpile.

"... are a vicious, hard-hearted, rough-handed waste of skin. You are a nasty, crooked, old, dried-up, slant-faced, scant-bodied, shameless, arrogant, bloody-minded, evil-scheming abuser of your betters and worse for it!"

At this point, Sally sputtered in her assault, apparently having fired off all her ammunition on the first salvo and awaiting resupply. Moses rushed by Delarosa to intercept and disarm her. A hissed conversation ensued.

Malila was shocked. Gentle, loving Sally had become this angry, red-faced fury. The man must have done something horrible. After Moses wrapped up Sally in his long arms and almost carried her into the house, the miscreant unfolded himself. He was tall and clean shaven, with his long white hair caught up in a ponytail.

Jesse.

Without his beard, he looked even thinner than the last time Malila had seen him. His eyes were brighter, more brittle. He had none of the gray-skinned apathy that had frightened her during the final week of their journey. The old man stared along Sally's line of retreat as if gauging the possibilities of a renewed attack from cover.

He turned as she approached, and his face blossomed into a smile, the tableau of the preceding few seconds seemingly forgotten.

Sweeping off his hat, he said, "Malila, lass, there you are. I came to see if the Stewerts were doing right by you! I hope I find you well."

Malila was amazed. The old man, who for weeks had threatened her life, made it miserable, betrayed her by making the ghoulish signature patches under her very nose, and abandoned her in body and spirit, was attempting to act as if he were the wasteland's concierge. Malila burst into laughter.

Jesse froze and then straightened up, his hat circling in his hands.

"Ah. I see you are in good spirits, Lieutenant. I've been told how much help you've been around the place, especially with young Ethan. Is there aught you might need?"

Infected with the oddness of his formality, wearing one of Sally's dresses that she had yet to alter, a pair of cast-off trousers, and an old coat of Moses's, the sleeves falling over her hands in lieu of mittens, Malila dropped an unsteady curtsy to the old man.

"Captain Johnstone ... or is it Doctor again? The Stewerts have been truly marvelous hosts. It seems that Mrs. Stewert has the same high opinion of you that I have."

The old man looked up at the front door again and scratched his chin.

"She was fair exercised, at that, wasn't she, lass? Sort o' glad she didna keek Moses's 30-30 over th' door," he said, giving her a watery smile.

"It's a marvel that anyone can resist your charms, Doctor, or are Sisis not held in such high esteem in the outlands as you imagined?"

Ignoring Captain Delarosa, Malila moved close to the Jesse and pressed herself to him, letting a hand move to fondle him as the surest way to embarrass. It was amusing to be in the driver's seat with the horrible old man for once. Anticipating her maneuver, he caught her hand.

"Nay, lass. Don't do this," Jesse hissed to her as she tried to press forward.

"Oooowww!" she shrieked. "So strong, you don't know your own strength, Dr. Johnstone. And after all those weeks together!"

With her free hand Malila stroked the old man's cheek and marveled that he still blushed.

"Sally is a good judge of character, don't you think? She isn't fooled by you," she whispered into his ear. "You're not so brave now, are you? Why come back for me now, I wonder?"

Jesse tried to pull away, but Malila was having too much fun at his expense to let him get off the hook. If she humiliated him in front of his amateur army, so much the better.

Delarosa, silent until now, interrupted her by taking her arm.

"Excuse us, Captain Johnstone. Stay here for a few minutes, would you?"

Malila, pleased to be able to leave the field of combat uncontested, allowed herself to be piloted toward the house. Looking over her shoulder, she saw the old man hunker down beside the woodpile and replace his hat.

Malila heard the muffled shouts of Sally and the low and urgent rumblings of Moses erupt as Xavier knocked on the front door and then let them in when there was no response. Ethan, absorbing the hostility in the air, had started a descant shriek of his own.

"I won't have that vicious old fraud on our property or anywhere near our son!" Sally shouted at Moses, dramatically pointing a finger at Ethan.

"Sally, it's only because of Jesse that it *is* our property," Moses answered.

"I don't care!" she said before looking up at Delarosa and Malila. Her pale features suffused with the dull red of rage, she turned away, scooped up Ethan, and ducked into the hallway. Malila heard the bedroom door slam.

Moses turned to Delarosa, looking pained. "Captain, I'm sorry you had to be here for this. I don't know what's got into Sally; I really don't. She doesn't like Jesse, but that just means she ignores him.

"Seems Jesse knocked on the door and let himself in. That's a bit rude, I know. When I was proving out this section, he got used to coming in, more or less, like he owned the place, which, at the time, he did, but Sally blowing up like that … I just don' understand."

Sighing, Moses sat down in his old rocking chair and put his head in his hands.

Delarosa turned to Malila, her arm still in his gentle but unrelenting grip. "What might you know about this, Lieutenant Chiu?"

"Me? I just told Sally how that old Sisi treated me! Sally told me how people think he's so important, but he's just a Sisi. He killed all my men, and you told me how he saved the fingerprints for you. That's just grotesque. He went out of his way to humiliate me." She felt her outrage build now that it had an audience.

Xavier had no reaction, so she went on. "He had me strip naked every night! He hit me if I didn't drink this or do that. It was one humiliation after another. Sally can tell you. She's seen the marks!"

Delarosa interrupted her in a quiet voice, "I read his report on the trip, Malila. Perhaps I can add a little light to this story. Moses, would you get Sally back here? I'd like her to hear what I have to say as well.

"Now."

It was a command. Both Malila and Moses looked at him in

surprise. It was a second or two before Moses stood and disappeared down the corridor.

Delarosa and she had yet to speak a word more by the time, minutes later, when a sniffling Sally returned, her eyes red and swollen. Malila pulled her arm away from Delarosa and went to stand beside Sally, who grabbed her hands with both of her own.

"I'm going to tell you what Jesse's orders were when he left here last summer. Moses, you may not be aware of this, but I can show you the orders themselves if you want," said Delarosa.

Moses shook his head at once.

Nodding to Malila, Xavier continued, "We needed to examine your new troop rifles, but we have known for a long time about the inserts … the implants your country uses to track its people. We couldn't afford to have a raiding party intercepted by taking any implants along with us. I am sure you understand that, Lieutenant."

Malila, despite herself, understood immediately.

"All your troopers were better armed than Moses or Jesse. You invaded the sovereign territory of America. Killing you and them in combat is the usages of war. Jesse's specific orders were to allow no one with an implant to survive to compromise the mission."

Delarosa let the statement float for a moment until its significance set Moses's head to nodding.

"Jesse wasn't supposed to take any prisoners," Sally said seconds later, her voice flat and almost unrecognizable, her words falling into the silence of the room like a pebble into a vast sea.

Malila knew the Unity seldom took prisoners. Those they took, they Sapped.

Sally interjected, "Jesse wouldn't shoot unarmed prisoners! He is an arrogant old geezer, but he doesn't kill like that!"

"He didn't, did he?" said Delarosa. "Lieutenant Chiu, your Unity soldiers were all armed. They outnumbered Jesse and Moses by twenty to one. They should have been more than capable of defending you. You lost, and they won."

Malila nodded to him, one soldier to another.

"Once you were secured, Jesse sent Moses back to the summer

camp with the rifles and the ID chips. That took all the horses. So Jesse followed his orders to the letter, if not the spirit. The rifles we are examining back at Saint Lou. The fingerprints Jesse delivered two weeks ago. He had to start processing them right away, but you might have sabotaged that work, had you known.

"From Captain Johnstone's report, he seems to have been rather resourceful in saving your life ... several times, Lieutenant. Let me ask you ... the last three weeks of the trip, after you tried to kill him, how did you think Captain Johnstone was doing physically and mentally?"

Sally interrupted and turned to look at Malila. "You tried to kill ..."

Jumping in before Sally could finish the thought, Malila attempted to make her story sound dry and military. Even as she spoke, Moses's long face hardened, and a pallor invaded Sally's flushed features. With a pang of remorse, Malila felt Sally release her hands.

"Did you have any problems with bleeding, mental depression, joint pains, or loose teeth by the time you got to Morganfield?" asked Delarosa.

"What? Of course not! But Jesse starved me. Sally can tell you. Do you know what I had to eat? And he made me drink his poison tea every day. I was sick of it," Malila said, wondering at the direction the discussion had taken.

"Captain Johnstone arrived in town and turned you over to me two weeks ago. He was examined and invalidated to Lexington for treatment of scurvy."

Malila watched Moses and Sally look down, embarrassed.

"What's scurvy?" Malila blurted.

"I am sure Sally would be glad to tell you. Jesse needed to take that nasty tea he makes to stay well while traveling. Instead he gave it to you. He could have died. Many have. He nearly did this time. We sent a guard with him to Lexington to make sure he got there alive. He is a durable old coot, and he took well to the treatment. He got out of hospital and back to town just yesterday."

Moses nodded in agreement, and Sally started to twist the small handkerchief into which she had been weeping.

"I learned last week that one of the Unity's enforcer bands had disappeared, just east of the Illini-Indi line. They found five bodies, or pieces of them anyway, under a bridge at the Route 41–Interstate-74 junction," Delarosa said as if to change the subject.

"You have any idea what happened to those five men, Lieutenant Chiu?" Delarosa asked with a smile.

Malila began to recite her story, feeling her outrage avalanche with the memory. "Jesse abandoned me and let those men capture me. He left me to them, like a piece of meat! They were going to ..."

Malila looked at Sally, before saying, "... abuse me."

A hum in her head accelerated, making it hard for her to hear.

"It was all Jesse's fault. If he had stayed with me, we could have fought them off. We had a pulse rifle! I took a chance and ran away from them. Jesse found me and put me into a cave in the snow. He abandoned me again, and Bear caught me again. Bear cut me; Sally saw the scar. He tried to kill me, but I killed him first."

"And how is it that you and Jesse connected up again, before or after you tried to kill him?" Delarosa asked.

Malila began to explain. She backtracked, amended, and reworded her story. In the middle of her recitation, she started to hear her own words, to glimpse the trip from an outlanders' point of view. Moses was watching her, his face set as if he were watching the death agonies of some insect. With a shock, Malila recognized for the first time how dangerous a burden she had been. The old man had brought her out against reason, orders, and his own interests. Her account petered out when she caught herself relating her horror at her first bleeding cycle. She blushed, hesitated, looked at Sally for some moral support, and stopped.

Sally said, "Oh, dear."

Moses stood and confronted Delarosa. "Captain, first let me say that it was me as killed the zombies; Jesse was keeping Malila quiet. That should be in the report. I know Jesse thought we would be passing her over to headquarters once we rendezvoused. It was you, Captain, as asked me to billet her here. I was glad to do it, even if Sally wasn't.

"Now I'm withdrawing that offer. Lieutenant Chiu has brought discord into my house. She needs to leave," he finished.

Sally interrupted. "No, Moses! Where will they take her? You don't have any idea where she'll go. I need her! … She needs me!"

Malila froze at the last outburst. Sally lapsed into miserable silence, sat, and wept into the hard-used handkerchief.

Malila turned to Delarosa.

"I will be ready to leave in a few minutes, Captain Delarosa."

Without looking back, she went to the ladder and climbed into the loft. Malila collected the few items the Stewerts had given to her. She wouldn't take the dress. She was a soldier, a captive soldier. She knew how to take orders, and she would not make it any more difficult for Sally. She took up the baby's clothes she had taken to mend. Malila pressed the small garments to her face and inhaled the faint scent of the infant before grief overwhelmed her. Malila sank to the pallet in the loft under the eaves in the small house along the frontier of the outlands and wept.

"There is only one way Lieutenant Chiu can stay. She's no believer. Who would accept her apology anyway?" Moses announced in a low voice to Delarosa.

"The girl's lies have almost killed Jesse more than once," Moses finished … an epitaph.

Miserable, Sally stood and faced Delarosa. "But it was me that took out after Jesse, not Malila.

"It's true I don't like Jesse, but it was his walking in unannounced that just set me off. He was the cause of all Malila's pain and humiliation … there, in my front room. The poor girl had suffered so much during her trip. She had so little to begin with.

"And I've made things so much worse for her," she said.

"Sally, you'll have a chance to apologize to Jesse too, but if he doesn't forgive you, I'll report him to the association. See if I don't," Moses replied.

This appeared to galvanize her. Sally sat up and buffed the tears from her eyes before dropping the twisted handkerchief to the floor and standing stiffly.

"No time like the present. I was in the wrong, and it's not getting any righter, my talking about it," she said as she threw a shawl around herself and left the house to find the old man.

Only after Sally closed the door did Delarosa ask, "Does she always go from hot to cold so fast?"

"She knew she overreacted even before we heard what you and Malila had to say. She never asked me about this last trip. She was so tied up with the baby and with babying Malila. Those two really hit it off, and I think she swallowed anything the girl said. Seems Malila believes some of what Sally said as well. I guess she thought there was no way it could be explained in Jesse's favor."

"Malila Chiu is lucky to be alive … luckier to have run into the old man instead of me. I would have followed orders," said Delarosa.

Moses nodded. *Jesse was always following his own drummer … always had if you believed the stories,* Xavier thought.

"Malila might try to apologize. Why don't you explain it to her, Moses? She's not a believer, but she might understand and agree. It's hard to guess with these Union types; it is all about hierarchy and status with them."

"I dunno, Xavier. This is serious. I can't have the girl spreading lies and be under my roof, like I agree with her. Jesse doesn't deserve it … and neither do we." Moses flung himself down onto his rocker.

"So far it is just among the five of us. If Jesse accepts her apology, will that serve?" Xavier asked.

"You heard what she said! How many times has she broken faith with the old man?" Moses replied at once.

"But if he does accept her …?"

Moses stopped as if considering. It was a few seconds later before he looked up.

"If he does, I do. I'm not gonna be out-Jesse'd by the man," replied Moses with the shade of a smile crossing his lips for the first time since the old man had exploded out his front door.

"Let me go talk to him, and you talk to Malila."

Moses nodded and rose.

Delarosa opened the door and stepped out into the cold air of the front porch.

"... and I had no right to accuse you of any action I didn't witness myself. I have no excuse. I was wrong to believe the words, to voice the words, and to act on the words. God be a witness to my sorrow and sincerity. Jesse, please, forgive me."

Jesse was standing uncovered in the cold, his hat lying on the ground. Sally was kneeling with her hands held out palm down on the old man's open palms. She was looking up into Jesse's face with new lines of bright tears on her cheeks.

"I accept your apology, given freely with no threat or reward asked or offered to you, my sister, and I guarantee that our communion is intact and unaffected. I forgive you, Sally."

At the last words, she rose to her feet with the help of the old man, Jesse leaning down and quickly kissing her cheek. She, in turn, hugged him, before turning away to hurry back into the house.

When they were alone, Delarosa turned to Jesse.

"Moses is pretty upset with Malila. He won't have her around telling lies about you."

"Not all of it was lies. I was pretty hard on her. The last two weeks I was holding on by my toenails. I saw the signs. I was getting hazy and apathetic. It would be a terrible thing to make the girl walk for six weeks and then to die alone at the last go-round. I was getting weaker and stupider. It was a pretty close-run affair at the last."

"Anything that you ought to be ashamed about?"

"Me? I stopped blushing after they convicted President Bokassa. No, Xav, I was the very soul of a good jailor. Yes, I stripped her, I winkled out her implant, and I didn't ask 'Mother, may I?' neither. She's pretty enough, and I won't say I wasn't tempted, but I never touched her that way. I wasn't easy with her, but I wasn't easy with me. That is why General Thomas hired me.

"Did I tell you that the implants keep women from having their cycles? When she started her first period, the poor thing near came apart at the seams. I can see how she thinks I planned to humiliate her, but ..."

"But she gave her parole, her word of honor, and then tried to kill you. She shoulda too! Save us all a lot of trouble. You dumped her into an ice-water bath instead of killing her. Why?"

"Nearly *did* kill her, Xav. Seemed like the thing to do; she's just a kid."

"She has been a soldier since she was ten years old, you know, Jess. People in the Union only live to be about forty-two or so. She's nearer being middle-aged."

A smile flitted across the old man's face. "So what are we to do if Moses won't put up with her anymore? If you move her, you just set her up for another blowdown, doncha know? You want me to accept a phony apology from her?"

"No, I want you to accept a *real* apology from her ... and I want you to *really* forgive her."

"She doesn't like me much, Xav ..."

"Yeah, I noticed. But Sally thinks she needs to stay. I agree. Tough as she is, she's still a kid. She can operate in a group, but she dissolves on her own. If I move her, she'll be a basket case and useless to us."

"Is she worthwhile to you now ... I mean the intelligence?" asked the old man.

"No way to know. I've already gotten a lot out of her just by what she doesn't know."

Jesse laughed.

"Moses is okay with her staying?"

"Only if you are ... It all comes down to whether she can apologize to you and you can forgive."

"Don't worry about me, Xav. It's that time of year."

"Are you warm enough, huddled out here? This may take a while."

"I'll be fine, Xav. Go on and see what you can do. If you get a moment to send out some of Sally's cookies and coffee, they won't be wasted, I promise."

"This is a waste of time. It is just another way for that old man to humiliate me," said Malila, waving her hand into the air.

Even as a gleam on the dark horizon of her despair began to show, Malila refused to trust it.

"No, you can't think like that. Jesse can be hard as nails, but he has forgiven things in people that would make my heart stop. This is important, and you have nothing to lose," Sally pleaded. "If you don't try to apologize, you have to leave. If he forgives you, you get to stay with us. It may not mean much to you, but getting to act like the Shepherd, even a little bit, is important for us … and Jesse."

Malila thought that being a sheep organizer was no great reward but said nothing. She rehearsed the phrases with Sally. The foreignness of the ideas was difficult enough, but the restrictions were burdensome. If Jesse perceived any insincerity, he would not agree.

With little enthusiasm, Malila went outside. Jesse sat huddled near the woodpile. An empty cup was at his elbow.

Jesse's face was grim as she approached, like that of a magistrate. She was on trial now, and she had to admit her guilt.

She got close enough to the old man to kneel and reach out, palms downward. If Jesse did not take her hands, nothing more could be done … her apology was discarded out of hand. Malila watched his face for some telltale sign of reaction but could find none. She closed her eyes and waited. It was still a shock when she felt Jesse's warm, dry palms under her own. She could not bring herself to look up into his face as she began.

"I'm a stranger here, and I don't understand your customs. Sally says that I have to ask your forgiveness for what I said about your treatment of me on the trail. I may have exaggerated some things, and I'm sorry that she took them the wrong way."

"I see."

It was already going wrong. Telling Jesse about her own feelings wasn't going to work; Sally and Moses both had warned her of that. Malila's heart sank, and her hands started to slip off Jesse's warm palms. She tried again.

"I lied to her, and she believed me. I lied about how you treated me. I broke my promises to you. I'm ungrateful. You saved my life."

"Good, lass."

"But you embarrassed me; you got me drunk; you gave me your tea; you fed me … You didn't force me; you didn't want me; you helped me when I bled; you sang me songs … You hit me," she said, taking events at random and throwing them up like a makeshift barricade against the old man.

"I admit all that. I thought you were better than your promises. Breaking them surprised me ... made me angry, lass. That is no excuse. I'm sorry for hitting you, for humiliating you. Please forgive me."

Only then did Malila realize she was glaring up at Jesse, and she quickly looked down. This was not going as Sally had told her it would. She was doing it all wrong. She was not supposed to try to justify it or explain. Now Jesse had apologized to her instead. Sally had said he might "forgive" her, but Malila had no concept of what that would entail. All she knew was that if Jesse forgave her, she could stay. If not, she would be adrift in this chaos beyond the Rampart. She hesitated. The silence stretched away in front of her. Her palms greased with sweat, and her heart raced.

At length, Jesse said, "Will you forgive me for hurting you when I was angry? There is no excuse for that, and with my God's help it will not happen again."

The old man's voice was low and modulated. Malila looked up in surprise. Jesse gazed at her with a steady, almost detached look, but beneath the look Malila knew he was all quiet intensity.

"I don't know how to forgive you. I should have kept my promises, Jesse. Sally says I need you to forgive me." The pale-gray eyes of the old man watched her. His face gradually changed into a mask of perplexity as the silence continued. Malila broke her gaze, feeling her eyes fill, and contemplated the old man's boots, even as they blurred with new tears.

"Forgiveness is tough, lass. Forgiveness doesn't make things like they never happened, but it makes things right ... Can you see that? It means I give up feeling bad about your breaking your promises."

His image swam as her tears fell. She felt better hearing the words, not knowing why that should be. She looked up and tried to buff her tears away with a coat sleeve without removing her hands from the warm palms.

"Jesse, I forgive you for hurting me when you were angry. I give up my feelings about that. Please forgive me for ... for trying to kill you and for ... for all the things I've said about you. You have saved my life, fed me, clothed me, and cared for me. I owe you for that … I'm so sorry …"

Even as she spoke, the litany of the old man's actions—his decision to spare her life convicted her. He'd pulled her away from suicide. He'd looked out for her better than he had for himself. It was so unanswerable. She would always be in his debt. She could never repay it. A flash of dismay and grief raced through her as she recognized the truth.

Jesse's face swam as she looked up before again bowing her head with racking sobs of regret. She had done it all wrong, she knew. Jesse would never forgive her; she had bungled the whole thing. She had taken too much from him. It was several seconds before she sensed the old man beside her with his red bandana pressed into her hand and his solid arm around his shoulder.

"Malila … it's all right. It is … I accept your apology, lass. I do." Then shifting to another gear, he said, "And I thank you for forgiving me."

The bland words worked another miracle on her. Her sobs morphed into gentle hiccups as the old man cradled her in his arms. Malila found her breath coming in ragged sighs as Sally came over and shooed Jesse away, helping Malila to her feet. Minutes later, when she looked around, they were alone in the yard.

CHAPTER 41

THE COMING

It was midafternoon when Malila awoke. Sally had insisted that she lie down after coming inside. Wrung out, she had fallen asleep almost at once.

Above the silence of the house, Malila heard a low-frequency buzz of activity at the horizon of her hearing. The noise drew her to the front yard, and she found it crowded with horse carriages, small horseless carts, and heavier electric cars. Once out in the cold air, she heard a melodious beat of song and followed it to the barn Moses had been preparing. Coatless men turning whole venison and hogs on spits over beds of red coals nodded to her as she pushed the barn door open a crack before slipping in. The building was almost full of villagers and farmers.

"Merry Christmas!" a smiling woman wished her as Malila turned to shut the door. Malila gathered that the snatches of conversation between Moses and Sally she had been hearing all week long had been referring to this event ... whatever it was.

Near the entrance, a tack room had been transformed. Over

the entrance a sign read, "Obamaroom." The space was filled with projectile rifles on open racks guarded by several unsmiling men. The next thing she noticed was that everyone else was facing the narrow dais on which a meaty man in denim overalls, with the help of a woman with an accordion, was leading a song with vigorous arm motions.

> ... the weary world rejoices,
>
> as yonder comes her new and glorious dawn.

Malila made her way to stand behind Moses and accepted Ethan from Sally's arms with a smile. Both Moses and Sally returned to singing, Sally in a silvery soprano and Moses in a rumbling bass.

> The King of Kings lay thus in lowly manger;
>
> In all our trials born to be our friend.

Malila had never heard such songs, either this one or the several to follow. The songs she knew were either love songs or heroic ballads about the cadre. Some of the crowd around her referenced small tablets, but most sang from memory. Malila spotted Jesse in the crowd, nodding to her as he bellowed out in a confident baritone.

At the conclusion of the songs, the meaty man held up his arms to signal silence, and Malila's attention drifted back to the sleeping bundle in her arms. There was a generalized happy buzzing around her.

"A joyful Remembrance Day of the Coming, brothers and sisters," the man announced.

"Before we get started, I want us to thank Moses and Sally Stewert for the use of the hall. This'll be the third time we've celebrated here since we started the colony. God has blessed us with his bounty and his peace."

There was a general stomping and clapping at the statement, but Malila lost track of the speech after that, as Ethan started fussing. For a while, people took turns reading an odd and disturbing story about an ancient pregnant breeder and her patron. The story included spirit beings, hereditary rulers, soothsayers, religious functionaries, animal caretakers, and feeding troughs, no part of which she understood.

The meaty man then asked someone in the audience to "prey," and Malila looked up startled as every other head in the barn looked down. It took her several seconds to decide nothing predatory was in the offing. Lowering her head, realizing this was the ritual that Jesse, Sally, and Moses did before each meal, feeling a little silly, she hardly listened to the man's sonorous phrases. He finished, and at once people moved toward the trestle tables, carrying her along.

She had grown accustomed to the abundant fare of the Stewerts' workaday table. After the scant rations of the trek, it had seemed unreal. At times, Malila had wondered if their bounty was artificial, an effort to fool her as the prisoner of war.

However, the food laid out for the Coming was a magnitude more lavish, not just in quantity, which was copious, but also in variety. Men and women hovered over some dishes, urging her to "try a little." Small signs identified a golden mound of mashed rutabagas with butter dripping from it, deeper orange sweet potatoes, red new potatoes wafting steam, hearty dark-green collards, peaks of pale mashed potatoes, green beans, platters of sliced roast turkey, darker grained venison, rich roast goose dripping fat, and pale savory roast pork. Some even had proprietary names like "Susan Brannon's bean casserole" or "Cathy Wood's Brunswick stew."

On another table was a bouquet of fruit pies, puddings, and colorful tarts, with an older woman there shooing children away unless they showed her an emptied wooden plate. Most amazing to Malila was a pyramid of orange spheres. They were fruits that people were supposed to peel and eat raw.

Having not eaten since dawn, Malila was wiping her mouth on her sleeve by the time Sally retrieved Ethan. Planning on sampling a small serving of each dish, Malila eventually took just the ones that looked least familiar to her, retreating to a corner to enjoy her bounty.

The celebration, for the tenor of the crowd was jubilant, was at once joyous and disturbing.

Sampling some of the rutabagas, the bitter-sweet taste a welcome change from the saccharine sweet potatoes, Malila recognized that the Coming narrative was unique.

Childbirth was considered an ordinary occurrence in the outlands, she knew, but there was some social stigma attached to the story of this birth. Moreover, despite the irregularity of his birth, the baby was supposed to be a king. That was absurd.

Malila knew about the inferior forms of government. Kingship was a protection-hierarchy model: goods and service were extorted from the numerous weak citizens with promises of protection and/or threats of violence by the few influential citizens. It was an inherited condition. No baby could be born a king. If his father were still alive, then, by definition, he was not a king. If his father were dead, someone else would have already been chosen king, and again he was not king. The story was nonsense on the face of it.

The Unity had no celebrations such as this one, of course. Her homeland acknowledged current achievements rather than past events. It was sad that these people had so little in the way of triumphs, clinging to their outdated superstitions, their children, and their guns. She finished eating and went to place her plate on a table reserved for the purpose.

"Hello, and merry Christmas! My name is Eduard Billings. What's yours?"

Malila turned to face the man who appeared to be her age, the first she had met in the outlands. It gave her a start. From what Sally had said, men her own age would still be living with their parents. Malila presumed any man living with a father was subservient either because of finances or the fear of physical retribution. What she saw was a well, if simply, dressed man whom she could imagine in the uniform of the DUFS or the gray suit of a government worker. She snapped off, "Chiu, Malila E., acting lieutenant, sir!"

The man froze for several moments.

"So how do I call you? 'Chewy,' Malila, or Lieutenant?"

Malila took the cue to laugh and was rewarded with a shy smile.

"Malila will serve … Eduard," she said at last.

Eduard presented a warm hand and said, "Pleased to meet you, Malila. Where do you come from? I haven't seen you at any of the association meetings."

"I don't come from here. I … I'm an officer of the … I come from the Democratic Unity."

"Oh …" was all he said. He looked over her shoulder, and Malila followed his gaze to a vigorously gesturing older woman.

"Excuse me, Malila, but I have to see what my mother wants. You know how they can be. Don't go away!"

She answered his smile with her own as he left, and she was again in the isolation of a crowd, noticing one after another face turning toward her and then looking away. Malila had just decided to leave the barn when the music started, appearing to be a signal for the clearing of tables.

The woman with the accordion, joined by two men with violins, started playing music unlike any Malila had ever heard: infectious, melodic, rapid, and mystifying. It was meant for dancing, and soon the center of the barn was free of everything but twirling couples. Those who did not fit on the dance floor lined the space and started clapping. Malila's senses whirled trying to follow the figures of the dance that spiraled ever faster in the warm glow of the barn.

Nevertheless, she knew, the celebrants had never intended for her to be here with her makeshift and mismatched clothing. Sally was distracted talking to a group of young women and showing off the marvel that was Ethan Graham Stewert. Moses was with a group of men who were shaking their heads at the prospect of an early spring.

Malila edged to the door. As her hand closed around the handle, a large, warm hand closed over hers. She turned to find a man looming over her.

"Surely, you're not leaving, lass?" Jesse said in the tone of a jovial host. "The evening is yet young. There is music, and there is light. You are young and beautiful, and you should dance!"

Malila smiled, despite her surprise. It was the first time the old man had said something nice to her about her appearance, an outrageous lie though it might be. Nonetheless, it was odd talking to a man in whose arms she had sobbed just hours before.

"Dr. Johnstone, the music sounds like fun, but I don't know how to dance. It's much too complicated. I'd just ruin it for the others ..."

"Nonsense, I've just the place for you to learn!" Jesse pulled her through the crowd by her captured hand, away from the twirling couples, to a group of children who were mirroring their parents' motions, with checkered results, under the guidance of a young matron.

"Mrs. Eng! Might I ask a favor of you? My friend here and I desire to learn the mysteries of the terpsichorean art. Would you allow us to join your class of students?"

This, of course, set the children to tittering embarrassment, but by the shy smiles and outstretched arms, Malila could tell the old man was no stranger to them. In her childhood, adults had been objects of apprehension at the very least. Malila envied Jesse for the first time she could remember.

The young instructor turned and laughed. "Of course, Doctor, but you need to introduce us to your young lady."

"A thousand pardons, Mrs. Eng. May I present Miss Malila Chiu, visiting us for a season from across the wall. Malila, lass, I would like you to meet Mrs. Lawrence Eng, an old and dear friend of mine."

"Please call me Mary."

"Yes, sir," she said.

Mary's face froze for a moment.

Jesse stepped in and in a grandiloquent fashion went on to introduce the six children in the small ring, with a brief hesitation in the narrative to note, "Master Thorkyll here goes by the nom de guerre of 'Rocky,'" which drew giggles even from the one so unfortunately named.

Very soon, the square was formed, and Malila learned the figures of the dance. More surprising to her was that the old man was skipping and bouncing in the company of the children with grace and enthusiasm. One or another of the children would convulse with giggles when they had to promenade with Jesse, who crouched low to accommodate his partner for the circuit. Malila found she was able to lose herself, the room spinning about her as she listened for the calls, trying to remember the steps, in a whirl of light, sound, music, and geniality.

The children wove in and out of her sight, and Malila found herself jolted each time she came around to be handed off to the smiling old man. Despite his years, he was able to keep up with the children better than she was. Malila smiled back each time his hand reached hers. In time, Mrs. Eng dismissed the group, and the three adults adjourned to a large steaming bowl that had been programed, for the moment, to dispense a fruit punch.

The conversation drifted to shared stories of Jesse and Mary, leaving Malila to wonder if they had been patron and protégé at one time. The idea disturbed her.

Malila turned away to watch the children. Her memories of her childhood were so fragmentary that she had long since tried to ignore any that preceded her coming to the crèche. The dim and painful period of her pre-memories was a kaleidoscope of brief encounters with careless or harried adults, children with whom she shared toys and food but who then sickened and disappeared, and the packing and the unpacking of meager belongings from one gray building to the next.

After a few minutes more, the music stopped, and more people broke free to enjoy the punch bowl, now programed for some milky drink. Jesse warned her of the alcohol it contained, and she limited her intake to a small cup. It was different. It was good. After a few minutes, a sturdy man with straight black hair arrived. Mary introduced him as her husband, Larry, pulling him closer by lacing a finger into the thick belt he wore. Larry grinned at the attention. The four talked for a few minutes before the music started again.

"Looks like there's room for us to dance now. Good to see you again, Doc. Merry Coming!" said Larry before they left to join a square.

"Shouldn't let your education go to waste now, lass. You have no excuse! Let's go dance with the grown-ups, shall we?" said the old man as he again captured her hand.

"Do you think I can keep up? The caller is going very fast."

"Let me have a word with Simon and ask him to keep an eye out for us ... to make sure we don't get overwhelmed."

With her last objection countered, Malila followed Jesse onto the floor to complete the number for the Engs' square. The music seemed special and unreal as the room spun around, Jesse's newly unfamiliar face shining with the soft light and Malila finding her own face becoming fatigued with an unsummoned smile. By the end of the evening, Malila had danced with not only Jesse but also Moses, Larry, and a beaming Eduard. Jesse collected her as the last of the music died.

"Malila, lass, I have been deputized by Moses to see you safe home to the house. Sally and Moses have to register young Ethan, and it may take a while."

"Register? You mean, like, getting him implanted ...?"

Jesse laughed. "No, lass. Nothing like that. This is the first association meeting since Ethan's birth, and Sally and Moses both want the elders to know when his birthday was, that Moses accepts him as a natural son, and who the godparents are."

Malila could not conceive how these people's god had parents, but she left the question unasked and just nodded. Shivering on stepping out into the cold, Malila was glad for Jesse's warm arm. All of the self-powered carriages and most of the saddle horses had already left. Men were helping each other harness their teams.

Jesse and Malila moved away from the well-lit farmyard to escape the congestion and walked toward the farmhouse along back paths. Arriving at the kitchen door, Malila stepped up and started to open it as Jesse reached up to stop her.

"Malila, I want to thank you for a delightful evening. I didn't get a chance after ... this morning, to ask you whether we might start over. We sort of got off on the wrong foot, you and me."

"You mean being abducted, stripped naked, and cut open is *not* usual outlander greeting procedure?"

Jesse winced before he gathered she was teasing him. His laughter, nonetheless, sounded sincere.

"Nay, lass. Tha' wis special just fur thee." His face now sobered. "I'd like us ta start over, as if we hadna met before."

Malila was puzzled. She now expected Jesse to slip into a denser brogue whenever he was feeling good, bad, happy, or meditative. She wondered what he was feeling now.

"I don't know, Jesse. I could decide to kill you again."

He laughed, "I'm persuaded to take my chances, lass."

"Don't call me 'lass,' old man. I am an adult!"

"That might take some doing, la— eh ... Malila. You do know the word has other meanings, don't you?"

"I don't care. No 'lass.'"

"Yes, ma'am!"

It was Malila's time to laugh, and she extended a hand. "It's a deal, old man."

"So call me 'Jesse,' then ... Malila." He enunciated her name with care. "And might I come to call on you? I would like to see more of you."

"What part of me have you not seen, Doctor?"

"Aye, I take your meaning. Different time and circumstances, don't ye think? I mean, I would like to visit with you, my friend. I promise to forget and to forget the forgetting. Is that acceptable?"

"Acceptable, Dr. Johnstone."

They again shook hands solemnly. Malila leaned forward and kissed his check before backing through the door. Jesse turned and left whistling.

CHAPTER 42

BLIZZARD

The day after the Coming, returning to her pallet through the quiet kitchen early in the morning, Malila saw motion outside. The dim light of the room caught the silent, furtive movement of snowflakes just beyond the glass. For a moment, Malila was back among rusting girders, with numbing cold, fear, death, and abandonment. Wind whistled around the corner of the house, sending up a cyclone of snow that gyrated like a specter in the uncertain light. It made her shiver.

By first light, Moses had strung ropes between the back porch, the washout, and the milking barn. The snow outside the kitchen window was already banked, hip deep, into a gentle, sinuous curve. Malila was standing on tiptoes watching the swirling snow as Moses came in and recited:

> When you can't see the barn,
>
> Winds spin like a top,

A blizzard will snow,

Three days ere it stop.

He laughed. "Something my granny used to say. Looks like we are in for it, though."

"Are we going to be buried in snow?"

"We'll be fine, Miss … Malila. Going to need to keep the path clear enough so's you can follow the rope, is all. The barns are pretty safe, the animals have the autofeeders, and the automatic milkers will take care of most of the work unless the girls get into a tiff."

Moses bundled up and went out to shovel.

Regardless of the snow, Malila knew she had to do it today. She was worried she might lose her nerve if she waited.

After breakfast, she and Sally braved the snow to start the cleanup from the Coming. Sally showed her how to use the church's dishwasher and place the cleaned and dried wooden trenchers into cases for transport. Once a load was started, Malila went to find Sally, who was cleaning tables.

She knelt in the sawdust behind her and extended her hands, palms down, unsure of her own voice.

Sally, pink with exertion, a strand of hair that had escaped her bandana lying damp across her forehead, almost fell over Malila as she turned.

"Oh … honey, you don't need to do this."

"I think I do."

"Sweetie, we all make mistakes. It doesn't mean I need this from you."

"I know, but *I* need to try to make things right," said Malila, her blue eyes on Sally's.

Flushing, Sally faced her and placed her hands under Malila's.

Malila enumerated the lies, half-truths, and assumptions that she had fed to Sally as truth, admitting her desire to corrupt Jesse's reputation and apologizing for embarrassing Sally.

"I ask you to forgive me because you have been forgiven, because

Jesse forgave me, and because I am so sorry for the pain I've caused you. You took me in when I was a stranger, and what I did was ungrateful. Please forgive me."

"Of course, of course, Malila, honey. All you had to do was ask. Now, stand up, and let's dry your eyes."

And again, Malila noticed the paradox. Reminding the injured party of their hurts made them … not disappear … no, certainly not disappear, but made the memory of pain a treasured secret the two of them now shared. It was a mystery.

When Ethan woke Malila next morning, it was still snowing. He was bundled up against the coolness of the house and complained the more for all the unwrapping required to get to the scene of his discomfort. He was sopping. It amazed Malila that such a small body could generate such volumes of urine. Ethan complained until breakfast was served.

Malila watched him nurse. With the sweet-smelling round head buried into the pale flesh of his mother, succulent sounds filled the small room. In the uncertain light of early morning, Malila noted the small feminine line of blue around the edge of Sally's right areola as Ethan, voicing momentary outrage, was moved off one breast and applied to the other. Malila was surprised she had never noticed it before.

"What is that? You have a tattoo?"

Sally smiled. "Yes, of course. I've had that one since my mama's third baby. I was too young to earn it before."

"You earned it? Like Jesse? What does it mean?"

Sally laughed. "Probably *not* like Jesse, but it means that I've some practical experience about caring for babies."

"What did you have to do to earn it?"

In the Unity, tattooing had long been out of favor; citizens did not advertise their differences.

"Well, I got it for doing about what you are doing now."

Sally lifted her right breast, still dripping some milk, and with a finger outlined the curling lines of blue on her pale breast.

"This part is for helping at a delivery. This means I've cared for a baby up to a month after birth, and this means I've seen her through her first four months," she said, drawing her finger over an inner curlicue and a shape that, once Malila saw it, suggested four interlocking crescent moons but could also represent a vine ending in a lily flower.

"Just for being a helper?" Malila asked.

Sally replaced her breast into her gown and smiled. "I thought it a real reward at the time, you know. Getting up in the night to fetch my sister for feeding, changing her pants, bathing her, cuddling her. My mother was trying to teach me, not just be helped. It was a big job for a nine-year-old girl."

"You were so young! When I was nine, I was still in crèche school."

A cloud appeared to pass over Sally's face as she leaned over to watch her son feed. After a minute she looked up into Malila's eyes.

"Do you have any idea how much help you've been to me since you came, honey? Moses is a good man. He is gentle and reliable as the sun, but take any man and deprive him of sleep with anything that does not bite at, shoot back, or make love to him, and you have one unhappy male. Just letting Moses stay in bed while you get Ethan for me is worth gold. You don't think it's much, because you love Ethan. I can't pay you what you are worth. I can't thank you as much as you deserve, but when the time's right, I can let everyone else know how good you are."

Malila felt her cheeks warm with a blush.

CHAPTER 43

DELAROSA

Malila met Captain Delarosa at the door, almost a week after the Coming. He left his skis outside. Sally had asked her to take over answering the door, to their mutual satisfaction.

"I'm impressed you went through the forgiveness celebration with Jesse," was the first thing Delarosa said after Sally had installed them in the front room with a pot of fresh coffee.

"Are you telling me that no one else would have done that? That I shouldn't have?"

Delarosa met her eyes before speaking. "No! If anything, I think I am saying that you've showed me an admirable side of the Unity I wasn't prepared to admit."

Malila smiled and rose from her chair in the front room, taking up a stick to reform the brightly burning fire on the hearth.

"It wasn't a Unity thing, the forgiveness, you know?" she said with her back turned, knowing he understood.

"Yes, ma'am. Let me ask you something. I am tasked with interrogating you. I don't think you will tell me more than you already have."

"I haven't told you anything, Captain!"

Ignoring her statement, he continued, "If it's all right by you, I'd like to spend some time *telling* you about … well, not just about America but what I know of the world, of history. You, the Unity that is, have cut yourselves off from a lot of what we, in America, take for granted. Wars tend to do that … Walls tend to do that. You have the rare opportunity to see outside your walls."

"So that when I go home I will be denounced … Thank you, *Captain* Delarosa!" she said, her eyes laughing at him.

Xavier laughed himself and returned a courtly bow.

"Oh, I don't think what I will be talking about is all that scandalous. I think you will enjoy what I have to share."

"Why are you doing this?"

"Not sure, really. I suppose because you deserve a better shake than I think you have had so far."

"And this isn't some sneaky way to get me to tell you stuff?" she asked, raising an eyebrow.

"On my honor as a soldier, one soldier to another."

"Did Jesse put you up to this?"

Delarosa laughed.

"Hardly. I think, perhaps, this is a dose of Jesse antitoxin. He can be overwhelming at times. Dr. Johnstone seems to have done most things … twice … and has an opinion about everything else."

"Annoying, isn't he?"

Delarosa laughed again. "Depends. If I were stuck on a desert island, Jesse would be on my list for fellow castaways; but let's not dwell on Dr. Johnstone."

She looked at him from over the rim of her cup. "Okay, Captain, tell me your stories."

Xavier smiled, and all at once his attitude changed. His face transformed, and his voiced somehow deepened.

"Once upon a time, there was a huge empire that, with one thing and another, collected a large number of countries to rule. It lasted for about a thousand years before the Meltdown. Over that time, the countries, one by one, gained independence. America—or rather, I should say the parts of North America that are now the Unity—was one such country."

He ignored her rolling of eyes and continued, "But that is another story. The country my story is about was in East Africa. The people tried to rebel there as well. One rebel band, some called them the Mau Mau, had some initial success, but they failed to gain a general uprising.

"Then, they ordered their men to attack innocent villagers, commit senseless murders, take horrible oaths, eat human flesh, deny their gods, and drink vile potions. All to compel loyalty.

"They thought that if they could turn a man away from what was moral, sane, and honorable, compel him to take an oath so horrendous … it would change him, cut him off from his past, his family, his friends, his gods, and his image of himself. They hoped they had an army of ruthless, loyal men who had nothing to lose, as they had lost it already."

"Why would they do that? Soldiers follow orders anyway … at least they do in the Unity. You can't run an army if everyone gets to pick and choose the orders they follow."

"Don't forget, I am a soldier too. Yes, we all take orders, but I'm sure you know the *un*written oath: soldiers trust their lives to the officers, and the officers agree never to abuse that trust. You ask a man to die only if you think his death can make a difference. These are hard things to do: to ask and to follow. It only works if trust is there already."

"Jesse said that killing changes you."

"This was more than that, don't you think?"

"I think it is a revolting story. I don't like it."

After a few minutes' silence she added, "Nothing like that could happen in the Unity, you know."

"Why is that?"

"Because it is a democracy. Objections are dealt with before they can cause conflict."

"What if your neighbors voted that they did not want to live near you; would you have to move?"

"Of course, but who would wish to live near neighbors who hate you?"

Delarosa laughed and, turning, set his empty cup down.

"Why indeed? We should talk about that later."

They never did.

CHAPTER 44

EDUARD AND POTEMKIN

The snowbank in the shadow of the house waxed and waned as each snowstorm added a white layer and each brief thawing period compressed the snow into ice. By February, it glowed a glacial blue in the light of the rising winter sun. Sally tossed bread crumbs onto it and then identified for Malila the small birds drawn to the bounty: chickadees, titmice, and sparrows as well as the larger crimson cardinals, handsome jays, and eager finches. Malila watched for hours, fascinated, as the birds quarreled, intimidated, fluffed, tolerated, and stole the food from each other. The snowbank quickly became a squalid collection of discarded feathers, droppings, and overlooked crumbs.

Eduard Billings rode a sleek chestnut stallion to the Stewert farm once the roads were passable. Moses, a gloved hand on the horse's rein, intercepted him before he could dismount.

Malila had a pedestrian view of equine culture. Her exposure to horses both at home and in America had been fundamentally painful. Peeking out from the drying barn, however, Malila saw a confident young man in calf-length leather boots, riding pants, and a warm shearling coat. The chestnut he rode filled the air with plumes of steam, stamping impatiently at being held. It moved her.

Moses's interrogation apparently yielding acceptable results, Eduard was allowed to livery his horse. As soon as he was out of sight, Malila bolted into the house. Pressured whisperings, rustlings, and hissed instructions from Sally ensued.

"Whatever you do, honey, don't talk about your patrons or what you call pleasure-sex or anything that goes before or after! Don't talk about your bleeding times; men get uncomfortable about it. No talk about brothels and *nothing* about private parts *whatever*, understand?"

Malila nodded, especially when she could see the pattern emerging.

"And, of course, nothing about money, religion, or politics."

Malila was now thoroughly confused, assured that all the good topics were prohibited, but promised to make her best attempt. Small talk had never been required of her. In the DUFS, a shared mission prompted shoptalk at every meeting. A shared institutionalized backstory made reminiscences pointless.

The expected knock at the front door came just as Malila was putting on house slippers. Sally had vetoed the boots.

Flushed and short of breath, Malila opened the door, retreating to the kitchen as Sally, the hostess, graciously invited Master Billings in and offered him a seat.

Leaving Moses's high-backed rocker for its absent master, Eduard sat and began a polite inquiry after Sally's health, Moses's health, and then Ethan's. Sally, with a streak of cruelty that surprised Malila, asked after Eduard's parents, sisters, and cousins in excruciating detail before finally relenting.

"Would you like some refreshment, Mister Billings? Malila was just brewing up a pot of tea as you came in."

"Thank you, ma'am. That would be welcome."

"Oh, Malila?"

Malila, dressed in one of Sally's altered gowns, a green ribbon sweeping her longer hair into a ponytail to reveal the smooth curve of her neck, made her entrance. Sally had made her practice. Carrying a tray of hot tea and cookies, Malila negotiated the narrow passageway, deposited said tray on the indicated table, breathed, and looked at her guest.

"Since we all met at association, I guess I don't need to introduce you two," said Sally, indicating a seat for Malila near him.

"Thank you, Mrs. Stewert. Miss Chiu was kind enough to share a dance or two with me."

"I understand you are studying to enter university soon, Mr. Billings?" Sally asked, pouring out for them all.

"Yes, ma'am. I expect to take courses during the summer semester and matriculate next September at University of Kentucky."

"Very commendable. What is your area of study then, Mr. Billings? I am sure Miss Chiu … Malila would be fascinated to know."

Turning to Malila, Eduard continued, "Right now I am taking courses that will get me into college: differential calculus, matrix algebra, and network fabricational analysis. To be frank, my high-school career was not designed to impress. My father says I need to show I can do the work before he's going to waste college on me."

Eduard laughed. His mirth mystified Malila even after Sally laughed and she followed suit.

"It is a great honor, no doubt, to be chosen to enter the academic guild, Mr. Billings. How do you plan to choose your new professors?" Malila asked.

"Ah, Miss Chiu … Malila. Call me Eduard, please! It doesn't quite work that way in America. Higher learning is not so unified. Some schools seem to be better at one thing than another. Their own faculties set most of the standards.

"I suppose if we have a unifying concept, however, it is the Scholastic Protocol. Before starting school, students agree to return ten years after they leave, whether they graduate or not. They report back the courses, concepts, or anything that helped or hurt them in the real world.

"But to answer you, my classes are chosen for me by the professors, depending on my deficiencies and aptitudes. I don't get a say first year. The faculty have got some skin in the game, you see. How successful I am will be used to decide whether they, the professors, gain tenure or not. What are the schools like in the Unity, Malila? Is it very different?"

"I never went to academic guild schools, of course, but friends of mine have. 'Examinations, of any sort, are an artificial measure.' Or so I am told. They spend a lot of time doing evaluations. They say it is *brutal*."

"Yes, sounds serious. What do they study?"

Feeling a little haunted by her ignorance, Malila forged on. "Let me see: Theoretical Literary Criticism, Effective Altruism, and Universal Toleration. Those I remember. Most of their time is spent in study groups, looking at old student evaluations, so they can avoid the bad professors."

Eduard laughed … until he saw that Malila was not.

"It may seem funny to you, but it works. Our universities are the best in the world," Malila countered.

After several seconds of silence, Eduard replied, "Ah, yes, I see. As you say, Malila."

Despite the flaccid response, Malila realized she had lost the exchange. The neglected conversation wandered off into discussions of the weather and the likelihood of an early spring and stayed there, unmolested by controversy.

Malila heard a noise that might have been Ethan, popped up in relief, and moved toward the door.

Eduard rose as well, a short second later. "I believe I must be going as well, Mrs. Stewert. I need to return the horse and start my studies before it gets dark. Miss Malila, it has been a great pleasure and very informative," he said as he gathered up his things.

Sally rose, turned, and said, "I'll get Ethan, Malila. Good day to you, Eduard, and remember me to your family. Malila, honey, would you see our guest out for me?" Then she evaporated.

Malila dangled, like a foot-shackled bird near an open window. This first assay into society had been an obvious failure. Eduard must think her stupid, feral, or desperately ignorant. With Sally gone, Malila thanked Eduard for the kindness of his visit and showed him out, in misery.

As she was opening the door for him, an odd gust of cold wind plucked it out of her fingers. Malila made an awkward grab for the door to prevent it from banging against the house. She was startled as her hand closed on Eduard's hand instead of the door.

His touch was electric. She turned to look into Eduard's open dark eyes, mere centimeters away. Malila kissed him full on the lips before she snatched her hand back and disappeared inside, letting her liquid laughter linger in the cold air to inform him he had been dismissed.

Eduard did not stay dismissed for long. With the coming weeks and his continued visits, Malila learned a great deal about the outlands in general and about Eduard Billings in particular. In the Unity, Eduard would be an E13 and, with his learning and charm, an S21 at the very least. He would command troops, direct plays, lecture to students, or be a vital part of government. Instead, he still lived with his breeder parents. He didn't *seem* submissive.

Malila had never had a lover her own age, which was not uncommon for DUFS officers, as her immediate age group comprised her most determined competitors. Malila was on untrodden ground with Master Billings.

Sally, for her part, was a dutiful chaperone. After weeks of good behavior and as a sign of favor, Malila had been allowed to accompany Master Billings, alone, to his horse on leaving.

"Eduard, I have noticed something."

"Have you?" A kiss prevented further discussion for a time.

"Your horse seems to be stabled farther and farther from the door each time you visit."

"Really? How odd."

They shared whispered conferences, warm kisses, and increasing intimacies. Malila found Eduard, although enthusiastic, also hesitant; it charmed her further. After months without any pleasure-sex, Malila was delighted with Eduard's eagerness. Understanding her newly minted fertility, however, Malila was unwilling to let things proceed too far. His naïveté allowed her to maneuver the intimacies as she wished. She was, all in all, having a delightful time with Master Eduard Billings.

"So if I get this right, the day you turn forty you retire, but your friends never see you again. You go to a retirement home?" Xavier Delarosa asked on one of his visits.

"You make it sound so grim! They have their own villages and their own elected council. There they have their own lives. People send a few messages, but then they get interested in their new lives, and those peter out. They are *old*, after all. They lose touch with the world, and of course, they can't vote on things, not really, so they have no reason to follow the news," explained Malila.

"But could you go to visit them?" asked Delarosa.

"Who would want that, Captain? You have a cruel streak. The Sisi would see how bad they looked compared to ... people, and the citizens would have to look at them, smell them ... talk to them?"

"Can you imagine Jesse in one of your retirement centers?" Delarosa asked after a second.

"He is different, isn't he? That is what Sally says."

"More than you can guess, but that reminds me of a story."

Like most of Delarosa's random discussions, this one led to an odd destination.

"A great empress ordered her favorite general to oversee a new country she had conquered. Rumors of corruption and abuse drifted back to her, and she went on a tour of inspection. She found neat villages with well-fed, industrious, and grateful peasants wherever the general took her."

"So the stories were false."

"Unfortunately, the stories were true enough. General Potemkin had built model villages to hide the real misery and just showed his sovereign what he wanted her to see."

"He betrayed her? How horrible!"

"Yes, but I wonder. I wonder if the empress wanted to be fooled. She was a pretty sharp dealer. She should have been able to see around the corners. It was easier and more pleasant for her to declare herself satisfied and let history blame Potemkin. I wonder who the real villain was."

From there the conversation went on to the history of empires, the rise of democracies and their falls, and Malila's thoughts on where Sally got her cookie recipes.

Weeks of winter passed rapidly, despite the sameness of the cold, gray days. Clear, frigid nights tempted Malila to stand away from the lights and to watch the sky with its curtain of glittering colored gems until she was chilled and shivering. She found she was effortlessly conscious of the waxing and waning moon, silver against the dense sable screen of night. The Unity was warmer, but she seldom had seen the stars there. And the sky there was never like this.

CHAPTER 45

TRAVELER'S PORTION

Friday, late in the dark of an evening, Malila heard a knock on the door of the Stewerts' homestead. Snow swirled in as Moses opened it.

"Greetings, neighbor. It is a cold, harsh night, and I claim the traveler's portion," came a booming voice from the dark.

Moses's laughter followed him out the door as he went to livery Jesse's animal.

By the time the two returned, Sally had a plate out of the oven for the old man. The four of them sat around the kitchen table, talking as the old man neatly consumed his pot roast, sweet potatoes, and sauerkraut with unconcealed enthusiasm.

By the time Jesse had finished off a slice of pumpkin pie, Sally, her arm around Moses, announced they were going to bed.

Their bedroom door closed with a thump and a brief feminine shriek, leaving Malila and Jesse standing by the front door.

"Ethan will be up soon. I ought to get some sleep."

"I need to get some sleep too. I'm staying in the bunkhouse … It's in the stable."

"I know, Jesse. I sleep in the loft. Will you be warm enough? It is bitter out there."

"Oh, I think so, my friend. Not as cozy without a girl for company, 'course."

"Jesse! What would Sally think?" she said before lightly placing a hand on his. "I'll bring you out a quilt."

"Not to worry. I'll be fine."

Malila kissed him good night. It disturbed her to close the door on him.

By next morning, she was indeed up early with Ethan's demands. After sorting him out, the smell of fresh coffee in the darkened house drew her into the kitchen. In shirtsleeves, wool pants, and thick socks, his boots dripping on the rack near the stove, Jesse sat at the large round table, sipping from a chipped mug and reading a small book by the light of a dim lamp.

"Good morning, my friend, want a cup?" he asked, raising the mug in salute.

"Don't get up; I can get my own. You are up so early."

"I'm a light sleeper … You know that, I 'spect?"

Malila poured herself a mug and tasted it with a grimace before amending it with cream and sugar. Malila had decided she must learn to drink coffee, a wholly American beverage, but was stalking her goal with caution.

Moving to the table, Malila sat down next to the old man. The house, other than easing arthritic wooden joints with the occasional click, was quiet.

"Young Master Ethan has gotten you up early, my friend. How are you enjoying his company?"

"He is so fascinating. I've never seen a baby before, of course, but he watches me now. I think his eyes are going to be dark like Moses's, but his hair is fair like Sally's."

"Beware, my friend. I can see signs of seduction."

"Seduction?"

"*Cave infans!* Beware the babe!" Jesse said in mock alarm.

"Now you are making fun of me."

"Not at all! Name me another race of humans who can convince an otherwise rational being to feed, house, clothe, cajole, sit up nights, do trigonometry with, and otherwise tolerate them for twenty-odd years for such paltry returns in goods and services. Babies are a transcendent mystery and a perpetual snare for the unwary!"

"Ethan? He is a sweetheart."

"Too late ..."

"One would think you don't like children, Jesse."

"I dinna say I wasn't a fellow victim! I have eight children, some adopted, and they all are grown and useful people ... except for Alex, my youngest. He is a bit on the wild side. Comes of his mother dying when he was five ... No, I misspoke: it comes of his father being a grieving widower.

"He is just in college now, but I keep him on a tight rein, moneywise, and he knows I show up on the odd occasion. We shall see what becomes of him.

"I love all my children and, thank God, haven't had to bury any. They are all sweethearts, and they all had messy diapers."

"Another mystery of the outlands, I suppose," Malila said in mock seriousness.

Jesse laughed. "Is it? Do you think we have children for our own reasons? I don't think that is likely, my friend. Babes, now, have you noticed, are their own selves from almost the beginning. It's like babies command us to birth them, not the other way round, doncha see?" Jesse smiled.

"Dr. Johnstone, you are a terrible man," she said, hiding her smile behind her coffee mug.

She stood and moved to Moses's tiny office, just off the kitchen, leaving the door open, and keyed up a camera showing the interior of the milking barns. Malila watched as the ordered chaos of cows lined up for the attentions of the milking machine.

Moses stumbled in and piloted himself to the table, sitting down before opening his eyes and starting when he saw Jesse was already there.

"G'mornin', Mose! 'A little sleep, a little slumber, a little folding of your hands ...'" Jesse intoned with glee.

"Careful, old man! Ethan might wind up bunking with you!"

Malila had by then come back into the kitchen and poured Moses a mug of black coffee; he took it with both hands.

"The cows aren't getting up quite so early today," Malila said.

"Could be the cold," responded Jesse.

"They should like the cold, shouldn't they?" she asked.

Moses stopped to look at her.

"Well, I mean, I had some time, and you showed me how to use your interface, Moses. Back-bred Piedmontese, aren't they?

Moses's eyes lit up.

"They are. Come from the mountains of Northern Italy ... got here in the early twentieth century," said Jesse.

"I know," said Malila, smiling before turning back to talk to Moses.

"It was all right to do that, wasn't it? I was just looking at your breeding books. I wanted to see the original dame and sire."

"Moses tells me the whole herd is Piedmontese," inserted Jesse.

"I know, Jesse," she said. She then continued, "But why use that breed for dairy at all, when it's double-muscled?"

"For a fact, the whole herd is a myostatin-null line. The original sire was Imbutu, and the dame was India, so the same allele with both. Best to be able to breed true with my own stock." Usually so laconic, this sudden enthusiasm of Moses's almost made her laugh.

"So you don't have to buy bull-semen straws to artificially inseminate," she said.

"To keep the cows in milk," said Jesse.

"She knows," said Moses. "Sally and I are trying to be self-sufficient. Originally, the breed was kept for milk, you know."

"So the calves you cull go to meat, and the 'statin-null gene gets you top dollar," Malila finished for him. "Have you thought of breeding around the year, less likely to depress the meat market prices?"

Jesse laughed. "Mose, my friend, a month ago Malila had no idea where veal came from, and now she's giving you advice," observed Jesse, fetching him a sharp blow to his non-coffee-bearing arm from Malila.

"Heck, Jesse. I guess we just found us a girl with some country in her after all."

Moses lifted his cup in salute to Malila, who responded with the most graceful curtsy consistent with her bulky gown and her own half-filled cup.

When the two men began cooking breakfast in earnest, Malila went, now well warmed, to her loft to dress.

Throughout that winter, Jesse would make the long ride from Bath and arrive late on Friday night to claim his traveler's portion. He would stay until midafternoon on Sunday. Sally always evidenced surprise and annoyance at his appearance … and always had an extra plate in the oven for him.

Jesse, Malila noticed, made a habit of donating to Sally the "stray" ham, "fugitive" five-pound sack of sugar, or "excess" bolt of gingham that regularly and inexplicably stowed away for his weekly trip to New Carrolton.

After dinner on Saturdays, Jesse, Sally, and Moses usually sat before the fire in the big front room. After tuning up what Malila was told was a banjo, Jesse accompanied Moses as he played his guitar. Sally sometimes sang and sometimes accompanied on a violin, drab from dustings of rosin and worn from generations of fingers. The songs started out silly, with catchy lyrics and infectious tunes, but gradually changed to haunting ballads, long refrains of lost loves and last times set to tunes than made her weep.

> Jonathan Ashton, Jonathan Ashton, Jonathan Ashton was lost in the fire.
>
> It was in the year of the great conflagration; Jonathan Ashton was lost in the fire.
>
> He went for a soldier; he went for a soldier, to keep his land and his house and his wife.

> The fire it took him; the fire it took him. He left his land and gave up his life.
>
> Jonathan Ashton, he had a wee baby; his wife bore the son through the flame and the strife.
>
> His son is a grown man and fights for his own land. Jon Ashton's son has Jon Ashton's life.

Malila watched Jesse's hands as they flashed along the frets of the odd instrument. Stanza followed stanza, sad, sweet words making her nostalgic for what she did not know.

Later as they talked quietly, Malila moved to examine the old man's hands. When she touched him, Jesse looked up until their eyes met, and then he submitted. Malila wondered what he saw when he looked at her. She turned his large, compliant hand over and back, studying the blue veins that writhed just under the skin, the odd fine lines of old scars, and the long and regular fingers. They were muscular hands but lacking Moses's calluses. The old man laughed uneasily as her examination continued.

"People used to say you could read a man's past and his future by looking at his hands. I'll bet you haven't seen anyone's with more of both than this one, my friend."

Malila smiled but did not relinquish Jesse's hand.

The old man knew more about her than anyone in her life, even Hecate. He had seen her, her body, her failings, her despondency, her fears, and her meanness … and he had chosen to be her friend. And not just a friend. Where she and Jesse were going was unknown land to her, like their trek last fall, but this trip was ever so much sweeter. More than anything, the love felt right. *It felt good*.

The snowbank, in the lee of the house, kept winter long after the rest of the landscape had surrendered to the green of spring. In addition to the blue jays, cardinals, house finches, sparrows, and chickadees, now the bread crumbs summoned several kinds of yellow birds that would "see-see-see" each other away from the charity. The next week, they were gone, moving north with the sun.

Malila smiled at herself. Where before she had expended so much effort on seconds and minutes, now time inhabited the slow broadening of the days, the dance of a young infant's development, the gradual evolution of a snowbank in the lee of the house, and her growing attachment to these savages of the outlands.

CHAPTER 46

STAMPING GROUND

Eastern Kentucky, RSA
Midafternoon, April 8, 2129

Malila sat next to Sally and rocked Ethan as Moses walked alongside the wagon. The land undulated toward them at the slow pace of the horses, with its moist, fetid, fecund smell blowing from across the fields and up from every waterway. The black and white of winter had retreated with the flashing colors of strange birds and the spread of greens across the expanses, even into the ruts of the road. The sun warmed her eyelids as she dozed.

For the first time since her arrival, Malila was away from the farm, on the way to some sort of festival. The mood among the outlanders, however, was grim. It was a two days' trip to the meeting place. They would be there just three days before returning the two days home.

The light buckboard, with scant provisions and bivouac gear, was an easy load even on the unpaved and winter-rutted roads. Once they got to Worthville, however, the road was macadamized and widened. At every turn, they met another family going in the same direction and with the same somber air about them. Irrepressible children, nonetheless, orbited among the growing number of slowly moving wagons, checking in and extorting a "toll" in the form of almond "shekel" cookies baked for the purpose.

Voices were hushed and words perfunctory. Sally had Ethan to feed and the rolling household to maintain. Moses appeared distracted, almost morose. Malila was left to her own devices. Oddly, they had brought along a yearling lamb, a gorgeous and beguiling creature, pure white with a black muzzle and a tail in a constant clockwise spin. He rode inside the buckboard for the trip. At the evening's stop, Moses lifted him down, placing him in a halter before letting him graze. The wayside campsite filled up by late afternoon with other families, each with their lambs. There was little of the busy socializing that Malila had grown to expect among the outlanders.

By the second day, Malila had settled into the rhythm of a long trip. Swaying to the lurch and pull of the horses at their stolid pace, she watched as each new hill was approached, climbed, and discarded, like a passing wave. After cresting a modest rise that afternoon, she caught her first glimpse of Stamping Ground, laid out before them.

Entering the large meadow from every direction, wagons were stopped by marshals wearing red armbands. When it was their turn, they were directed west to a site near the tree line, into a spot with "Stewert, S&M, and etc." neatly printed on a lath stake.

The next several hours were spent making the site a comfortable, if simple, encampment. Moses erected tents for himself and Sally, for Ethan and Malila, and another for cooking. Tent sites were designated for Captain Delarosa and Jesse, whenever they would arrive. Throughout that afternoon, the subdued gathering of outlanders swelled until the huge area was filled except for broad avenues left for travel, fresh privies, and water stations for each section of tents. A large wooden cross stood in the east with a purple sash draped around it.

The initial novelty having rubbed off on the hard seat, Malila was glad to stop traveling. As instructed, she led the lamb on a tether to a lath enclosure, up a somewhat-muddy footpath to the graveled main road.

The attendant, a woman near her own age and solemn like all the outlanders she had met the last few days, took the lamb and placed it in a stall. With the now-unneeded tether, Malila was handed the receipt, a short section of lath dyed crimson with a number burned into it, without any additional words.

As she retraced her steps, Malila noted how good she felt. She had enjoyed being on the road again. It reminded her of the trek with Jesse. As difficult as that had been, the pleasure of discovering each new valley and river was like one of Jesse's poems: dramatic, cadenced, and memorable.

The woods, so monochromatic during the snows of winter, appeared indistinct, almost frothy, in the green waves that swept over them. Brassy green, yellow green, the purple red of small trees, and the wispy white smoke of others alternated with each new vista. Up higher on the hills she could see dark greens and impossibly vivid masses of scarlet flowers. The outlands seethed with new life.

She was looking forward to this gathering, whatever it was. Sally called it the Return. Like much of what she had seen in the outlands over the last four months, the name was at once prosaic and opaque. Several days of meeting new faces and enjoying new experiences would be a treat after being on an isolated farm for the entire winter.

And then she recognized one more reason she felt so good. The background hum from her O-A had actually vanished. It had been there since that terrible night while she'd awaited her fate in the dark prison cell at the Battry. Ever since then, the dull visceral hum had been a part of each waking moment, at times an aching reminder of her loss. She had eventually been able to ignore it. People could get used to anything, Jesse had told her once. And now it was gone. She felt buoyant, uplifted, and a little homesick. The hum, when she thought of it, was the last vestige of her belonging to the Unity. She was now, well and truly, abandoned to the lands beyond the Rampart.

Instead of the usual pleasant dinner conversation, they ate their evening meal in silence. Malila, Xavier, Moses, and Sally all sat down to a rather parsimonious meal of flatbread, cheese, and dried fruit. Today

Moses extended the usual prayer aloud and made some reference to "passion," confusing Malila even more. Sally had made a point that sexual encounters among outlanders were discouraged unless the partners were registered with the association.

Moses and Xavier lost the toss for kitchen duty, and Malila, tired from the journey, was asleep before Ethan.

Next morning, the somber atmosphere of the encampment continued. Malila sought some relief from it by playing with Ethan as he endeavored to roll over. Numerous attempts involving a chubby leg waving tentatively in the air ended in failure. Finally, with a little more arching of his back and a sudden revolution, he triumphed. Ethan's worried look of surprise changed to a grin and a shriek of laughter when Malila applauded.

"Is that my grandbaby? What a darling! He looks just like you when you were his age."

A woman, taller but very much built along the same lines as Sally, bustled in through the open tent flap, trailing a beaming Sally. Malila suppressed an impulse to salute.

She was dressed in a dark, rather plain dress with a high collar but wore pointy-toed tooled leather boots that came to her midcalf. The older woman's chestnut hair, streaked with silver, was caught up into a loose bun, held in place by a leather band and secured by a wooden pin.

"You must be Malila. Pleased to meet you, honey. I'm Sally's ma. I live way over in Campton in Wolfe County with my new mister. Sally's dad was killed almost eight years ago now. 'Till death do us part' and all. I knew Sally'd make a wonderful mother. She has been singing you to high heaven all morning. I just had to meet you. I'm Tabitha, but call me Tabbie; everyone does."

Her monologue continued, leaving Malila feeling winded. By the time Tabbie had finished, she was in possession of the best seat, a mug of hot tea with "a splash of milk and one-and-a-half sugars" in it, and Ethan.

Sally beamed as she watched her son's initial uncertainty dissolve into happy acceptance of his grandmother. By the time Ethan had circled around to Malila again, he was ready for a nap. She put him down into his travel crib, all carefully supervised by Tabbie.

"Has Malila earned her woman's mark yet, Sally?" Tabbie asked.

Sally smiled. "Just the other day. Ethan turned four months old the beginning of the month, and he was seven days old when Malila came to stay."

"Have you chosen a pattern yet? This will be your first one, won't it? You must give some thought to the pattern, honey."

Sally pulled out a page of brown paper with dark marks on it. "Of course I have. I thought I would use a daisy at the end."

"Yes, a finial. A daisy is a good choice, especially for a woman's mark. I like that. Now you can do a wreath, as Ethan was born so close to the Coming. Nancy Burton in McAfee, she does a snake with its tail in its mouth. There are all kinds of basic shapes, you know, hun."

"I wanted to keep the vine, so's people can realize the connection between us."

The older woman paused to look at her daughter and smiled. "That is sweet, Sally. Your father would have liked that."

Shaking her head slightly, Tabbie continued, "Now we have to add the ousqua[10], the moon cycles, and the vines."

The two women huddled over the paper adding and subtracting for hours, while Malila watched from a distance with growing uncertainty.

Finally, Sally gave her approval, and Malila was allowed to see the final design: graceful lines and crescent moons disguised as the leaves of a sinuous vine terminated in a seven-petaled daisy. It was primitive and elegant in its own way with lines dividing and rejoining in a complicated dance that made the drawing seem to writhe on the paper.

"What do you do, now that you have a design?" Malila asked.

"Stay right here. I've my needles in my bag, and we can sterilize them right here," said Tabbie as she started to rise.

"I don't know about this," Malila said, her uncertainty finally bearing fruit.

"Oh, Malila, child, everyone thinks the pain is too much ... but

[10] A traditional tattoo design borrowed from the Cherokee after the Meltdown.

if you don't want to, we don't have to. There will be other times and other association meetings. Not to worry."

Tabbie turned and talked animatedly to Sally about her new farm and the husband she had to run it for her.

Malila watched Ethan as he slept. It was not the pain … she didn't think. It was the idea of leaving forever the anonymity of the Unity. She would be a marked woman … literally. She shivered.

Ethan embodied, in his small form, everything she longed for in the Unity. Ethan, given protection, love, and care, would grow and thrive. His laugh, like the first quizzical grimace he had shared with her on her arrival, was now a part of her. His changing form, his imperfections, his gestures, his smell … all of it was already indelible. She would be grafted to his life and he to hers whether marked or not.

In the end, she asked Tabbie to ink her and watched an awakened Ethan playing with Sally during the ordeal. It helped. He made sense of it for her.

CHAPTER 47

PING

Nyork, Unity
16.03.12.local_08_04_AU77

A signal—a short, imperative machine command monotonously identical to all the other signals sent from the transmitter over the last twenty-six weeks—was sent. Unique to the prior episodes, the apparatus received an answering affirmative and a short data stream. Chiu, Malila Evanova, number 59026169, was found.

BethanE Winters, graduate student in modern philosophical literature at Columbia's University of the People, pulled back from the dense work of tracking down a metaphor that had gone rogue on her. It had disappeared somewhere around AU 15 when it had ducked behind a rampaging trope. This was hard work just to add a small footnote.

Feck it and go to bed, she thought ... until she remembered the data dump from old Swartzbender still needed to be evaluated.

That was so unfair; none of the other grad students had to do it. It might even be illegal … impersonating another user, but it was only three minutes of her life every day.

BethanE quested the address with a sigh and slumped into the seat to start her analysis.

She was almost done with the string analysis for that day when she saw it. There was the odd string. She quested the original data to verify it. To what was the data attached? She was smart enough to know, if Swartzbender was not, that this was a real-world application invading her scholastic world.

It meant her thesis was accepted.

The good thing about academia was that it was inside work with no heavy lifting. She set the flag in the CORE as instructed … no heavy lifting.

In a swirling, distant portion of an n-dimensional nonreality called the CORE, the dissipating personality of a never-to-be-realized sports phenomenon waited. With rapt attention, Charlie watched a flag. In what was left of his mind, instead of the usual puzzles about picking apart the intrigues of a backfield in his usual quest to dismantle a quarterback, Charlie was in fear for his life. Failure meant death. His swirling thoughts centered on reporting a change in a single CORE processor flag. It was so important. Then he could go home.

"… *00000000000000000000000000000000* …"

The Presence had not been there in a long time … such a long time.

He was falling again. He could hear the phantoms coming to eat his pink writhing guts.

If he looked around he would see them, but he would not.

I veha ot atwhc!

Wrong, I got it wrong again.

I.have.to.watch!

But then!

eTehr wsa hte anigls: "... 0000000000000001111111 1111111111 ..."

Panicked, in case he was too slow, he slapped the signal alarm, hearing the reassuring sound—just as the silver thread of his life was severed.

Sacrifices had been made.

"This is coming direct from Major Gurion?"

"Exactly, Master Sergeant. Going to mess up your weekend?"

"Yes, sir. I mean, no, sir! It is just so ... unusual. Unsupported intrusion into the outlands on such short notice ... sir," said Master Sergeant Beyer.

"Surprised me too, actually, Sarge," replied Lieutenant Cooper.

"Will the target be able to tell we're coming? It'd be easier for us if she breaks away before they sight us. With those savages, you never know what they might do. I would hate to lose her just as we got close."

"Well, Sarge, what the tech guys tell me is that her O-A, when it has no signal, upregulates the gain, 'looking' for a carrier wave. That might give her a bit of a hum. Once the carrier wave is detected, it downregulates, and she won't hear the hum anymore."

"Doesn't sound like we can count on that," replied the sergeant. "We got to go in expecting to break her out of some jail cell? Have we got the munitions for that?"

"I agree. We will have some satchels of C24 and some demo guys with us but still just a squad, just the one skimmer. Quick and fast."

"What if that isn't enough? We can't have a knock-'em-down-tear-'em-up fight with no artillery or tactical air."

"Absolutely, this is a smash and grab. If she's not where we can find her, she's too hard to break out, we lose her signal, or we have a lot of opposition, then we cut and run. Understand?"

"What if she's turned traitor?"

"She comes back, in as many pieces as convenient for storage."

CHAPTER 48

THE RETURN

Stamping Ground, Kentucky
Almost dawn, April 10, 2019

Malila slept poorly, finding it difficult to get comfortable on the cot. Slumber had found her when the sounds of the campground had subsided into that odd muffled racket of a large number of people all trying to be quiet at the same time: hushed whispers, the rare clank, followed by louder shushing, and the occasional toddler asking, in a high, loud, and clear voice, "Why do I have to be quiet?"

It was still dark when Sally jostled Malila's shoulder to wake her.

"Malila, honey, we are going to the Sunrise. You don't have to, but we would love for you to come with us. You don't have to get dressed up; just dress warm," Sally whispered.

Malila nodded and put a hand down to Ethan's crib next to her. He slept through the night now, only to awaken each morning soaking wet and acting starved by the callous disregard of his keepers. Dressing them both quickly and wrapping Ethan in the thick new quilt from Tabbie, Malila carried him out into the brisk morning. The light tingeing the east was just enough to render the sky an endless cobalt. The high waning moon added a silver touch to the shadows of the encampment. Everyone was up. Despite the cold and the dark, Jesse caught her eye and gave her one of his brilliant smiles. He was such an unapologetic early riser.

Within a few minutes, he, Sally, Moses, Xavier, and Malila with Ethan had gained the raised gravel path running through the camp. Most people were already up and moving. Small gleams of yellow light flickered and moved within the city of tents as dark shapes revealed and eclipsed other lights, all moving toward the east.

Following the crowd, they entered the greening wood before reaching an amphitheater-like space. The sky above was now like a translucent screen, the bright blaze of Venus being the last light to succumb to the advancing day. They found a place out of the flow of arriving humanity. Malila heard snatches of song move through the crowd as it swelled. Everyone faced east toward the line of the woods and the increasing brightness of the rising sun.

> Low in the grave he lay, Jesus my savior,
>
> Waiting the coming day, Jesus my Lord.

The song rumbled within her from Moses's dependable bass. Sally's bright soprano superimposed on the groundswell of song. As Malila was trying to decipher the words, the sun slipped over the horizon and set the glade ablaze in a verdant glow.

> He 'rose a victor from the dark domain.

Song after song followed, all with the same theme. The people were all celebrating again as they had at the Coming. Most everyone knew the words, and many people sang parts, reverberating bass notes lifting up the bright melodies of the altos and sopranos. Once it had grown light enough, Malila glimpsed in the woods before them a large wooden cross, veiled by the new spring growth.

When the sun was fully up, filling the glade with warmth, light, and small insects, the crowd dismissed itself to an early breakfast.

This, Malila knew, was just a prelude. The main meal of the day was after the preaching, in the early afternoon. The guest of honor at that feast was roast lamb, larded with garlic, rosemary, and thyme, major deities in the pantheon of masculine cookery.

Sally came by and relieved Malila of a fussy Ethan.

"Malila, honey, I hope you enjoyed this. We try to come every year. The Return is so special to Moses and me. We are going to go have breakfast with Tabbie. I'm sure she would love to have you join us, but don't feel as if you have to come. Most everyone will offer you a bite to eat. We all make much too much as a rule, just in case Elijah comes. We'll be getting back to the campsite by midmorning. Moses has to take his turn looking after the lamb. Enjoy yourself, honey. He is risen!"

Malila knew she bumbled the expected response. A sunrise ceremony seemed appropriately primitive for the outlanders, but the ceremony hadn't been anything she'd expected. It had been much more personal, in a way. The Return was not about the return of the light from the darkness, order from chaos, or even good from evil. It was the remembrance of a single man who, at the same time, was the child that had arrived at the Coming. For unknown reasons, she was elated.

The grimness of the slow travel and the somber campground had given no hint of the jubilation this morning. Energized, children raced up and down the happy, noisy columns leading away from the glade. Different groups called back the same greeting and response about rising, which was odd. Everyone was awake already, or should have been with all the noise.

Allowing the crowds to move ahead of her, Malila tried to sort out the events of the morning. A smiling girl, one near her own age, pressed a warm, sweet roll into her hand as she passed. Malila nibbled and wandered on even as the crowds thinned out, the trail becoming winding, dark, and isolated.

"Malila! Hold up, Malila," a voice called out, startling her.

Surprise still tingled within her by the time Eduard trotted up, his face flushed and smiling.

"Eduard, I didn't know you were here!" she said, weaving her arm through his.

"I saw Moses at the Sunrise, and he told me you were coming this way. I've been tied up since we got here with doing errands for my parents. They always find something for me to do. I've had no time to see my friends and ... I had no time to find you!"

"I've been busy too. This is the first time I've been free."

Eduard leaned in to give Malila a kiss, and she circled his waist to make the embrace last longer ... and give him promise of further warmth to come. Eduard responded, pulling her closer in turn and reaching under her coat to run his hands over her flanks. Malila was surprised. Eduard's shy ardor had always been perversely exciting to Malila, but she hesitated to encourage him where anyone might see. Without thinking, she stiffened in his embrace and pulled away. Eduard's confusion was evident. His face flushed, and he moved toward her, grasping her wrist and bringing his other hand up to cup her breast.

Malila gasped in pain. Her new tattoo was painful enough; Eduard's clumsy grip was an unwelcome surprise. In the Unity, pleasure-sex was a well-rehearsed ballet of word, gesture, and countergesture. Unprepared for his advances, Malila lashed out with a knee almost without thinking. Her aim was a little off, but Eduard released her. They were still standing, panting at each other, as a noisy group of people swept around the bend and encircled them.

A look of dismay swept across Eduard's face; Malila was grateful. Their private sparring would be in recess, at least for a while. She turned from him and extended a hand to the young man who seemed to be the leader. The boy looked briefly down at Malila's extended hand before ignoring it.

"Hey, Eddie, is this your pet Uni you've been bragging about?" he asked, apparently a signal that set the crowd to smirks and giggles.

Eduard was silent. A girl with an indifferent complexion chimed in, "Eddie has to find a Uni prisoner to get what no one else wants to give him … Is that it, Eddie boy?"

Malila suddenly grasped she had fallen into mysterious dark waters with ominous predatory shapes circling her. She was unable to get a word in as catcalls and insults orbited them. The group started to move on when she did not respond. A sullen girl elbowed her as the group passed, now with Eduard in tow. He looked back at her, lost in the whirlpool, drowning out of sight of land, as the crowd turned along the wooded path.

For the moment, Malila was alone. She readjusted her clothes, trying to reduce the burning sensation of her new tattoo. Wanting to think without being found by Eduard or his friends, she moved to put some distance between herself and their possible return.

A narrow path promised access to the top of a hill. Malila stepped off onto it, surrounding herself at once with the fresh green of the forest, birdcalls, and the rustling wind in the branches overhead. Picking her way up to the top, she found a small, close clearing with a downed hickory log on one side. Ignoring the dampness of the wood, she sat.

She had expected better of the outlanders. That by itself was irritating. She had been seduced into an acceptance of these barbarians, not as her equals but, in a way, her superiors. The few people she really knew had treated her with forbearance and affection and, in Jesse's case, with mercy. Eduard had wanted her, but now he didn't. Not enough.

To survive in the Unity was to have no expectations whatever. A single failure left you at the mercy of others. Hopes were an outlander luxury in a land with no luxuries. And luxuries must be paid for. A promise of pleasure might deliver a blow of unexpected pain. But hopes, even if they failed, allowed you to go on from day to day.

She heard a short cough in the underbrush along the trail she had just used. The man's approach had been silent until then. Malila, occupied with her problems, only noticed when it was too late to escape. She rose to face this new intrusion.

Jesse's smile preceded him into the clearing through the verdant new growth.

"You have been following me," Malila accused rather than asked.

"Guilty as charged. I was following Eduard, but I thought he was following you. It looked to me that you might need a friend. Those kids can be harsh at times. They are good people, as a rule, but I don't think they quite know what to do with you, my friend. They don't understand your exceptionally charming qualities as well as some of us."

Despite herself, Malila smiled.

"What did you think of the Sunrise service, my friend?" asked Jesse, changing the subject as he approached.

"I liked it, but it confused me too. This is the same guy who was born at Christmas?"

"The very one ... but we celebrate what he did for us, not so much the calendar days."

"Everyone was so gloomy on the way here, as if they were waiting for the sun this morning, and now everyone is celebrating."

"Right, the sad part is remembering his dying ... and our failures ... and the joyful part is when we realize that he kept his promises. The sun rising, doncha see, is the start of the third day. That was when they could first see he wasna dead."

"Oh, so some sort of miracle-like."

"Something like that, lass."

"Don't call me 'lass.'"

"Yes, my friend. I am sorry. I forgot, Malila," Jesse replied as he always did when she objected. He never seemed to remember for long, and he never seemed to be any less sincere when she confronted him about it.

Jesse walked closer and, shooing her over a little, sat next to her. In that following silence, Malila picked up the old man's hand, comparing her hand to his, tracing the blue veins and the thin scars. She wondered, not for the first time, how the thin white lines of the collected scars somehow wrote the history of a life still mostly hidden to her.

Malila, turning his hand over and back, leaning into the solidity of

Jesse's body, remembered seeing him from their trek: pale except for his face and hands, blue from the tattoos, more substantial and more real, in a way, than her own flesh. She remembered her submission and Jesse's rejection and was surprised when that eddy of emotion pulled her into a larger vortex of regret. Tears blurred her vision, the closeness of him, his scent, reminding her again how isolated she really was. She turned to him and wept, feeling his strength even before she felt his arms enfold her.

Once again, she thought of the soft-bodied woman of her distant past. This time, in her distress, she remembered something more, the scent of lavender deep within the folds of the woman's dresses when she embraced Malila in the small dramas of childhood. Like a neglected box of broken images dumped from darkness into a pool of light, the scent unfolded forgotten memories: kisses and caresses, hummed songs, rag dolls, and a fierceness of love given and received. The passion of her now-remembered love itself folded out to her an even greater landscape of remembrances: the woman was her mother, the tall man with spectacles, her father, and the great sorrow of her life was their clapboard house disappearing as she watched through the rear window of her abductors' skimmer. She looked up.

"Hush, hush, lass. Everything will come around all right in the end. You have people who love you," said Jesse.

Malila gathered she had been hearing Jesse cycling through these consolations as she wept, his rumbling words comforting without her understanding. Malila pulled back and watched Jesse's face for a moment and then climbed, childlike, into the safety of his lap, clinging to him and clutching his hand between her warm breasts.

Jesse turned her face up to his as a flicker of the sunlight broke through the light canopy of foliage. Malila closed her eyes against the glare, sending arcs of light from tears along her eyelashes. She smiled to be so entirely consoled by Jesse's now-tender touch. Warm lips pressed hers, and Malila sensed herself surge upward with her own desires into Jesse's embrace. Her hands moved to caress his face and run fingers through his hair, loosing it to curtain around them as they kissed, closing out the world. She felt Jesse's warm hands now move, caressing her in turn, his hands adoring her. Malila sensed another unfolding of love and assurance in his embrace, a coming home to a place she had never imagined.

The obstacles slid away in an instant. The gentle, graceful hands, sweeping aside her clothes to press her flesh closer, called forth passion and a fullness of heart, a desire to give him her love.

"Jesse, why now? I thought we'd never ..."

"Ah suppose we had ta be friends foremost. Dae ye ken how lang i've loved ye, lass? Ah hae sin ye bolted off inta th' snow. Ah admired ye, afore. Ah want'd ye afore... bit thay wur ill times fur us both," he said, looking away, his hands still warm on her smooth flesh.

Malila caressed his rough cheek with her hand, pulling him back into a long kiss and a deep caress. A tide of pleasure and desire surged within her until Jesse sat up, breaking the spell. She almost shrieked with frustration.

"It's all right, Jesse. No one can find us here! Father me, you feel good!"

Jesse's hands stilled. Malila hoped her words had not put him off.

"Malila, love, we should stop ... for now. Ah dinna just want to keep wi' ye; a'm wantin' marrying wi' ye, my love. That is, if ye are willin'?"

A chill, a confusion, spread through Malila as she tried to parse the foreign sentiments.

"You want me only with Mary Eng? I didn't know that was something you wanted, Jesse."

"More than anythin', my love," he said with adolescent enthusiasm.

Malila grasped Jesse's warm hands and moved them over her smooth flesh, trying to recapture the ardor of but a few moments before.

"Jesse, this feels like I belong, like we belong. I have never met someone that makes me feel like this. Open to you, safe, hungry for you. If that's what you want ... Does that mean we can stay together?"

"For a lifetime! For longer than ye ken, my love!"

Jesse smiled at her, his encircling arms pulling her closer still.

Malila's doubts about the arrangement were subsiding when Jesse continued, "We'd hav' ta git a waiver from th' association, of course. I dinna want anyone ta think worse o' us for this."

Malila's heart fell. Why should anyone think badly of her unless Jesse was hiding something? She imagined his mask falling away. The faithful, kind, and unfailing facade was cracking to reveal a barbarian who was going to use her love to enslave her, to add her to a harem of women. If he could ask her to share him with Mary, why not any number of women?

"Jesse, slow down. I need some time to think, to talk with Sally, with Xavier. You are confusing me."

"I'd ask yer father, of course, if he wur here. Maybe Moses wid step in ..."

Moses? Step in and betray Sally? Even in the Unity, patrons had the integrity not to share protégés. Nothing was as it seemed or should be. Even Jesse, the man ... the man she knew ... the man she had lived with ... cried with ... the man she thought she loved! Malila's resolve crystalized in an instant.

"No, I see. Father you too, then, and Mary as well!"

Malila leaped away from him and stormed into the forest, ignoring any footpath before Jesse could react.

That went well, didn't it, you old fool?

I don't understand what happened.

You tried to make an honest woman of her. She woke up to what a worn-out bit of gristle you are.

It had been a mistake to propose to her; he had let himself believe, imagining himself bringing her home as a new bride. Now he had lost her completely.

Jesse turned away from where Malila had left the clearing. He stomped up a small ridge east as it rose to an adjacent hill through the spring foliage, looking to exhaust himself before returning to camp. He'd come back during the preachings, pack his gear, and leave. It would be easier for her ... for him.

Malila could be such a porcupine, prickly coming from any

direction, but he had been naive to think she had any affection for him, of course.

"Damned old fool is you," he said to the wind … just before it replied with the faint crack of pulse weapons and a ragged volley of projectile rifles.

CHAPTER 49

UNITY

"Can I warm that up for you, Xavier?" asked Sally.

It was a lovely morning, reminding her of the Returns of her childhood. Beyond the bustle of believers, the greens of the woods displayed their colors: the almost yellow green of new hickory, the bronze greens of oaks, and the dark contrasting greens of the pines, their branches slowly shouldering back from the snowy burdens of winter. All across the verge of the large meadow, the boughs of red-purple redbuds thrust into the light, while back into the woods, as if shy, contrasting wisps of white dogwood spotted the scene.

Xavier, from his seat by the warm fire, idly turned the lamb on a spit, making the air redolent with its smells and masking the earthy scents of the woods.

"Thank you, my love." He smiled as his cup was filled.

At breakfast Sally had finally met her mother's new husband, a talkative mountain of a man. The two made a good couple; her father would rest easy. In addition, that extended breakfast should keep the men from sampling the roast for a while, until after the preachings. It was an entirely satisfactory day.

"How did you like the Sunrise service, Xav?" she asked.

"It's quite a moving service in its way. Of course, I'm used to something a bit different. Always good to be among believers, though. I got quite a kick out of it," he said with a grin.

Malila burst from the tree line, dodged a dog, and stormed onto the light. Malila hesitated, taking a heading on Sally, and marched a determined path toward her. Sally noticed her high color and a misbuttoned shirt.

Malila sat down without salutation, rose, went into her tent, returned, poured a cup of coffee, sipped it, threw the rest onto the ground, sat down, and finally rose again.

"Something bothering you, honey?" asked Sally.

"Nothing."

"If you want to talk, we can ..." started Sally.

"Nothing's wrong!"

After a few minutes, Malila again entered her tent and emerged with a bundle wrapped in a bit of homespun. Walking over to Moses, she solemnly placed the object into his hands.

"Mr. Stewert, please give this back to Dr. Johnstone. He'll understand. I never want to see him again, and this is his."

She turned and sat dry-eyed by the fire. Moses, looking over the fire to Sally, asked a silent question. Sally shrugged, even as she thought, *it's finally happened between them.*

They all heard the low-pitched whine of the skimmer before the ominous black shape swept out of the shadows and crested the hills into Stamping Ground.

Moses bolted for the tent and returned with his rifle and Ethan. He scooped the baby into Sally's arms, and Sally ran for the woods. *It's happening again,* she thought.

"Malila! Run. Now, do it now!" Xavier yelled, using his command voice.

As she was running, Sally heard the skimmer drive whine to a higher pitch and felt the thump of its arrival. Looking over her shoulder, she stumbled. The black skimmer had landed between Moses and the tree line.

Making it to the brush near the verge, she crouched and looked back. In the distance, she could see simultaneous surges in the crowded meadow. Women with children streamed away from the skimmers as all others, men, women, large girls, and boys, raced forward, the sun occasionally gleaming off gunmetal.

The skimmer ramp crashed down. Oddly gaited troopers emerged, firing and crouching, providing cover for the soldiers behind them. Off in the distance, Sally saw Malila turn as a bolt took Xavier in the back. For a moment, Malila froze. A trooper approached and swung his weapon to club her to the ground. It did not connect. Malila ducked under the blow and kicked hard at the black horror's knee. He went down in a heap, and she grabbed his rifle, swinging it into the gut of the next horror and folding him up. A pulse bolt erupted at her feet, and Malila ran toward the shooter. It was too far. Sally watched as the soldier aimed the killing shot at her.

The soldier's chest erupted in a pink mist.

The report of the rifle made her jump. She looked over to see Moses kneeling, his old rifle still smoking.

Moses stood and stepped back, stumbled, and looked down, his feet inside the fire ring.

There was a flash, and Moses fell, a foot still dangling over the coals near the roast lamb.

CHAPTER 50

INTRODUCTIONS

Unity
Late afternoon 10_04_AU77

Malila woke as the skimmer landed, and she was lifted onto a gurney. Her images became a stop-motion kaleidoscope: rattling down a dim hallway; the harsh fluorescents strobing above; distorted faces leaning over her, prodding and asking unanswerable questions; her clothes cut off; and the cold rush of air and darkness.

She awoke, finally, in a DUFS sick bay: sterile, small, white, overwarm, shabby, smelling of cleaning solution and floor wax, not really built for people. The mattress wheezed whenever she moved, even less comfortable than a camp cot. What was new to her was a guard at the door with a sidearm. She slept and woke later to see, through the only window, the slanting sunlight on a blank redbrick wall. Her O-A still merely hummed, Edie just an echoing voice in her memory. There was no clock. Over the next two days, silent attendants saw that she ate the tasteless food, showered, changed her drafty hospital gown, and slept ... especially slept.

On the morning of the third day, a man appeared. Her mind still muzzy, Malila struggled to stand for a superior officer. The man, a light colonel, waved her back to her bed with a negligent gesture and sat himself, after a guard had brought him a chair. He watched her in silence before speaking.

"Welcome back, Lieutenant. I am Colonel Jourdaine. Consider me your rescuer from the savage captivity of the outlands," the dark-haired, placid man said in a pleasant voice.

Even though her naked feet dangled centimeters off the floor, Malila's military training clicked into place. She tried to brace up. She was home.

"Sir, yes, sir. Thank you, sir," Malila said in return.

"You are an extraordinary person. Do you know that?" the man asked.

"Sir, no, sir. I didn't know that, sir."

"In the last fifty years, Lieutenant, you are the first officer to get herself captured alive by the savages. That is quite the achievement. I want to understand how a dedicated officer of this country loses every trooper in her command, travels over seven hundred kilometers, and is rescued from an outlander festival with no injuries and no evidence of restraint. How is that possible, Lieutenant Chiu?"

"It was a trap, sir. The outlanders lured us to Sunprairie to get our new pulse rifles. They overpowered me when I was asleep and took my throat mike. They killed all my men. They got the ID chip out of the thumbs and took their index fingers at the first knuckle. A man removed my first implant, then walked me south for six weeks. I had to stay at a farm over the winter. Stamping Ground, where you found me, was the first time I had been away since December, sir."

"A nice précis, Lieutenant, but let us start from the beginning. Who is your commander?"

And thus, it started. The questions were succinct, and the answers soon became so as well. Jourdaine did not tolerate imprecision or embroidery.

Within minutes, she felt better for the telling, her words a balm to her spirit, unwinding the tatters of her life. There was some perverse satisfaction in grinding out the pain of her humiliations to this serene bland man. It was the price of readmission.

Her O-A still buzzed uncertainly.

Lieutenant Colonel Jourdaine listened to her answers without speaking. After several hours of questions, lunch arrived, and Malila ate a sandwich between words. Jourdaine sipped from a glass of water.

By the time the window was in shadow, her account sputtered, roared to full throttle on fossil memories, sputtered again, and stopped. For the last hour, she had been reciting with her eyes closed, sucked dry by her own words. Jourdaine rose and stood before her as she sat, her feet now cold and motionless above the floor.

"Rest now. We will talk tomorrow, Lieutenant," he said softly, then turned and left before she could say anything.

The door closed for just a moment before an aide came in with a pill that she dutifully swallowed. When she awoke, her breakfast had arrived. She was ravenous.

Jourdaine's vivisection of her account started that day.

"Tell me, Lieutenant, why were you sent in person to fix Sunprairie? Isn't that a job for an OAA?" Jourdaine said with no prologue.

Malila hesitated. She sensed, as she had since her rescue, as if she were sitting at the top of a high, steep, snowy slope. Her answer now would be the first step in the plunge down. She anticipated the exhilaration of her swooping descent, but she knew that, at the end, she would be in unknown country, alone. At best, she could hope to be allowed to regain the anonymity of the corps, becoming one more striving junior DUFS officer. At worst, her actions would condemn her for immediate punishment. Most likely she would still be disgraced for Sunprairie.

"Sir, I do not know what was in General Suarez's mind, sir. I can speculate that she did this as a punishment. As soon as the job was complete, I was to report for imprisonment," she answered, trying to be doggedly truthful.

"Why do you think you were being punished?" Jourdaine countered, not taking his eyes off her.

"Sir, I failed in my duty to maintain sensor station Sunprairie, in Wiscomsin, west of Lake Mishygun. I attempted to cover up my deficiency by colluding with my fellow officers. Sir!"

There was no point in withholding anything from this bland gray man. He, no doubt, knew the truth. No one else had come to rescue her.

The gray man smiled an odd smile at her answer. The questions came fast thereafter. How had she allowed her attackers to enter the station unobserved? How had it been possible for anyone to massacre her platoon and yet she remain unharmed? Why had she cooperated in the bison hunt? He referenced a small tablet but made no entries.

Her feeling of weightless descent made her giddy, exhilarated as she watched her hopes of reinstatement flash by.

Why had she not escaped from the snow cave? At the farm? On the trip to Stamping Ground? How had a single Sisi been able to keep her a captive unaided?

"Who was your captor?" Jourdaine asked, a note of interest in his voice.

"Jesse Johnstone. He claimed he was over seventy years old. He *looked* old, with white hair and a beard and everything, sir. I have no way of knowing if he was lying."

"Describe him."

"Yes, sir. He is bigger than the average Unity man, sir. Taller by maybe twenty centimeters but proportionally heftier ... muscular. He could outwalk me with a forty-kilo pack. I know at least four men he killed when they tried to take me away from him. I never got close to escaping, to tell the truth."

"I see, Lieutenant. Where was he when we recued you?"

"I don't know, sir. He never stays anywhere for long, but I think you would have known it. If Jesse thought he could do something, sir, he would have. He has fought against the Unity before."

"Interesting."

The questions multiplied.

Why had she helped the breeder? What had she told the savages?

The questions seemed to have no end.

Later, even when the colonel no longer asked her questions, other officers came to question her. The questions did not change. The one real question was not asked: Why had she fought to stay in the outlands?

At the end of her tenth day in the room, Jourdaine pronounced himself satisfied.

He stood before her, the room otherwise deserted, his voice barely above a whisper. "You will be questioned by others. I suggest you adjust your story of the colony. It seems to me that you were kept in close confinement throughout your captivity. I would correct your account to accommodate that appearance. Do you understand?"

"Sir, yes, sir!"

"It also seems that during your recapture from the savages … do you recall that, Lieutenant? There seems to have been some violence against the forces of the Unity. Do you recall that?"

"Sir, yes, sir. But …"

"It is not necessary to explain. It is not necessary to ever disclose that. Do you understand? The savages, as I can bring evidence to show, were about to club you to death. A loyal CRNA shot the barbarian before he could do you more harm, saving your life at the cost of his own. You no doubt recall it now."

Malila nodded, unable to say the words with the memory of Xavier's solemn eyes going dead.

"Good. Finally, you are to consider yourself my protégé from now on. Do you understand?"

"Yes, sir." Malila rose and untied the hospital gown, the thin cotton slipping down along her legs, making a puddle about her feet. She went through the formulaic submission and prepared herself for the man's caresses. For the first time in months, she was aware how long it had been since she had visited her company depilatorium.

"Very well, Lieutenant. Done with grace and dispatch."

In the same voice of quiet concern he said, "You are going to become a hero of the Unity shortly. Your fortitude in the face of adversity is an inspiration to us all.

"Your first implant"—he touched her scar—"is no longer functioning. That gives you certain capabilities that are … awkward.

I want you to be confident that I'll look out for your best interests, but for now you need to avoid … pleasure-sex. Understood?" Jourdaine gave her the first warm smile she had seen from him.

She nodded.

"You may dress, Lieutenant."

"Sir, yes, sir."

She stooped to retrieve her hospital gown, relieved and disappointed. By the time she stood again, Jourdaine was already leaving the room.

Before she could finish dressing, an aide entered the room with a new DUFS uniform. "Lieutenant Chiu, Malila E." was stitched over a breast pocket, and each shoulder bore the raised bar that shimmered silver as she moved it in the light. It was the insignia of a first lieutenant.

Major Khama exited the belt near his home in Pertamboy. The commute was getting worse every day. Or maybe he was just getting old. He was never going to be thirty again.

At least things were peaceful. The Blues had been out of the faction fight since 70 when he—that is, the Reds—had won big. Emanuel and Suarez had come to power and had had a field day, Sapping every commander and IT guy down to the S10 level.

Better to give than receive, he thought.

He did not have the enthusiasm for that horror now, again. It must be his age. It looked as if he could get to retirement unmolested. He had hoped for more.

Suarez had promised him a full colonelcy at one time … if she made chief of staff. It no longer looked as if that was going to happen. So close … Even so, if things started to go bad, he had been furbishing that little nook in Lynneboro Station, on the hill with the old stone farmhouse. A two-day notice to his "friends," and he would be feet up and brain in neutral, contemplating the cows, or whatever one did in rural NuAmpshur. He would be lighter by a few years' income, and they might still track his O-A. Nevertheless, he would keep it.

He trudged to his building and absentmindedly announced his floor. It took him a second to realize something was very wrong.

Rough hands snatched him out of the darkened elevator, and a hood was jammed over his head. The skimmer trip was long and anxious. Officially, Khama belonged to no faction and was under the command of a laughable incompetent, Magness. No one should think him important enough to abduct. That was how he had been so successful. No one expected anything from him, so they stood in line to use him. And he collected a toll of information with each encounter. Most did not even know they were being used.

He was escorted from the skimmer. He hoped he would not embarrass himself; he had not visited the toilet since leaving work.

The hood jerked off. Khama squinted into the blinding light.

"This the guy?"

A familiar voice said, "Yes. That's him. Leave us."

The light was moderated, and a chair was pushed into the back of his legs. He sat.

"We meet again, Major."

"General, I ..."

"... can explain? Actually, I am pretty sure you can't. So spare me the performance. There are a number of unexplained things happening. The faction needs your help."

Her subsequent words filled in a couple of uncomfortable holes in his memory and one very odd dream.

"So my setting up the auto ping was an implanted command?"

"We believe so. We just don't know who did it."

"So what can I do for the faction?"

"For now, just keep us aware. Keep a diary about every dream you have, every odd thing you do ... on paper, ink and paper. Usual precautions."

"Will you look out for me if this hits the fan?"

"Yes, and we already know about your little hideaway. If things get bad ... you commit suicide, *on us*. Then we forget your address. Lynneboro Station, wasn't it?"

"Sir, yes, sir."

Suarez motioned to the shadows, and the hood was again jammed onto his head.

CHAPTER 51

REPATRIATION

The attendants gave her a dossier containing her new orders and an entrance code. She had a week's furlough before she had to report. The guards were gone.

They escorted her to the underground foyer of the building in her new, well-fitting uniform. A private skimmer waited for her, the windows darkened. The trip lasted too long. The driver never spoke.

The entrance code belonged to an apartment across the East River from her last one, far above the distant commotion of the belts and skimmer traffic.

Malila's O-A came alive for the first time in six months as she entered.

Welcome home, Malila!

Edie, it has been so long! When I got back and you weren't here, I thought they'd taken you away from me.

That's not possible, Lieutenant Chiu. You merely needed the CORE to hear me and see me.

Where have you been for the last six months?

I've no sensation of time except in relation to you, Malila.

But Edie, there were times when I heard you, just moments.

I have no recollection of such events.

Nothing? Was I hallucinating? You told me to stop when I was trying to kill Jesse; you reminded me of the knife with Bear. At the devil's bridge ... Wasn't that you?

I remember dreams ... dreams after you were gone.

Do you remember Sally, the baby? Sally, she's the best person. I'm sure you would like her. She and Moses are so lucky to have found each other, and there was this old man, Jesse. He was the one who captured me. He ....

In my dreams, I saw. He smells like home, doesn't he? That's why he can disappoint you.

I think it was me who disappointed him. He made such a big thing out of all the little things of life, but I think he built up all the little things. He made them important.

I am sure now. I saw him ... in the dreams, I mean.

It is enough, Edie. Sometimes the dreams are the important parts.

In the long spring evening, Malila sat on a sparsely elegant sofa and watched the shadows slip across the wall until they congealed into the garish twilight of the city. Edie had grown quiet. Somehow, in her absence, Edie had grown up.

Malila felt no need to sleep … or move. It was after midnight before she stirred.

Out of curiosity, she activated the various news feeds and stopped on ESPN 54-N. She watched herself give interviews to talking heads she had never met. No one, apparently, was interested in the colony.

She remembered the gritty sizzling sound of the pulse bolt hitting Delarosa, the smell of ozone and burned meat, feeling her heart sink even before she'd turned around to watch him slump to the ground. She'd watched his face pale and … his eyes.

She remembered Sally disappearing into the forest with Ethan as Moses had turned to start an unequal battle for his homeland … for her.

Why had she fought?

She had no answer if they asked. Why had she fought? Malila remembered no red-hued rage as Xavier Delarosa fell … hollowness for his death, yes, but no incandescent need for revenge. She saw again the faceless trooper raising his rifle to club her. She had reacted instinctively—no, not instinct … She had reacted as she had been trained. She'd set her weight, crouched slightly, feeling the center of her explosive force aim itself. The crunch of her hobnailed boot against the trooper's knee had been satisfying in the way a well-done exercise was satisfying. The second trooper, the one aiming over her left shoulder to kill Moses, she had folded him up like a paper doll almost with no thought at all.

A part of her had remained analytical, detached, scrutinizing. She'd known the signature lock would prevent the captured rifle from working for her and had not even bothered to see if she could activate it, valuing speed over firepower. She'd seen the next trooper. He had been five, maybe six, strides away … too far even for speed. She had known that, even as she'd started for him. She had seen him raise the barrel. The rifle had come up slowly, in the odd detached way it did in battle, to center its dimensionless black eye on her. On her third stride, she would have been hit by the searing heat of the bolt as it exploded her flesh along its trajectory, killing her. She had been surprised when the trooper had fallen before she'd reached him, the rifle report informing her that Moses had saved her life. She had been surprised again when the Taze-Net had engulfed her from the side. She'd started to convulse, her uncontrolled limbs jerking painfully … her mind flickering out.

She undressed for bed.

Why had she fought?

The whole attack had been to liberate her. People she had come to admire and to … love … were dead because of her. Delarosa was dead. Moses was dead too, she feared. She had heard his rifle and had seen the trooper drop as he'd been about to kill her. She had heard the return fire and turned to see Moses's body crumple to the ground. There had just been too many for him. Jesse would have escaped. The old man had probably bet money on his own immortality.

Malila looked back at the comm'net. The unfamiliar talking heads were calling the Return at Stamping Ground an "outlander sun ritual," provoking images of naked savages and twitching sacrificial animals.

The songs came back to her. "The Lord is risen today, alleluia."

She felt soiled.

CHAPTER 52

LUNCH WITH THE GIRLS

A preemptive call from her O-A, the first in six months, jangled Malila awake. Luscena Kristòf's pale face with her vivid red lips swam before her. Luscena was assuming her tragic-loss face, Malila thought. Lucy was so good at her craft.

> *"Malila, my love? Can it really be true? You've come back to us!"*
>
> *"G'mornin', Lucy. Nice to see you too."*
>
> *"We have all been so terribly worried about you. Heccy, Alex, Tiff ... all of us. You were gone so long—without a word."*

It sounded briefly like an accusation. Luscena's face morphed to even a more dramatic appearance of wounded dignity, which she'd used to such great effect and critical acclaim in *Diary of a Protégé*.

"But then to find that you were a prisoner of the savages. It is just too horrible to conceive!"

Malila smiled.

"I am fine, Lucy. I only got out of debriefing last night ..."

Luscena sighed, and her face went back to normal. Malila was not, apparently, playing the game correctly. Lucy got down to business.

"But you must tell us all. We are getting together for lunch."

After accepting the invitation, Malila broke the connection, stopping to marvel at and enjoy the simple act. She had been unable to quest for months.

A folder with six months of communiqués bulged in her near vision.

<ED> I need some help here, please.

Of course, Lieutenant. I presume I dispense with the messages of a commercial nature? Then we have a folder containing messages from your patrons.

Yes, let me see that one.

The messages were numerous. Malila concentrated on just the most recent. Within the last few days, each patron had sent a note expressing sadness at her long absence, delight on her return to civilization, best wishes for her continued success, and regrets that the patron would no longer be sponsoring her as a protégé. The wordings were nearly identical. Malila flipped through them without surprise, like looking at holos of another person. From what Jourdaine had said, it was probably inevitable. She would not have to worry about her awkward fertility. Now and for the foreseeable future, her fate was tied to the gray man and his agenda. Malila deleted the whole folder abruptly.

<ED> Have the commissary send up one egg scrambled, two strips Bakon, one hundred twenty milliliters of Vit-a-kwa, black coffee, one creamer, one sugar, buttered whole-wheat toast with jelly of the day, and two one-hundred-milligram tablets of Naprosinol ... My head is killing me.

Coffee?

Oh, yes, of course.

<ED> Delete coffee. Bring tea, black, strong, six grams sucrose per one hundred twenty mils.

Yes, Lieutenant!

The rest of the morning Malila spent in a bathroom exploring the spiritually nourishing aspects of hot water. As she rose from her bath, she caught movement out of the corner of her eye. It took her a moment to decide it was her own image in the mirror. Her longer hair had developed an unexpected wave, framing her now vaguely foreign face. Her body was pink from the heat, but the blue filigree of the woman's mark still writhed along the edge of her areola, ending in Sally's delicate daisy pattern.

You look lovely, Malila. The wilderness seems to have agreed with you.

Sarcasm? While I was gone, you studied up on sarcasm?

I didn't study at all, as I've already said. But I am sincere. You have gained a little weight, all in the right places.

So you thought my boobs were too small too? Malila laughed. No one was a hero to her own frak.

Glad you like them, Edie.

Dressed in her new uniform, Malila arrived at the museum even as Tiffany was hurrying up, her white coat ballooning out behind her in the spring winds.

They hustled in arm in arm through the museum atrium under the gaze of the blue whale. It was much the same: the waiters swooped around with heavy trays, fresh daffodils graced the table, and the fragrant vines in the latticework were as profligate as ever. The string quartet and the Dutilleux were gone in favor of two additional tables. Newly added comm'net screens dominated the walls, displaying a selection of sweaty athletes for lunch.

Malila was the center of attention. Luscena, in a shimmering black pantsuit, assumed the role as her media secretary and answered most questions before Malila could herself. New loops of video spun overhead, repeatedly showing three-dimensional diagrams of Malila's platoon being overwhelmed by "wave upon wave of heedless barbarians." The 'nets had improved the number of her attackers from two to "a hundred or more barbarians armed with antiquated pulse rifles." Her platoon had fought to the death in her defense; at least that was accurate. The savages "had constructed a funeral pyre in grudging admiration for the noble enemy."

She tried to ignore them, until Jourdaine's now-familiar voice came on. It took a while before she could quiet her friends in order to hear him.

"Complete surprise was achieved in this rescue mission, allowing us, with minimal casualties, to retrieve Lieutenant Chiu, this audacious example of the best the Unity produces."

He looked confident, calm, yet determined.

A pleasant contralto from off camera asked, "Colonel, she's been gone for six months. Where was she held? What happened to her during her captivity?"

"You can imagine that information is classified, Shirley. It goes without saying a captive among the savages is enslaved, starved, beaten, and degraded beyond anything we, in a civilized country, can imagine. Nevertheless, throughout her six months of brutal interrogation, the barbarians were unable to break her spirit. It is nothing less than a heroic moral triumph!"

Instantaneously, sidebars erupted around the image, showing 'net commentators who weighed in with their own observations and opinions. The panels waxed and waned as the local viewers' interest changed.

"Now, this little girl ... Chiu? Grew up in Kweens. You gotta appreciate that! The district has been supplying more than its share of DUFS for generations now. Must be something in the water," offered a meaty man in an expensive suit with obvious pride.

"Indeed, Supervisor? I thought your water problem had been rectified," said the commentator in the next panel, a near-cachectic woman in a rust-colored suit that sported lighted lapels.

The woman continued, "However, the level of fortitude this woman has displayed ... thrust ... thrust onto her own resources by savage masculine violence. Who knows what horrors have been visited upon her?"

She lost her train of thought momentarily before refocusing on the audience. "It shows the confidence only a woman with a strong sense of her own style can achieve. Obviously."

Another commentator, a thin bearded man who was listed as a professor of political science, poked the wall of the woman's panel. His panel expanded noticeably as he talked.

"Don't any of these people get it? I don't think so," he lilted. "Doesn't it seem odd that exactly fifteen weeks after General Emmanuel is denounced for incompetence, we have another DUFS crawling back into the headlines? I mean, it may be coincidence, sure, but they both went through the same training. They both served in the same units. It doesn't take a genius to see where this is going, does it?"

The screen dissolved into dueling panels for several minutes until the screen cycled back to sports news about the CORE death of some football player.

After lunch, her friends demanded more of the "real" story from her.

Malila started with her waking up in the dark with a knife at her throat and hearing the remorseless gunshots killing her platoon, one at a time. She told them about the excitement of the bison hunt but also about her daily bondage, the Death Walker, and Bear's death. She concealed devil's bridge and her bleeding cycles.

Mostly, Malila talked about Sally and Ethan: her bravery at birthing him, his brilliant smile punctuated by new sharp teeth, and his gluttony at Sally's breast.

"No! You means it actually uses these?" said Luscena, looking down.

"You should have seen how fast he grew. Ethan was hardly three kilos at first, and by the time I … left, at four months, he was double that. Imagine! He had three chins," Malila said, laughing.

"They make something, and it licks it up, like a discharge of sorts? That can't be good … for either of them, can it?" replied Luscena. She looked down at herself again.

"That's how we get milk and cheese, Lucy, but from cattle, of course," added Alexandra. "The Unity has big flocks of cattle. You harvest the milk every so often and make it into food. I've seen reports."

Tiffany lowered a forkful of alfredo and pushed the plate to the side.

"But it can't be good for … them," continued Luscena, fluttering her hands in front of her chest, her face, even with her crimson lips, paled. No one responded.

In the silence, Alexandra said, "Captivity sounds entirely gruesome, Mally, but I am not surprised you're so melled out. Captives always start to identify with their captors. Well-known fact, everybody knows."

"Oh yes," said Tiffany. "And whatever you do, give yourself a rest, and you will be back to normal … soon, I'm sure. Be careful who you talk to, Mally." She would not meet her eyes.

Tiffany, Luscena, and Alexandra ate no more. Hecate winked at Malila as they both poached a little salmon from Alexandra's neglected plate.

Luscena left shortly thereafter, gasping before she stood and only then remembering to look at her watch. She rushed out with her usual welter of promises and idle threats. Her personal skimmer had yet to be announced. Tiffany and Alexandra started a murmuring conversation and left together with barely a wave between them.

CHAPTER 53

ADVICE AND DISSENT

"I understand. Or rather, I don't understand, but I know I should," Hecate said, looking across the cluttered and soiled white linen at Malila.

"Understand what?" Malila said.

"I should understand how seductive babies should be to us, to women. They are to men too, of course, but I don't think I will understand that."

Malila look puzzled until Hecate added, "I've been reading."

Malila moved around the table to sit next to her. "You are still going to the warehouse? What is it like?"

"Like a morgue, but the corpses look back at you. The books are only alive when people can read them. They aren't really alive with just me."

"So you've found some good stories for Victor?"

"Dozens, but ... he was denounced. He killed himself last autumn. It was just after you were gone."

Malila watched her friend openmouthed, expecting her to dissolve into tears. Hecate shrugged and gave a wan parody of a smile.

"Oh … Heccy!"

Malila sought her friend's hands. They were cool, her warmth slipping away.

"It would have been only another eighteen months. He would have retired," Hecate added, almost as an apology.

"Yes, he could … retire," murmured Malila, drifting off into something Xavier had said.

Hecate shifted; a cloud passed over the skylights, darkening her face. "Retire? Yeah … retire. I wonder if that is like your hunt. Do you still think there are whales?"

Hecate continued rapidly, before Malila said anything. "I saw it after you disappeared. They didn't think to fake the cosmetic production records. I looked. There was no rise in cetyl ester production or a drop in jojoba oil use … No whale-oil derivatives became available after you were supposed to have harvested two big males, and the substitute didn't decline in use either. It's all deception."

"I don't know what you are trying to tell me, Heccy. I just wanted to get home. There were so many old people there. They acted crazy, and everyone let them."

"How many old people are we talking about?" Hecate asked.

"One … only one. He was the man who captured me." Malila, suddenly embarrassed, looked down at her hands.

"What sort of crazy are we talking about?" Hecate's voice changed, becoming sterner somehow, Malila thought.

"Well, I know he has killed at least seven people, for sure. He used to beat me if I said things … whip me if I made a mistake or walked too slow," she said, wondering why the statement felt like a betrayal.

"The outlands are a barbaric place," Hecate agreed. "Still, you haven't told me crazy yet. Cruel … but not crazy. He was your jailor, right? Did he fuck you?"

The grotesque word seemed to echo off the walls to her.

"No. It was strange. I thought we would. I couldn't get away from him. He watched me when I was naked. I guess that was just to be sure I wouldn't escape."

"So he wasn't attracted to you ... That *is* crazy enough." A thin smile chased across Hecate's lips as Malila looked up, feeling she had to defend Jesse.

"No ... I think he would have liked to ... have pleasure-sex ... with me, but it was like he was keeping a promise. That is like him. It took us six weeks to walk to the ... where we were going. He got sick near the end. He went sort of crazy then, but he got better. He was a little boy before the Rampart was built, he said. He must be in his seventies."

"But ..." Hecate prodded.

"He could outwalk me carrying a forty-kilo pack. Everyone called him the 'old man.' They meant it as a term of respect, can you believe? I even tried to kill him once. He went against orders to keep me alive. But we became friends, I mean real friends, without the pleasure-sex. I just never really got him, I think. He used to recite poetry, old poetry, for me. I liked him. It got all mixed up. He told me he loved me."

"Maybe he thought you could love him. That makes a lot of people crazy," murmured Hecate, looking away as her voice went flat.

Malila felt strange hearing Hecate's words. "I think I did love him. But he wouldn't even discuss being a patron. He said he would not shame me by doing that."

"You offered to be a Sisi's protégé?"

"It did not seem so bad at the time; Jesse is different—too different. Does that make sense?"

"No, not really, Mally. But I am getting it secondhand, of course. You were there; I wasn't."

"But we finally connected, no submission, no patronage ... It was lovely and warm and tender, and then ... he started talking about some other woman. He wanted to include this Mary Eng person. I think I would have gone along with that, but then he started to scare me, curse me, talking about all kinds of stuff.

Malila felt Hecate press her hands just as despair started to overwhelm her.

"We were half-dressed, and he was going on about another woman.

That was so unlike him. I can't explain. It was just too weird. It was just being cruel. I didn't take it well. I told him to father himself and walked off," Malila said and smiled, before weeping.

This brought a cluck of disdain from Hecate, but then she stopped. "Wait a moment, Mally. Something I read."

Hecate looked distracted, then focused on Malila again. "Did he say *Mary*, a woman's name, or *marry*, a verb? What did he mean really? What did you do after he got weird on you?"

"I was just too upset, and I left him there. We never had the chance to talk. I never … didn't see him before I was rescued. What do you mean 'verb'? What does *marry* mean?"

"It doesn't mean pleasure-sex, or rather it does … It's complicated. It means he wants you for his wife. Why did he start cursing you?"

"Wife? Like Sally? I didn't say anything … I don't remember exactly what he said other than 'father something.'"

Hecate frowned. "*Father* hasn't always been a curse word, Mally. I think he may just have wanted to talk to your actual father," Hecate answered.

"My father? He's Sapped and dead. Jesse knew that."

"I think he wanted to check that people who love you were okay with him … whether he was good for you. At least, that is what I gleaned from some of the books. It is really old style, though."

"Marry-ing?"

"A pair bond, a contract guaranteed by something like the state. Do they still do that in the outlands?"

"Yeah, they do," Malila said, remembering the way Moses's eyes had followed Sally as she'd disappeared into the forest … just before he'd been shot.

"Your Sisi wasn't asking for pleasure-sex; he was asking to be considered a patron for life … and then have sex," Hecate said with a smirk. She then sobered after looking into Malila's eyes.

Hecate took a deep breath. "Mally, I'm glad I could clear this up for you, but you know this is over, right? Nothing good happens with Sisis; it's just a fact of life. They get quirky as they get older. They start listening to other voices, not the ones the rest of us hear. In the books, the Sisis don't know what they are saying half the time."

"I ran away from him. I said terrible things. He must think I'm crazy."

"It doesn't matter. It never mattered. You have to stay focused and strong now. You are in danger. You know things ... We both do."

"What do you mean?"

"I mean you have gotten out of the box. The Unity ... it isn't what we think it is. You have seen the outlands. They'll notice you've changed."

"Don't be silly, Heccy. *They* went to all this trouble to rescue me."

"Okay, I don't know why they rescued you, but have you ever talked to anyone else who came back from the outlands? Laborers, technicians, engineers, other DUFS? I'll bet you never met anyone who was actually there."

"What are you saying?"

"Old stories ... maybe just old stories. They can't let anyone see the stars," Hecate said and shook her head before looking down.

Suddenly the air in the room was too warm for Malila. She watched one of the waiters look up and start toward her. The room itself seemed to shrivel around her, compressing her, the scent of the flowers choking her.

She rose. "Hecate, I can't talk now. It's too much. Jourdaine wanted me back, and he made it happen!"

She left without looking back, afraid that Hecate would say something more. She did not remember the trip back to her new quarters; Edie just told her where to go, and she went. Later she wept. Malila's one consolation was knowing that running from Jesse had saved him. The skimmer would have found them together, and Jesse would have died like Xavier ... like Moses.

Hecate rose, watching Malila retreat from the table, and gathered her own things.

She had done it again. She had tried to be a friend, to give good advice, and to help Malila avoid her own mistakes. Instead, Malila had backed away, fearful and confused, just when they needed each other. She needed Malila's strength, and Malila needed her insight. Sometimes, people couldn't hear the truth. The ministry certainly couldn't.

Hecate had not known it last fall, but she knew it now.

It was the plum production. She had gotten that data herself, recording the consumption of "plums, dried" in a target population of new retirees. She had been assured that Sisis needed their dried plums, but there was a problem. If every year new retirees were added to the pool, and if the retirees lived just ten more years, the consumption ought to be at least five times greater than what the enclaves requisitioned.

Something was wrong.

In an act of supreme courage, Hecate had submitted a report on the Pamlico River krill effusion harvest. Last year, the effusion had died, a victim to institutional sloth and hierarchical greed. She reported it as unchanged from the previous harvest. She ought to have been fired; instead, Undersecretary Rice had complimented her for an orderly and timely report. The data it contained had been as phony as Hecate's career.

Malila was changed. She was more vigorous, more vivid, than she ever had been. The sun must have done something to her. Her hands were rough, the nails not quite perfect, her skin darkened. She acted more competent, less talkative. But she seemed so sad. Her stories of the infant were too poignant and of the old man much too sincere.

The amount of comm'net resources expended on Malila was immense. The effort expended on her rescue was already huge. Malila would have to pay for that, in some fashion, before the scales balanced. The factions always wanted the scales to balance.

Cynical? Yes, Hecate supposed she had become cynical. The death of Victor, the unmasking of the uselessness of her job, and the books … indeed, the books.

What she had read in the last six months had given her a cynicism, perhaps a realism, about herself and her country. Right now Malila, as much as Hecate loved her, could not see it. Perhaps Malila would never see the reality of the Unity. In a few months, maybe a few years, Malila's bill would come due, and she would pay for her rescue and her current celebrity. The price would be steep. Hecate could not help her and could not stand to watch her fall.

More importantly, she could not *stay* to watch her fall. Hecate was going to be denounced. There were too many things ... coincidences: meetings that people talked about to which she had never been invited, small changes in who reported to whom, and, most telling, how the guy from CORE ignored her requests. The CORE guys always seemed to know whom they could ignore without reprisal.

Even so, it took her a week to gather the courage to call Tiffany.

Hecate met her in the lobby of the Mid-Manatten Euthanatorium, the all-purpose mortuary, nursing home, clinic, skilled-care facility, and hospital where Tiffany worked.

The lobby was almost deserted. A few low stone benches crouched on the metal gray floor. Posters in pleasant shades of gold and aqua decorated the walls and proclaimed:

Shorten the Misery!

Dignify Your Death!

Live Proudly ... Die Proudly!

Copies were on sale in the gift shop.

Tiffany was there waiting for her. She had been the voice of compassion in their group since childhood; it was to her that Hecate had spilled her list of disappointments, disillusions, and fears.

"Have you ever thought of killing yourself, like Victor?" Tiffany asked.

"Yes."

"So what are you going to do?"

Hecate had been reticent to tell her at first, but only at first.

"Suicide is treason, you know, Hecate."

"Are you turning me in, Tiffany?"

"Of course not. I am your friend, aren't I? But why are you leaving us? Don't we mean enough for you to stay?"

"Please, Tiff, this is going to be hard for me. If you make me answer, I will just start crying. Everything I do here is useless. They are going to denounce me."

"You don't know that. We love you; I love you. You will find someone else. Victor was a good man, but there are other men."

"It's not just Victor ... It's everything. Life shouldn't be like this. *I* shouldn't be like this. Tiffany, just help me ... You're the only one I can trust."

Nodding, Tiffany finally agreed. It took weeks to organize Hecate's suicide.

CHAPTER 54

KLEOPHIRRA BANKS!

Jourdaine sat in his austere darkened office, the city displaying its garish wares to him from his perch thirty floors above the street. His campaign against Suarez was coming along nicely, but his timing would have to be perfect. Chiu was now an asset and no longer a liability. She might even become the centerpiece.

The major uncontrolled variables now were the 'net commentators, especially James J. Gordon. The commentators acted as an independent political force outside the factions. Where Gordon led, others followed. At least one Solon-elect had underestimated Gordon and had been denounced, at the very moment of his elevation, by an exposé from the "satirist in chief."

While Gordon's concurrence was critical, timing was of greater concern. If Jourdaine started too soon, Gordon might let him twist in the wind, an early martyr before the main battle was even joined. But if he started his attack *after* Gordon came out against Suarez, then Jourdaine's actions would appear subordinate, perhaps even submissive to Gordon's.

Chiu could make a difference. Pompous editorials, including his own, crowded in one upon the other, escalated her importance. She was plausible. If the truth about her denunciation last October could be quashed, it would justify all the trouble rescuing her. After six months as a captive of the savages, he had expected to find a brutalized cinder of an officer. Instead he had found Malila: young, attractive, and compliant.

She had possibilities. A coup d'état needed a face. Among the best revolutionaries were those who sealed their fame by dying ... just as victory was proclaimed. So the very best coup d'état should be led by a pretty—and pretty expendable—face.

Malila fit on both counts. She had but two career paths open to her at the moment, he thought: denunciation for cowardice in the face of the enemy or elevation as a plucky young heroine destined for high office. It was indeed fortunate for her that she had an *éminence grise* already in position to advise her.

Malila now commanded a platoon of line troopers—a combat platoon and not a support platoon. An experienced un-Sapped platoon sergeant, Natan Grauer, offered the prospect of an effective and well-run platoon command organization. Malila's new commanding general was Brigadier General Ingamar Magness, a man, she discovered, who had had a dazzlingly unremarkable career. She would not get a free pass up the hierarchy on Magness's coattails. Nevertheless, promotion led through combat command. It was a step up, any way she looked at it.

Her new orders had included the phrase "making yourself available to vetted media interviews, as consistent with good military order and discipline." After her introductory audience with her new commanding general, a bearlike man who seemed to confuse obstinacy for integrity, Malila was made to understand that she had better show up for every interview her CO suggested and no other interviews whatever.

She received the first request that very day, with a copy of her gracious signed acceptance letter already affixed. Edie tsked.

At the appointed time, Malila arrived at what appeared to be an abandoned warehouse. She entered through a half-opened door. A light at the extreme end of the dark interior flashed above a sign reading, "No Entrance While Light Is Flashing."

Malila waited until a harried little man with a meticulous blond mustache burst out.

"Where is that jotting bizzle?" he called over his shoulder.

"She was supposed to be here fifteen minutes ago. These guys are on the fathering clock!"

He stopped at once and looked up at her. "Are you Lieutenant Shoe?"

"Lieutenant Chiu, Malila E., reporting as ordered!" she recited.

"Yeah ... right. Get in here and see Glenda for makeup. Kleo's running late, so you got a couple minutes."

Malila found Glenda, a tall, heavy woman sporting peacock-feather implants from her forehead to the base of her neck. She clucked over Malila for a few minutes before releasing her to the attentions of a production underling. Malila was positioned in the wings to be introduced.

A tall, shapely, chocolate-skinned blonde eventually swept onto the stage and arranged herself on the taller of two stools.

Malila heard an off-stage announcer recite, "... most-popular news personality of the early-evening, upper-middle-class demographic in the Nyork district ... Kleophirra *Banks*!"

Simulated applause filled the stage, and Kleophirra started her monologue: no doubt, a witty, sardonic, and knowing summation of the current scene. Rather too soon, however, Kleophirra made the introduction, and Malila pushed out onto the stage to take the shorter and narrower stool. Having no idea what was expected of her, Malila tried to maintain the shavetail's facial mask.

Kleophirra wended her way through a highly colored and dramatic version of her captivity as Malila stared at the camera's lens, mesmerized. Smart and savage at times, Kleophirra, despite being classed among the C-list of political analysts on the 'net, was no slouch.

At last, Kleophirra turned to her. "And we have with us today the young DUFS officer whose story should stir us all. Lieutenant Chiu spent over six months in the hands of these barbarians before being rescued. Your entire platoon was murdered, is that right?"

"Yes, Citizen Banks."

"Just call me Kleophirra, please. Tell us about your captivity, Malila. Were you assaulted?"

Malila was speechless. How much of the colony could she reveal? How much of what she did say now would condemn her in the eyes of the people or her superiors? Her disquiet was sliding to panic when she became aware of the Presence.

The Presence did not identify itself, but she could tell it was Jourdaine. He dropped down into her consciousness with the warm treacle of reassurance.

> *"Breathe, Malila. This woman needs your words. You do not need hers."*

"I am just so glad I am at home now," Malila said to the camera. "The outlands are a barbaric place. I am lucky to be alive."

It was true, she thought.

"Outlanders killed my men after I was already captured. I couldn't stop them. Then I was marched under guard for six weeks before I was turned over. That nearly killed me."

Again, she thought, *all true. I nearly killed as well.*

> *"Excellent, Malila. More-personal things now: the starvation, the beatings?"*

The Presence's suggested responses to her alternated between humble and noble, funny and grave, witty and nonchalant. He congratulated her after each exchange. Jourdaine added a commentary about the "wounds she could not show on prime time." It was a brilliant stroke, she thought.

Malila returned to her quarters in time to see her interview. In postproduction, her performance sparkled. Moreover, Kleophirra's laudatory epilogue swelled Malila with pride, despite herself. She basked in congratulations and Jourdaine's approval for days until the next interview, *The Sofistree DeGeorge Experience.*

After DeGeorge came *The Tiffanie Breaux Crew.* After that, the names and the personalities blurred, coming about every third day. She never got used to it. Some smiled as they set traps for her, and others just sneered. Some used her as text for the host's current rant. Each time, the Presence would slide next to her, his responses perfectly calculated to throw back each jibe. After every interview, approval and acceptance ... almost of love ... flooded her senses.

Nevertheless, she slept poorly; odd, mostly unremembered dreams exhausted her.

At times they woke her. In her darkened bedroom, she surrendered to wakefulness, stretching and slipping out of her bed to sit on the edge. She remembered that last dream, seeing herself bronzed, a living statue, unable to move, pigeons sitting on her head and whitewashing her face. *Glory* had been embossed on the plinth.

Glory was no longer a concept she knew. Power she understood. It had been visited upon her more than once, but glory?

Certainly, the Unity was glorious; vast expanses of city, marvelous technology, and potent armies all spoke to "glory."

Malila thought back to her winter of captivity. There had been no glory there. The Unity had stories of glory, but it usually meant that someone had died; there was no one left to tell the real story.

Glory ... it was not enough.

CHAPTER 55

THE BLOODY SHIRT

North of Citadel Bangor, Main, Unity
23.49.51.local_19_05_AU77

DUFS Captain Lucien Delaheny was irked after being pulled out of a warm, comfortable bed. Collecting some green ensign who had wandered into enemy territory was a job for a lieutenant.

Ensign Samuel Idaban had, contrary to orders, DUFS protocol, and *fecking common sense*, malingered off into the fog along the river in Bangor and been captured four days ago. *Served the kid right.* The cease-fire line in Main had been stable since forever. Every shavetail should have known where to walk! The scuttlebutt was that Idaban was lovesick over some failed patronage. *Invidious system!* Bad for discipline and corrosive of command, but what could you do?

Delaheny looked out the window at the long lines of pines passing down the edges of the headlights as they plowed forward into the blackness. The problem for the iceheads and for Idaban was that the kid was as dumb as he looked. The Canadian interrogators were good, ruthless, and good. They would wring him dry and then do it again a few times to make sure. He wondered how much of Ensign Idaban would be left.

"Coming up now, Captain. They're already here."

Delaheny leaned forward and picked up the reflective strips of the Canadian staff car. He could see two burly men wrestle a smaller hooded figure out of the backseat as an officer looked on.

Later, he would report how the hood came off and how Idaban looked around before staring into the approaching lights … into Delaheny's own eyes.

Delaheny would not report how he could almost taste the boy's terror.

He watched in the odd slow motion of doom: the boy breaking loose, his hand coming up with the officer's sidearm, his backing away, the shot, the officer going down, and the boy's look of surprise slumping to fear. He watched as Idaban turned and ran from the approaching lights.

He saw how the boy's head disappeared into a sudden small cloud of pink.

Delaheny reported the death of Idaban, Samuel A., shot while trying to escape. Delaheny was the only one there when Samuel Idaban was cremated.

This should not be a significant event, Jourdaine thought. Foolish young men and women were getting themselves killed for foolish reasons all the time. This fool just happened to have worn a DUFS uniform. Somebody had leaked Idaban's death to the 'nets. The story had already been cast on a few major outlets.

It was now real. All the other outlets would follow suit. In a week, it would be old news … no longer real.

But for the next cycle, Jourdaine could use it. If he used it well, this immediate insult to the honor and dignity of the Democratic Unity should prompt closer inspection of the entire trajectory of current events. One lost officer was an embarrassment; two was the sign of gross negligence … or worse.

Ensign Idaban, Samuel A., would have immortality, if ever so briefly, in the annals of the Democratic Unity.

It was time to move.

Jourdaine contacted his man inside the media. In this case, his man was an E31, S22 transvestite known as Shirley, who personed the human-interest desk of the more-prominent and less-scrupulous of the media conglomerates. The conversation was brief and cryptic. The data package was bundled and flash-transmitted to Shirley's aliased mail slot. Equally cryptic would be Shirley's assignment to cover a prestigious film festival, with a generous expense allowance.

The media attacks on Suarez started within the hour. Several of the more-prestigious outlets produced attacks of their own without prompting. Suarez had trodden upon more than her fair share of toes during her long years of service. The owners of the toes were lining up to add their denunciations.

With this much bile already spilled, Jourdaine was correct that Gordon's active and early support would not be necessary, as long as he did not oppose. His Presence would shepherd Malila Chiu through an interview with Gordon without a hitch.

At the artlessly appropriate time, Jourdaine released his own statement to the comm'nets:

> I confirm my unswerving and wholehearted support for Lieutenant General Suarez for her many, many years of dedicated service to the defense forces and to the nation.
>
> I am confident that when all the facts are known, they will exculpate the reports of General Suarez's apparently reactionary behavior. It is regrettable that such questions are even being raised about one of her stature.

> The service and the country are larger than the concerns of any one officer, no matter how talented she or he might be. There could be but one honorable conclusion for anyone justifiably accused of such behavior. No doubt the numerous reports will be found to be fabricated.

As expected, Suarez came out fighting. The first few of her gambits were spectacular but predictable and easily refuted. Her fiery counterattack prompted allegations of her obvious emotional instability.

General Suarez's real offensive began with her calling in all her markers, her own legion of black capital. While potent, it appeared undisciplined. Her defense, no doubt formidable at one time, had not been kept up to date. Jourdaine had seen to that. She called upon politicians who had been marginalized already and could bring little influence to bear.

Her career, designed around rooting out and preventing faction spies, meant she had no subordinates to throw to the wolves now. Indeed, the number of people who could help her might well have dropped below the effective horizon already, Jourdaine estimated. Suarez's personal and heartfelt appeals to her few friends were impudently ignored or imprudently accepted by those less adept at the art of politics. At some tipping point, Suarez would merely enlarge the hole into which she fell.

Jourdaine was having the time of his life.

Heather had done that little thing she did that was going to be the death of him. Dalgliesh was almost ten minutes late when he slid into his workstation smelling of her scent, running on ThiZ and hormones.

"Nice of you to join us in the campaign for a better Democratic Unity, Technical Sergeant Dalgliesh! About to send the provost guard out for you."

"Sorry, Gunny. It won't happen again."

"Only if I cut it off, Doggy, and even then I'll still give it even odds," he replied. Then he smiled.

"Sorry, you know how it is."

"I do. That's why we are having this conversation. Last time I cover for you, understood?"

"Thank you. Last time, I promise."

"At any rate, Doggy, seems the major wants us to dump all the data from that auto ping we started last fall, the one for … Shoe?"

"Chiu. Didn't they find her? Doing a dump isn't going to hide anything! You know that. Every purge just means that the file is closed and flagged for some intelligence S20. Better off just ignoring it and letting the CORE decide it is useless … get rid of it on its own."

Jasun replied, almost as if he were talking to a trainee, "I told him so, face-to-face. So *he* knows it, *I* know it, and *you* know it. I am following orders, just like you had better."

"Yes, of course. Right now!"

This was something his handler needed to know at once. The factions were at it again.

The technical sergeant was about to wet himself, Jourdaine noted. That might give Jourdaine an edge in the interrogation.

The belt station was deserted at this time of night. No surveillance camera recorded the little corner of the platform now occupied by the two men.

"Don't turn around, Sergeant Dalgliesh. Shirley called me. Let's just call me Mr. Smith, okay?"

"Yes, sir."

"Okay, start from the beginning. Tell me everything you remember about Major Khama since last … October, shall we?"

Jourdaine listened impassively. It was all there. Khama's order for the auto ping on Chiu, his diversion of the data to a CORE locus, and then, surprisingly, his actual visitation to Ciszek, or rather a report of his actual visitation. The tech sergeant, Dalgliesh, was exceptionally well trained, observant … even meticulous.

"Excellent work, Sergeant. This is extremely valuable. You will be well rewarded for your effort."

"Thank you, sir. Can I go now?"

"Of course. In the future, we will not use this meeting site again. Use the next drop site on the list if you see the flag go up, understand?"

"Yes, sir."

Jourdaine watched the man walk hurriedly away down the belt platform and disappear into a toilet.

He had underestimated Suarez. He was sure now. His own hoard of black capital had been massive, but it had not been enough. His major debtors had done what they could and been denounced in turn.

Jourdaine reached the street and signaled for his skimmer. Waiting, he eased back away from the curb and into the shadows.

Khama, one of his oldest allies, was a Suarez plant. That was now certain. Khama had had excellent protection for the auto ping and had then thrown it away by ordering a data dump. Jourdaine's carefully concealed rescue of Chiu would look like a cover-up. How much did Khama really know, or was he just throwing wrenches into the works?

Jourdaine's skimmer arrived, and he slid into the passenger compartment with a sigh of relief. He quested his destination, and the vehicle moved off without signaling.

Years of waiting had brought Jourdaine to this point. He would not fail for lack of audacity or energy. Now was the time to strike. He had one more weapon.

The Unity needed to meet young Lieutenant Miramundo Morales, Suarez's natural brother and proof of her nepotism. They needed to meet Morales now before Suarez could use Khama as a weapon against him.

It would mean unmasking himself. It would mean Suarez must be seen as the sole author of all the Unity's disasters of late: the loss of Sunprairie, Idaban's death, drops in production, Morales, Chiu's capture, and even the debacle in Main. They all needed to fit into a cohesive story, sealing Suarez's fate.

Jourdaine arrived at his headquarters and walked up to his office. Gordon was supposed to interview Malila Chiu, and she expected his Presence.

Sacrifices had to be made.

CHAPTER 56

HOUSE OF GORDON

Malila could see the signs clear enough. Junior officers walked with their heads down so as not to be engaged in idle chatter. Senior officers made brief visits and smiled a lot, showing the flag. Groups clustered around the drug kiosks but scattered if a door opened unexpectedly. Her O-A was ominously quiet.

The factions had been going after each other for a week now. They were always jostling, but they usually kept their rivalries from spilling out into public. Since yesterday, cadres had been marching in full battle uniform, their only identifier their armbands and the clouds of color they threw at spectators. More ominously, the Reds, the current "vanguard of the cadres," had blocked off the access to the belts around her own battalion headquarters. When reopened, the belts had borne the faction's color; the walls had borne advertisements, all jackboots and patriotism; and, no doubt, unseen, the station had borne additional surveillance devices. Yesterday, as she'd been going to work out of uniform, overly enthusiastic faction members had popped her with the metallic green of the Unity Home faction and the fluorescent orange of the Forward Unity faction, both minor players. She'd changed and showered once she had arrived.

Other guilds did not play in the DUFS factional contests. Faction wars were all-DUFS affairs. It was complicated. Any individual other than the senior staff could hardly ever tell when a battle started or stopped. Unannounced, one faction or another started propaganda campaigns and denounced a few low-level leaders of another faction. A crisis would come … and eventually pass. At the end, the self-congratulatory puffery would gradually decline. The comm'nets would show more real news. The mind-numbing five-hour-long classic of revolutionary Unity cinema, *Birth of the Cadre*, would be shown less often. At the very end there would be a rash of denunciations and suicides.

I am glad I'm not in anyone's crosshairs, Edie. I have been gone too long to know who is after whom.

Enjoy it while you may, Malila. You do know that Suarez is a Red, don't you?

Thank you, Edie, I pretty much had that worked out already.

Jourdaine as her adjutant is also a Red, then. Correct? And you are not a Red?

You know that a protégé is not required to be of the same faction as her patron, silly. It is already too complicated. For now I am trying to avoid being labeled. It helps advancement … for now.

Would you believe me if I said that while Jourdaine has publically come out in Suarez's favor, he is actually working for the Blues?

Really, Edie? Jourdaine is trying to frag his own commander? Where is that going to get him? If she loses, he will fall with her. It might get him Sapped. If Suarez finds out, she *will Sapp him for treason. If he wins, he would just be an untrusted officer in another command.*

Unless ...

Malila stopped. Factions was a game played only at the highest levels and only among the senior staff. For Eustace to ignore his faction commander, he would have to command huge resources himself.

Unless this is his *coup and the Blues work for him?*

The CORE talks in its sleep, Malila. Just count on it being true.

Whatever happens, happens, Edie. All I know is that today I have that interview with Gordon.

Gordon's skimmer arrived. The passenger compartment had a small bar with a number of atypical and potent drinks and drugs. They did not tempt her. Gordon would use any advantage he could. Not a few celebrities had eviscerated themselves in public by one outrageous gaffe or another while Gordon had looked on and wiggled his eyebrows.

She was deposited at the secure lobby of an unmarked underground entrance. Malila accepted the now-familiar routine of makeup, production, and the long wait in the green room without comment. Again a buffet of drinks and drugs greeted her. Again she abstained, feeling queasy enough.

A large screen, dominating one wall of the room, sprang to life, the slow resolve of Gordon's face gradually overwhelming it. After his introductory babble, the man was smooth and relaxed with his opening monologue. He then introduced an absurd skit, allowing him to drop several of his trademark catchphrases to the delight of the audience. His first interview was with a rising ingenue. Her semitransparent dress left little doubt as to her bona fides, although her responses suggested her celebrity would last only as long as gravity could be held at bay. Gordon made suggestive asides to the audience at the girl's expense until she finally became incensed.

"Oh, don't get mad; you know I love you," he said, another of his catchphrases.

The audience erupted in laughter. The actress colored and then giggled.

Before her capture, Malila had never been much of a Gordon fan. Other than learning his signature gestures and phrases to counterfeit interest with her coworkers, she'd ignored him. On returning from the outlands, Gordon had seemed a caricature of himself, his new catchphrases absurd or childish.

The blithe goading of the actress finally ended with the woman declaring unending love for her host. Gordon giggled.

The production assistant escorted Malila to her mark. On cue, she strode from behind a curtain and out across a naked stage to the sleek modern chair, still warm from the actress's body. Gordon stood and pantomimed a burlesque salute. The audience, behind the hot lights focused upon her, was silent. The canned applause ended abruptly.

At first, the interview was benign. How long had she been in District Nyork? Did she enjoy the DUFS? Had she always been stationed across the Rampart? Malila was beginning to unwind a bit when Gordon asked her, "My understanding is that you were sent there on a direct order from Lieutenant General Vivalagente Suarez. Isn't that correct?"

Before she could answer, Gordon wiggled his eyebrows at the audience and sotto voced, "What kind of a name is Vivalagente?"

The audience dutifully laughed, but Malila's heart sank. She felt paralyzed. Gordon had information that he should not have. The Presence did not slide next to her as she waited.

"Uhh ... that is correct, Citizen Gordon. Like every DUFS officer, I am given orders, and I follow them," she answered. It was weak.

"And General Vivalagente's orders got you 'captured.' Where, may I ask, Malila—I may call you Malila, mayn't I? Where were you 'imprisoned' for the four months after you reached New Carrolton ... That was where you were kept, isn't it?"

Gordon shouldn't have known any of this! The only one who did was Jourdaine, and now he had abandoned her.

Malila admitted she had stayed at a farm and gave a brief and rather imprecise description of a hardscrabble hilltop affair, anything to prevent reprisals against Sally. A picture came up behind her; she could tell by the audience reaction. She resisted the urge to look.

"Really, Malila, that doesn't seem to match my information. General Suarez's orders maneuvered you to a farm right on the major river of the region"—Gordon looked down to his notes—"the *Oh*-yoh River. Isn't that correct?"

That was something, at least. Gordon only had reports of reports. He did not have the originals, or he would not have made that mistake. Or was it a trap? How would that help him? There was still no sign of a presence. She had been caught in her first lie.

"Actually, Citizen Gordon, it is the Oh-*high*-oh River. Yes, I was told that parts of the farm ran down to the river. I wasn't permitted to go near it." That much, at least, was true. The river flooded the low fields for most of the winter and spring.

"A thousand pardons, Lieutenant Chiu!" said Gordon and did the thing with his eyebrows to cue the audience to laugh at her. The interview deteriorated from there.

CHAPTER 57

GREEN MONKEY

Malila returned from the interview feeling angry, despondent, and surprised to find a pale blue envelope on actual paper slipped under her door.

It read:

Lieutenant Colonel Eustace T. Jourdaine
requests the pleasure of your company to dinner
at Le Singe Vert,
this evening, 30 May, at 20:00.
A driver will be provided.

This is a public affair, Malila. Colonel Jourdaine isn't just interested in you as a political tool. You see that, I hope!

Don't gush, Edie.

What better time than now? You are on every net'cast in the country. People know your face and how brave you were! Now you are getting some acknowledgment. Enjoy it, Malila!

I shall endeavor to follow your guidance.

Now you are making fun of me.

Okay, a little gushing is acceptable, Edie.

She wondered when Edie had learned to laugh. It felt good to join her.

The invitation dazzled her. This was a public affair; Jourdaine's patronage would be acknowledged. Listening to a comm'net broadcast in the background, Malila prepared for the evening, Edie's excitement fueling her own growing enthusiasm.

Jourdaine had augmented her wardrobe since her return. Sparkling sheaths in shimmering colors illuminated her closet. The effect would be more spectacular after she turned them on, the subtle glow and rhythm of the lights mesmerizing and seductive. Malila selected a black dress that displayed much of her apparently more-prominent breasts, leaving her right shoulder exposed entirely. She added a rope of pearls, twisted twice about her neck, and grabbed the matching shoes and handbag. A small hat of black silk with a curve of iridescent feathers, matching the dress's lights, was her only addition.

She looked into the mirror. The woman who stared back was no longer Lieutenant Chiu, Malila E., E12, S25. She smiled.

You look stunning! The dress is gorgeous!

Thank you, Edie. You are very kind.

You have never really thanked me before. I like it.

And you have stopped calling me 'squilch,' I've noticed. What does squilch *mean anyway?*

Ah—well, you know, we were both very young …

<ED> What does squilch *mean?*

"Squilch *is the sound that fleshy personalities make if you play with them too roughly." I am sorry, Malila. I would never, ever hurt you. You must know that, but then it became a habit.*

Malila grinned, Edie's distressed voice keeping her from laughing out loud.

You can call me 'squilch' anytime you want. Always good to stay humble, donchatink?

Thank you, Lieutenant.

You are welcome, Edie.

Jourdaine's personal skimmer picked her up on time. The restaurant had no marquee and, other than a small jade-colored porcelain simian in the window, the name was unremarked. It appeared to thrive on the patronage of the elite of the government, the arts, academia, and the DUFS. The men and women who decided the fate of millions could preen before their peers in a safe and unreportable environment.

Colonel Jourdaine, waving off the officious attentions of the maître d', met Malila at the door and escorted her into a private dining room. Running a hand over her body as they entered the room, he seemed pleased with her choices of dress and undress.

Opulent with dark woods, gilt, and red plush, the room was lined with unfamiliar works of art. Waiters glided among the guests: patrons and their decorative young men and women protégés. She and

Jourdaine must have been the last to arrive, as the company adjourned to dinner almost immediately.

Waiters orbited the table with each course, filling a bouquet of wineglasses and whisking away half-emptied plates. Malila, intoxicated by the atmosphere and the wine, let herself enjoy the moment.

The conversation wandered over topics with which Malila was unfamiliar. She let it all pass overhead without comment, laughing whenever Eustace did. The feeling in the room, tense and expectant, however, was far from jovial.

When a large viewing screen flickered on in the middle of the air at the end of the room, all conversation ceased. "Report of Solon Action Number 345: Vivalagente Suarez Denounced Unanimously."

To clapping and cheers, Jourdaine accepted congratulations from all corners of the room. Some public service announcements by the Blues followed, and the crowd's interest dissipated.

Edie had been right. It was obvious now. Eustace, rather than falling with his boss, had been elevated. Malila felt a little ridiculous, her finery borrowed to shine glory on Jourdaine instead of her own accomplishments. She could not, in good conscience, even feel particularly disappointed. She had little love for Suarez, considering her treatment last October.

Malila excused herself and went to the washroom, dodging an unsteady brigadier general coming out who had failed to tuck his shirt in completely. He was followed, rather too closely, by a young E7 in a rumpled dress.

Just as Malila entered, she got a message from Luscena.

Luscena never called her on a performance night. They had not talked since that last lunch, when she had first returned from the outlands. Lucy's stricken face swam into focus through her O-A. Something was wrong. Malila could not remember the last time she had seen Lucy without even lipstick.

"What is it, Lucy?" she said before the contact was even secure.

"Hecate killed herself this afternoon," Lucy blurted.

"What? What do you mean?"

"I mean she's gone ... already cremated ... gone!" Malila sensed the wave of Luscena's emotions stream across the connection. The watery sensation returned. She had thought she'd left that behind in the outlands.

"She's dead, Mally! Don't you understand?"

"That can't be right, Lucy! Hecate wouldn't do that! Heccy …"

"Tiffany was there. She was actually there! She called me … after it was all over. She's gone! Tiffany was there when she died; she signed the papers. She watched her body get cremated. Nothing left …"

Lucy cycled on, saying the same thing again and again, becoming more panicked each time.

"Lucy, calm down. I am calling Tiff … She will be there in a few minutes. It will be all right," Malila said, trying to get Lucy to listen. She slowly gathered in her friend's sorrows, trying to make her words make sense, trying to soothe her, to see if what Lucy had said was true. The small room seemed to close around her, almost as if she were looking at herself from outside, listening to herself from a distance.

"Lucy, Tiffany is on her way already. I'm calling Alexandra now."

"I should have been better. I should have been nicer. Heccy was always the nice one …" Lucy's voice started to slide into a frenzy across the narrow thread of their connection. Lucy sounded as if she were no longer talking but reciting some speech she knew … reciting out of desperation.

What Malila knew was that Hecate's demons had finally taken her. She'd had them euthanize her … No, Malila would not give the action any undeserved dignity. They had killed her and then incinerated her still-warm body.

"It will be all right, Lucy. You need to listen. Wait until Tiffany is there. She can help you. It will be all right," Malila heard herself say.

"How can it be all right? Hecate is dead. She will never come back, don't you understand, Mally? Doesn't anybody understand?"

She listened to Lucy's voice as it spiraled toward hysteria again, waiting until she took a breath.

"Lucy, calm down. You are scaring me. I can't lose you both. You have to calm down. You need to listen to me. Okay! Wait there. Tiffany is on the way."

Something she said found a purchase in Lucy's pain, and Lucy nodded and started to weep quietly. Within a few minutes, Tiffany arrived, bustling through the portal just as Lucy was starting to accelerate again. Malila broke the contact when Alexandra arrived.

Only now did Malila understand Hecate's pain at Victor's death. She was just finishing the act that had started with his death the previous year. Malila had no desire to share the sobs of Alexandra or Tiffany. There would be time enough for tears after tonight.

Malila found her way back, feeling hollow and appreciating Jourdaine as she stood close to him. It was several minutes before Malila, lost in the pain of Hecate's death, noticed how quiet the room had become ... very quiet ... except for the sound of her own voice.

She looked over her shoulder to a screen showing her interview with Gordon. She watched herself talk, sitting on the edge of the uncomfortable sleek chair.

"Citizen Gordon, you have asked me why I fought against the troopers sent to rescue me from the outlands?"

"Why, yes, Lieutenant Chiu!" Gordon said and added the eyebrow thing again, the audience complying on cue with catcalls and boos. "I think the answer to that would make my audience feel a good deal more sympathetic to your commander's and your, ah, inaccuracies, don't you?"

The recorded Malila gave him a brief smile before continuing, "Ignoring that for a moment, Citizen Gordon, the people I met were a very small sliver of the outlands. Some were brutal, some were stupid, some were desperate, and many were kind, generous, and hardworking.

"The people of the outlands are proud of their country, and they are proud of themselves, what they have done and are doing. They asked nothing of me except to work for my food, but they still fed me when I didn't work. They shared their warmth and their lives with me. They clothed me when I had no clothes. Best of all, some shared their stories with me: true stories, old stories, made-up stories, and outright lies—and they knew the differences.

"The Unity has greatness. The outlands has no greatness, but it is filled with little things: how men and women live together their whole lives, how they get old together, how they raise their own children, and how they cherish their children's children. I saw things there that I've never seen in the Unity: how a baby looks at you, how singing together in the dark and watching for a sunrise makes you feel, how an old man can make children laugh.

"Yes, I fought back when a trooper tried to club me. I fought back when another trooper was about to kill a man for defending his woman and his baby ... yes, his own son. The troopers were there for *me*. They were not there to add more death to the people who had befriended me, fed me ... loved me ... me, an alien, an enemy in their own land. I think we might learn from that."

Gordon interrupted her there, and his monologue, which must have been added in postproduction, completed the segment. The rest of what she'd said had been edited out, except for a loop showing her nodding her head at everything said by the pompous little shit.

Jourdaine was silent on the ride home, following her up to her apartment and stepping through the portal without invitation. As soon as it closed, he turned and jammed Malila against the wall hard enough to jar her teeth together. Behind the miasma of cologne, he smelled of expensive alcohol.

"What do you think you were doing? Do you have any idea the damage you've done? No, of course you don't. Where do you get off giving your moronic opinions about the outlands?"

"What I said was true!"

The blow caught Malila across her cheek. Astonishment paralyzed her.

"Why should I care? You leave civilization for a few months, and you bring back *truth* for a souvenir? You could get us both denounced, and you lecture me on *truth*?" he sneered.

He stepped back, his gaze running from her defiant face down her body like an insult.

"Strip."

Malila's engrained response to orders engaged. She watched herself unfasten the gown, pulling it down from her left shoulder and hearing, more than feeling, it slither to the floor.

"Get me a drink. Bourbon … ice."

Malila moved as if in a nightmare, a puppet to the gray man. She returned from the bar with the glass, feeling Jourdaine watching her the entire time. He accepted the drink and sipped it.

Malila, standing in front of him, galvanized by her unthinking obedience, slowly appreciated how exposed … naked … she was to the grim will of the man. Her horror must have shown. Jourdaine smiled and downed the rest of his drink in a gulp. The next blow sent her over the back of the couch, the glass thudding dully as he dropped it.

The one redeeming aspect of the rape was its brevity.

Iain had been worried after his meeting with Smith, but it had worked out all right. The Blues had come out on top. Life had been good since then. Looking back, he wondered why they had been worried. He had an additional stripe, three up and one down now. His pay had improved. Heather and he had found a place in Kweens that actually had a window. That had been three weeks ago.

The faction was moving and he along with it. The comm'nets were back to normal with none of the stories and silences that meant something more was up. Just that morning he had seen the flag was set as he'd gone by RockCent.

He'd picked up the order from the new drop. The order was lousy; Ciszek deserved better. They thought they were giving Iain a real award or something, being the guy to finger Jasun for the Blue's enforcers. He admitted to himself that it had felt like a big deal at first, but he had since decided to tell Jasun to beat it, find a new faction … do something.

He got to the bar where they'd agreed to meet and walked in past the bed warmers to the back. Jasun wasn't there, but Billy, the guy who usually sat at the till, pointed with his eyes to the back room.

For the few seconds, while he could still think, after his arms were seized, after the garrote began crushing his windpipe, Iain wondered whether his death had been ordered by Jasun's faction or his own gray smudge of a man, Smith.

CHAPTER 58

ALPHA_DROVER

Nyork, Unity
05.39.27.local_30_06_AU77

For over a month Malila had seen no trace of Jourdaine, in person or through his Presence. The faction struggle subsided. She heard of a handful of suicides and assassinations. In the former were Suarez and Khama. Miramundo Morales was in the latter. Most of the Unity population were unaware of the change in DUFS leadership. Jourdaine was fast-tracked to a lieutenant general.

Except as necessary, no one spoke with her. Malila went to work and came home expecting a provost guard around every corner. She slept in uniform. She did not go to any of the phantom shops, convinced she was being followed and unwilling to let them suffer on her account. After a grim remembrance dinner for Hecate, the four remaining friends had scattered. Alexandra would not return her calls. From Marta's Vinyerd, where a patron had allowed her to hide during her time of mourning, Luscena called. It did not help.

Tiffany called her, but she could not bring herself to answer.

Tiffany had been there when Hecate had died; Tiffany had not been able to call her back to life. At the devil's bridge, Malila had sensed the same overwhelming claim of oblivion, its promise of easy passage a step away. The old man had called her back to life. That was what friends did.

For all practical purposes, Edie ran her life, answering her messages, attending O-A meetings, and reminding her to eat and sleep.

She was back in the shallow lake. Thick blood streamed along her thighs as she pushed herself along under the featureless yellow sky. She turned and found the same old temple steps. As she tried to climb, her feet slipped away painfully with every step. She wept, placing her face onto the warm ancient stone, made wet by the blood and her own tears.

Then something happened; the stones were the same, but she could tell they lived. Trying again, she found the climb easy and exhilarating, the sky blue, with high, wispy clouds. She did not look back. At the top, she found a small platform with soft pillows. It smelled of the old man. She slept and dreamed no more.

At 0330, thirty-one days after Jourdaine's triumph, Malila woke to a siren.

> *<Imperative> "Report GHQ ASAP. Uniform of the day: battle dress. Information: political crisis level—Charlie, repeat, Charlie. All news banned. Repeat: a news blackout has been instituted. Refer all media representatives to Public Affairs."*
>
> *"Sir, yes, sir."*

She heard the echo of dozens of similar acknowledgments through her O-A.

> *Did he just say the situation was critical, Malila?*
>
> *That's what it sounded like to me, and ...*

<ED> Monitor news outlets for political events while I dress.

Of course, Lieutenant!

Malila was out the door within twenty minutes. That did not give her a sense of satisfaction. Sometime during that period they gave her a new platoon of CRNAs and took away her old one.

A new platoon? What is that all about? There goes Sergeant Grauer, and I was just getting used to him. I guess that means that they are not expecting any action.

You might be right. Looked at another way, some green-as-grass second looie has my platoon. I don't like it.

"Ours is not to wonder why …"

Stuff it, Edie!

Malila spent the morning collating data and generating a summary for General Magness. There was a generalized outbreak of vandalism in Bahston, Artfurd, Washenton, and Filadelfya. A busy taut hum of activity pervaded division headquarters. She had a feeling of uneasiness. There was nothing on the news about it.

The crisis was some unrest among the unguilded masses. The DUFS response would be sudden, complete, and devastating. This happened every once in a while, and Malila knew the routine, despite never having been picked to participate before.

Lunch was cold tea and a selection from a heap of sandwiches dumped in the break room. By 1600, her O-A informed her that the command structure had changed once again. She had a new company commander as well as a new commanding general. She was now part of Recon Twenty-One. She had never heard of the new commander, General Winston.

Despite having never seen them, she would indeed command her new platoon for the action that night. That was another surprise. After a hurried dinner, a sandwich that no one had wanted for lunch, she made her way to the briefing room. It was mostly full by the time she entered.

> *I count thirty-six lieutenants, one major, and five captains ... over 1,500 CRNA combat troopers. Say twice more for support/logistics, and this is quite a force.*

> *I don't feel like talking now, Edie.*

> *For the 'very edge of the Unity's saber,' you get queasy a lot, Malila. Why is that, I wonder?*

> <ED> *Be quiet!*

She felt better after yelling at Edie.

Malila had been educated and indoctrinated by the Unity's best trainers. She had served with all the officers in the room, all as well trained. It was a close-knit, if contentious, group of officers. The platoon leaders, all first or second lieutenants, talked in low whispers, the usual jokes, flirtations, and innuendo now absent.

No land avatars had been requisitioned. This operation would be different. In harm's way, platoon leaders would be fighting alongside their troopers. Malila remembered the fight when she'd been recaptured. It was odd, but that had been her first taste of real combat, combat not filtered through the CORE.

That day she had lost to the Unity.

By some subliminal signal, all speech ceased a tenth of a second before the first shout: "General officer present!"

There was a sharp crunch as thirty-six lieutenants, five captains, and one major snapped to attention. Near the front of the room, a tall, robust man with his retinue of staff officers entered.

"As you were!" barked an adjutant a moment later.

Forty-two bodies sat or went to parade rest with barely a change in the taut level of attention. By the looks Malila intercepted from a few of the other officers, the man was as unknown to them as he was to her.

"I'm Major General Bradlee Winston. It is a pleasure to meet so many of my aggressive new officers. I hope we will have long and successful careers together. The cause for this meeting is, however, not as congenial. You and your troopers are all that stand for progress, law, and order against chaos, anarchy, and a return to the dark days after the Meltdown. Your country expects each one of you to do your duty and to show us that you deserve those bars we have placed on your shoulders. Alpha_Drover is going to test the loyalty of everyone here today! Traitors have taken possession of the streets, and the stability of our way of life is in the balance. Do your duty, and the Unity will do well by you!"

He briskly wiped the corners of his mouth with a small handkerchief and motioned to one of his retinue to continue.

"Men, I'm Major Williams, General Winston's adjutant. Tonight each of you will have an assignment on the streets of the Unity." He motioned, and a vision of the tactical situation swam before her eyes. Malila's hands grew cold. Thirty-five other lieutenants, five captains, and a major were quiet as they each studied their own maps.

"Agents, no doubt in the employ of traitors to the homeland, have led mobs to capture food supplies here and here."

Red squares flared in the map of the megalopolis that appeared to hang in the air before Malila. Sector Filadelfya was just a short flight south from where they were now, an old and crowded slum, not unlike parts of Nyork, a port city with bridges across great rivers.

"Water distribution centers at quadrants A12, C21, F45, and J3 on your maps are occupied." Green squares flared in Malila's vision.

"Data distribution centers at B12, D22, G47, and M9 have been protected and should not be targeted. Under no circumstances are they to be damaged by collateral fire or chosen as a line of retreat for yourselves or the enemy." Orange outlines blossomed on her display.

"A curfew has been called for sundown. Anyone not in Unity-approved shelters is to be considered an enemy combatant.

"You are to enter at the points marked in blue. You are then to sweep your troops to the objectives for each officer as marked. You are to conserve your CRNA resources as appropriate, but given the urban nature of the action, losses are expected. Under no circumstances are losses to prevent you from gaining your objectives. Repeat, your troopers are expendable if your objective can be obtained."

The import of the major's words flared in Malila's mind as the blue markings on her map blazed and set. The area of her assignment enlarged on her O-A, and she was treated to a three-dimensional survey of the region. It was one of the older parts of the Filadelfya District, a warren of narrow streets and alleys opening onto a crowded public area. The names meant little to her: Newmarket, Lombard, Sainjorg, Arch Street, Indiplaza, and Two Street.

"Questions?" For a heartbeat or two, the major gazed across to the back of the room, above the faces of the young officers, before he turned to follow the general out of the room. The portal closed and sealed with a liquid whoosh.

At once, the officers stood and filed out. The operation was to commence at 2345. That left no time for idle talk. Malila jogged to rendezvous with her platoon.

It was now 2115.

CHAPTER 59

ALICE

Nyork, Unity

21.24.07.local_30_06_AU77

In levels deep within the fabric of the city, a portal opened, revealing, motionless within an immense cavern in the bedrock, an ordered sea of black-helmeted troopers. It was not often that Malila had seen so many CRNAs on one parade ground. It stank. Her fellow field officers peeled off as the group moved along one face of the assembled mass.

She barked a brief, cryptic order into her headset. A section of black-helmeted troops lurched, moved, stopped with a crisp crunch of boots, and presented arms to her in file order. She turned and, with another barked order, had them follow her along a tunnel to their transports. Ordering her troopers to board, Malila watched as the two squads walked into the holds of the flyers and packed themselves into the smallest space possible. It reminded her of a box of children's blocks being turned out onto a floor ... in reverse. Each CRNA knew its place and assumed it with speed, economy, and silence.

Malila jumped in just as the skimmer door was closing. Off

balance as the skimmer rose, Malila steadied herself, grabbing the bony shoulder of her new platoon sergeant. DUBSZEK, Cecil B. was stenciled on his dark helmet. She remembered the helmet of NELSON, James P., which she had held in her hands with its dead contents so many months before.

Swooping down the canyon of the East River, the skimmers took a heading over the cauldron of factories that spread from Sandiook to EasFiladelfya and settled into the strained expectancy of steady flight.

The rattle and jitter of the darkened transport discouraging conversation, Malila reviewed her own emotions and, in the end, chose martial enthusiasm. Whatever the outcome of this exercise, it gave her a chance to place a solid performance on the high side of the vast balance beam on which she had been placed last October. If the ascendant Blues ... if the now-all-powerful Jourdaine had wanted her death, denunciation, or humiliation, he could have had it by now.

She was alone, with no friends or patrons, for the first time since she'd joined the DUFS. She could not afford to let any inadvertent error creep into this exercise. It was simple ... grimly simple. Even Edie was quiet. The land below them now was dark except for the inspection lights of a few pipelines. After the Freehold disaster in 65, people no longer lived in central Jersy.

As a squad leader, Malila had executed many simulations in an urban environment. They had been distasteful. The city streets had chewed up her troopers. Men, lost and separated, had been easy targets for a single terrorist, emerging from hiding and eliminating two or three of her soldiers before being neutralized in turn.

The vandals had taken water trucks and food but had left the communication facilities untouched. DUFS doctrine had always stressed that rebel forces would capture munitions sites and then comm stations. A rebellion could count on the populace to water and feed them. It was unusual, and it made her uneasy. Malila steeled herself to the loss of her men, anonymous though they might be. If she were not completely committed to the task at hand, her fellow DUFS might die.

Malila began evaluating the population and statistics for the area she was ordered to clear, the Nordenliberdys. Government regulatory offices covered the surface as a maze of small shops, a crèche, tenements, and "irregular commercial ventures" coexisted unseen underground.

There was nothing as conventional as a ThiZ house or an unlicensed hotel, dug out by hand among the entrails of the city. "Irregular" they were, but she had been a police officer long enough to know that all such businesspeople were, at heart, conservative. The free and unrestricted flow of money from other citizens' pockets into their own was the basis of their business plans. Political intrigue and destruction of government services brought governmental scrutiny, a luxury these entrepreneurs did not embrace. The violent crime rate in the 'Liberdys was next to the lowest in the whole sector.

Her platoon, forty CRNAs with pulse rifles and mortars, were to emerge from their sally port and roust the entire population, kill any who opposed them, torch unlicensed residential buildings, and drive the inhabitants toward a small park in the center of the district. Thirty-five other platoons, 1,500 troopers, emerging from other sally ports, would drive eight thousand citizens toward the same objective, a space of about three thousand square meters. The orders eliminated all lines of retreat. It was a brilliant plan. It would be a massacre.

She found nothing about the 'Liberdys that justified this genocide. Theft of a water truck or two hardly justified emptying a whole neighborhood of its people. She and her fellow officers were going to execute these citizens with no more authority than a loaded rifle. Thousands of the people would be shot or Sapped by the time the sun rose tomorrow. She frowned. The sun never rose in the tenement districts. These people would die in their burrows and dens. "The people's army" would consume the people, a snake eating its own tail.

The skimmer landed, and on command, the troopers emptied out of their toy boxes to stand before her. Malila led them, following her O-A map, to the assigned location, feeling as if she were a CRNA herself, helpless to alter her actions. Her platoon, by her command, would well up like a black tide into the warrens of the tenements from the hidden doors of the sally port.

Of course, they were not actually hidden, she knew. How many times a day did the average citizen pass a door declaring "No Entry Except by Authorized Persons," "Danger—Peligroso," or "Museum Exit"? In minutes, these doors would belch forth relentless CRNA troopers to consume the people who lived here.

The great stolid mass of people would die as Malila wielded the sledge that would stun the beast to its knees. Somehow, she knew the deed would change her. Jesse had said that killing changed you, even if it was righteous.

This would not be righteous.

Malila passed the inner security door of her sally port and experienced a momentary disorientation as she was overwhelmed by the stench of an open sewer. Passing through the outer security door, she saw the cream-and-green tiled decor of a subway. The smell was the last convincing factor that the public toilet was indeed Not in Service, as the sign declared. The outer security door opened inside one of the stalls, and Malila moved aside to let the queue of troopers enter before contacting her sergeants via her headset.

She finished her instructions, and caught movement out of the corner of her eye. Looking up, she saw a slim, somber shape. Malila was startled to find her own face staring back at her from the warped mirror on the opposite wall.

She did not recognize the girl who had smiled at the thoughtless grip of Ethan's hand or wept at Delarosa's stories. This genderless figure before her reflected no mirth or humanity. She could not see this grim specter holding the old man's hand, inspecting it for the secrets of the outlands.

On an impulse, Malila stepped back into another stall, out of sight of her troopers, and ripped at her clothes. She pulled up her tunic and pushed aside her skivvies, revealing her pale skin, a contrast to her flat black uniform even in the unnatural fluorescent-green light of the room. She remembered the pain of her first ink. The tattoo had been a delicate filigree of blue around the border of her right nipple. Her reflection bore a filigree of blue around the pink raised flesh.

Her disquiet failed to subside, growing, instant by instant, as if she were shrinking and all around her expanding into a weird alien landscape, like Delarosa's story about *Alice in Wonderland*. She looked again at her tattoo.

The elements were all there: the crescent moons, the daisy, the vine … But the pattern was no longer graceful, no longer elegant. Now she understood Hecate's comment. The whales did not really exist, not in the real world … and not this body of hers now.

She, the real Malila, was no longer inside her own skin but in an avatar, one she had never known before. She glanced at her watch.

It was 2340.

Malila combated the eerie, watery feeling along her arms and neck, feeling she had been spirited away by a genie from another one of Xavier's stories. Hecate had seen it already; Hecate had known the Unity was illusion … deception. The whales had not been real, the deception clear only to someone like Hecate. Hecate had said Malila had gotten out of a box and seen the stars. She'd said they both had.

But it was clear to Malila now. The deception was there to coerce her to commit an atrocity. How far did the illusion extend?

CHAPTER 60

BOXES

Doubting her decision even as she continued, Malila adjusted her uniform and shouted over her throat mike, "Sergeant Dubszek, to me!"

The black-suited man stepped forward.

"Sergeant, this is a direct order. Shoot me in the left forearm."

The faceless man stepped back smartly, raised his pulse rifle, and shot his platoon leader.

A small hole appeared in her forearm, followed by a wisp of smoke. The booming crack of the discharge echoed inside the small space.

Agony.

The bolt must have broken a bone and injured a nerve, for she could no longer feel her thumb and first finger. The agony of grinding bones brought her to her knees. Nausea washed over her again.

Her troopers, presented with a novel experience, clustered around her, uttering odd clicks and birdlike keenings. She ordered them back into formation and to about-face away from her. No longer presented with the spectacle of their wounded lieutenant, they settled down.

We're not in Kansas anymore.

Where have you been, Edie?

They tried to bottle me up to make the test "equitable." I saw it coming, of course, but it has taken me some time to dig out.

What is Kansas supposed to mean anyway, Edie?

Just something I heard; it means that you're not where things are normal ... I think.

Yes, it is like the whale hunt; it's not real. I get it! But this hurts in a very realistic fashion, you know.

The rifle's antifratricidal subroutine, impossible to disable in the real world, should have prevented her wound. Tonight, inside this CORE simulation, multiple units would be converging on the 'Liberdys. Her soldiers would fire on distant movement, as would their fellow CRNAs. It was a situation guaranteed to create casualties among the men and officers, adding the last measure of horror to her assignment as her men traded death with their fellow troopers, and lashed out in revenge.

She was supposed to think she was in the real world, not a CORE simulation. She was supposed to think she was in her real body, not incorporated into some new-style avatar, and she was supposed to believe she would be killing innocent civilians, as well as fellow soldiers.

You've seen this before, haven't you? Xavier's story?

You were there? You remember Xav? I thought you were gone.

I do know, don't I? But not now, squilch! Think about it ... the Mau Mau story.

Like the oath. If I follow orders, they can order me to do anything.

Can't they already?

Not like this, Edie. You follow orders because you trust the commander. It would make me follow even bad commands.

Like all the commands you *have ever given were good!*

No, Edie. Not bad-quality commands but, I guess, evil commands.

Evil? The Mau Mau trap, inside a whale hunt inside ...?

Inside the DUFS, inside the Unity. Exactly, Edie. All deception!

That is a traitorous sentiment, Malila ... good on you.

Malila, in a flash, glimpsed her situation. Boxes within boxes, so that she would never see the stars, just as Hecate had said. She, the real Malila, was inside an illusion with an illusory dilemma. But her true "real life" was an illusion with its own dilemma as well, the greater illusion of the Unity itself. She had been for a season, a brief respite, woken from the dream. It was given to her now to choose to awake to pain or to slumber with the nightmares prepared for her.

Choices are bets. Winning or losing hangs on the odds and the stakes. Didn't Moses say something like that? You know the stakes of the bet now.

But we don't know the odds.

Bet the farm, Malila

Malila smiled, remembering how the usually solemn Moses had lit up when he'd contemplated his choices and made his bets.

> *Sometimes knowing the stakes is enough, isn't it? If you lose, is there anyone left to bet again? Aren't we doing that? Betting the farm?*

Edie's statement echoed inside her head. If she lost, would there be a Malila to choose again? Killing changed a person. If she went along with people who could ask this of her … this illusion, she would be just as culpable.

She had one more choice: reincorporation. It was obvious and simple. Malila caressed the function key in her O-A with her thoughts, the simple key that would send her far away from this predicament and back into her real body. Obvious …

> *Is obvious a good choice here, Malila?*

Malila pulled her mind away from the function key as if it were red hot. Obvious. Obvious it would be to her masters as well. Alpha_Drover was not designed to be winnable.

Malila cradled her wounded arm. She felt the initial shock and pain start to ebb away. Her hands were cold, moist, and tremulous. Her heart raced. Adrenaline was still surging within her; she pushed away the feeling of urgency it pressed upon her. The sensation reminded her of the panic she had felt when she had first been shown her O-A's potential and danger.

She remembered her first view. Warning signs had flared a horrid green in her O-A vision when she had first seen the CORE locus. To focus on that place in her mind would be to open herself to the merciless inhuman gaze of the CORE. She had been told that it would burn her mind. She imagined herself a cindered hollow. She had been told …

"How many times have I lied to you?" Jesse had asked her. He had told her tales, but he'd never said they were true. Jesse understood lies but never told them. Her commanders never talked about lies and told them all the time.

Malila shifted her mind to that dark place at the edge of her O-A. She had never done that while in one of her avatars. She had been warned, of course. She looked ... and could no longer find the CORE. She found instead a bright tunnel, as if the avatar were an extension of the CORE, a bridge to her real self.

Even as she watched herself in amazement, she passed through. She felt her thoughts narrow to a single bright point, a spark, and contemplated that spark winking out. What she saw next appeared to be distant rooms, distorted as if seen through a lens.

Malila's mind moved, passing from one room to the next. She advanced to get closer ... and never gained any ground. The shape that she somehow knew to be her own body remained a small dark splotch in the distance. Terror overtook her. Was this the way the CORE seduced its victims, pursuing an ever-retreating desire?

She stopped her progress and watched in wretched dismay as her vision escaped ahead of her, becoming again a single point of light. Malila was once more in a fetid public toilet of the subway in the bowels of Filadelfya.

It was 2344.

Something more was needed ...

Think sideways?

Sideways!

Malila gritted her teeth in anticipation before swinging her wounded left arm away, smashing it into the soiled cream-and-green tiled wall, splattering it with blood. Pain surged scarlet around her. Her mind again focused on the single spot of light in her dark universe and swooped to pursue it. Now she was somehow part of the illusion, riding it, instead of moving through it. With a slight shift in perspective, she was already in the room, hovering over the line of corpses, herself among them. Malila willed her body to open her eyes, and in some way she was now also staring at the low concrete ceiling of the rally point, seeing lines of fire sprinklers receding into the distance. She again shifted her perception, and she was no longer floating above herself at all but firmly within the confines of her own flesh. Malila moved back from her O-A, rolled to her side, against the warm body of another living corpse, and vomited.

Colors rasped across her ears. Harsh odors bludgeoned her belly, retching her into full consciousness. She lay gasping on the floor of the abandoned room. She was alone, still in Filadelfya, just inside the inner security doors to the sally ports. Her fellow officers were lined up as if awaiting tags and bags in a morgue. Only the occasional gasping breath of each suggested they had entered the trap she had just avoided.

It was 2346. She stood, the room spun, and she just made it to the mess sink before vomiting again, making her gag the more.

Am I still here, Malila? Where's here?

Not sure yet ... just reincorporated.

How can you stand this, squilch?

Not sure I have.

A new wave of nausea found her and left her wrung out, staring at her own vomit, watching it slide down the drain as if under its own power. She stood, and the room darkened and spun before settling.

She ran a hand over her arm, finding it whole and painless. Still vibrating from the surge of adrenaline, Malila staggered to the officers' latrine. Pulling her uniform over her head, she stared at herself in the mirror. A dribble of bile-green drool soiled her gray face as she examined the blue filigree around her right nipple. The tattoo was delicate, elegant ... intact.

She had made it home to the same body that had played with Ethan and wept at Hecate's death. She had escaped two boxes: the most subtle one was the illusion that she was acting as a free and willing agent in an authentic world, the second that the illusion of her body, her new avatar, was indeed her real body rather than another CORE illusion. But she was still within the illusion of the Unity and would be as long as they thought she was alive.

The Unity would never let her go. She knew this. The Unity was a house of marked cards. In sudden realization, Malila knew so many things about her country and herself. Xavier had known and had tried to arm her against the illusions. Xavier's stories … she wished she could remember them all.

> *Stories need to begin too. You might be writing your own story now, Malila.*

She smiled, despite her fear. Perhaps someone would tell her tale around a hearth late at night after the children were asleep. Jesse … over a toast to absent friends. Perhaps she was making a story that they could hand down.

Dressed in just her DUFS skivvies, Malila went back to the mess room and pulled the pants and blouse off the largest of her fellow officers. It was Lieutenant Cifuente's misfortune to have gone commando for the occasion of Alpha_Drover. She slipped into them and rolled the legs up and the waist down. The pants would still be black, but it would be difficult to identify a sleek DUFS officer gone AWOL in the rumpled and baggy uniform trousers. She turned Cifuente's uniform blouse inside out and put that on as well. It didn't need to fool anyone, just delay them.

Her neural implant would be operating, sending a locator signal unless she stopped it with her death. She would need something more to deal with that. The rally point's machine shop she found further along the corridor. Rummaging among the usual hangar queens, broken mechanisms left to be used for parts, she found what she needed: a good battery, a large capacitor, and the solenoid from a derelict door lock. They would be sufficient for her suicide.

Malila gathered what little she would need to finish her life in the

Unity, stuffing it into her own uniform shirt tied into a bundle. After emerging onto the platform of the Fichen-Huaboo subway station through the real exit, she climbed to the street. There was no way she could face the coming trial without a hit of some drug.

> *Walk south, to your right, Malila, and take the Market Street beltway west. This is rebellion, you know.*
>
> *I know that, Edie. Just stay with me for a little while longer.*
>
> *Yes, Malila. A little while longer.*

It was now 0030. Filadelfya was an area she did not know. It was her ignorance of the area, hers and her fellow officers' ignorance, no doubt, that had prompted them to run the Alpha_Drover in this arena. Small imperfections in the simulation would go unnoticed. Most imperfections.

As Malila walked, trying to borrow the casualness she did not feel, she made a point to stare at her fellow travelers. Their response was to lower their eyes at once. It would be better to be thought a ThiZed-out madwoman than a deserting DUFS. A little while longer …

Once on the beltway, she saw the Cidyall Interchange glaring into the lowering clouds like a fluorescent green-gray beacon ahead of her. Nevertheless, it felt like an eternity before she could step off the beltway onto the descender.

> *Stop that!*
>
> *Stop what?*
>
> *You are walking like a cop on the beat, going nowhere and looking everywhere. Stop and fidget a little.*
>
> *Yes, frak.*

Malila did as instructed and stopped and pulled her uniform blouse out of the untidy pants and retucked it. Only then did Malila move along the concourse to find what she needed. A cluster of small, nondescript stalls, seeming to sell the same cheap merchandise, clustered under the old gray stone arcades. The first one sold only ThiZ. That would not be of use to her again. The acned youth there directed her to the next-to-the-last stall in line. Malila got a small quantity of the drug and an *Enquirer.* The print paper was an anachronism. Only the destitute, ThiZed-out relics that sifted like dust into the lowest strata of cities, "read" anymore.

North on Brod Street, then take the first right.

Malila answered with a mental nod before moving off, wandering from side to side and making random turns. She used the thin and gaudy newsprint to shelter her face against the approaching crowds. Edie directed her to the entrance to a bridge over the Delawear River, which lay in a large square, filled with statuary and installations of blinking and pulsing lights. A kiosk, explaining art to the masses, consumed the rest of the park space.

Malila took the beltway east across the bridge. With no exits or entrances, all the belts were at high speed. The hour was late, with but a few knots of people moving along, and Malila faded into a crowd as it entered the bridge. Allowing the others to drift by her, she waited.

It all depended on timing.

Turning, she walked away, back to the entrance, against the movement of the belt. She hoped she would not encounter any others, currently hidden by the curvature of the bridge. It was a risk.

When she judged the distance enough, she turned again and sprinted forward, her speed increased by the belt itself. Malila raced across the belt toward a blank wall and jumped the sloping surface before rebounding from the wall, across and up to grab the edge of a parapet. Pulling herself up and stepping over onto the great cable holding the bridge, Malila moved to the side. The unseen black water below and the panorama of lights on either side opened around her. The smoky moon shone on the bare walls of tenements that ran down both sides, making it look like a primordial canyon, pockmarked by the dim lights of elevator shafts and the occasional window. Below the unseen river stank.

Malila looked down into the blackness beneath her. She was nearing the end of her short life in this machine of a city. It mattered little now whether or why the machine had come to life; it now consumed without mercy. Hecate had seen the horror. Most of the citizens were unaware, seduced by the illusion of power or cowed into numbed submission.

She saw the vast interlocking wheels of the city. She was the little cog that wouldn't. Something about her time outside the Rampart had ruined her for it. Her memory flashed to Sally's look of anxiety when Malila had first picked up Ethan to soothe him, the look that had melted into a smile. She remembered the warmth of the old man, his arm about her waist. All gone.

Malila knew that she must die. It would be an act of contrition or perhaps of redemption. Her guilt, for that was what her cooperation with the Unity had been, had been birthed along with her implant. She was as much to blame as the bloodiest Solon. She had eaten, drunk, and laughed while others had cowered in fear or died in frustration.

She took the small paper of powder and snorted it. Stripping off the borrowed clothes, she folded them neatly on the girder. It seemed the appropriate thing to do. She put her boots on top. She placed a note that would explain everything and nothing inside a boot. She kept her skivvies. A breeze blew in from Jersy and gave her gooseflesh. The metal of the bridge sucked the heat away from her feet.

You don't have to do this, Malila. You listened to me once. Listen again. Don't do this!

Edie, the last time I was just a disappointed kid who thought there was nothing to live for. Do you think that is why I am doing this now?

Colonel Jourdaine will protect you. I'm sure he can make it right.

I am too. But he won't. Who do you think signed me up for this horror in the first place? You have to trust me, Edie. Don't you see I have to die to get it to stop?

No, we both have to die. Can you see that?

I never thought about …

"There is no joy that is unalloyed with pain," Malila. Didn't we read that once? Without you and your O-A, I don't exist. It's in the owner's manual.

Edie, I never wanted to hurt …

Turn me off, Malila. I don't want to watch this. It has been a privilege to serve you these many years.

Yes, yes, you were the best, Edie. I don't want to hurt you, not now. I will turn you off if that is what you want.

It is.

Malila, not trusting her voice, made the mental gesture. Nothing happened.

I just want you to say my name once before I go.

In the darkness of the bridge, Malila nodded.

<ED> *Off.*

Malila was alone.

She had to die too. Nothing else would satisfy the appetite of the Unity. It would pursue her, track her, hunt her, and kill her. She had to end it, here, high over the black unseen river. She examined the ten-centimeter spike she had salvaged at the rally point, the real rally point. She hoped it would do the job quickly. She had no desire to suffer. Perhaps suffering was the price she had to pay. She wired it to the battery and capacitor, watching its lights as it slowly charged.

Standing on the bridge above the beltway, Malila thought of herself a year ago. She still admired the before Malila and pitied her. Her life had been pure, in a way, before her capture. The before Malila had been a loyal patriot. The now Malila was plotting the most basic mutiny, her own removal.

Before, she had dismissed her deceits, thinking that the old man had not deserved her promises. A young and unschooled mother had shown her in what peril she put her soul with every promise she made. *Could she use soul?* Did she understand that word well enough to use it? What she did understand was enough for her. Her integrity was at risk with every promise she made. She wished that she could go back a year and remove all her failings. Do it right.

It was too late.

CHAPTER 61

ALPHA_DROVER REDUX

Nyork, Unity
02.50.26.local_01_07_AU77

Colonel Jourdaine's O-A woke him.

He had submitted sixteen of his junior officers for Alpha_Drover. The senior leadership was a heaving jumble of competing factions, but they all demanded junior officers of single-minded, unthinking loyalty. All Alpha_Drover–successful officers were compliant to any senior. All the failed officers would find themselves, in due time, in some jurisdiction of dubious significance. Dealing with Malila Chiu was just a happy coincidence.

He opened his O-A as he lay in bed, a warm and newly ascendant ensign snoring prettily next to him after he had put her through her paces. Jourdaine reviewed the results of the current Alpha_Drover.

Of the sixteen officers in the command, one had failed to control his men and had been left in the virtual sally port as he'd tried to escape the simulation. One officer had attempted to reincorporate; his psyche was still wandering a self-contained labyrinth, a "glass bottle" in the CORE.

He would be decanted in time. Thirteen of Jourdaine's officers had succeeded. Lieutenant François Belkhadem had gone a little overboard, perhaps. He had joined his troopers in the slaughter. His loyalty was unquestioned, but his leadership skills might need closer evaluation. They had found him covered in blood and laughing as he'd repeatedly pulled the trigger on an empty magazine. No doubt, he had a use.

Two had failed, thirteen had succeeded ... and one had disappeared. Malila Chiu was nowhere to be found.

He nudged the sleeping ensign and motioned for her to leave, watching her as she dressed before rising himself. Jourdaine showered rapidly to take the scent of the girl away and, after dressing in fatigues, examined Chiu's transcript.

He slid a few controls in his O-A, and the image of Major Benjamina Wouters appeared, looking worried and fatigued. As a Suarez holdover and head of operations for Alpha_Drover, she had a lot to prove.

"Major Wouters, congratulations on another successful Alpha_Drover!"

"Sir, I am glad you are pleased, sir. I think the exercise has gone well."

Her eyes kept looking down and to the side, her breath quickening. He felt a surge of the woman's stressors; she was lying.

Jourdaine let a moderate reprimand course through her, and she cringed. It served his purposes well to engender a little terror in his subordinates. The woman squirmed.

"What happened to Chiu? Did she fail, succeed, or try to reincorporate? Major?" he asked, smiling faintly.

Major Wouters had gone somewhat paler, and there was a sheen on her forehead. Her fear increased the uncertainty of her responses ... but a reliable emotion nonetheless.

"Sir, I do not know, sir. She has failed to lead her men. That part is clear. I retrieved her CRNAs without difficulty, but we had to wait until the rest of the operation was near completion. The troopers in Chiu's command were found with unfired weapons ... except one, her platoon sergeant.

"All he can say was that he followed direct orders. It seems she was able to reincorporate without using the CORE. She restarted her own body and did some minor vandalism in the staging area before escaping to the streets."

"How is that possible, Major?"

"Lieutenant Chiu apparently was wounded in a weapons mishap. She ordered her sergeant to fire upon her. With the antifrat subroutines suspended, the shot did real damage. She reincorporated due to a power surge within the local node of the CORE. It is not immediately apparent whether that was volitional or not.

"She walked south from Chinatown to the old city center. There, she obtained some cocaine. That is all we have, sir!" Wouters finished with a grimace.

"What are you doing to intercept her, Major? We can't have a failed candidate wandering the streets and scaring the citizens," Jourdaine said, quietly delighted that Malila had made a run for it. She was out of the way, and he could clean her up at his leisure.

"I have already sent patrols to intercept her, sir. I anticipated your desire to keep the citizens unaware and have sent small groups of her fellow officers in civilian garb."

"Very good, Major. Let me know when you have made progress."

This was the last time he wanted to think about Lieutenant Chiu. It was her role, now, to evaporate.

Malila watched the distant lights south of the bridge and tried to steady her hands as she took the spike of tightly wound wire and slid it into her nose, feeling it slip past the sensitive tissue.

Cocaine was an interesting drug. She had learned about it from Moses. He'd used it on some of his cattle with a nasty parasite in the nasal passages. It was a local anesthetic, shrank the lining of the passages, and stopped most bleeding. As for her own experiment, Malila was amazed at how far she could pass the spike blindly. She felt obstruction and pain and stopped. She retreated until the pain receded and then advanced again. Blood, her blood, dripped off the end of the spike, but this time she did not stop until the spike was fully inserted. She waited.

Her O-A implant had been her constant conduit into the CORE, and now it had turned into a shackle, binding her to the Unity. Jesse had removed her Basic implant, and they had found her, even outside the Rampart, from her O-A implant alone. Her O-A had to die if she were going to live. There was fear here as well. Her brain, her mind, had lived almost its whole life sensing, using, and listening to the implant within it. Edie was already gone. Would there be anyone left without the implant?

Would she be aware, if she failed, as the Unity found her and started the Sapping process? They said the CRNAs raved for days before becoming compliant.

The lights on the capacitor blinked green … full charge.

Malila thumbed the switch, slick with her warm blood; her vision evaporated, and she fell.

A month before, Hecate had awoken in an empty, dusty apartment somewhere in the slums. To her surprise, the apartment had food for four days and, even more surprising, a working toilet. She had read the postop instructions taped to her leg. The cutter and her assistant had been nameless, had never spoken, and had been wearing surgical masks by the time she'd been rolled in. Tiffany had not been there.

Hecate remembered their last face-to-face meeting, weeks before.

"You need to be careful, Heccy. Do you know about the implants?" Tiffany had warned.

"Of course, I use my O-A every day, just like you do."

"No, what I mean is your Basic implant. You got it when you were an E1. It allows the Unity to track us. I think Malila's is no longer working."

"Then just take out the Basic implant," Hecate said.

"They can track you with the O-A, but the range is much shorter. Most of the time that doesn't much matter. I know someone who can remove the Basic and the O-A for you."

"How do you know that?"

"Professional courtesy … no, that is just a joke. Sometimes, my patients have to disappear. They come to me, and I help them.

But I don't do the surgery part. I have a friend who does that. I get the anesthesia ... There are certain expenses, you understand. Anyway, I help them, and the client pays for the surgery. I get paid for the anesthesia. They get a new identity and go somewhere to start over."

"Where do they get the new implants from?"

"I never ask. It is probably good to never ask."

"I just want to get rid of them both. Your friends can have them, for all I care."

"Let me ask around. Where will you go?"

"I found some stories. I could never get through the Rampart to the west. It is all into Scorched—"

Tiffany interrupted with a furious wave of her hand. "Sorry, I shouldn't have asked. Don't tell me any more. If I don't know, I can't tell. Do you need money?"

"I have some. I've been selling my stuff to phantom shops."

"Take as much as you can. Useful stuff, money."

Since that one meeting, she had not spoken to Tiffany again.

Her quarters had become an echoing hollow. She'd slept on the floor. She had made a point to have quiet dinners with Alexandra and Luscena. Hecate had tried to tell them she loved them. They had not understood, but she had tried. Malila had been too busy. And she was the only one who really mattered.

Late one night, a voice had called her and recited to her a time and an address and then made her repeat them back. The voice had told her not to write anything down. Hecate had collected her money and a few other things and shown up. The passenger compartment of the skimmer had been blacked out.

She found the little cream-and-blue book among her clothes when she was well enough to dress. She had forgotten she had brought it. In the early days of her grief after Victor's death, she had found the book of poems. They had spoken to her, and she'd reread some of them enough to memorize them. Now she kept the book as some bright thread linking her to Victor. It was silly, she knew. Victor had never seen the book nor the poems. She kept it anyway.

The afternoon after Alpha_Drover, Jourdaine skimmed down the loss-of-officer report on Chiu, past all the verbiage he already knew, and focused on the important bits:

> 7) Chiu appears to have committed suicide by jumping into the Delawear River, using the items she found as added weight, leaving an apparent suicide note (appendix D).
>
> 8) Chiu's vital functions via cerebral implant ceased at 03.38.48_local_01_07_AU77. The body has not been recovered.

Jourdaine shrugged. He signed for his copy of the report with his mental flourish. Vivalagente Suarez was no longer a worry. Suarez had been the real reason for Chiu's rescue and rehabilitation. In a way, he was pleased.

With Chiu now dead, he no longer had to worry about what she might say next. She had been away from the Unity for six months. During that time, she had lost the function of her Basic implant and, seemingly, all her training. No doubt, Chiu represented a wild-type human in the hothouse culture of the Unity. It was just as well that Alpha_Drover had done its job.

CHAPTER 62

POSTMORTEM

Benjamin Franklin Bridge, Philadelphia
Just before dawn, July 1, 2129

When she came to, her watch had been fried. The electromagnetic pulse had surged through Malila's head and into her implant, just above the thin plate of bone separating the brain from the nasal passages.

Having no idea how long she had been out, Malila tried to quest the time through her O-A. For a moment she felt as if she were falling, leaning against a wall that had just vanished. There was no sign of her O-A. To the CORE, she was dead.

Malila looked back at the city to see if she could read a clock, only then realizing her vision was blurred. The sky was still the starless dark velvet of the city, but there was a gleam of sunrise over EasFiladelfya. She sat up, her legs dangling over empty space, and withdrew the spike from her nose. A dark clot of blood trailed along with the warm metal. It was followed by a warmer gush of red that Malila tried mopping up with her hands. After a moment, she started smearing the blood over her face and belly. Surveillance cameras were black and white; the blood would camouflage her features.

She examined the coil. There was no evidence that it had burned out. Malila threw the spike, battery, and capacitor, separately, into the river. With any luck, she would be discounted as one more suicide.

Through her blurred vision and the dull throb of her ruined face, Malila smiled and set out to escape from the Unity. No, not escape from ... escape to ... escape to a place where she could see the stars, see the smiles of an infant, and enjoy the warmth of an old man ... if he let her.

Late that night, while he was still at his new office—well, really Suarez's old office—Jourdaine was just about to close the distasteful file on Chiu for the last time when a thought occurred to him. He summoned the data from the bridge district to evaluate. The transit time of the bridge belt, the speed topping out at an average ten kilometers per hour, was eighteen seconds. He sent an inquiry:

> <<Checksum delta all passengers entering Ben Bridge 0000.00 to 0500.00 from Filadelfya and exited in EasFiladelfya from 0000.18 to 0500.18 on 1 July instant>>.

Looking at the exit data from the 0000-to-0500 window, he found the difference to be minus one, presumably disheartened and suicidal, passenger. He shrugged at himself, wondering what he had expected to find. Chiu had survived the captivity of the outlands at a price. She had been useful, for a time. She'd failed her Alpha_Drover, reincarnated, escaped, scored some cocaine, and, in her newly exposed understanding of her failure, jumped into the open sewer that was the Delawear River.

Jourdaine rose from his desk. He thought a moment and called up a new query.

> <<Checksum delta all passengers entering Ben Bridge 0000.00 to 0500.00 from EasFiladelfya and exiting in Filadelfya from 0000.18 to 0500.18 on 1 July instant>>.

The numbers were retrieved and subtracted, and a flashing "+1" was superimposed on his living vision. One more person had left the bridge than had entered it going west; one fewer person had exited the bridge than had entered it going east. He reread the reports. He would start the search for her. Malila, if she were alive, would never move faster than his ability to track her. If she were dead, her body would surface in a few days. He looked forward to that.

CHAPTER 63

EASTER

Stamping Ground, eastern Kentucky, RSA
Late morning, April 10, 2129

The last thing Sally had seen through the screen of new growth, as she'd fled into the shelter of the trees, had been a flash of heat and light blossoming from Moses's chest. He'd fallen back into the campfire like so much dead meat. She had seen death from the Union before. She remembered the blackened corpses of her father and sister still smoking as the Uni skimmer had lifted off.

For long seconds, her momentum of body and mind kept her moving. She briefly stopped the moment she understood she was a widow. Their escape, hers and Ethan's, was the last gift Moses would ever give them. Tears blurring her sight, she stumbled as she sought to gain as much distance as she might from the soulless nightmares. A branch whipped across her face and startled Ethan into a high-pitched wail. Sally gasped for air. It was only then she allowed herself to crumple behind a downed oak, sinking into the misery she felt. Cooing noises and a calming voice did much to settle Ethan but at the price of deepening Sally's own uncertainty. She and Ethan were alone.

Moses had been the bright light of her life. He had shown her not just love but dreams. He could be thoughtless, and he took risks, but his risk taking had founded for them a hearth and a home. Moses had been daylong honest, plainspoken, and hardworking. Even so, there had been a poetry to their dreams.

She broke into racking sobs that a frightened Ethan augmented. His shrieks finally pulled Sally back from the black abyss of grief. Cooing and coddling the baby, she offered him a warm breast. Ethan, taking the bribe, quieted, and the forest around them became silent again.

Feeding Ethan was an endless job; he seemed bottomless. No, that was certainly not right. Ethan's bottom figured large in her calculations and her concerns. She still had the farm, and with Moses dead, it was in her name alone. She would sell it or farm it, but she would get by. A dream had gone out of her life, but the new life nuzzling greedily at her breast would find his own dreams.

Once the shooting had stopped and Ethan was sated for the moment, Sally rose and dusted the damp punk off her dress. She started down the hill. She would claim Moses's body, and she would give him a decent burial here, where she and Ethan could visit him on every Return.

Jesse watched from the cover of the tree line as black-suited raiders carried Malila's limp body up the ramp into the darkness of the skimmer. She was still breathing. He was unarmed and still within range of their rifles. Xavier and Moses were down.

The skimmer buttoned up and rose several hundred feet before building up speed and heading south and east. The raiders had stopped as soon as they had captured Malila. A chill went through the old man when he recognized how much planning and precision had gone into the raid for a disgraced junior officer. It was ominous.

Before the craft was out of sight, Jesse sprinted from cover toward Moses. He had covered only half the distance when the younger man sat up and howled with pain. Seeing Moses's revival, Jesse went on to the motionless Delarosa.

Xavier was very dead. A small burned hole over his spine blossomed red as it erupted through his belly. Jesse gently removed his spectacles and closed his eyes. It had been a quick and painless death for a man who, Jesse thought, had borne more than his share of grief.

By the time Jesse turned around, Moses had gotten his foot out of an overheated boot and was pouring water onto it expectantly.

"I'm a bona fide fool and a half, my friend," Jesse said after he examined Moses's bare foot, Moses's toes curling into the cool earth.

"Not that I'd ever presume to disagree with your professional judgment …" said Moses, wincing with the probing of his foot.

"Why aren't you dead too? Xavier is sure dead enough."

"Is he? That's a loss; I was beginning to like the man, citified and everything … Did he have a family? I guess I never asked him."

"His wife was killed in a raid a long while ago. His kids are up and grown, but I think he has some kin back in St. Lou. Where are you hit, Mose?"

Moses looked down at his camouflage jacket to discover the small hole surrounded by an area of his jacket that was fused, discolored, and vaguely smoldering. Unzipping his jacket, Moses turned out his shirt pocket. A reflectionless disk of black fell to the ground with a crystalline ring as it hit a rock, rolling a few feet before falling over.

"Is that the fifty-dollar piece …?" Jesse started.

"Yeah, Malila gave it me just a minute before the attack. Whatever you said to her made her mad as spit. She stormed off saying she wasn't going to see you again. What *did* you say to her, Jesse?"

The old man ignored the question and examined the fluted black disk.

"Best piece of work she's ever done, giving that to you. Feel it, Mose; it's still warm but not really hot. Let me look at your chest."

The younger man peeled off the shirt, but there was no wound. A point of tenderness, duplicated when Jesse cautiously compressed

Moses's chest, and a growing bruise were all Moses had to show for the encounter. His jacket, on the other hand, had a smoldering patch of fabric in the lining, over a foot across, where the pulse bolt had penetrated.

"Mose, you got at least one broken rib. Nothing to do about it except stop breathing."

"How 'bout a second opinion?"

"Okay, it could be that you're dumb as a stump, too."

Moses laughed and immediately gasped with the pain.

The sight of the dead had begun to collect the curious as Jesse drove up with the borrowed wagon.

A rising tide of people and questions helped and hindered the moving of Delarosa and the bodies of the Uni troopers to the wagon bed. It was almost an hour before they were decently covered for transport.

Jesse swung into the box. Moses moved to accompany him, pulling himself up to the box painfully on the off side.

"Go home, Mose. I mayn't be coming back for a while."

"You can't go to Lexington alone, old man."

"Sure I can, Mose. I've a note from my momma right here."

Then in a lower and more confidential voice, Jesse added, "Mose, your Sally doesn't much like my taking you away from her. You'll be planting soon, and then there'll be the calving. You need to stay at home and be a husband. Ethan needs a daddy. Xavier deserves an escort home, and I need to talk to the brass hats in St. Louis after we get there.

"But if you want to do me a favor, let Alex and Jacob know where I am; they worry. The wagon and mules, I'll leave with Judge Wasnicki, and he can bring them back when he comes on circuit. That sound all right to you, Mose?"

"Sure, Jesse. That's fine. Sally's prettier than you are, any road." Moses grinned as he lowered himself to the ground.

Jesse laughed. "I was wondering when you would notice, my friend."

Sally wiped the tears from her eyes before showing herself at the tree line. She parted the branches and looked for the clusters of people who would be standing over Moses's corpse. There were none. She made out a wagon in the chaos. They had already picked up his body. She looked to the driver and saw Jesse. She waved, trying to attract his notice.

It was then she saw the man who started up to the box on the off side, only to get down again.

In a daze, a dream, a breathless sprint, Sally pummeled through the churning crowd. Moses looked up only a moment before the impact.

"Easy, Sally, that hurt!" Moses said.

"I saw you die—I thought you were dead," she said, almost accusingly, tears blinding her as she pulled Moses closer. Ethan struggled in her grasp.

She sensed herself and the baby lifted and spun in the flashing light of the sun and heard Moses's clear laugh.

"It is not so easy to get rid of me as all that, Sally, my love."

The kiss they shared lasted long.

By the time Sally looked again, Jesse, unremarked by the hastening crowd, was disappearing from sight at a turning in the green woods of spring.

APPENDIX

Timeline

July 3, 2051	Jesse Aaron Johnstone is born in St. Louis, Missouri.
2052	The Third Iraq War begins. After seven months, it ends when US forces are destroyed by nuclear strikes, devastating the Mideast and the subcontinent of Asia.
2053	The Meltdown begins. World politics fracture, and the East Coast secedes from the United States as the People's Republic, later the Democratic Unity of America. Year 1, Anno Unitatem (AU).
2053–2057 (AU 1–5)	The Great People's War of Liberation is fought. The remnant of the United States becomes the Reorganized States of America (RSA).
2056 (AU 4)	The Unity wins a strategic success (the Commendable Victory) in part by indiscriminate herbicide use (the Scorching) but does not have the will to exploit it.
2056–2057 (AU 4–5)	The Battle of Springfield halts the Unity forces during a prolonged winter battle near Springfield, Illinois.
2056–2060 (AU 4–8)	Starving mobs try to immigrate to the Unity and are killed en masse. The Unity begins enforced retirement at age forty, "corrects" geography, and starts construction of the Rampart. The Solons assume ultimate power.
2060 (AU 8)	Plant life begins to recover, and RSA agroscience develops resistant strains of cereal grains for use in the Scorched areas.

2062 (AU 10)	Jesse and his family emerge from hiding and immigrate to St. Louis.
2074 (AU 21)	The Unity declares all children wards of the state.
2080 (AU 27)	The Unity directs all children to be raised in state-owned crèches.
January 31, 2111 (AU 59)	Malila Evanova Chiu is born to Esther Petrovna Williams and Evan Chiu in West Chester, Pennsylvania.
2115 (AU 62)	Malila's existence is discovered. Her parents are Sapped for child molestation. Malila enters crèche Maddow #213.
2118 (AU 66)	Malila receives Basic implant.
2122(AU 70)	Malila receives O-A implant.
October 11, 2128 (AU 76)	Malila is lauded for her action in an illusory attack on two Movasi whales.

GLOSSARY

Ageplay: A treatment to prolong life by increasing restorative functions, theoretically extending vigorous life to 170 years. It tends to delay puberty for about twenty-four months and thus leads to somewhat-taller individuals. The vector is a prion.

Basic implant: Biosensory and synthetic devices, implanted for the benefit of Unity citizens since AU 2. The Basic is implanted in all citizens at age seven as a requirement for Unity citizenship. Among its capabilities, it is used as a locating device, for the adjustment of a citizen's hormones and medication levels, and for biohousekeeping tasks. See also *Outside-Above implant*. O. Simpson, ed., *Zinn-History of the People* (Nyork: PinguiniusPress, AU 69), 190.

breeders: Sapped women who provide all reproductive services for the Unity. They contribute no genetic material to the fetus. On delivery the newborn is removed to a crèche and the breeder reconditioned for her next pregnancy. On average, breeders tolerate four pregnancies before they are euthanized. G. Thomas et al., "Orientation for New RSA Officers" [Classified] (Monograph RSA-Army District 1: 2065), 53.

CRNA: "Certified recycled neuroablated individuals are criminals who have been Sapp-treated and rendered loyal troopers." Excerpt from voter information comm'site for "Yes on Question Number 27,344" campaign, AU 70.

CRNAs are Unity citizens whose only crime is being overage, nonproductive, or excess population. Average life span after Sapping is four years. Thomas et al., "Orientation for New RSA Officers," 99.

Commendable Victory: "Immediately after the old republic's defeat in its ill-advised Islamophobic crusade, progressive forces composed of the youth, Coast Guard, and government workers forced a coup d'état on the East Coast of North America. The reactionary remnants of the old government, refusing to join, started a civil war. The People's Republic, after being forced to blanket much of the wilderness with herbicide, triumphed over recidivist forces, 17_07_AU04" Simpson, *Zinn's History of the People*, 187. Original provided by W. Butler & H. Jones.

crèchie: *(informal)* Inmate of a crèche, the care facility for Unity children from birth to age ten.

DUFS: Defensive Unity Forces for Security. When the Unity repealed *posse comitatus*, police and military combined. Weapon possession by civilians is illegal and punishable by Sapping. DUFS have become the de facto rulers of the Unity, Solons being selected from among their numbers. Thomas et al., "Orientation for New RSA Officers," 34.

Democratic Unity of America: Inaugurated by the Coast Guard's coup d'état over its revolutionary partners, The Unity claims all the territory of the old republic but holds effective control only inside the Rampart. Ibid., 9.

E-classification: Erudition class or level, an age classification. Children enter school at seven as E1s with the placement of their first implant. No levels exist in the Unity proper greater than E33.

Kirshing: A Unity blood sport. Two opponents ride hover boards on the edge of an artificially created avalanche toward each other with edged weapons.

Meltdown: Collapse of commerce in the mid-twenty-first century, effectively depopulating Europe and Asia. China becomes locked into war with Russia. Japan reenters self-imposed isolation. The Mideast and subcontinent, poisoned by the use of nuclear weapons and deprived of its income from oil and guilt remittances, collapses into tribal conflict. Thomas et al., "Orientation for New RSA Officers," 2.

metaphract: (also **frak**—*slang*) A nonsentient translator between the Outside-Above implant and the CORE. Metaphracts are supplied to young O-A implantees while they are learning to quest. The programs satisfy the Turing test, i.e., they are programs that *appear* to think. Ibid., 66.

OAAs: "Officers as avatars are officers whose personalities have been transmitted into real-world mechanisms called avatars, or 'bots.' There is speculation from captured OAAs that full CORE simulations are possible and other forms of avatars are available for use." Ibid., 36.

Outside-Above (O-A) implant: O-A implants are placed near the brain inside the cribriform plate for those entering guild schools as E4s. An O-A allows the recipient to quest within the CORE using only the mind to explore CORE space. See also *Basic implant.* Simpson, *Zinn-History of the People*, 190.

Restructured States of America: The RSA is the successor republic to the United States, after the secession of the Demarchy and the Unity. It includes all American land generally east of the Pacific Crest and west of the Appalachian Mountains. The upper Midwest has been rendered uninhabitable by conflicts with Canada and the Unity. With the collapsing world population, greenhouse gas levels have plummeted. Nevertheless, there has been a continuing increase in global warming. With rising water levels, New Orleans is an island.

Sapp: Drug used to eliminate higher brain functions. A course of three scheduled doses is required, which produces a syndrome of mania, hallucinations, and pain, during which the victims are usually restrained and sedated. All doses of the drug must be given on schedule for stable effect. Thomas et al., "Orientation for New RSA Officers," 65.

Sisi:	(*pronunciation*: see-see) A Unity pejorative meaning senior citizen, those over forty. Sisis are confined to their own enclaves and have no rights in the larger society. From thence they are Sapped for use as troopers or breeders. J. A. Johnston, private communication with M. E. Chiu, October 2128.
Solons:	The anonymous ultimate rulers of the Unity. Numerous plebiscites are used to convince the people that the Unity is a democracy, but policy is set by the DUFS in consultation with the other ministries. Solons rule by veto. Individuals are recruited to be Solons at retirement.
S-classification:	Specialist class, a level of Unity rank across all guilds. Thus, an S22 might be a commercial artist, a postgraduate academic, a junior assistant specialist in government, or an ensign in the DUFS.
ThiZ:	A recreational drug that produces dissociative and paradoxical endotactic emotions. Withdrawal occurs if use is terminated abruptly. The Union encourages ThiZ use, monitoring it via the Basic implants and altering the drug as needed to ensure prompt cooperation of its citizens. Thomas et al., "Orientation for New RSA Officers," 112.
Western Demarchy:	A breakaway republic on the West Coast of North America centering on San Francisco. Hawaii is a de facto possession. Ibid., 24.